Signs of Love

BlackThorpe Security

Book 2

Kimberly Rae Jordan

THREE**STRAND**
P R E S S

A CORD OF THREE STRANDS IS NOT EASILY BROKEN.

A man, a woman & their God.

Three Strand Press publishes Christian Romance stories

that intertwine love, faith and family.

Always clean. Always heartwarming. Always uplifting.

1

"**H**I, JUSTIN."

Justin Morrell dropped his bag onto the seat of the truck and pushed his sunglasses to the top of his head as he turned around. "Hey there, Mel. How's it going?"

Melanie Thorpe approached him with a smile. "Not too bad. Just stopping in to check on the guy that came over earlier. Duncan Miller. Did you work with him?"

Justin rested his arm on the edge of the bed of his truck. "I got him set up on the range. Mitch was with him when I left. I'm heading into the city for the night."

Melanie nodded. "Meeting tomorrow, eh?"

Aside from church, the Tuesday morning BlackThorpe team meetings were really the only reason he went into Minneapolis most weeks. Since he had to be in the city the next morning anyway, Justin planned to head to his apartment, take a long hot soak in his Jacuzzi tub and do some laundry. He'd spent the last two days training with a team of possible recruits for the company. To say he was sore and dirty was an understatement.

"Yep. I'll see you there."

"Yeah. Got flack for the last one I skipped out on." Melanie smiled ruefully. "Guess I'd better get in there and see how Duncan is doing. Have a good evening."

"You, too." After she'd walked away, Justin shoved his bag to the passenger side of the seat and climbed behind the wheel.

Lowering his sunglasses over his eyes, Justin started the truck and sat for a moment waiting for some heat to flow from the vents before heading out of the BlackThorpe compound. The physical activity over the past few days had worked up a sweat even in the cool spring air. However, now that he wasn't moving around as strenuously, he was grateful for a little more warmth in addition to his leather jacket.

He'd barely reached the highway when his phone rang. Using the hands-free capabilities of his truck, he answered it.

"Justin! Are you coming into the city tonight?"

"Hey, sis," Justin said when he recognized his sister's voice. "Yes. I'm on my way in now."

"Can you come by the house for supper?"

Justin stifled a sigh. "I'm kind of beat, Beth. We've been training hard the past few days."

"Please, Justin? I'd really like to see you since we've missed you at church the last couple of weeks." She paused. "And I want to talk to you about something."

Even though he was pretty sure the argument would be shot down, he gave it one more try. "I'm a mess. I'm covered in muck from the obstacle course, and I haven't had a shower in three days."

"You can take one when you get here. I'll even do your laundry."

She definitely knew him too well. He sighed, not bothering to muffle it this time. "You win, but consider yourself warned, okay?"

Thankfully, he'd stuck a clean set of clothes into his bag so he'd have something to wear while his dirty stuff was being washed. And hopefully, his brother-in-law had some masculine soap and shampoo so he didn't get out of the shower smelling like vanilla and roses...or toddler scented products.

Since Elizabeth and her husband, Daniel, lived between the training compound and his apartment in Minneapolis, it wasn't long before he pulled into their driveway. He grabbed his duffle bag and laptop case and headed toward the front door of the two-story house they called home.

Having accepted the inevitable, Justin found himself looking forward to it. He always enjoyed time with Daniel and Beth, but more than that, he loved seeing his two-year-old niece, Genevieve.

The door swung open before he could even press the bell. As he got a look at his sister, he realized something was off. He hadn't picked up on it from their conversation earlier, but she looked tired and...sad?

"What's wrong, Bethy?" Justin asked as she stepped back to let him into the house. He kept his gaze on her as she pushed the door shut.

"Why don't you get cleaned up first and then we'll talk," Beth suggested, shoving a strand of brown hair behind her ear before crossing her arms over her waist.

He didn't like the sound of that. What was going on? And how was he going to fix it?

"Hey, man."

Justin swung around to see Daniel standing in the entry to the kitchen with his daughter in his arms. He headed over to them and pressed a kiss to Genevieve's downy soft curls.

"Hello, baby." She smiled up at him and reached out, but Justin didn't take her since he was still so dirty. "After my shower. Okay, sweetie?"

Justin shrugged out of his jacket and heard a muffled sound to his left. He turned in search of the source of the noise and froze. A woman who looked vaguely familiar stood with a young boy pressed to her side. Her dark blonde hair was pulled back from her face which only served to emphasize her delicate features and the size of her green eyes as she stared at him. Her flowing skirt almost reached the floor, and she wore a long sleeved shirt that fit her loosely. His gaze moved to the boy at her side. He looked like the male version of her with curly dark blonde hair and green eyes.

How had he not noticed them when he'd walked in? Usually, he scanned any room he entered to be aware of who was present. He had been too distracted by Beth's obvious distress to check out what he'd assumed was a safe environment.

He turned back to his sister. "Beth?"

She frowned as she moved to his side. "First of all, you need to lose the guns. You know the rule."

He arched a brow at her. That's what she was focusing on? Since it hadn't been his plan to stop at her place, he hadn't taken the weapons off before leaving the compound, and he'd forgotten to remove them before coming inside. He looked back at the little boy who was watching him with wide eyes that seemed to be stuck on the shoulder harness he wore.

"Let me get a shower, and I'll put them away." The two strangers just added to the mystery of the evening. His gaze met the woman's again briefly before he turned back to his sister. Under different circumstances, he might have thought she was trying to set him up, but something told him the woman wasn't there for his benefit.

"You can use the bathroom off the guest bedroom in the basement," Beth said.

With his thoughts racing as to all the possible explanations for Beth's apparent distress, Justin made his way down the stairs. His dreams of a leisurely soak were gone, so he made the best of the hot water and tried to keep his mind from going to the worst case scenarios, but it was a challenge.

Alana Jensen felt a tug on her skirt and looked down at her son, Caden. She watched as he signed the words for big, strong man and guns. Before replying, she searched his face for any sign of distress, but the expression on his face seemed more curious than anything.

That is Beth's brother. His name is J U S T I N. She signed back to him, spelling out the individual letters in Justin's name.

Caden's mouth turned up at the corners as he lifted one arm and made a muscle then used his other hand to do the sign for the letter J against it. Alana smiled as she mimicked the movements. Caden didn't always come up with a sign for someone's name so quickly. That he did for Justin spoke clearly of his interest in the man.

"Sorry about the guns, Alana," Beth said with a sigh. "Justin knows I don't like him to wear them in the house."

"You need to cut him a little slack, babe," Daniel said as he set Genevieve down on her feet. The little girl headed straight for Caden, who took her by the hand and settled onto the floor with her toys. "Those weapons are just a part of who he is. You know he didn't mean any harm by wearing them in here today. He hadn't been planning to stop by."

Alana felt bad for Beth and her husband. They'd been through a rough couple of months and from the looks of things, they hadn't been keeping her brother abreast of the latest developments in their life. Unfortunately, from the brief look she'd gotten of him, something told Alana that Justin wasn't a man who appreciated being left out of the loop.

Justin Morrell had come as something of a surprise to her. Given Beth's small, though rounded, stature and open, expressive nature, Alana had expected a male version of that, but Justin appeared to be the opposite of his sister in every possible way.

The second he'd stepped into the room, he'd dominated everything. Daniel wasn't a small man, but even he looked short next to his brother-in-law. Alana guessed Justin was a good four to five inches over six feet with a build that suggested hours of work in the gym. Even relaxed, she had been able to see the definition of the muscles of his arms...as, apparently, had Caden. The man's firm jaw and square chin gave him a chiseled look that, when combined with his deep-set dark blue eyes, definitely made him an attractive—albeit dangerous looking—man.

She was glad Caden's mind seemed to not have retained the memories of their past that might have made him afraid of a man like Justin. Too bad the same couldn't be said for her.

"Let's get dinner prep finished up so we can eat when Justin's done. I'm sure he's hungry," Beth said. "When he comes off these training days he seems to be half-starved."

"Does he do them often?" Alana asked, a little uncertain where the question had come from. She told herself she was just being polite.

"Yes. He's in charge of the security teams that are part of BlackThorpe as well as the ones that are sent to them for training from outside agencies. He does have other staff who work with him who could do more of the training, but he seems to like to get in there with them," Beth said as she set a bowl of salad on the counter.

Alana picked it up and moved it to the table in the dining room adjacent to the kitchen. She had been at the Olson home for dinner several evenings over the past couple of months. By coming into their lives at such a stressful time, she'd been able to see the raw dynamic between the husband and wife. Now she'd get to see the one between Beth and her brother.

Conversation stopped for a bit when Daniel used the electric knife to slice up the huge roast he had pulled from the oven. She took the spoon Beth handed her and scooped the vegetables out of the large pan into a bowl.

Alana had her back to the entrance of the kitchen, but she didn't need eyes in the back of her head to know that Justin had walked into the room. Something in the air around her changed, and when she looked over her shoulder, she saw him there. His imposing presence was only emphasized by his stance. Even in stocking feet, with his legs spread and fingers splayed across his hips, he was a formidable figure.

He wore a pair of camouflage pants that had a variety of different pockets and a black long-sleeve T-shirt. Thankfully, the weapons were nowhere to be seen.

"Now I'll hug you," Beth said with a smile when she spotted him. She set down the whisk she'd been using to make the gravy and went to her brother.

His arms wrapped around her, and she all but disappeared into his embrace. He bent down and kissed the top of her head.

When she stepped back, she said, "Where are your dirty clothes? I'll stick them in while we eat."

"I took care of them. They're already in the wash."

Justin's gaze moved around the room, and Alana froze when it landed on her. His eyes narrowed briefly before he took a couple of steps in her direction. "Hi. I don't believe we've met. I'm Justin Morrell."

"Oh, I'm sorry," Beth said. "Justin, this is Alana Jensen. She's a friend from church."

Justin held out his hand. "Nice to meet you."

After a brief moment of hesitation, Alana reached out toward him. His hand totally engulfed hers when she slid it into his grasp. His fingers and palm were large and rough against hers. His grip tightened briefly before he released her hand.

Before Alana could say anything, Caden walked in with Genevieve, who, upon spotting her uncle, immediately abandoned her friend and made a beeline for Justin. A smile—the first she'd seen—crossed Justin's face as he scooped the little girl into his arms and held her close to his chest. Genevieve put a hand on either side of his face and gave him an enthusiastic kiss. Seeing their closeness gave her a better understanding of why Beth was worried about sharing their news with Justin. It was clear that this big, strong man was securely wrapped around the finger of a two-year-old pixie of a girl with blonde curls.

Caden came to stand next to Alana and when she looked down at him, she saw that he was also watching Justin and Genevieve.

"And this handsome young man is Caden," Beth said with a smile at the boy.

Justin held out his hand. Caden hesitated then took it for a quick shake. Looking at her son standing next to Justin was a startling reminder of just how small and defenseless he was.

"It's nice to meet you."

Caden looked up at her, so Alana quickly signed what Justin had said. He signed a reply, and Alana turned her gaze back to Justin. "He says it's nice to meet you too."

There was no expression on Justin's face when he said, "Your son is deaf?"

Alana glanced at Beth then back to Justin. "Yes, he is."

Caden tugged her skirt and she looked down, following his rapid signs. Alana hoped that Justin had some patience and tolerance for curious little boys. "He wants to know if you shoot your guns."

Justin's gaze moved back and forth between her and Caden before settling on her son. "Yes, but usually only for target practice."

She signed Justin's response for Caden then added on *we're going to eat. No more questions for now.*

Disappointment flashed across Caden's face so quickly she almost missed it, but he nodded his understanding.

"He didn't like my answer?" Justin asked.

Alana turned to him, more than a little surprised that he'd recognized Caden's reaction when it had been so fleeting. "Your answer was fine. I just told him no more questions since we are going to be eating."

With that, Beth told them to take the rest of the food into the dining room while Daniel brought the large platter of meat. Alana breathed a sigh of relief when she realized the seating arrangement didn't put her right next to Justin. His presence was overwhelming in a terrifyingly familiar way. If she had known exactly what sort of man Beth's brother was, she would never have agreed to this. As it was, it took everything within her to keep her hands from shaking as she passed bowls of food and dished up her plate and Caden's.

Conversation between the three others at the table swirled around her while she tried to eat what she'd taken, but her appetite had long since fled. A touch on her arm drew her attention from the food she was pushing around on her plate. She looked down at Caden, waiting for him to begin to sign something.

Instead, he left his hand on her arm, his eyes asking all his questions. From very young, he'd learned how to decipher her expressions and body language. With it just being the two of them so much, he'd always been able to pick up on her moods. And right then, she knew he sensed her unease...her fear.

He lifted his hand from her arm and signed to her. *Why scared, Mama?*

Underlying the question in his eyes was a bit of anxiety as well. She hadn't wanted that for him. She had to do a better job of keeping her emotions tamped down. Taking a deep breath, she smiled and then tried to ease his worries. *Not scared, baby. Just thinking about something. But you don't need to worry. Mama will take care of it.*

She could tell he still wasn't totally convinced but eventually, after a quick glance at the man sitting on his other side, Caden turned his attention back to his food.

"Everything okay, Alana?"

"Everything's great." Alana gave her friend a quick smile. "You're such a great cook, Beth."

A tense silence fell over the table, and Alana knew she wasn't the only one responsible for it. She shot a glance at Justin and saw that as Beth had promised, he had polished off a whole lot of the roast. But now he set his knife and fork across the empty plate and turned his gaze to his sister.

"What's going on, Beth?" When she didn't answer right away, Alana saw Justin shift his attention to his brother-in-law. "Dan?"

The other man cleared his throat and took a drink of water before looking at Justin. Alana held her breath, knowing what was to come. She wanted to move Caden away from Justin, uncertain of how the large, muscular man was going to react.

"Someone tell me what's going on." The firm tone of Justin's voice brooked no further delays.

He glanced at her as if she would be the one to tell him. At the sight of the barely contained frustration in his gaze, Alana felt a vice tighten around her throat. Would the frustration flash into anger and then into violence? Right then all those emotions seemed to be rolling off him in waves.

"Uh, a few months ago Beth and I noticed something about Genevieve—"

"Something's wrong with Genevieve?"

Since her gaze was already on him, Alana saw the momentary panic on Justin's face.

"Yes." This time it was Beth who spoke. "She's experiencing hearing loss."

"Hearing loss?" Alana saw Justin's gaze shoot to Caden then back to Beth. "She's deaf?"

She slipped her arm around Caden's shoulders. When she looked down at him, she could see the confusion on his face. She'd already explained to Caden about Genevieve's diagnosis, so when she signed that they were telling Justin about it, he understood immediately what was going on.

Both Beth and Daniel nodded in response to Justin's question, but it was Daniel who gave him more information. "We'd been noticing over the last several months that she wasn't responding as she should to noises...sounds. When we took her in for her two-year appointment, we mentioned it to the doctor. Since then, we've been taking her for a variety of different tests."

Justin crossed his arms. "Why didn't you tell me?"

Alana could see emotion swirling in his eyes, but his face looked like it had been carved from granite. She noticed that he still hadn't looked at Genevieve. Was he going to reject the little girl over this?

Beth lifted her chin. "We wanted to have some answers before we told you. There's nothing you can do. There's nothing any of us can do at this point beyond accepting the diagnosis and adjusting to the new normal of our life."

Justin's lips thinned as his brows drew together. "Why did she go deaf? She wasn't born that way."

"They don't know. We've gone through genetic testing and all kinds of other tests for her and still don't have a definite answer to that," Daniel explained. His jaw tightened, and Alana knew he was trying to keep his emotions in check.

She'd come to know Daniel and Beth well during the past few weeks. Beth had seen her at church signing in the service and then later with Caden and had approached her. She still remembered seeing the weary, sad and confused look on Beth's face when she'd asked her about Caden's deafness. Alana had offered to come and talk with them both about her experiences parenting a deaf child.

Of course, she hadn't known then that Beth had a brother who would trigger memories she'd rather not have.

"I can't accept that. They must have some explanation. A child doesn't just go deaf for no apparent reason."

Beth laid her hand on his arm. "We're still looking for answers, trying to figure out what has happened to her. But in the meantime, we're doing what we can to make sure we can still communicate with her and help her communicate with us."

Justin's gaze landed on Alana with such force her lungs constricted, holding the air there captive. He stared at her then looked at Caden before turning his attention back to Beth.

"Alana knows sign language. You might have seen her signing during the services at church. We've asked her to help us learn it and to also begin to teach Genevieve." Beth hesitated then said, "I'd like you to learn as well."

He shot another look at her, and Alana found herself hoping he'd say no.

"I want a second opinion. If it's money, I can—"

"No." Daniel spoke softly but firmly. "We've had second and third opinions, Justin. And money won't fix this. Nothing will."

Justin pushed back from the table and got to his feet. "I need to go."

"Justin, please," Beth pleaded as she and Daniel also stood. "Don't leave. Talk to me."

"I have to go." Justin turned and disappeared through the doorway.

Beth's shoulders slumped as she looked at her husband. "Well, that went about as well as I expected."

Daniel put an arm around her shoulders and pulled her close. Alana felt a flash of envy at the gentle way he gathered Beth into his arms and stroked her hair, whispering to her. She wondered what it would be like to have that kind of tenderness in a relationship.

There was a sudden movement in the doorway, and Justin stepped back into the room. He wore his leather jacket again and had the duffle bag he'd arrived with in his hand. With a grim set to his features, he walked to where Genevieve sat and dropped into a crouch next to her high chair. The little girl smiled at him, and Alana saw pain flash across his face as he leaned forward and pressed a lingering kiss to her forehead.

Then he went to where his sister and brother-in-law stood and rested his free hand on Daniel's shoulder as he bent to kiss the top of Beth's head. "I'll call you."

And then he was gone.

For the first time since Justin had walked into the house and dominated it with his presence, Alana felt the tightness in her chest ease, allowing her to take a deep breath. Somehow she was going to have to tell Beth there was no way she could help her brother learn sign language.

2

JUSTIN grabbed the handle and with a vicious jerk slammed the door of his truck closed. He twisted the key in the ignition and backed out of the driveway, barely waiting for the vehicle to stop reversing before throwing it into drive and peeling away from the house. When he got to the highway, he was sorely tempted to return to the compound where he could make use of the wide range of exercise equipment there to help him burn off the emotions that raged inside him.

But he had a bag full of wet laundry and a meeting he had to be at the next morning, so he turned the truck toward his original destination. As he drove, Justin let loose with all the words he'd kept locked up while listening to Dan and Beth explain what had happened to Genevieve. The habit of swearing he'd picked up while in the military had been something he'd worked hard to overcome through the years, but in that moment of emotional...weakness, it was what seemed to fit the situation. Only it didn't make him feel any better. If anything, he felt worse.

Forgive me, Lord.

He pounded on the steering wheel with a fist, still needing some way to vent his anger and frustration. There had to be *something* he could do. He liked Dan and believed the man thought he'd done all he could for Genevieve, but Justin needed to know he'd done all *he* could do for her himself. He just didn't want to believe that his beautiful blue-eyed, blonde-haired niece was going to be sentenced to a life of silence.

He couldn't accept that.

He just couldn't.

And the woman who had been there to help them adjust could just go away. They wouldn't need her. He would find a way to make sure Genevieve could hear again if it was the last thing he did. Tragedy had already rocked their lives. He couldn't let this be one more.

Justin stalked into the boardroom at the BlackThorpe building the next morning. He looked around the room, noting that all members of the team were present except for Than Miller.

"Morning, Justin," Marcus Black said, his voice deep. Though he didn't have Justin's height, the man carried himself in such a way as to dominate any room he entered.

"Marc," Justin said with a nod of his head.

Marcus's lips thinned at his use of the shortened version of his name, but Justin didn't give a flip. Most people didn't understand the relationship between them, and that was fine by him. The fact that it was none of their business seemed to be the only thing he and Marcus agreed on anymore.

Justin dropped down into the chair next to Melanie, knowing she shared his impatience with these weekly meetings. The two of them spent most their time out of the main BlackThorpe complex and hated being dragged in each week.

Melanie stared at him, her eyes going wide. "Wow, Justin. Everything okay? You look...rough."

Justin rubbed his fingers over his chin, knowing the day's growth of facial hair when he was usually clean-shaven gave him that rough look. Unfortunately, after sleeping in later than usual, he'd skipped shaving in order to be on time for the meeting. He'd take care of it when he got back to the compound once this infernal meeting was over.

After he'd gotten home the night before, Justin had spent a lot of time on the internet trying to learn more about hearing loss in children. The results had not been encouraging and without having more information about the tests that had been done so far on Genevieve, he'd been searching somewhat blindly. The one thing that had stood out to him though was the large percentage of cases of *unexplained* hearing loss where the cause was unknown. That didn't sit well with him at all. How could he fix things for Genevieve when he didn't know what was wrong?

"Everything's fine," he told Melanie. Never one to share much of his life outside of work, he certainly wasn't going to start now.

If he had shared anything with anyone, it might have been Melanie, but he preferred to keep his personal life separate from his job. He had a congenial relationship with most members of the BlackThorpe team except for Marcus, but he rarely socialized with them.

Melanie gave him a skeptical look, but she didn't say anything further as Marcus started the meeting.

"First up, as you know, Than is currently over in the Philippines. We've just received word that there is a super typhoon closing in on his location. We are monitoring the situation and will make arrangements to evacuate him and Lindsay Hamilton if it becomes necessary. In the meantime, he has been in contact via the sat phone and doesn't seem to feel that evacuation is imminent at this point."

Though Than could be a pain in the butt with his easygoing, carefree attitude sometimes, the man excelled at his job. Given Than's persistent attempts to get him to go out to socialize more, Justin never felt guilty about giving him a weekly beat down when he'd come to the gym at the compound. Still, he wished no harm to the man and hoped he and the woman he was protecting would be safe for the duration of the storm.

Justin tried to focus on the discussions that went on around him, but he didn't contribute. That likely surprised no one present. If he had comments to make, he usually reserved them for after the meeting and spoke with the person they pertained to. It drove Marcus crazy, but Justin knew he would never call him on it. The bottom line was that if he ever felt something was worth commenting on, Marcus knew what he said would have weight and value.

As he drew circles on the notepad in front of him, Justin accepted that his distraction wasn't solely because of the news of Genevieve's hearing loss. The presence of that woman—Alana Jensen—only added to his unease over the whole situation. To him, she signified his sister and Dan's capitulation to Genevieve's diagnosis. Instead of wasting time and money learning sign language, they should be spending that time contacting doctors and anyone else who could give them the answers they needed to make Genevieve right again.

But it wasn't just that, there had been a flash of what his instinct said was fear when his gaze met Alana's for the first time. The boy at her side hadn't seemed to share that feeling, but there had definitely been something about Justin that alarmed her. He wasn't unaware of the visual impact his size and countenance had on people—in fact, Justin counted on it. People didn't question him, didn't disagree with him. Most of all, they tended to just leave him alone. But usually when his presence inspired fear in someone it was because they had done something wrong, or they had something to hide.

Was she out to scam Beth and Dan? Beth had said they'd met at church, but in his mind, that made absolutely no difference. In fact, what better place than church for scam artists to find people willing to accept a person without question? His sister's horrible habit of embracing everyone, accepting them at face value, would get her into trouble sooner or later. Dan wasn't much different even though he was an FBI agent and should know better.

And the fact that Alana was an attractive woman with a young son didn't lessen the feeling that she could be a threat to his family. He had never allowed himself to be swayed by a woman's beauty before, and he wasn't about to start now.

There was no way he would let this woman take advantage of his sister and Dan in the midst of everything else they were going through. His job gave him the resources to do a background check on her, but Beth would be furious if he just presented her with facts. He needed to get his sister to see for herself what this woman was doing.

Because he had little doubt she was up to something.

Alana pushed the cart through the aisles of the store, trying to ignore the knot in her stomach. She hated grocery shopping anymore. Prices seemed to be constantly going up and though she wanted to buy lots of good food for Caden, it was hard to stretch her money in that way. In the end, she usually bought what she could of the fresh fruit and vegetables, knowing that Caden would be the only one to eat them, and then added in the cheaper, less healthy, foods like mac and cheese and ramen noodles.

Shopping for groceries also served to remind her of what she'd given up when she'd grabbed Caden and run from the only home he'd ever known. As she stared blankly at the shelf in front of her, Alana wondered if she'd made a mistake. Maybe Craig wouldn't have turned his abuse to Caden. At least when they'd lived with him, they'd had money for food—good, healthy food. Craig may have had a nasty streak in him, but he'd also wanted the best for his *temple*, so he'd insisted Alana only buy the healthiest food for them. She'd taken Caden from that because she told herself it was only a matter of time before her son felt the pain of Craig's heavy hand as she had for the past five years.

But had that been the real reason?

An overwhelming ache settled over her. Every bruise, cut and burn her body had ever borne, every bone that had ever been broken, once again pulsed with pain. She pressed a hand to her chest. In truth, Craig had ignored Caden ninety-nine percent of the time. From the minute he'd discovered his son was deaf, he'd wanted nothing to do with him. However, he put on a good front when around his friends and business acquaintances. Caden had gone to the best school in Miami, and everyone had complimented Craig on how well he cared for his deaf son.

Unfortunately, they didn't see behind the scenes.

Maybe she should have been able to endure more for Caden's sake. He'd still be going to the school he loved instead of being homeschooled by her. He'd have lots of good food and a nice home instead of the run-down one bedroom apartment they lived in now.

Alana blinked back the tears as she reached for the boxes of mac and cheese on the shelf in front of her. Thankfully, she even had coupons for them this week. With a resigned sigh, she shook off the hurt and doubt-filled thoughts. She wanted to finish this up and get back to the apartment. The older woman next door watched Caden when she needed to go out, but she never liked to leave him for too long. She'd stopped bringing him with her to go grocery shopping because she'd been unable to deal with his repeated requests for all the treats she couldn't afford to buy him.

Hopefully, this food would last the week, and next week she should receive some payments for work she'd done. Enough to cover rent and more groceries. As she stood in line, Alana prayed her math had been correct and that her wallet held enough money to pay for what she'd placed in her cart.

When it was done, her wallet was empty, but she had her bags of groceries, so she said a prayer of gratitude and headed back to Caden. Thankfully, they were going to the Olson's later that afternoon. Beth always served them delicious and healthy meals. Though Beth and Daniel tried to pay her for the time she took to teach them sign language, Alana hadn't felt right taking advantage of their situation. Beth's suggestion that she at least provide them a meal in exchange for the lessons was one Alana could live with.

She just hoped Justin wouldn't be there. It was clear he wasn't interested in learning sign language, so there was really no reason for him to join them again.

Justin stared at the documents on the screen of his laptop. It hadn't been quite a week since he'd asked his contact in the research department at BlackThorpe to do a background check on Alana Jensen. Unfortunately, the report didn't contain what he'd hoped it would.

Justin ~ Attached is the information I found through our normal channels for Alana Jensen. However, it appears she obtained a legal name change just over two years ago in Florida, but the records are sealed. There is no indication of any sort of criminal activity since the name change. I didn't find any record of employment for her, and her son isn't registered in any school that I could find.

The file was thin, even electronically. Justin sat back in his chair and considered the little bit of information that had been unearthed. Usually, a sealed name change meant there was a concern for the safety of the person requesting the name change or for a child. His eyes narrowed as his hands clenched into fists. Now in addition to wondering if she was taking advantage of Beth and Dan, Justin wondered if danger might be following Alana Jensen and her son. If so, would it end up at his sister's doorstep?

That definitely couldn't happen.

Justin snapped the lid closed on the laptop and shoved it into his bag. Since it was Monday, he was heading into the city once again. He had a standing invitation to Beth's for dinner, so he planned to stop there on the way to his apartment. He needed to talk to her, to find out just what she knew about the woman she let into her home on a regular basis.

As he strode down the hallway to leave the building, Justin called Beth to give her a head's up that he was stopping by. He'd called her a couple of days earlier, but they hadn't talked long. She seemed to be giving him some space to come to terms with Genevieve's diagnosis. He'd spent a lot of his free time researching hearing loss in children, but without knowing what tests she'd already had and what had been ruled out, what he read didn't make much difference in how he felt about it all. He was still convinced there was a diagnosis and a cure out there. He just had to find it.

"You're welcome to come for dinner, Justin," Beth said when he told her of his plans, "but try and dial back the macho man stuff. And leave the weapons off. Alana and Caden will be here."

"They'll be off, no worries." His guns were already in the locked case he carried along with his duffel and laptop bag. "What's for dinner?"

He didn't want her on the defensive, and he suspected that if he said anything against Alana, that's what would happen. Justin could bide his time until he gathered more information, but the end result would be the same. He would protect what remained of his family, whether it was from a scammer or something worse. Beth and Dan might be ready to invite a perfect stranger into their home, but Justin wasn't nearly as trusting. However, their past had also taught him it wasn't always a stranger who walked in and tore lives apart.

"Lasagna." Beth's response pulled him from his thoughts. She'd cooked one of his favorite dishes. "I had a feeling you'd be showing up."

Justin grimaced as he pushed the button to unlock his truck. It should please him that his sister knew him so well, but for some reason it made him feel predictable. And in his line of work, that was not a good thing. Of course, if he were honest with himself, he'd have to admit he *had* fallen into a somewhat predictable pattern of late. Most particularly with his regular trip into the Twin Cities on Monday nights. He needed to mix that up even though he had to be at the BlackThorpe offices every Tuesday morning. Marcus and his tedious team meetings.

"I'll be there in twenty minutes," Justin said gruffly as he cranked the key in the ignition.

At least knowing what he was going into this time helped him feel more in control than when he'd left the previous week. Genevieve's diagnosis would not alter the relationship he shared with the little girl. And now armed with a bit more information on Alana, he would see what he could draw out of her. There was no way he could change how he looked, but perhaps interacting a bit more with her and her son would encourage her to lower her guard.

Heavy gray clouds were hanging over the Twin Cities as he pulled onto the highway and headed east. Even though the calendar said spring had officially arrived, the weather hadn't gotten the message apparently. The past few days had been chilly thanks to a constant wind, and there had even been a light skiff of snow on the ground two mornings ago. It was May. They should at least be experiencing sunshine, not these gray fall-like days.

As he drove down the street to the cul-de-sac where Dan and Beth lived, he noticed two figures making their way along the sidewalk. Even though they faced away from him, he recognized the wheat colored hair of both the woman and the boy. The long skirt Alana wore tangled in her legs as she walked, no protection at all against the wind. He hit the button to lower the window on the passenger side of his truck, and after checking to make sure there was no traffic behind him on the quiet residential street, he slowed to a stop a few feet ahead of them.

In the side mirror, he saw Alana's arm go to Caden's shoulders as she moved him to the far side of the sidewalk. Justin realized she likely didn't recognize his truck and that the big black F450 with a diesel rumble might be a bit intimidating.

"Alana!" he called through the open window.

3

AT THE SOUND of her name, Alana's head whipped around. For a second, she and Caden stood frozen there. Suddenly, she looked down at her son, and he signed something to her.

After another glance in the rear view mirror to check for traffic, Justin got out and jogged around the hood of the truck to the sidewalk. Both mother and son watched him but remained in place. Figuring he had probably alarmed them with his weapons the last time they'd seen him, Justin parted the sides of his leather jacket so Alana could see he wore no guns. Then he reached for the handle of the front door and opened it.

"I think we're going to the same place. Hop in, and I'll give you a ride."

"It's okay," Alana said. "We can walk. It's not much farther."

Before Justin could say anything, she focused on her son again. Even without knowing any sign language, Justin could read the boy's fascination with his truck through the gestures he made toward it along with his wide eyes.

Alana's gaze moved from Caden to the truck then to Justin. He could see the indecision written all over her face. Just as he was going to shove the door shut—far be it from him to force a woman to do something she didn't want to—Alana gave a quick nod.

"Your son will need to sit in the back," Justin said as they walked toward him. He opened the rear door then stepped back so Alana could help Caden onto the back seat. He would have offered to do it, but something told him she still wasn't one hundred percent comfortable with him.

Once she'd buckled Caden in, Alana moved out of the way. Justin shut the back door then waited as she climbed into the front. Normally, he would have helped a woman up onto the seat since the truck was higher than most other vehicles, but again his gut told him to not touch her. After she was settled, Justin closed her door as well and rounded the hood to climb back behind the wheel.

The irony in all this was that if he'd just driven on and let them walk, they'd all be at Beth's already. He glanced over to see her slide her hands into the pockets of her bulky jacket.

"You don't have a car?" he asked as he slowly accelerated.

"No. It's an unnecessary expense when the transit system is more than sufficient for us. Plus, Caden enjoys riding the bus."

Justin looked into his rear-view mirror and saw the little boy's wide eyes taking in all the bells and whistles of his truck. He was reminded of the way the boy had looked at him when he'd taken off his jacket to reveal the weapons he wore. The kid's reactions made him curious about his father and what had occurred that led Alana to apply for a name change.

"Well, I hope you're not too hungry. Beth told me she's made lasagna for supper, and it happens to be a favorite of mine."

He caught the startled glance Alana shot him before she looked back down at her hands. "Beth is a great cook."

"The best," Justin agreed as he turned into the driveway of his sister's house.

He'd barely put the truck in park before Alana undid her seatbelt and pushed open her door. Justin stared at her back as she slid out. With a shake of his head, he got out then opened the rear door to get his laptop bag and the weapons case. He might not be wearing his guns, but he wasn't going to leave the case where someone could steal it.

By the time he locked the vehicle, Beth had the front door open for them and stood there with Genevieve in her arms. The little girl waved with both hands and a big smile on her face.

"Did you give them a ride?" Beth asked, her gaze going from him to Alana.

Justin shrugged. "I saw them walking on the street so offered them a lift."

Beth reached out to give Alana a one-arm hug. "I wish you'd let us pick you up and drop you off."

Alana glanced at him before she looked back at Beth. "You know we're fine to ride the bus. Remember our deal."

Beth gave an exasperated sigh as she set Genevieve down. "Well, come on in. Supper's almost ready."

As Justin inhaled the rich, tomato-y scent in the air, he wondered about the deal his sister had made with Alana. He watched as she helped Caden take his jacket off and then removed her own. Once again, it looked like she wore clothes that were two or three sizes too big for her. Caden, on the other hand, appeared to be about ready to grow right out of his.

He slid his laptop bag and weapon case onto the top shelf of the closet next to the front door. When Beth held out her hand toward him, he took off his jacket and handed it to her. After hanging it up, she stepped close and wrapped her arms around his waist. They weren't the most demonstrative siblings—or rather, *he* wasn't the most demonstrative sibling—but for Beth's sake, he tried. He put his arms around her and held her for a second before letting go.

Once they moved from the foyer into the living room, Caden dropped to his knees in front of Genevieve and signed something to her. Justin watched as his niece mimicked the action.

Caden spun around and quickly signed to his mother, a wide grin on his face. When Alana smiled back at him, it transformed her features from tense to beautiful. Justin glanced at Beth and saw a similar smile on her face.

"We've been working with her on that sign as well as a few others this week," Beth said, pride evident in her voice.

Justin felt as if he stood on the outside looking in. He was used to it in other social situations, but being with Beth and Dan had never felt like that...until now. Until Alana and her son had shown up.

He felt small arms wrap around his right knee and knew it was Genevieve. With a smile, he scooped her up and cuddled her close. She was probably the only person on the planet he felt comfortable showering affection on. And now he was losing the ability to communicate with her.

Even so, he looked right at her and said, "Hi, baby."

He pressed a kiss to her forehead and then waited for her to take his face in her hands like she had started doing. She didn't disappoint him, and Justin felt a rush of love as she planted a quick kiss on his lips. Pain edged that love as he thought about what lay ahead for his little niece.

He tried to squash the thought. Even entertaining it in that way made it seem as if he accepted her diagnosis, and he hadn't come to that point yet. Or had he?

Ever since tragedy ripped through their lives and left just him and Beth, Justin had vowed to protect what remained of their family. What Genevieve was going through was something he couldn't keep her from, and it ate at his heart like acid. He also struggled to understand how God could let them go through yet another heartbreaking experience when the last one nearly shattered them.

"Why don't we eat?" Beth suggested as she moved toward the kitchen.

Keeping Genevieve in his arms, Justin followed the others to the dining room. He slid her into her high chair then pressed a quick kiss to her satiny curls. After they were all seated, Dan said a prayer for the meal.

"Caden," Dan said as he picked up the basket of garlic bread and passed it to Beth.

Justin glanced at his brother-in-law then at the little boy. He saw Alana touch the boy's arm and point to Dan. Caden looked at the man and smiled.

Slowly, Dan began to sign as he said, "How was your day?"

If possible, Caden's smile grew bigger, and his eyes lit up. Unlike the rapid signing he did with his mother, Caden moved his hands in slow, measured movements as Dan watched him closely.

"Okay, I think I understood that he had a good day," Dan said. "But the rest is a little beyond me."

Alana nodded. "He said that we did reading and science today which are his favorite subjects."

As the meal progressed, Justin found himself watching Caden's interaction with Alana, Beth, and Dan. This would be how Genevieve would have to communicate if he couldn't somehow find a doctor to figure out what was wrong with her and fix it.

The lasagna he normally would have enjoyed sat like a heavy lump in his stomach. He did notice that Alana seemed to be eating heartily. And Caden as well. At least they were enjoying themselves.

In his mind, Justin knew that Beth and Dan must have already worked through the emotions that had come with Genevieve's diagnosis, but he hadn't been included then. He had to deal with them on his own now, and he didn't know which ones to focus on. And even though he knew it wasn't right, he couldn't help feeling that Alana and her son were part of the problem. He resented what they represented in Beth and Dan's life.

"Justin?"

He looked up from his plate to find Beth watching him expectantly. "Sorry. What?"

"Caden wants to know if you shot your guns today."

He turned his attention to the little boy whose chin barely cleared the edge of the table by an inch or two. Caden's eyes were large with curiosity and, if Justin wasn't mistaken, a bit of awe.

Not sure how to communicate with him, Justin just nodded. Caden's eyes got even larger. Turning to his mom, he quickly signed something. Alana's brows drew together as she stared at her son then looked up to meet Justin's gaze. The tension was back on her face, and Justin figured she wasn't all too keen on Caden's interest in his weapons.

"He wants to know what you shot with them. And please, if it was a person, don't say that."

As Justin held Alana's gaze, he saw that flash of fear once again. "I shot them for target practice. Only thing hurt by the bullets was a piece of paper."

Alana relayed this to Caden, and Justin almost smiled as disappointment crossed the young boy's face. Obviously, he was hoping for something more exciting. Justin tried to remember himself at that age, but all his recollections seemed to get stuck on that fateful day ten years ago when his life had been permanently altered.

The memories he wanted to have were just shadowy images in his mind, but the ones he wanted to forget were still as sharp and clear as the day it had all unfolded. It wasn't every day that a guy was taken aside by his commanding officer and given the news that his family had basically been wiped out. And not only that, he was being discharged from the military in order to take care of the one surviving member, Beth.

At the tender age of twenty-three, he was thrust into the role of primary caregiver for his thirteen-year-old sister. His severely traumatized thirteen-year-old sister. Suddenly cut adrift from the military career he'd planned on, Justin had been at a loss as to how to provide and care not just for himself but for Beth as well. Desperation had led him to accept the job his cousin, Marcus, offered even though he had hated the man at that point for the role his father had played that left him and Beth with only each other instead of the family of seven they'd been before the tragedy.

He'd determined early on that no one at BlackThorpe would ever see him as a free-loader because of the family connection. In reality, he wasn't sure that any of the current staff—aside from the Thorpes—knew of the relationship between him and Marcus. Oh, they were aware that he got away with jabs at the older man that no one else dared make, but they didn't know why.

He and Marcus had been in the same boat in the aftermath of the tragedy. Marcus had a sister who, like Beth, had survived the massacre at the family cabin north of the Twin Cities. But instead of commiserating with the man, Justin held onto his anger toward him. Blaming Marcus for not seeing that his father—Justin's uncle—had been so close to losing his grip on reality. Surely there had been some indication of his instability before he'd gunned down both their families and then turned the weapon on himself. Beth and Marcus's sister, Meredith, only survived the shooting because they'd been up in the attic, the place they had loved to go to talk. The commotion had brought them downstairs in time to see Edward Black take his own life. That, in and of itself was bad enough, but they'd also come face to face with the carnage he'd left behind.

Eight dead. Seven at the hand of a suicidal madman. In addition to their parents, he and Beth had lost the siblings that had been between them in age. Michael, their sixteen-year-old brother who had just gotten his driver's license. Amanda, their eighteen-year-old sister who had been preparing to graduate high school. And Charlotte, their newly engaged twenty-one-year-old sister. Marcus had lost his parents as well as Meredith's twin brother, Mitchell. And in the aftermath of everything, Marcus's fiancée had broken off their engagement just two months before the wedding.

Justin looked over at his sister, pride flooding him at how far she'd come in the decade since that horrible day.

Meredith hadn't fared as well. No doubt in part because she'd lost the twin she had been exceptionally close to and had also seen her father take his own life.

Realizing he needed to stay in the present, Justin turned his attention back to the conversation going on around the table. He almost checked out again when he realized they were talking about church-related stuff. Since hearing about Genevieve's diagnosis, he had struggled with how God could allow yet another traumatic event in Beth's life. Hadn't losing the majority of her family in a horrific way been enough? Surely she had been entitled to be able to live out the rest of her life without any more heartbreaking trials.

But she didn't question any of this. Her faith remained strong. When he'd returned to Minneapolis to take care of Beth, she had insisted on still going to church. After five years in the military, Justin hadn't exactly been interested in attending at first. He'd gone just for her sake, but soon he was listening to the sermons and eventually, he'd reconnected to the faith his parents had raised them with. But that didn't mean he didn't still have some questions for God when stuff like this happened. Because not understanding was one of the hardest things for Justin, and he definitely didn't understand why Genevieve had to go through this.

"Would you be willing to take some sign language lessons, too, Justin?" Beth asked.

Justin looked from Alana to his sister. What could he say? He didn't want to. He wanted to believe that he could find a cure for Genevieve. But what if he couldn't? Sign language would be the only way to communicate with her. His gut clenched at the thought.

"I'll think about it," he said, not wanting to make any promises he couldn't keep.

"Alana is a great teacher. And Caden has even been good helping with Genevieve," Beth told him.

"I'll think about it," he repeated, his voice gruff.

Alana watched the exchange between Beth and her brother. She could see the firm set of Justin's face as he responded to his sister's suggestion about learning sign language. As far as she was concerned, she'd be just as happy if Justin didn't want to learn from her. The less she had to do with the man, the better. And even less contact between him and Caden would be a good thing.

Still, she couldn't miss the disappointment on Beth's face when Justin refused to commit. Alana knew it was important for the relationship between Justin and his niece that he learn how to communicate with her. And it was easiest for them all to learn now because they would learn together at a more natural pace. Genevieve was young enough that she would only need the most basic of signs to start. The adults would pick it up more quickly and would always be able to communicate with the little girl even as they encouraged her to expand her vocabulary.

If Justin refused to learn, his relationship with Genevieve would suffer. It had probably been a poor decision on Beth and Daniel's part not to let Justin know sooner what was going on. They'd worked through the process of coming to accept Genevieve's diagnosis already. Beth needed to give her brother time to catch up to where they were in the grief process. Because, in a sense, that's what it was. They'd had to grieve the loss of the future they thought their little girl had in front of her.

Alana would have had to be blind to miss the way Justin doted on his niece, so he needed to grieve the loss of that future as well. Maybe she should talk to Beth a little bit more about it. She'd hesitated to say anything until she'd actually met Justin, but now that she had, she could see that he was struggling with it all. And unless she was way off base, he wasn't dealing well with her and Caden's presence in their life—and what that represented—either.

Well, the feeling was somewhat mutual. She'd been hoping that Beth's brother would be some nerdy geek who would be excited at the prospect of learning something new. Not a mountain of muscle who reminded her a little too much of her past. Beth's brother was the type of guy she really didn't want to be around. At all.

She hoped that he left soon because she didn't like staying much past seven-thirty. Any later meant they had to make the walk from the bus stop to the apartment in rapidly fading daylight. After Justin had stopped to give them a lift, Alana was afraid he'd offer to give them a ride home. And she really didn't want that.

"Marcus called the other day," Beth said, interrupting Alana's thoughts.

"He did?" Justin responded, his words as tense as the expression on his face. "What did he want?"

Beth shredded the piece of garlic bread she held. Without looking at Justin, she said, "He wanted to know if everything was okay. He said that when you'd come into the office for the meeting you looked a little worse for wear."

"Did he now?" Anger laced Justin's words. "Why did he feel it was necessary to call you?"

Alana saw Beth did look at her brother then, an eyebrow arched. "Seriously? You guys don't talk. Ten years and you still haven't talked to him about what happened."

"There's nothing to talk about," Justin ground out as he tossed his napkin on the table. "If I wanted Marcus to know what was going on, I would have told him."

"Well, I told him what was happening with Genevieve," Beth stated firmly.

Alana could feel the irritation emanating off Justin. She glanced at Caden, but thankfully he was busy making faces at Genevieve. For a seven-year-old, Caden was remarkably adept at picking up on what people were feeling. She really didn't want him picking up on this though.

"Why would you tell him that, Beth? It's none of his business."

"He's family, Justin." This time it was Daniel who spoke, his voice low and firm. "You can choose not to share about this, but Genevieve is our daughter, and if Beth wants Marcus to know about it, that is her right."

Alana held her breath, waiting for Justin to lash out at the other man. He was definitely one who wanted to be in control and fix everything—that much she'd figured out already. And she sensed that anger bubbled near the surface of his emotions when it came to Marcus and whatever had happened in the past.

Strangely enough, even though Daniel's words should have riled him up further, Justin just took a deep breath and let it out before settling back in his seat. Alana was still trying to figure out the dynamic between the three adults in this situation, so Justin's response didn't make much sense.

His face completely devoid of emotion, Justin said, "You're right. Genevieve *is* your daughter." He pushed back from the table. "I need to be going. Thank you for dinner."

"Justin..." Beth reached out to her brother. "Marcus was just concerned."

"It's fine, Beth. Dan's right. Who you choose to communicate with regarding Genevieve is your business, not mine." When Beth and Daniel started to get to their feet, Justin waved his hand. "No need to get up. I know my way out."

Once again, he paused long enough to give Genevieve a kiss before walking out of the kitchen. None of them said anything as they sat listening to him gather his things from the closet. The front door opened then closed with a soft thud.

For the second week in a row, Justin had left the evening early. The first time around, Alana had chalked it up to anger and disbelief. This time though, while it appeared to be fueled once again by anger, Alana got the feeling that underlying it all was hurt and confusion on Justin's part.

Beth took a deep breath and let it out, her shoulders slumping. "I don't know why he won't give Marcus a chance."

Daniel reached out and slid his hand along the back of his wife's neck. "Might have been better not to bring Marcus up, babe. You know he's already having a hard time dealing with all this."

Beth shot Alana a rueful glance. "Sorry you keep getting dragged into this mess with Justin."

"It's okay. I know family dynamics can be a challenge at the best of times."

"And this is definitely not that," Beth said then sighed.

Alana bent her head then looked back up. "I know it's really none of my business, but I think you need to give him a little more time."

Beth tilted her head. "More time?"

"Yes. You and Daniel have known about Genevieve's diagnosis now for a few months. Do you remember how it was when you first found out? That shock? The disbelief? The feeling of not wanting to accept—or even share—the news? Well, that's where Justin is right now. He needs some time to catch up to where you guys are in dealing with all this. It's obvious he loves Genevieve very deeply...perhaps as much as if she were his own daughter. This has got to be very difficult for him to go through, and he's processing it on his own. You two had each other."

Alana remembered how alone she'd felt when the news had come that Caden was deaf. Craig hadn't seemed to care at all. He'd just told Alana to keep the kid away from him. She'd been trying to deal with all her emotions of the diagnosis on top of trying to still care for Caden. More than once she'd longed for someone to be there at her side to share the burden of the news. Not that Justin was likely to share that burden with anyone, but that didn't mean he didn't feel it as deeply and keenly as Daniel and Beth had.

"I know what you're saying is right, Alana," Beth said as her head dipped. "The problem is I can't go back to where he is. My own emotions are still too raw even though I've worked through a lot of it. I can't allow myself to be dragged back to the anger and grief he's going through now."

Alana understood where Beth was coming from. Unfortunately, she had no answers for her on how to deal with the situation with Justin.

Daniel sighed. "I guess we likely made a mistake in not having him be part of all of this right from the start."

Beth laid her hand on Daniel's arm. "You know why we did that. I was afraid he'd just take over everything. As much as I love my brother, we are Geni's parents. You know how he likes to take control of everything."

"I do understand, sweetheart, but maybe if he'd heard what the doctors told us and had gone through it with us, he would have had an easier time accepting things."

Beth shrugged, a helpless look on her face. "We can't change that decision now."

Alana met Daniel's gaze when he looked at her. "I know we've already asked a lot of you, Alana, and really appreciate all you've done for us. Could we ask you for one more thing?"

Even though she knew what was coming—even though she knew she should say no—she just couldn't. Instead, she nodded.

"What are you thinking, honey?" Beth asked as she turned to her husband.

Daniel looked down at his wife. "I think maybe Alana might be able to offer support to Justin in a way we can't. She's gone through this, but maybe she's far enough away from her emotional turmoil over it that she can help Justin during this time."

Yeah, that's what she figured he wanted from her.

"There's no guarantee he'd want to talk to me," Alana felt obliged to point out.

Beth nodded. "That's true, but I guess we won't know until you try. Are you okay with that?"

She wasn't, but Alana also got the feeling Justin would turn down any attempt on her part to help him, so it was really no biggie. With that in mind, she said, "Sure, I'm willing to give him a call to see if he wants to talk."

Even as she said the words, Alana sent up a prayer—just to be safe—that Justin would turn down her offer.

4

HOW WAS IT that two weeks in a row he managed to leave Beth's house feeling like his emotions were wrecked? Justin felt like he was losing control of everything. Why had she insisted on telling Marcus about what was going on with Genevieve? The problems facing their family were *his* responsibility, not Marcus's.

He let himself into his apartment and dumped his laptop bag and weapon case onto the couch before taking his duffle bag into the hallway. After jerking open the closet doors that hid the stacking washer and dryer, Justin began to dump his dirty clothes into the machine. He started the washer then went to his bedroom and found a pair of clean work-out clothes and changed into them.

Once in the second bedroom that he'd converted to a work-out space, Justin found the playlist he used while running and got it set up with the speakers. As the music pulsed through the room, he stepped onto the treadmill and set it to his usual setting and began to run. He probably should have stretched first, but right then he just needed the soothing motions of working out to help him deal with the jumble of emotions in his head.

There were two things that meant the world to him: his family and his job. And while things were fine with his job, it certainly didn't feel that way with his family. He and Beth seemed to be at odds for the first time in...forever. He couldn't remember the last time he'd left her angry, but that's what had happened twice now in as many weeks. And on top of that, his efforts to find out more about the woman who'd made her way into their life had been thwarted.

Justin hit the button to push the treadmill past his usual comfort level for running. His heart rate was already elevated, but he needed to feel the burn. He needed to force his breath in and out in order to loosen the tightness of his chest. Sweat beaded on his forehead and torso and ran unchecked down his neck and back. He clenched his fists as he pumped his arms to keep up with the rhythm of his feet.

He needed to make things right with Beth and Dan. They were the only people in the world—along with Genevieve—who mattered at all to him. Without them, his life really had no purpose. From the day he'd gotten the call about the tragedy, Justin's life had been centered on doing what he could to help Beth work through it all and to give her as normal a life as possible in spite of everything. He'd had to adjust some when Dan had come on the scene, but, strangely enough, the man had seemed to understand his need to care for Beth, and they had found themselves on common ground. They both wanted what was best for her.

But now it was Beth and Dan standing firm together while he stumbled around in quicksand trying to figure out what on earth had happened to his family.

The music dropped in volume as his ringtone trilled through the speakers. Justin hit the button to stop the treadmill and slid off, grabbing the towel he'd left on the handle and wiping his face while he still gasped for breath.

He picked up the phone from the stand and stared at the unfamiliar number a moment before answering. "Hello?"

"Justin?"

"Yes." He tried to keep from panting, but he didn't recover that quickly from an intense workout. "Who's this?"

"Uh, this is Alana, Beth's friend. Is this a bad time?"

Knowing he couldn't carry on a conversation while breathing so hard, Justin said, "Let me call you back in a minute."

Not wanting to stand there breathing heavily in her ear like some perverted caller, he ended the call without waiting for her response. Justin draped the towel over his shoulders then opened the French doors leading to the large balcony that looked out over the Twin Cities. The fresh air that greeted him helped to cool his heated skin. He took several deep breaths in an attempt to slow his heart rate and breathing

When his heart no longer pounded and his breaths didn't come in pants, Justin pressed the button on his screen to call Alana back. When she hadn't answered after two rings, Justin wondered if she'd decided she didn't want to talk to him since he'd ended their call so abruptly.

After the third ring, he heard her soft greeting. "Hello?"

"Hi, Alana. It's Justin. I'm sorry about earlier. What can I do for you?"

There was silence for a couple of seconds before she said, "I'm hoping it might be more what I can do for you."

"For me?" Justin lifted the edge of the towel to wipe any remaining moisture from his face.

"After you left earlier, Beth and Daniel realized that maybe things could have been handled differently."

"What things?" Justin walked to the railing that ran along the outside edge of the balcony. He gripped the metal in one hand.

"I think they both realize now that maybe they should have told you about Genevieve's diagnosis sooner."

"You think?" As soon as he said the words, Justin let out a harsh breath. "I'm sorry. I know you had no part in the decisions they made back then."

"No, I wasn't part of that nor did I realize the closeness of the relationship between you and Genevieve or I would have suggested they let you know when they told me."

So far, nothing she said actually made him feel any better about the situation. "There's nothing we can do now. Decisions made can't be undone."

"Yes, that's true. And Beth and Daniel know that as well."

"So why did they have you call me?" The urge to get back on the treadmill or lift some weights slowly crept over him again.

"Though they understand where you are coming from and how you feel about Genevieve's diagnosis, they—Beth especially—is struggling to let herself feel those emotions again with you. The impact of them is still too close." She paused, and he heard her take a quick breath. "In a way, the news of Genevieve's hearing loss was a bit like a death."

"A death?" Justin stepped back into his apartment and shut the doors.

"They had dreams of a future that their little girl would have—something I'm sure you also had for her—and now the dreams are gone. They had to grieve the loss of that as well as the type of relationship they had envisioned having with her. They experienced the stages of grief, although to a lesser degree than what they would have with an actual death. But they did deal with the denial, guilt, anger and such. They're in a place where they're accepting what has happened and are trying to make adjustments for a different future than they planned. I think Beth is scared to go back to the denial and anger stages that you're likely experiencing."

Justin's chest tightened. He knew all about the stages of grief. Though he hadn't wanted to, he'd sat through counseling sessions with Beth after the death of their whole family. Was that really what he was going through once again? "Are you a shrink or something?"

"No, I'm not. I'm just someone who has been through what you, Beth and Daniel are dealing with."

"Did your son lose his hearing like Genevieve?" Justin asked as he walked toward the kitchen. He pulled open the fridge and stared at its empty interior. Well, not quite empty. There was an egg carton—holding how many eggs, he had no idea—and a couple bottles of water. He grabbed one of them and quickly twisted the lid off.

"No. Caden was born deaf."

"So do you know what caused his hearing loss?" Justin swallowed half the bottle as he waited for Alana to reply.

"It was genetic. Apparently both his father and I carry a gene for it."

Justin wanted to ask where the boy's father was now, still curious about the reason for the name change, but he sensed that this conversation needed to stay centered on the current situation. "So you don't think you'll have the same problem as Beth?"

"No. I'm far enough removed from all of those feelings that I don't get caught up in them like Beth might. Other things might trigger my emotions, but not helping someone else come to grips with the diagnosis of permanent hearing loss."

"And you think you'd be able to help me?" Justin sat down on a chair at the kitchen table and ran a hand through his damp hair.

"Maybe. I can answer questions you might have about adapting to life with hearing loss. Over the years, I've met people of all ages who are deaf, and I can share their stories with you. It might help you to understand that life isn't over for Genevieve. She can live a full and happy life even with hearing loss."

Justin sincerely doubted she'd be able to do that for him. If the psychologists couldn't help him after his family's death, there was no way this woman would be able to either. However, he saw in her offer the opportunity to find out more about Alana and the secrets she hid. He had to make sure that whatever was in her past wouldn't end up hurting his family.

And all the better that the suggestion came from her and Beth. He'd been trying to figure out the best way to draw her out but knew it wouldn't be easy to ask her questions without raising red flags. Thankfully, she was offering of her own accord to talk about her experiences, opening the door to questions about her past. He might not be able to do anything about Genevieve's diagnosis, but he could make sure Beth and Daniel were not taken advantage of in the midst of it all.

"Maybe it would be helpful to hear about things like that," Justin said, trying not to seem too eager. When there was silence on the other end of the line, he realized that in all likelihood she'd assumed he'd decline her offer. He could still picture the fear in her eyes on the two occasions he'd interacted with her. "When would be a good time for you?"

"Uh… Maybe Saturday afternoon? Caden is going to a friend's house for a couple of hours."

"Should I come by your place?"

"No." There was no hesitation before she responded that time, and the trace of alarm in her tone had Justin making a mental note to find out where she lived.

"Why don't you decide where to meet and then let me know," Justin suggested.

"Okay." Her voice was more subdued now. "I'll let you know by Friday."

"Sounds good." When she didn't reply, he added. "Guess I'll see you on Saturday."

After she'd said goodbye and hung up, Justin sat staring at his phone for a bit. In truth, he wouldn't have minded having someone to talk to about this. The problem was that he wasn't close to anyone but Beth and Dan. Of the guys at work, he was probably closest to Than and Trent, but not close enough to be able to spill his guts about what was going on. Still, he wouldn't be spilling his guts to Alana Jensen either. He just wanted to get her comfortable enough to spill hers.

Well, that certainly hadn't gone as planned. Alana tossed her phone onto the daybed and paced over to the kitchen. She grabbed a glass from the cupboard and shoved it under the tap, cranking the handle to start the flow. As water filled it, she replayed the conversation she'd just had with Justin. She was usually so good at reading people. According to everything she'd seen of Justin, the idea of talking over his feelings should have sent him running in the opposite direction. But the reverse had happened, and now she had to meet with him face to face.

Not at all what she'd planned. She sat down at their small dining table and propped her elbows on it. Squeezing her eyes shut, Alana tried to ignore the growing ache in her head. She still had work to do after putting Caden to bed. Thankfully, he'd been happy to play some games on his tablet while she'd called Justin.

With a sigh, she pushed back from the table and went to the tiny bedroom of their one bedroom apartment and sat down on the mattress next to Caden. When he looked over at her, she signed that it was almost bedtime. His brows drew together, and he gave a quick shake of his head before pleading his case for staying up...again.

Not in the mood to argue, Alana let him know he had thirty more minutes and then it was bedtime. Though she had things to do, she curled up next to him on the mattress and watched him as he played his game. It was one of two luxuries she'd brought with them from their old life. The other was her laptop that she knew she'd need in order to support them. She just hoped that neither of them stopped working anytime soon.

She looked around the sparsely furnished room and couldn't help remembering the home they'd come from. Caden had been just five years old when they'd left, but she was certain he must have memories of Florida even though he never spoke of their home there. The spacious and beautifully decorated rooms. The toys his father had allowed her to buy for him. The swimming pool where he learned to swim.

When they'd fled their home, she'd been limited in what she could take. But he had his tablet, and along the way she'd picked up a bucket full of Legos. Now that they were settled in one place, he also had all the books he could want from the nearby library. It didn't seem to bother him that his mattress sat directly on the floor instead of a bedframe. Nor did he seem at all concerned that his clothes were put away in plastic drawers instead of a real wood chest of drawers.

When they'd moved into the apartment ten months ago, Alana had given him the bedroom since she'd be staying up later than him most nights and needed to be able to work without keeping him awake. Though she did keep her clothes in a set of plastic drawers in his room, she slept each night on the daybed in the living room. It had been left by the previous occupants and she'd put it to good use once she'd replaced the mattress. It wasn't much, their little apartment, but it *was* theirs.

Since they'd moved around for the first year or so, finally putting down roots had been a blessing. She'd used up all the money she'd saved before leaving Florida, so it had been necessary for her to find some work and she really could only do that once they had settled down somewhere. Plus, she'd needed to start teaching Caden, and homeschooling while they hopped from town to town had been challenging. Since setting up their home in Minneapolis, Caden had thrived with his schooling.

And things had actually been going very well. Though the church hadn't been part of her life when she'd left Craig, she'd made friends with a woman at one of the shelters where they'd stayed who had shared about her faith. It had amazed her that someone who had gone through something similar to her had such peace and joy. She had wanted that for herself.

Since settling in Minneapolis, she'd found a church with a strong deaf ministry and quickly got involved. The church even gave her a small salary to sign during the church services. The rest of her money came from doing things on the internet. She had a blog and an email list where she featured books that were on sale each day. She was able to earn some money through affiliate sales that way and also through some advertising spots on her blog. Freelance writing jobs that she acquired made up the balance of her income.

They wouldn't be able to survive on just one of those things, but all together, they generally brought in enough money to cover rent, the few bills they had and groceries. She also tried to put aside a few dollars each month...just in case.

It certainly wasn't how she'd envisioned her life unfolding, but at least now she and Caden were both safe. And they'd stay that way as long as she didn't let Justin into their life. She'd meet with him this once and after that, she'd only agree to see him when she was at Beth and Daniel's. Never again would she allow herself to be in the position where a man could use his strength against her. Justin had Craig beat in the muscle department, and she sensed the underlying tension in him that was just like her ex had exhibited.

God had given her a brain, and she intended to use it when it came to dealing with someone like Justin.

"Something on your mind?"

Justin looked up from the mat where he'd landed flat on his back after Alex Thorpe had managed to get the better of him. Normally, Marcus was the only one who could do that to him. When Alex held out his hand, Justin took it and came to his feet.

"Seriously," Alex said, concern in his blue eyes, hands on his hips. "Is there something going on? Because I really doubt I've improved that much."

Justin walked over to a nearby bench and grabbed the towel he'd left there earlier. He used it to dry the sweat on his face before looping it around the back of his neck, holding onto each end with his hands. "Just dealing with some personal stuff."

"Personal stuff?" Alex arched a brow as he reached for a towel. "Dude, did you go and get yourself a personal life? A girlfriend, maybe?"

Justin gave him a frustrated look. Alex and his sisters were the only ones in the company who knew his history and his connection to Marcus. He was kind of surprised Marcus hadn't shared anything with Alex since the two of them were best friends. "No. No girlfriend. Just stuff going on with Beth."

Concern crossed Alex's face. "She okay?"

Justin picked up his phone and checked the display as he nodded. "Yeah. We'll work it out."

He felt Alex's hand on his shoulder and looked at him. The man had obviously gotten the hint that he didn't want to talk about it.

"Well, if there's anything I can do, let me know."

That would never happen, and they both knew it. "Sure. I'll do that."

"I expect you to keep the upper hand next week or we'll be doing coffee so we can chat."

"Well, that's definitely an incentive," Justin said with a laugh.

Alex grinned. "I figured it would be."

As the other man walked away, Justin flipped his phone over and over in his hand. There was still no text or call from Alana. He wondered if she was going to back out and found himself feeling strangely disappointed at the thought.

"Hey, Justin!"

Justin looked up to see Dan walking toward him, dressed in a suit and carrying a briefcase. Though the BlackThorpe compound was heavily secured, he had put both Dan and Beth's names on the approved list of visitors so they would be let in without a hassle. They didn't visit often, but Dan had come by a few times to work out with him.

"Dan," Justin said as his brother-in-law came to a stop in front of him.

Dan's gaze went from the top of Justin's head down to his feet. "I swear you just keep getting bigger and bigger, man. You really should share the wealth, you know."

"You want the muscles, you gotta do the work. I ain't gonna hand you anything I've worked for," Justin said with a grin. He crossed his arms over his chest and stared at the other man. "What's up? I'm sure you didn't come all this way just to admire my physique."

With a sigh, Dan nodded. "You're right. I do have a reason for bearding the lion in his den."

Justin arched an eyebrow at that comment. "Everything okay with Beth and Genevieve?"

"Yes. All things considered." He motioned to the bench. "Can we sit for just a minute?"

Trying to ignore the tightness in his chest, Justin sank onto the hard surface of the bench. "What's on your mind?"

Dan stared out at the room, his profile tense. "I realize now that perhaps Beth and I made a mistake when we didn't include you sooner in what was going on with Genevieve."

The pressure in Justin's chest increased. "You're her parents. There was no need for me to be included."

Dan turned to look at him, sadness in his gaze. "You know that's not true. You love Genevieve as if she was your own daughter."

Justin couldn't maintain eye contact with his brother-in-law, so he looked over to where a couple of guys were sparring on a nearby mat. He wondered if Dan was recalling the moment they had placed newborn Genevieve in his arms for the first time. It had been a long labor for Beth, but Justin had stayed in the waiting room the whole time. And when they'd finally come and got him, his own exhaustion had thinned the cover he usually kept over his emotions. He'd taken one look at the little girl's face and cried.

He'd cried for the hugs from his parents she'd never experience. He'd cried for the fun she'd never have with his more easy-going and fun-loving siblings, all of whom would have doted on her. He'd even cried for the cousins she'd miss out on having. And he'd vowed to be everything she'd be missing in her life since it was just him and Beth left in their family.

"Justin, Beth and I made the decision out of equal parts concern and selfishness. And I want to apologize for that. We should never have kept that information from you." Dan lifted his briefcase onto his lap and opened it. He reached in and pulled out a folder. "I want you to have these."

Justin took the folder and gave Dan a curious look. "What is it?"

"These are the results of all the tests Genevieve has had done. I know you've probably been trying to research on your own, but you won't know what to look for if you don't know what tests she's already had. You're welcome to go to a doctor and see what they say about the test results. I wish I could tell you that their answers will be different from what we've heard, but I think that's highly unlikely."

As he flipped through the thick stack of papers, Justin saw a lot of terms he didn't understand but give him a couple of days and he'd have it figured out. "Thank you, Dan. I really don't want to step on your or Beth's toes in this situation, but I just can't process this without more information. I just need...to understand."

Dan slapped his back. "I get that. I put myself in your shoes—something I should have done on day one of all this— and knew I would need more than just some vague information to work through it all."

Not for the first time, Justin realized just how glad he was that this was the man his sister had married. He was a decent guy and since he worked for the FBI, he understood a lot about what BlackThorpe did. In fact, Marcus had tried on more than one occasion to woo Dan to the company. Dan was smart and super tech savvy. While Trent was their computer guru, Dan was all that and also very knowledgeable about all the latest gadgets used by the good *and* bad guys. A lesser man might have been intimidated by Justin's presence in Beth's life, but Dan had accepted him without question, understanding that in a way, they were a package deal.

"Does Beth know you've given this to me?" Justin asked as he lifted the folder.

"Yes."

The text tone sounded on his phone, and Justin glanced down to where he'd put the phone on the bench beside him. He couldn't really read the text, but he'd leave it to reply to once Dan had left. "Is it okay if I ask you questions once I've read it."

"Certainly." Dan cleared his throat. "But it might be better if you direct those to me instead of Beth."

"Understood."

"Well, I'd better get home. Hope you'll join us for supper again on Monday."

"As long as nothing comes up work-related, I'll be there." Justin got to his feet when Dan did and shook the man's hand.

"Good. See you then."

Justin stood with his arms crossed, folder tucked under his arm, as he watched Dan make his way from the workout room. Armed with more information, he was eager to get in front of a computer as soon as possible. He and Google were going to be spending some quality time together.

As he bent to scoop up his phone, he remembered the text message and pressed the button to activate the screen. Sure enough, it was a message from Alana. She wanted to meet at three o'clock the next afternoon at a restaurant not too far from Beth and Dan's house.

He quickly typed out an offer to pick her up. So far he'd come up blank in a search for her address. Apparently, Alana Jensen had no driver's license, which might explain why she took the bus everywhere. She also didn't appear to be employed anywhere, nor was Caden enrolled in a school that anyone could find. While he realized it was possible she was homeschooling him, what was she doing for money?

And that was the main reason he was meeting with her. Two and two were not adding up to four in the case of Alana Jensen. He needed to find out why.

5

IT DIDN'T SURPRISE Justin that the text that came back almost immediately was to decline his offer. That was fine. He had other ways to find out where she lived that he hadn't explored yet. Sooner or later, he'd have her address in his hand.

Before leaving the gym, Justin tapped out a quick message to Trent Hause to let him know he wouldn't be available the next afternoon if he and his fiancé, Victoria, planned to come out to the compound to shoot and spar as they usually did on Saturday afternoons, unless they wanted to come earlier.

Trent's reply came quickly. *Got a date, man?*

Justin rolled his eyes as he walked into the changing room. *Nope. More important things to do.*

Oh, my friend, you really should make time for a woman in your life.

Sure, Trent would feel that way. He was engaged to a great woman. The first time Justin had met Victoria, who also happened to be his co-worker, Eric McKinley's younger sister, he'd been a bit curious about her. Given that she had a form of dwarfism that no doubt made life a bit more challenging for her, Justin had wondered about Trent's desire to teach her to shoot. But then he'd gotten to know her during her visits to the compound, and he quickly realized that Trent would do absolutely anything for her. He was glad his co-worker had found a woman that made him happy.

That didn't mean Justin was in any rush to find a woman for himself. His last relationship had ended a couple of years ago. She just hadn't been able to deal with the time he put into his job. He'd accepted Marcus's offer of a job because it paid well, and he'd needed a way to provide for Beth. In spite of that—or maybe because of it—he'd worked hard to prove that he deserved the job. That meant long hours and spending most nights of the week at the compound and no time for a social life outside his family.

Maybe one of these days. In the meantime...I'll be there next Saturday to keep you humble.

I look forward to it.

Justin pulled a pair of sweatpants and a sweatshirt on over his workout clothes. He grabbed his duffle bag and left the change room. He lifted his hand to the few remaining guys in the gym before pushing through the door to the long hallway that led to the stairs. He took them all the way down to the basement and then followed the tunnel that led between the buildings. And then it was back up another three flights of stairs to his small apartment on the third floor of the barracks building.

There were three other apartments on the floor. All fairly sparse in décor and furniture, just as his was. The other apartments were usually reserved for overflow from the barrack-style rooms on the second floor. Occasionally, they were used for important visitors or if they had a married couple in for training. His was the furthest away from the staircase.

Natural light flowed into the hallway from the large glass windows that lined the wall to his left. He pulled his keys from the pocket of his duffel bag and let himself into his apartment. All he planned to do was shower and change before heading back down to the cafeteria. He didn't always have that option on the weekends, but they currently had a group in who were there for a solid two weeks, so they had staff come in to cover the meals on the weekends. Justin was happy with that since it meant he didn't need to try to drum up meals for himself in the small kitchen of his apartment.

Justin's stomach rumbled appreciatively as he walked into the cafeteria and got a whiff of what was cooking. Thankfully, BlackThorpe didn't skimp on the food they provided for the groups that came to train.

After getting food and something to drink, Justin found an empty table and sat down. He pulled out his phone to check for any emails that might have come throughout the afternoon. Between bites, he followed up on a couple of inquiries about possible training dates later in the year. He'd just sent the email when his text alert went.

You available to spar tomorrow?

Justin grinned when he saw the text was from Than. That must mean the man was back from his adventures in the Philippines. *When did you get back?*

Haven't landed yet, but feel the urge to punch something.

Justin chuckled. It looked like two weeks with Lindsay Hamilton had been more than Than could handle. *I have a meeting at three but could meet up with you around noon if you want.*

That would work. Thanks, man.

Justin set his phone down and picked up his fork. Once he was done with his meal, he gathered up his dishes and stood. After placing his tray on the counter by the kitchen, Justin left the cafeteria and returned to his apartment.

He made himself a cup of coffee and took it to his desk where he opened up his laptop and then laid the folder from Daniel next to it. He hoped that the contents would help give him direction when he went to look for a cure for Genevieve.

Between the file of information and the planned meeting with Alana the next day, Justin felt more in control than he had since that day almost two weeks ago when Beth and Daniel had dropped the bombshell on him.

Alana slid into the booth the hostess led her to.

"You're waiting for someone?" the woman asked as she set a laminated menu down in front of her and then one across from her.

Alana nodded. "He might ask for me. My name is Alana."

After the woman had left, Alana rubbed her palms along her thighs that were covered by the long denim skirt she wore. This was the last place she'd wanted to be, but she was a woman of her word.

"Hi! I'm Hope. Can I start you off with a drink?"

Alana looked up to find a petite woman standing next to the booth, a wide smile on her face. "Could I have a glass of water and tea?"

"Sure thing. I'll be back with those in just a minute." She gestured to the other menu on the table. "Is someone joining you?"

"Yes. He should be here in a few minutes."

Alone again, Alana gazed out the large glass window beside the booth. She had purposely chosen mid-afternoon to meet Justin so she could get away without having to order a meal. She bit her lip. Never before in her life had she had to watch her pennies so closely. Her parents had been well-off, but when their seventeen-year-old daughter found herself knocked up and decided to keep the baby, they'd quickly cut her off. She'd had no choice but to marry Craig, who, at twenty-three, was out of college and already doing fairly well at his job as a computer programmer along with some modeling on the side. Of course, his family was well-off so even without his work, he'd have still lived comfortably. The fact that he'd gone to college and then got himself a job—despite having a trust fund—had been a point in his favor, and even though he hadn't been the most generous man, she'd always had enough money to buy the things she and Caden needed.

The past year had been a crash course in couponing and stretching a dollar. Most the time she was okay with it and sometimes even relished the challenge, but lately, as Caden had begun to ask for things, it had become more than a challenge. It didn't help any that his eighth birthday was three months away, and she'd be lucky to be able to get one thing from the list he'd already given her.

The other stress from it all was trying to keep up the pretense around people. None of her friends from church— people like Beth and Daniel—had any idea of her financial circumstances. She never invited anyone over for coffee. She never accepted the offer of a ride home. She didn't want anyone's pity. Or worse...their charity.

She alone had made the decisions that had brought her to this point, so she alone would be the one to deal with the consequences.

"Alana?"

Alana jumped at the sound of her name and turned from the window to see Justin sliding into the booth across from her. His short dark hair looked damp like he'd taken a shower right before coming. He had on the same black leather jacket he'd worn the last two times she'd seen him, and she wondered if it concealed his weapons.

Before she could say anything, the waitress returned and slid a glass of water along with a small teapot and mug onto the table in front of Alana. The woman then turned to Justin and Alana watched as she smiled at him, the dimples in her cheeks prominent as she said, "Hi, there. I'm Hope. Can I get you something to drink?"

Justin glanced up at her. "Coffee, please." Once the waitress left, he said, "Have you ordered already?"

Alana shook her head. "I already had lunch."

Even as she said it, she willed her stomach not to growl. In reality, she'd been too nervous to eat anything but a granola bar before leaving the apartment. There was leftover spaghetti waiting for her and Caden once she picked him up.

"Well, I hope you don't mind if I order something. I'm starving."

As he picked up the menu to look at it, Alana took the time to study him. She still found it hard to believe he and Beth were related. Never mind just being different genders, they were opposites in pretty much every other way too. Beth was bubbly and outgoing while the only smiles she'd seen on Justin's face had come when he'd held Genevieve. And he looked to be about twice the size of his sister. He still hadn't taken off his jacket so Alana figured that he was, indeed, armed. She wasn't sure how she felt about it, but he didn't strike her as a man who would shoot someone or something without provocation.

Suddenly he looked up, and his intense blue gaze met hers. Alana felt a flush rise in her cheeks, but she fought the urge to look away.

"What's the verdict?" he asked.

Alana clasped her hands in her lap. "The verdict?"

"I could feel you studying me like I'm under a microscope." He said the words without any inflection. Just a statement.

She should have known that with a job like his, he'd be acutely aware of what was going on around him. "You're very different from Beth."

His eyebrows rose slightly at her response. "Yes, that's true."

Then it was her turn to feel like she was under the microscope. It was only fair, she supposed, but that didn't keep her skin from heating and her stomach from clenching.

"Do you have any siblings?"

The question took her by surprise. She hadn't anticipated having to answer any personal questions during their meeting. This was supposed to be about Alana's experience with hearing loss and how that related to Genevieve.

"I have an older brother and sister." Neither of whom cared about her the way that Justin obviously did for Beth.

"Do they live here?"

"No." Knowing what the company Justin worked for did, she wasn't all that keen to give him too much personal information. He could likely find out all he wanted about her without much trouble. If he hadn't already.

She sucked in a quick breath. Had he checked out her background? Now that she thought about it, it made sense. After all, she'd seen how overprotective he was with Beth. He would want to make sure no one in Beth's life presented a danger to her or Genevieve. The thought that he might already know the ugliness of her past made her nauseous.

"Have you decided what to order?" Hope, the waitress with the dimples was back, smiling broadly at Justin.

He looked at Alana. "You sure you don't want anything?"

"I'm fine."

Alana felt a rush of relief when he turned his attention back to the menu. She had to get this meeting back on track. She'd promised Beth and Daniel she'd try to help Justin understand what was going on. But that hadn't included talking about herself except in relation to her experience with hearing loss.

"I'll have the double cheeseburger with fries and a bowl of the chicken noodle soup. And a vanilla milkshake."

Alana fixed her tea with significant amounts of sugar and cream before taking a sip of the hot liquid. Hopefully adding more calories to the beverage would calm her stomach.

Once the waitress was gone, Alana said, "I'm sure you've been doing some research on hearing loss in children. Do you have any specific questions about it?"

Justin stared at her. His expression hadn't changed, but Alana didn't doubt for a minute that he knew what she was doing.

"Actually, Dan came by yesterday and gave me copies of all the tests Genevieve has had done and what the doctors have said about it so far. I spent some time searching on the internet last night."

Alana nodded. "The most difficult part of Genevieve's diagnosis is that what caused it is unknown. I know Beth and Daniel are both concerned about future children also having hearing loss even though it doesn't appear to be a genetic form of deafness."

"You said your son's was?" Justin asked.

She hesitated. Any questions about her and Caden opened the door to revealing too much about her past. "Yes. In his case, we found out fairly quickly he was deaf. He hasn't known anything else. Genevieve likely won't remember being able to hear either."

"Where is Caden's father?"

Hope walked up then with his order, distracting him from their conversation. Alana held her breath, hoping he'd move on to something else. However, when they were alone again, he picked the burger up—but before taking a bite—he prompted, "Caden's father?"

"We're divorced. Something like this can cause strain on a marriage. I'm glad to see that Beth and Daniel are so close. They are definitely taking this on as a team."

"So your son being deaf caused your divorce?"

"Yes. Among other things. As I said, Beth and Daniel seem to have a pretty strong marriage. I doubt something similar will happen with them." Alana took another sip of her tea. "Genevieve will have a good support system in place with them and you. They are eager to learn sign language which will help keep communication open with Genevieve."

"I suppose you think I should learn as well," Justin stated as he lifted his milkshake.

Alana tried to ignore the smells drifting across the table toward her. She pressed her hands against her stomach. "If you take lessons now at the same time she's learning, it will be easier. I learned when Caden was a baby which made it easy to incorporate it into his natural learning process. I'm not saying you couldn't learn at a later date, just that it would be easier if you start now."

"Did Caden's father learn it as well?" Justin took a bite of his burger, his gaze expectant as he watched her.

Frustration grew within Alana. This was what she wanted to avoid. But if she appeared reluctant to answer questions, it was likely to raise alarms with him. "No. He didn't."

Justin's brows drew together briefly as he set his burger down. "So how do he and Caden communicate?"

"They don't." Alana hoped there was nothing in her voice that betrayed the sadness she felt about her son not having a father who loved him. "He is not part of Caden's life."

Alana braced herself for another question directed to her personal life. This was not going well at all. She realized now that it was likely Justin hadn't seen their meeting so much as an opportunity to learn more about how to adjust to Genevieve's diagnosis as it was to find out more about her. He wouldn't let some stranger waltz into his sister's life without making sure they were safe.

Her shoulders slumped, and she stared down at the table. She was trying to do a good thing for Beth and Daniel—trying to help them—but to have her own life come under scrutiny was a little scary. It wasn't like she was hiding a criminal past. She just wanted her past to stay in the past. She was working so hard to set up a new life now. It hurt to have someone like Justin come along and rip it all open again.

She took a deep breath and looked up to meet his clear blue gaze. "I get that you're concerned about who Beth and Daniel might have let into their life. I'm sure that by this point, you've at least tried to do a background check on me."

Something flickered in Justin's eyes, but he didn't say anything.

"If you stick to legal channels, you'll come across sealed documents regarding a name change for me and Caden." Alana paused and took another breath, forcing herself to keep her gaze on Justin's. "If you take a less above-board approach, you'll likely be able to get past the seal to find the file filled with the pictures taken of the injuries I sustained as a result of my ex-husband's abuse of me. Which is the reason for the sealed file."

Justin straightened and leaned back against the booth. She could read absolutely nothing from his expression, and he remained silent.

"And if you don't want to wait to see the proof in the file...here." Alana laid her left arm on the table, pulling up the long sleeve of the shirt she wore. She didn't look down to see what he was seeing. It was an all too familiar sight. There were puckered scars from the burns and cuts he'd inflicted on her, promising that if she protested, he'd go after Caden.

"Alana..." Justin's voice was rough, and she saw emotion in his eyes that hadn't been there before. Too bad it took stripping her soul bare in order to make him see that she wasn't a threat.

"I'm no danger to Beth or Daniel. All I'm trying to do is help them and to make a better life for my son than we had with his father. If you'd rather I didn't go around them anymore, just let me know." Her hands were shaking as she reached into her pocket and pulled out the twenty dollar bill she'd placed there earlier. Since she'd initiated the meeting, she'd planned to pay. She laid it on the table, hoping he didn't see her fingers trembling. Sliding out from the booth, she said, "You have my number. Call me when you make your decision."

"Alana. No."

He reached for her arm, but Alana evaded him. If just being near him brought about reactions she'd thought she'd moved past, she couldn't imagine what his touch might do.

She didn't look at him again as she moved as quickly as she could to the entrance of the restaurant. He called her name again, but Alana was no longer interested in talking with him. She spotted a bus approaching the stop she'd arrived at earlier, and she started running toward it. It didn't matter where the bus was going, she just needed to be on it. She'd figure out how to get home once she'd put some distance between herself and Justin.

"Alana!"

She was a bit surprised that he hadn't managed to catch up with her, but a quick glance over her shoulder showed he was only part way across the parking lot. As she climbed onto the bus, she flashed her pass at the driver. When his gaze went past her, she saw concern there.

"Please just go," Alana said, taking advantage of what the driver had likely deduced from the scene unfolding in front of him.

Justin's black leather jacket and large build gave him a scary look that no doubt helped make up the driver's mind to get going before Justin could reach them. As the bus lurched forward, she slumped down into a seat on the far side so that she didn't have to see Justin.

Anger coursed through her. Partly at herself—she should have been able to handle being around him—but she was also angry at Justin. Maybe she shouldn't have run off, but frankly, once she'd realized the sole purpose of Justin's meeting with her had been to get information on *her* and not to discuss Genevieve's hearing loss, there had been no reason to stay. If he had come right out and asked her about her past, she would have told him. From conversations she'd had with Beth, it had been apparent Justin was very protective of his family. With that perspective, it made sense that he'd be concerned about her presence in their lives.

As the distance between her and Justin grew, Alana slowly came to the realization she probably shouldn't have just run off like that. But her fear, anger and not wanting to see pity in Justin's gaze had pushed common sense from her mind.

She sighed as she rested her head against the glass window for a moment before straightening and pulling the cord to request a stop. She needed to get off this bus and on the one that would take her to Caden.

Justin stalked back into the restaurant. Though he'd left the twenty on the table—which would have covered the bill—he returned to the booth he'd shared with Alana and slid into the seat. Thankfully, at this time of the day there weren't too many people in the restaurant to witness what had just gone down.

He sat for a moment staring blankly at the table. In his mind, all he could see were the scars marring Alana's skin and the fact that her arm had been thin...painfully so. And her words still rang in his head.

If you take a less above-board approach, you'll likely be able to get past the seal to find the file filled with the pictures taken of the injuries I sustained as a result of my ex-husband's abuse of me.

Even though he'd suspected something along those lines, hearing her say the words and looking at the proof for himself sickened him. Justin was no stranger to violence. Between his time in the military and viewing the photographs taken at the scene of his family's murders, he had an up close and personal acquaintance with violence. But seeing the scars on Alana's arms and imagining what her son might have endured or seen troubled him more than he liked to admit.

"Is everything okay?"

Justin looked up to see the waitress standing beside the booth, her gaze going to his half-eaten hamburger and the empty seat across from him. "Yeah. It's fine. Could you just bring me the bill, please?"

Without waiting for her reply, Justin pulled out his phone and tapped the screen to get to his contact list to make a call. When his contact in the research department answered, he said, "Couple things. I need you to stop any in-depth searching you have in progress for Alana Jensen."

There was a pause, but the man didn't question Justin's request. "I can do that. What else do you need?"

"I still need an address for her. As soon as you find that, send me the information."

"Will do."

After the call had ended, Justin got his wallet from his rear hip pocket. He folded the twenty dollar bill and slid it into his wallet then pulled out a credit card. When the waitress returned, he handed it to her.

"Do you want any of this packaged to go?" she asked.

"No, thank you." Once the bill was settled, he slid out of the booth and left the restaurant.

He climbed behind the wheel of his truck, but as he reached to start it, Justin remembered that he had Alana's phone number from the texting they'd done earlier. Not at all sure what he would say beyond apologizing, Justin found her number and added it to his contact list before calling her. He wasn't too surprised when it went to voice mail almost immediately. It was just a generic system message, so he tapped the screen to hang up.

Justin sat for a minute trying to regroup. Clearly, he'd underestimated Alana. He had no doubt she'd figured out pretty quickly he'd agreed to the meeting for a reason different from what she'd originally thought. But now what should he do? If he didn't get this fixed, and Beth found out what he'd done, she would be beyond livid. It was rare that she actually got mad, but when she did, Justin knew to steer clear. Except in this instance, she would be justified in hunting him down.

He ran a hand through his hair. Without question, he had gone overboard in his desire to make sure Alana wasn't out to scam his sister. He'd just felt so helpless when he'd found out about Genevieve's diagnosis. Maybe there was nothing he could do about that—though he hadn't yet given up hope—but he knew he could protect his sister and her family from someone that might take advantage of them when they were in the midst of the struggle to accept the news. Except he'd rushed ahead of himself, and now disaster was looming if he didn't fix things with Alana.

Well, she could send him to voicemail and even ignore any message he left, but chances were it would be harder for her to ignore a text. He brought up their last text message exchange and stared at the phone trying to figure out the best way to start the conversation. He had a sneaking suspicion it was going to be a one-sided conversation, but hopefully she'd at least read them.

Alana – I apologize for asking questions I had no right to ask. He paused again. Should he explain to her why he'd done it? Really though, he'd had no excuse for delving into her past the way he had. She'd been pretty close to right on with her assessment of the paths he was taking to get information on her. Never before had he felt bad for taking steps to protect his sister. But this thing with Alana. Justin shook his head then pressed send.

He waited for a minute, but there was no response so he tapped out another message. *And it's not up to me whether*

you continue to work with Beth and Daniel. They both
clearly want your help so I won't do anything to disrupt
that.

He paused again before tapping the screen to send the
message. Once sent, he sat for a few minutes to see if she'd
reply. When she didn't, he slid the phone onto the console
between the seats and started the truck. He debated where to
go. His apartment? The compound? Beth's? Each had a
draw, but in the end, Justin turned the truck to the west and
headed back to his stark apartment at the compound.

6

ALANA STILL HAD an hour before she needed to pick Caden up from his friend's house. He didn't have a lot of playdates, so she hated to cut it short because of her problems with Justin. Peter, the boy he was spending time with, was a couple of years older than him, but he was also deaf so the two of them got along well. They'd met Peter and his family at the church where his mother, Suzanne, was the boys' Sunday school teacher. Caden had been able to participate in the program because Suzanne taught both verbally and with signs. The church's deaf ministry was the main reason Alana had chosen the church, and it had ended up being a great decision.

She got off the bus near a favorite thrift store not far from the house where she'd need to pick up Caden. There wasn't anything she needed, but it seemed that every couple of weeks Caden outgrew his pants. At least the warm weather made it easier since she could cut off his old pants and get a bit more wear out of them. He always outgrew the length before the waist. It appeared he was destined to reach his father's height which was fine with her as long as that was all he inherited from the man. In appearance, she knew he favored her with his hair and eye coloring. It also appeared Caden was more like her personality-wise because it was rare he ever got angry over anything. He'd been a fairly mellow baby and had grown into an easy-going, sensitive young boy.

The tension eased from her body as she looked through the racks of boys' clothes. She managed to find a couple pairs of jeans as well as three T-shirts. He would be particularly pleased with the one that had Spiderman on the front of it. Relieved that the day was turning around, Alana wandered through the store to kill a bit more time. When she eventually approached the cash register, she recognized the cashier.

"Alana, sweetheart! Good to see you again." Mary Ellen, a retired school teacher, always greeted her with a warm smile. "Where's that darling boy of yours?"

"He's with a friend for the afternoon." She laid her selections on the counter. "I found a few things for him though."

As the woman rang up the purchases, she said, "Did you see the new selection of ladies' clothes we just got in? I'm sure several of them would fit you perfectly."

Being fairly particular about what she wore, Alana shook her head. "What I have is serving me well. Fortunately, Caden is the only one growing out of his clothes these days. "

When the woman told her the total, Alana frowned. "I think you must have rung something in too low."

Mary Ellen smiled as she put the items into a bag. "Special sale today on boys' clothes."

Alana wanted to argue with her as she pulled her wallet from her purse. But honestly, after the twenty dollars she'd spent on Justin's meal and her tea, saving a few dollars here would be a blessing. As she slid the cash across the counter to Mary Ellen, she said, "Thank you."

"Next time bring the little guy with you. I've been learning a few signs and want to try them out on him."

Warmth spread through Alana. "Really? That's terrific. I know Caden will be thrilled."

As she left the store and headed to pick up Caden, Alana found she couldn't keep her thoughts from going to her meeting with Justin. Now that she had a little distance from it—and him—she realized that the overriding emotion she felt was anger. Not fear like she'd initially had when first meeting him but anger that he'd turned her offer to help him into an info-gathering mission.

The choices she had made over the past few years hadn't been about hurting anyone. She'd done it to protect her son. Beth and Daniel weren't the first family she had helped either. Regardless of what Justin thought her capable of, all she was doing was trying to support families who were dealing with something she had gone through herself. She didn't even take money for teaching them sign language. Why Justin was questioning her motives, she had no idea.

She'd read the two text messages he'd sent. It was hard for her to take his apology at face value. That was one thing she'd learned at the hands of her ex. His apologies after hurting her were meant to keep her off-guard. They had always been so sincere—sometimes accompanied by things he knew she loved. Flowers. Candy. A CD of her favorite group. Jewelry. And each time he stirred just enough hope in her heart to keep her chained to him so that she was still there the next time he had to vent his anger.

Verbal apologies meant nothing to her.

Suddenly, Alana realized she was stomping down the sidewalk. She rotated her head, trying to ease the tension in her shoulders. As she took a couple deep breaths, a verse popped into her head. One she'd struggled with the most since becoming a Christian.

It was the verse where Jesus told Peter to forgive a brother who sinned against him not seven times, but seventy times seven. Four hundred and ninety times. She'd used the calculator to figure that one out. Did that verse mean she should have just stayed with Craig and forgiven him each and every time he hurt her? Meeting with a counselor at one of the Christian shelters had helped her see that forgiving him didn't mean she had to stay with him when her life was in danger. She'd also come to realize that her unwillingness to forgive Craig held her trapped to him even though they were far apart. Forgiving him was to free *her* heart. It wasn't for his sake at all. She still struggled with that verse a lot.

And now Justin was on the receiving end of her inability to trust in apologies. If she never saw him again, it would be too soon. But as soon as the thought popped into her head, it was followed by the image of him cradling Genevieve in his arms. Of him pressing his cheek to her curls. Of Genevieve planting a big kiss on him. Surely the little girl wouldn't be so affectionate with someone who would hurt her. Even Caden had known to get out of the way when his dad came around. And Beth certainly adored her brother.

Could she accept his apology? Just this one time?

Before she had a chance to decide her answer to that, the house where Caden had spent the afternoon loomed in front of her. Pushing aside her thoughts to deal with later, Alana climbed the porch steps and pressed the doorbell. It was answered quickly by a slender woman with blonde hair. She smiled as soon as she saw Alana.

"C'mon in."

"Thanks, Suzanne. How was he?" Alana asked as she stepped into the foyer of the beautiful home. It was almost as nice as the home she'd left behind in Florida.

"He was perfect. As always." Suzanne motioned for her to follow as she walked toward the kitchen. "Can I get you something to drink? The boys are just playing a video game. They played some basketball, too."

"I'm good, thanks. I really appreciate you having Caden over for the afternoon. And I hate to drag him away, but we do need to leave."

Suzanne gave her a curious glance as she nodded and headed out of the kitchen. Alana knew that the women she'd met at the church couldn't quite figure her out. Considering the way she dressed, the fact that she took a bus everywhere and never had anyone to her home, made Alana a bit of a mystery to them. Which was the way she liked it. Disclosing the life she'd come from was like admitting she was weak. That she'd stayed with an abusive man for five years would no doubt make her look pathetic to them.

Beth and Suzanne wouldn't understand. They both had husbands who doted on them. Men who loved the children they had together regardless of the fact that they were deaf. No, they wouldn't understand where she had come from. One look at her scarred body would send them running scared. Just like her friends in Florida had done.

These women—along with the others at the church—were acquaintances more than friends, really. Their children were the only connection they shared. Her secrets kept her from getting too close to any of them because she knew abuse was a subject that made people feel uneasy. Hadn't she discovered that when she'd revealed what was going on to the two women in Florida who she thought were her best friends?

It had been shocking to sit there and listen to them tell her she must be mistaken, that Craig hadn't meant to hurt her. She'd laughed then—a hysterical, panicked laugh—when she'd realized they wouldn't help her. No, she wasn't going to risk that kind of reaction again.

Only now Justin knew about her past. She'd *shown* him her scars. Whatever had possessed her to do that? And she had felt desperate to leave before the look on his face could change from shock to pity. It was almost funny that she'd been able to shake the granite expression that was usually on his face. *Almost* funny.

Alana sighed. What was supposed to have been simple had turned into something way too personal for her liking. All she'd wanted to do was help Beth, Daniel, and sweet Genevieve.

She heard movement and turned to see Suzanne lead her son and Caden into the kitchen. Caden's face brightened when he saw her, and Alana knew she wore a similar expression. She used her hands to ask him if he'd thanked Miss Suzanne. He gave a quick nod but turned and did it again.

"Thanks again, Suzanne," Alana said as she took Caden's hand.

"We'll have to get them together again soon, especially once school is out," Suzanne said and then paused. "Oh. Do you stop homeschooling for the summer?"

Alana nodded. "Yes, he gets a break too."

"Then for sure once it warms up a bit more he should come over to swim. Peter loves the pool."

After agreeing to call to set up another playdate, Alana and Caden left the house and headed down the sidewalk. Though she was sure Caden had all kinds of things he wanted to share with her, they walked toward the bus stop without communicating. Once on the bus where she could pay attention to him without distraction, he'd tell her all about what he'd done with Peter. And for just a short time, she'd pretend her life hadn't just taken a weird turn because of her revelation to Justin.

Justin grabbed his bags and left the compound apartment. Hoping he didn't run into anyone wanting to talk, he stalked his way down the stairs and out to the parking lot to his truck. He was tired and sore, but it was the frustration that overrode all of that. Frustration that Alana still hadn't responded to his texts. He would have kept texting her if he'd thought it would make a difference, but something told him it wouldn't.

Thankfully, he made it to the truck without anyone stopping him. He tossed his bags into the back seat and climbed behind the wheel. It took effort to keep to the speed limit as he drove toward the Twin Cities. He'd sent Beth a text earlier to let her know he was going to stop by. Though he'd thought about asking if Alana would be there, he'd decided it might be better not to.

Recalling the time Alana and her son had arrived the previous week, Justin had left the compound early in hopes he might have a bit of time with Beth before Alana arrived. He was going to have to confess his stupidity—if Alana hadn't already done it for him. When things had started spinning out of control two weeks ago, he'd tried to regain that control in the wrong way. He knew that now. Things were still out of control—especially where Genevieve was concerned—and Justin couldn't ignore the feeling that things were about to change in his life. He just wasn't sure if it was for the better or the worse, and that, more than anything else, contributed to an overwhelming feeling of unease in his gut. And it was that unease that had contributed to his bad decision where Alana was concerned.

He kept an eye out for Alana and Caden as he drove the last few blocks to Beth's, but there was no sign of them. And it was apparent they hadn't already arrived when Beth let him into the house, Genevieve perched on her hip. After stowing his bags, he reached for the little girl and gave Beth a quick one arm hug.

"Hey, sweetie." He nuzzled the curls on top of her head and tried not to think about what was happening in her ears. "How was your day, Beth?"

She didn't look upset as she led the way into the kitchen so Justin assumed Alana hadn't told her about their disastrous meeting.

"It's been fairly quiet," she said as she reached for a cucumber on the counter. "How about you?"

Justin settled on a stool on the opposite side of the counter with Genevieve on his thigh. "It was a pretty lousy day since it rained. It made our outdoor training twice as hard and messy."

"But it's important the trainees get to experience that too, right?"

Justin nodded as he snatched a slice of cucumber and handed it to Genevieve. "Yep. But that doesn't mean I like it any better."

Beth gave a snort. "Like you'd have it any other way. If it really bothered you, you would get someone else to do the training runs."

"True." He watched as Beth dumped the cucumber into the salad bowl and moved on to a tomato. "Listen, Beth, I need to talk to you about something."

She glanced up at him, a frown on her face. "What's wrong?"

"I sort of did something that I realize now I shouldn't have."

Beth rested her hands on the cutting board and looked at him. "What did you do?"

Beat around the bush or straight to the point? "I asked someone to run a background check on Alana."

His sister let out a sigh as a frustrated look crossed her face. "Why would you do that, Justin?" Then she shook her head. "Never mind. I already know the answer to that question."

"There's more."

"Oh my goodness, Justin." Beth thumped her hand that held the knife on the counter. "Do I even want to know?"

"No, probably not, but I'm going to tell you anyway because otherwise you'll have questions when Alana gets here."

"Does she know what you did?"

"She suspects." When Beth didn't respond to that, he said, "We met Saturday afternoon so she could help me understand a bit more about everything regarding Genevieve's diagnosis."

Beth tilted her head, her brows drawing together. "Yes, we discussed that she might be the best one to help you with that. I didn't know she'd made arrangements with you already."

"Well, she did and we met, but I guess I asked one too many personal questions of her and she kind of bolted after giving me a brief rundown on her past."

His sister's blue eyes widened. "She bolted? Did you frighten her?"

Had she been scared? That wasn't exactly the feeling Justin had gotten, although perhaps there had been a little of that. "I think she was...mad."

"Well, big surprise, Justin Robert Morrell. I would be mad too. Actually, I *am* mad. *What* is your problem?"

Justin met Beth's gaze head on. "It's not a *problem* to want to keep my family safe."

Beth's expression turned from anger to sadness. "But that's not your job anymore, Justin."

Justin clenched his teeth and hoped it didn't show on his face how much that statement hurt. For seven years, they'd only had each other, and it had been his job to make sure she was safe. But then she'd married Daniel, and while Justin still only had her, she now had a husband. It was the second painful reminder in the past couple of weeks that he wasn't a part of their small family unit.

"It might—*might*—have been different if Daniel didn't have the job he does. Do you think he doesn't know how to protect me and Genevieve? He might not be all muscles and guns like you are, but I have full confidence he could keep us both safe if it should come to that."

Justin knew she was right, but he'd been her protector for *seven* years. Daniel had only held that role for three. Did she really think it was *that* easy to step aside? He had to admit she was right though. Daniel was more than capable of protecting Beth and Genevieve. He couldn't have picked a better husband for Beth.

Before he could respond, the noise of the garage door going up reached them. Not wanting to continue this after Daniel showed up, Justin said, "You're right. As I said, I did something I shouldn't have. I realize that now. I just wanted you to know in case Alana says something."

Beth stared at him for a moment before nodding. She laid down the knife and moved to greet Daniel as he walked into the house. As he watched his brother-in-law slide an arm around Beth and bend to kiss her, a totally foreign longing struck him. But even as Justin acknowledged what it was, he knew he needed to ignore it. There was no place for a wife and family in his life. His job was his life, and it would have to be enough.

Daniel came to where Justin sat. "Good to see you again, man."

"You too." Justin lifted Genevieve to relinquish her to Daniel.

"How about you make yourself useful," Beth said, setting a stack of plates on the counter and scooting them toward him.

With a nod, Justin picked up the plates and moved to the dining room table and began to set them out. Considering there were five plates, it was a pretty good indication that Alana and her son would be there for dinner too. He was headed back to the kitchen to get the silverware when the doorbell went.

His gaze met Beth's as Daniel walked toward the front door with Genevieve in his arms. Alana would have known he was there are soon as she saw his truck parked on one side of the wide driveway. She'd still chosen to come in, but Justin had no idea how she'd act when she saw him. He wished she'd at least phoned or texted him so they could have gotten this straightened out before seeing each other again.

He gathered the silverware into his hands and went back to the table, listening as Daniel greeted Alana.

"Hi, Alana. C'mon in. High five, Caden!"

Justin heard the slap of hands and then a happy squeal from Genevieve. The two kids were the first to appear in the open area between the dining and the living rooms. Caden held Genevieve's hand and his expression brightened when he saw Justin.

The boy let go of Genevieve and then gave him what looked like a modified salute followed by another sign. When Alana stepped behind her son, Justin looked up at her hoping she'd help him out.

"He said, *Hi, Justin.*"

Justin turned his gaze to Caden and said, "Hi, Caden," before looking back at Alana. "One of those signs was my name?"

She nodded. "He came up with a sign for your name after he met you the first time."

"What is the sign again?" Justin asked, somewhat relieved that they'd dived right into this which helped to alleviate some of the awkwardness between them.

Alana laid her hand on Caden's shoulder. When he looked at her, she signed something to him. He nodded and then turned back to Justin. Smiling, the boy lifted one arm like he was making a muscle and then made a motion in front of it with his other hand.

"He chose to make a muscle because you have..." Alana gestured to him. "You have muscles. Then the sign he makes in front of his arm is sign language for the letter J. Which is, of course, for Justin."

"So you don't just spell out letters of a person's name?" Justin asked.

"Sometimes. But sometimes a deaf person will use a characteristic of the person to give them a name sign. In this case, Caden chose what he saw as your most distinctive feature and put it together with the first letter of your name."

"So if he makes that sign, he's talking about me?" Even though he'd hadn't been interested in sign language up to that point, Justin found himself being drawn in by the boy's initiative in giving him a sign for his name.

"Yes."

Justin glanced around to find Daniel and Beth had joined them. "So what are Daniel, Beth and Genevieve's name signs?"

"He hasn't really given them a sign yet. For the most part, he just spells their names. Although he has shortened Genevieve's to just Geni."

"And what about you?" Justin asked.

"His sign for me is the one for mommy." Alana did a motion with her hand as she looked down at Caden. He smiled up at her and repeated the sign. Then after a look in Justin's direction, he signed more to his mother.

Alana lifted her head and met Justin's gaze. "He wants to know if you like the name sign he chose for you."

Caden's eyes were wide, his expression expectant as he stared at Justin. With the exception of Genevieve, Justin hadn't really spent much time around kids, but he could see how important this was to Alana's son, so he smiled and nodded at the boy. Immediately, a huge grin lifted the

corners of Caden's mouth and his green eyes lit up.
Something flipped inside Justin as he watched the boy's
reaction to his response. Knowing what he did now about
Alana's ex, Caden's father, he couldn't help but view the
young boy in a somewhat different light.

He looked up at Alana and their gazes met. He saw
apprehension on her face but didn't know what might have
caused it. Hadn't she wanted him to say he liked what Caden
had given him as a sign for his name? His interactions with
the woman all seemed to end up in a minefield of sorts.
Okay, so their meeting on Saturday had been a minefield
he'd set up himself, but now...he had no idea what he'd just
done to put that expression on her face.

And if he was honest with himself, he didn't like to think
about causing this woman any more distress than he already
had.

"Justin, why don't you finish up the table while I get the
food," Beth suggested, interrupting the heavy silence that
had descended on them. "And tonight, Alana, how about you
teach us some more sign language while we eat?"

Without waiting to hear Alana's response, Justin turned
back to the table and began to put the silverware into place.
Dan brought over the glasses and soon the food followed. By
the time they were ready to sit down, whatever had been
bothering Alana seemed to have faded away as she spoke
with Beth and Daniel.

Justin watched as Alana finished pouring water into the
glasses on the table. Again she wore a long loose skirt and a
blouse with sleeves that ended at her wrists. Now that he
knew what the sleeves hid, Justin wondered about other
scars her body might bear. Anger burned inside him against
the man who could do something like that to a woman. He
glanced at Caden and felt a little sick at the idea that the boy
might have scars of his own.

While he had no problem dealing out a beating himself
when needed, it would never be against a woman or child.
And any beatings he did give were always against valid
targets. Ones who had as much chance of winning their
battle as he did. And right then he knew if he ever came

across Alana's ex, he would be more than happy to beat on the man.

As the meal progressed, Alana and Caden showed them a few signs. Beth and Daniel were quick to repeat the signs. Justin, however, just watched. He hadn't wanted to learn sign language because he'd seen it as accepting Genevieve's diagnosis as final. However, watching them sign to each other, he realized there were still people besides his niece—people like Caden—with whom he'd be able to communicate if he learned along with Beth and Dan.

"Justin, Caden wants to know if you will learn sign language too." Alana's voice drew him from his thoughts. "He'd like to be able to talk to you."

Justin looked at the boy and once again he saw that expression on his face. More used to people getting out of his way—well, except for the women who thought snagging a military man, even an ex-military man, was a good thing—Justin found Caden's fascination with him a bit perplexing. This kid was determined to interact with him and seemed to view him with a serious case of hero worship.

When he glanced back at Alana, he saw an almost pleading look on her face. "I'll think about it. I'm not sure I'll be much good though. Not as good as he is, that's for sure."

"He's had a lot of years to learn," Alana said, the tension on her face easing.

"You should at least try, Justin," Beth said as she placed more chunks of cut-up chicken on Genevieve's tray.

"We're actually starting off with fairly basic stuff," Alana said. "Being that Genevieve is still so young, we're learning the signs that relate to what she most likely would be able to communicate if she were a hearing child. Hi. Bye. Hungry. More. Mommy. Daddy. Things like that."

Justin knew that if he hoped to have any type of relationship with his niece in the years ahead, he would need to learn the language she used to communicate. Over the weekend, he'd had time to think over the whole situation. Not just about what had transpired with Alana, but also what was happening to Genevieve. He'd realized he needed to disconnect what had happened to their family in the past from what was currently going on with Genevieve. Though her hearing loss would definitely change the way her future might play out, she was still healthy. She was alive. She deserved to have the people in her life support her.

And none of this had taken God by surprise. But what could possibly be His plan for something like that? Justin wanted so badly to understand. That's always what it came down to for him. Needing to understand.

"I will try to learn as best I can," Justin said. "Languages have never really been my thing."

"Oh, Justin, thank you." Beth scooted out of her chair and came to hug him before Justin could even blink. "I knew you'd come around."

"You and I can practice together," Daniel said with a grin. "Languages aren't really my thing either."

He glanced at Alana, but her face was expressionless. He wondered if she'd been hoping he'd refuse to learn. Something told him this was the second time she'd underestimated him. Of course, he'd underestimated her as well. Though she gave off an air of vulnerability and, at times, fearfulness, Justin was beginning to see that she had strength underneath it all. It would have taken strength to leave an abusive situation and build a new life. From all appearances, she'd done a good job. Caden seemed to be a fairly well-adjusted child, all things considered.

The boy's only failing appeared be in choosing Justin as a person to be admired.

7

ALANA WAS THANKFUL for all the years of practice she had at managing her facial expressions. She'd learned to smile and be social even when every inch of her body pulsed with pain. It had taken her awhile to figure out that Craig had wanted a certain reaction from her. At first, she'd tried to keep from crying—tried to present him with a strong front—but that had only seemed to infuriate him even more. He usually stopped when she was a crumpled weeping ball on the floor. And once she realized that was what he wanted, she made sure to get to that point as soon as she could without raising his suspicions that she was manipulating him.

Unfortunately, she had a hard time reading Justin, which made her a little uneasy. Twice now she'd figured him wrong.

That was bad enough, but it was Caden's reaction to him that had her more concerned. She had no idea what exactly it was that had drawn him to Justin, but she had a feeling it had something to do with all the muscles, guns and macho-ness that made up Justin Morrell. Of course, added to that was the fact that Justin actually paid attention to him which no doubt made him rate pretty high in Caden's opinion.

Unfortunately, Caden wasn't the only one who was drawn to the man. Even though their own interactions had been a bit rocky, seeing how Justin was with Caden offset that for Alana. The way he'd looked right at Caden when replying— even though she had to translate—meant a lot to her.

So often people would look at her when answering since they knew she'd have to sign it for Caden. But Justin had looked right at her son and answered his question. The first time he'd done it, she'd wanted to thank him, and when he'd done it the second time she'd just about hugged him. He'd shown respect for Caden and that meant the world to her. It was almost enough to make her forgive him for what had happened on Saturday.

"Why don't we get this cleared up, and we can have a lesson while we eat dessert," Beth suggested.

Alana signed for Caden to help collect the plates. She could tell that he didn't want to but as soon as Justin stood up and started to help, Caden's reluctance disappeared. He moved around the table stacking the plates, his gaze on Justin. When the table had been cleared, Justin turned to Caden and held out his fist, knuckles up. With a wide grin, Caden made a fist and bumped it against Justin's. The man might not know sign language, but he definitely knew how to communicate with her son.

Dessert was an assortment of homemade cookies and brownies. Thrilled to be able to indulge her sweet tooth, Alana ate more than she probably should have, but they were just that good. Partway through, Genevieve began to get restless so when Beth took her out of the high chair, Alana asked Caden to go play with her for a bit.

She felt Justin's gaze on her as she went through a few signs. Beth and Daniel were quick to imitate her motions, but

Justin just watched. His dark blue eyes tracked her every movement, but his face didn't give away what was going on in his mind.

"C'mon, Justin," Beth said. "You need to practice the signs or you won't remember them."

His gaze flicked to Beth before looking back at Alana. "I'll remember them."

Alana shifted on the padded cushion of the chair she sat on, her hands in her lap. It was one thing for him to watch her while she was showing them signs but quite another when she wasn't doing anything. She could feel warmth spreading across her skin as she wondered what he saw when he looked at her.

It had been a long time since she'd really made much of an effort with her appearance. She couldn't remember the last time she'd had a haircut. The mass of curls nearly reached her waist if she left it down—which she rarely did. There had been no money in the budget for makeup and the lotions she'd once used, so she'd settled for a very basic skincare routine and left off the makeup.

Up until this point, she hadn't cared what people—men in particular—thought of her appearance. And she needed to keep that mindset. Wondering what Justin might think of how she looked was heading down a dangerous road. One that would, no doubt, lead to hurt. Even if she didn't have the past she had, Justin didn't strike her as the type of man interested in marriage and a family of his own. And she wasn't the type to get involved with a man just because he was attractive.

Because, man, if she didn't find Justin just a teeny, tiny bit attractive.

After what had happened with Craig, Alana never thought she'd be attracted to a man who had the same focus on building muscles as her ex. All it had taken was for Justin to be nice to her son and she was ready to ignore everything else. *Stupid.* Yeah, that's what she was. *Stupid.* She needed to pull her focus back to the reason she was there and ignore the muscled man sitting across the table from her.

"Can I give you and Caden a ride home?" Justin asked when they had finished their lesson for the evening.

It was tempting—oh, so tempting—but given how her emotions and thoughts were already running, taking him up on his offer would definitely be the wrong move right then. "Thanks, but we're fine."

"Are you sure? It's no trouble," Justin said, his head bent as he looked down at her, his gaze intent.

"I'm sure." Alana was glad right then that Caden couldn't hear their conversation. No doubt he would have been trying to convince her to reconsider. He liked Justin's truck almost as much as he liked Justin.

Apparently Justin realized she wasn't going to change her mind, so he straightened and stepped back. After saying good-bye to Caden and Genevieve, he gave Beth a hug, shook Daniel's hand and left.

Once he was gone, Alana got Caden's attention and signed that they were leaving. As he guided Genevieve to pick up the blocks they'd been playing with, Alana helped Beth clean up in the kitchen.

"I'm glad Justin agreed to learn sign language with us," Beth said as she put the leftovers into a plastic container. "I figured he would come around once he had some time to adjust to the idea."

Alana put the glasses into the dishwasher. "He does realize he'll actually have to use his hands at some point, right?"

"Yeah." Beth smiled. "This is just how he processes stuff. He studies things to get a grasp on them before jumping into anything." Her expression turned serious as she looked at Alana. "He told me about what went down on Saturday."

Alana couldn't help but lift a brow at her revelation. "Really?"

Beth nodded. "I'm really sorry about what happened. I should have known he'd do something like that. He's been responsible for me since I was thirteen and he was just twenty-three. It's a hard habit for him to break."

"I'm not sure why he thought I was a threat."

"Justin suspects the worst of pretty much everyone. He even felt that way about Daniel, and he works for the FBI." Beth gave her a rueful smile. "I hope you won't hold it against him too much. He was thinking of me and Genevieve and made a mistake. He knows that now."

Alana nodded. "Did he tell you about what he found when he did the search on me?"

Beth shook her head. "I didn't ask, and he didn't volunteer. I figure if you want me to know anything, you'll tell me."

"And Daniel?"

Beth shrugged. "I don't know what he knows either. Maybe it seems naive or like I have my head stuck in the sand, but I know that with those two in my life, I'll be safe. If either of them were truly concerned, they would have said something."

Alana wondered what that must be like. For Beth to be so confident of Daniel and Justin's ability to keep her safe. She had a feeling either man would lay down their life for Beth and Genevieve. There had never been anyone in her life who would have done that for her and Caden. Her heart clenched at the thought.

It wasn't her role to be protected. It was her role to protect, and she would do it until her very last breath. She swallowed and straightened her shoulders, giving Beth a smile. "No harm done."

"He really is a good man. Just a little intense at times. He was always a bit that way, but after the majority of our family was murdered, he took it to an all-new level."

Alana felt her eyebrows shoot up in surprise. "Murdered?"

"Yeah. We were all out at our family cabin—well, except for Justin and our cousin Marcus. Justin was in Afghanistan, and Marcus was here at his business."

Sensing this was a difficult thing for Beth to talk about, Alana held up her hand. "You don't have to tell me."

Beth lifted a shoulder. "I just want you to understand why Justin is so protective of me. My uncle—Marcus's dad—went completely nuts and shot all the family members that were at the cabin."

"Except you?"

"Me and my cousin, Meredith. We were up in the attic talking about boys and stuff like that. When we heard the noise, we actually thought it was firecrackers or a movie. We came downstairs to see what was going on and walked into the room in time to see my uncle kill himself."

Alana covered her mouth with her hand. Though she'd known it was only Beth and Justin, she hadn't imagined the circumstances under which her friend had lost the rest of her family. "I would never have guessed."

"Lots of counseling helped. I've been able to deal with it a lot better than my cousin. I suppose that was because in addition to seeing her father kill himself, she also lost her twin brother. "

Well, if nothing else, Beth's revelation explained so much about Justin and what he'd done. "I'm so sorry for your loss."

"Thanks. It was an absolutely horrible time, but thankfully I had Justin and friends at church who helped us out. It wasn't easy for Justin to step into the parent role either. The military discharged him so he could take care of me. Thankfully, Marcus gave him a job at BlackThorpe. More than anyone, Marcus understood when Justin needed time off. I mean, Marcus was dealing with the same thing with his own sister." Beth ran water over a cloth and wrung it out before gliding it across the counter. "Sometimes I feel like I've worked through it better than Justin. He really doesn't seem to have much of a life outside his job or any friends. And after he broke up with his last girlfriend over a year ago, he's never bothered to see anyone else. At least, not that I'm aware of. That was one of the reasons I worried about telling him about Genevieve's diagnosis. I had a good idea of how he'd react and, sure enough, that's pretty much how it's gone down."

"It seems he's coming around now," Alana said. "I think you and Genevieve are too important for him to not get on board."

Beth nodded. "I hope so. I just keep praying that he'll get to the point where he can relax and enjoy life."

Alana understood the responsibility Justin felt with regards to Beth. It was similar to what she felt for Caden. He had no one else to take care of him, so it fell on her shoulders. It was hard to not have it consume her life, and she didn't have the added pressure of trying to help him through such a traumatic event like Justin had with Beth. She guessed the difference in how they'd responded to that responsibility was that she was determined to give Caden as much of a "normal" childhood as she could in spite of everything.

"It's interesting," Beth began as she continued to wipe down the counter, "that even though Justin has always said he didn't want children, he seems to be most at ease with them. First it was with Genevieve and then tonight seeing him smile at Caden did my heart good. There may be hope for him yet."

Alana lifted a couple of containers so Beth could wipe underneath them. "I'm afraid Caden has developed a bit of hero worship for your brother."

Beth's brow furrowed. "I hope you don't think that's a bad thing. He really is a good man. He would never do anything to hurt Caden."

Despite having her own negative thoughts toward the man, Alana found that she believed Beth when it came to her son. "I just hope Caden doesn't annoy him."

"Though it may not be obvious, Justin has endless patience. I sincerely doubt that Caden could do anything to bother him." Beth pushed two plastic containers with food in them toward her. "Can you guys make use of these leftovers? I doubt they'll get eaten here. I made way too much food this time around."

"Oh, I'm sure we could. It was delicious. Are you sure?"

Beth pulled out a plastic bag and put the containers in it and held the handles toward Alana. "I'm sure. If it stays here, I'll just end up throwing it out, and that's just wasteful."

"Thank you. I'll bring the containers back the next time we come over."

After gathering up their things, she and Caden headed out to grab their bus home. Their ride consisted of a lot of questions and observations by Caden, mostly centered on Justin. Alana had mixed feelings about the information she'd gotten from Beth about her brother. On one hand, she was glad for a bit more insight into the man who had so captivated her son. However, she knew that the understanding that had come because of Beth's revelations made her vulnerable to Justin.

Surely she wouldn't be that stupid again. Not that it would matter. She had a feeling that even if she did fall for Justin, he'd never feel the same way about her since he didn't seem to be in the market for something serious, and that was all she'd consider. She just needed to keep her distance and focus on why she was in his life to begin with.

That was easier said than done though, when, shortly after she'd gotten Caden tucked into bed, her cell phone rang. She stared at the number for a moment before tapping the screen to accept the call.

"Alana? This is Justin."

She pressed a hand to her stomach. She did *not* just get butterflies. "Hi, Justin. What can I do for you?"

There was a bit of a pause before he spoke again, his words measured. "I understand now the importance of learning sign language in order to communicate with Genevieve." Another pause. "But what I said about languages not being my thing is true. I wondered if I might make a deal with you."

"A deal? What sort of deal?"

He paused again, but Alana suspected it wasn't because he was at a loss for words but more that he was trying to figure out the best way to present his deal. "I think I could probably benefit from additional lessons apart from the ones with Beth and Daniel. I would be willing to pay you for those lessons or if you're interested, I could teach you something in return."

Alana took the phone from her ear and looked at it for a moment. "Teach me something?"

"Well, uh...given what I know of your past..." Another pause, but this time it felt more awkward than the previous ones. "Um...if you were interested, I could teach you some self-defence and even how to shoot."

"Shooting? As in a gun?" Alana sank down on her day bed and tucked her feet up under her.

"Yes. As in a gun. BlackThorpe has a shooting range, and I could give you some lessons if you'd like."

The idea of learning to defend herself and even shoot a weapon held a strange appeal. And yet she knew it wouldn't have saved her from the situation she'd ended up in with Craig. But part of taking care of Caden was protecting both of them. Learning self-defence could be a good thing. Shooting wouldn't be much use since she couldn't afford to buy a gun.

"So? What do you think?"

"I can give you lessons without payment or you having to do anything in return," Alana said. When it came to teaching people sign language, she just couldn't bring herself to charge. It wasn't usually something people were learning just for kicks. For the most part, the people she came in contact with had to learn because they wanted to be able to communicate with someone special to them.

"I would prefer to think of it as an exchange of services. You can teach me something I need to learn, and I can teach you something every woman should know."

She should say no. She needed to keep her distance from a man like Justin. A man like the one who had ruled her life for far too many years already.

But Justin isn't like that.

Alana pressed her fingers to the spot right between her eyebrows. Common sense screamed at her to say no. But then she thought of how Justin held Genevieve and of how he'd smiled at Caden earlier. Teaching Justin sign language would mean that her son could communicate with his hero.

"Alana?" Justin's voice rumbled in her ear.

Realizing her pause had lasted longer than all of his put together, she said, "I'm here. Just thinking."

"What's to think about?" Justin seemed genuinely puzzled about why she wasn't jumping to take him up on his offer. "It's mutually beneficial. We each get something we need."

Of course, he didn't have the pitfalls in front of him that she did. After having a man in her life who used and abused her, to come in contact with one so protective of those he loved was like a breath of fresh air. And it tugged at her, made her long for things she had no right to. She wondered what it would be like to be loved by a man as protective and caring as Justin. Even though he had hurt her during their meal together, she understood more of why he'd done what he had. And he had apologized for what he did.

"Okay. I guess when you put it that way it really is a no-brainer." Alana pulled her knees up and wrapped an arm around them.

"Exactly." Justin's voice rang with confidence.

Too bad all she could see ahead was possible heartache. She cleared her throat. "How did you see this working? I don't really have anyone I can leave Caden with for any length of time."

"Not a problem. You can bring him along. We can meet at the BlackThorpe offices for the self-defence stuff. They have a full gym there we can utilize. Then we can go back to my place or yours or even stay there at BlackThorpe, and you and Caden can teach me sign language."

It all sounded so simple. Obviously, in Justin's eyes it was. If she could only keep it that way in her perspective as well. Having Caden there would help. He'd be a distraction, but with his serious case of hero-worship, spending even more time with Justin might not be a good thing.

"If you want to come by tomorrow afternoon, I can show you around so you know what I'm talking about."

Alana scooted to the edge of the bed and grabbed the notebook and pen she kept on the small table beside it. "Can you give me the address?" She scribbled the information down as Justin recited it, hoping there was a fairly direct bus route. "I can be there around two. If that works for you."

"That would be fine," Justin said. "I know I've offered already and you've turned me down, so I'm going to just lay this out there and say if you ever need a ride, just call me."

"Okay. Thank you." After the call had ended, Alana slid off the daybed and went through the motions of getting ready for bed. Her thoughts, however, were on what the next day held.

Justin made sure he arrived early for the staff meeting the next morning. He settled into a seat at the large boardroom table and glanced at the man sitting next to him.

"No word from the lovely Lindsay?" Justin asked.

Than scowled at him. "It's only been three days. I'm sure she'll call soon."

They'd spent more time talking than sparring when Than had come to the compound on Saturday. He felt a bit sorry for the man, but Justin figured things would work out for Than and Lindsay. However, he wasn't really great at understanding women himself, so what did he know?

Marcus and Alex walked into the room, and the conversations around the table faded out. Though they were partners, Marcus usually took control of the meetings and today was no different.

"Before we start, I believe you had something you wanted to share, Trent?"

Justin glanced across the table at the man seated beside Eric. He had a large grin on his face as he nodded.

"Yep. Victoria and I are getting married, and you're all invited."

"You two finally picked a date?" Than asked, sitting forward, his own romantic woes apparently temporarily set aside.

Trent nodded. "Yep. We finally just put all potential dates into a bowl and pulled one out."

"Seriously?" Adrianne asked, a skeptical look on her face.

"Yeah, seriously. We've been having a hard time settling on a date, so this just seemed the easiest way. It's nothing fancy and will be rather small, but I would like you all to be there if you're available."

Justin made note of the date on the calendar on his phone as Trent gave them the particulars.

"Well, congratulations to you both once again, Trent," Marcus said, a rare smile lifting the corners of his mouth. "I will clear my schedule to make sure I can make it."

"Thanks, Marcus."

Justin looked at the people seated around the table. Two down now with both Trent and Eric tying the knot. Something told him Than wasn't going to be too far behind. That left the three Thorpes, he and Marcus. He supposed it wasn't so surprising that people were dropping like flies in the romance department given their ages ranging from late twenties to late thirties. Prime marrying age. If he had to make a guess, Justin figured the next one to go was likely to be either Adrianne or Melanie Thorpe. Eventually, it was going to be just him and Marcus.

Justin pulled his thoughts from that direction as Marcus guided the meeting to the business topics on the agenda. Thankfully, things moved fairly quickly, and soon Marcus was tying things up.

"Justin, can I speak with you before you head back to the compound?" Marcus asked.

Now what?

Justin nodded his agreement then stood with the others. He spoke briefly with Alex and Melanie before he left the board room and made his way to Marcus's office. Might as well get it over with.

"Marc. What's up?" Justin said as he walked into the office.

Marcus looked up from the papers he was studying. He pointed his pen at the chair across the desk. Though Marcus was his boss and had four years on him, it still rankled Justin when he did stuff like that. But he sat anyway. Stretching his legs out, he interlaced his fingers across his stomach and looked at Marcus.

"So I spoke to Beth the other day."

"Yes, she mentioned that."

"I'm sorry to hear about what's happened with Genevieve. How are Beth and Daniel doing?"

"As well as can be expected, I suppose. They're in the process of learning sign language and doing what they can to adapt to the diagnosis and what it means for them."

Marcus's blue gaze was piercing as he looked at him. "Is there anything at all that can be done? Do they need money for tests or treatments?"

Justin shook his head. "They've gotten several different opinions, apparently. Dan gave me copies of the tests they've done and the results. I did some research using that information and everything I've read indicates it's a permanent condition."

Marcus's brows drew together. "Do they know what caused it? Is it hereditary?"

"No, it doesn't appear to be genetic. For now the cause of the hearing loss is unknown."

"Unknown? In this day and age, how can that even be a diagnosis anymore?"

Well, that was one thing he and Marcus agreed on. "Yeah, it was kind of hard for me to accept that myself."

"But you have?" Marcus asked.

Justin shrugged. "I didn't want to, but you know, the bottom line is that Genevieve is still healthy. There could be so many other things wrong that wouldn't have the outcome this one does. I try to keep that in mind whenever I start to get too angry about it."

"If there's anything I can do, let me know. We're family after all."

Yes, they were even if it didn't feel that way most the time. Justin wasn't altogether sure why he held Marcus at arm's length. They hadn't been close even before the tragedy, but it hadn't been this awkward then.

"If something comes up, I'll let you know."

He saw a flash of surprise on Marcus's face. Justin understood it since he usually rebuffed any offer of help from him. But they were talking about Genevieve here. Justin would do pretty much anything for her. Including make nice with Marcus and learn sign language.

They'd ended up having to walk a couple of blocks from the bus stop, but since the day was nice, Alana didn't mind. Caden was nearly dragging her along the sidewalk in eagerness to see Justin. He'd been thrilled when she'd revealed the plans for the day, and even though the hours had seemed to fly by for her, she had a feeling they'd dragged for her son.

She hadn't been sure what to expect from their visit to the BlackThorpe offices, but as they got closer to the address Justin had given her, Alana was a bit taken aback by the large wall that ran next to the sidewalk. Her grip on Caden's hand tightened as she spotted a sign reading "BlackThorpe Security" and then just beyond that was a large black iron gate. Justin hadn't given her any instructions on how to get inside. She'd just assumed she'd walk into a building and give his name.

"Can I help you?" A man's voice interrupted her thoughts.

She turned to see who had spoken to her. A large man in a black uniform stood in an opening beside the gate that led into the compound. It didn't escape her notice that he was armed and had a build much like Justin's.

Caden pressed against her side as she took a step toward the man. "I'm here to see Justin Morrell."

"And your name is?"

"Alana Jensen."

"Just a moment, please."

The man stepped back and closed a smaller black iron gate. She wasn't sure if she hoped they were in the right place or the wrong one. The level of security around the tall building was a bit overwhelming.

The man reappeared, a clipboard in his hand. "Do you have some ID?"

ID? She clutched her purse. "I only have stuff like a bank card."

The man arched a brow. "No driver's license?"

Alana shook her head.

"Passport?"

Another shake of her head. Even if she had one of those, she wouldn't have been carrying it around with her. "I didn't realize I'd need ID."

The man looked her up and down then said, "Just wait one minute."

When they were alone once again, Caden tugged his hand free. Alana looked down to see him signing to her asking what was going on. As best she could, she explained what the guard had asked her. She saw the worried look on Caden's face and any thoughts she'd had of just walking away and not bothering with the hassle vanished. Until the guard told her they wouldn't be allowed inside, she'd stand there with Caden.

He continued to pester her with questions as they waited for the man to reappear.

"Alana?"

She saw the huge grin on Caden's face just before she lifted her head to see Justin standing in the opening through which the guard had disappeared.

"Hi, Justin. I'm afraid that I didn't know I'd need ID to get inside. I don't have anything like that on me."

"It's fine. I'm sorry I didn't check with you about that when we talked last night." He stepped away from the entrance and waved them forward. As they walked passed him, he held out his hand to Caden and gave him a high five. "Hi, buddy."

Caden grinned and let go of her hand long enough to sign, "*Hi, Justin.*"

They walked into a guard shack where she spotted the man who'd been talking with them earlier. He smiled at her and gave a nod of his head.

She glanced at Justin. "It's okay that I don't have ID?"

"I vouched for you, so no funny business or it's my neck on the line."

Alana's eyes widened until she saw the corner of his mouth twitch up and his eyes spark with humor. "We'll try to behave."

They walked along a sidewalk that wound its way through a couple of parking lots to the doors of the closest building. Once inside, Justin addressed the two men sitting behind a counter. "They're with me, guys."

The men both nodded their heads, clearly aware of who Justin was.

After they had stepped into a nearby elevator, Justin waved a card over a scanner and then punched a number. The silence in the elevator was thick, and it was at times like this that Alana wished Caden could talk. He would no doubt have a billion questions.

Once the doors slid open, he motioned for them to precede him out. As her feet sank into the plush carpet, she was struck by the subtle elegance of the decor.

"You don't work here all the time?" Alana asked as Justin led them toward a set of doors not far from the elevator.

"No." Justin reached out and opened the door. "Most my work has to do with training out at the compound. I'm here once a week for an administration meeting. That's more than enough for me."

They walked into a huge open room that was obviously the gym he'd spoken about on the phone the night before. Different types of equipment ringed the perimeter, but there was a large open area in the center of the room. At that moment, a few of the machines were in use, but there was no one in the open area. This was where he'd teach her self-defence? Right out in the middle where anyone could see her?

As if reading her mind, he said, "Once we settle on a schedule, I'll make sure that everyone knows the gym is closed for that time." He motioned them to follow him as he walked to the right. "There are change rooms here so you can change if you need to. Sweats or something similar would work best."

Though Alana preferred skirts, she had some sweats that would probably work. "Is there a place Caden can sit to watch?"

"Sure. There are some benches around the room, but he can also sit on the floor near where we'll be working."

"Do a lot of people use this?" Alana asked as they walked back toward the door they'd come in.

"Not as many as should. We do try to encourage anyone who does field work to keep fit. Everyone in the first couple levels of management is required to take weapons training and self-defence."

Alana looked up at him, trying in vain to not notice the way his muscles stretched his shirt. This man took his job seriously. Craig had mainly done his workouts to compete in bodybuilding championships. Justin's were clearly there because of his job—not so he could pose in minuscule briefs and win awards. "Do you teach them all?"

"Not all, but quite a few. If they choose to come to the compound, I'll usually be the one working with them." As they approached the elevator once again, Justin said, "I'll take you up and introduce you to Marcus. I think you heard us talking about him the other day."

Alana nodded, remembering that it hadn't been a good conversation on Justin's part. She also recalled what Beth had told her the night before about exactly who Marcus was to her and Justin.

If she'd thought the elegance had been subtle on the previous floor, it was a bit more overt on this one. There was a large desk just outside the elevator, and the woman behind it looked up and smiled as her gaze took them in.

"You're still hanging around, Justin?"

"Just giving a tour. Alana, this is Kelsey. Kelsey, this is Alana and her son Caden."

Alana looked down at Caden and quickly fingerspelled the woman's name so he would know it. When she lifted her head, her gaze met Kelsey's and she saw the curiosity there.

"Nice to meet you, Kelsey," Alana said.

"Nice to meet you, too, Alana." She looked at Caden, a smile on her face. "And you too, Caden."

He smiled at her and gave a little wave. Caden always responded to friendly faces.

She felt a touch on her back and looked to see Justin holding his other arm stretched toward a hallway. "Marcus's office is this way."

As soon as she and Caden began to walk, his hand fell away. Alana told herself that was how it should be. They'd only walked a short distance when Alana spotted a man coming toward them. He had dark hair and eyes and a broad smile on his face as he came close. He wore a suit that looked like it had been made specifically for him.

"Well, Justin, who do we have here?" Like the woman at the desk, this man's expression held more than a little curiosity.

"Alana, this is Than Miller. He works here as well. Than, this is Alana and her son Caden."

Than held out his hand to her and when Alana slipped her hand into his he gave it a firm shake. He then turned to Caden and held his hand out, palm up. Caden grinned and slapped it and turned his hand palm up so Than could return the greeting. Then he looked up at her, an expectant look on his face.

Once again she fingerspelled Than's name.

"Is he deaf?" Than asked.

Alana looked up and said, "Yes."

Without any hesitation, Than lowered himself so one knee rested on the floor and began to sign with an ease that told Alana he was likely as fluent as she was. Caden's face brightened even more—if that was even possible—as he responded to Than.

"Seriously?" Justin crossed his arms and stared at Than. "You know sign language?"

Than didn't answer right away as he watched what Caden was signing then he said, "Yep. You know languages are my thing."

"Yeah, but I didn't know that included sign language," Justin commented.

"I don't use it much," Than said as he got to his feet. "But I initially took a few lessons because I met a cute deaf girl when I was a teenager."

Justin gave a snort of laughter. "Of course."

Than grinned without shame. "Even after she rejected me, I decided that it was interesting enough to continue learning."

Justin turned to Alana. "Than is our language expert. The guy knows more languages than anyone I've ever met."

"Maybe he should be the one to teach you," Alana suggested.

Than looked at Justin. "You're learning sign language?"

Justin shrugged. "I'm going to try. We just found out that my niece has experienced permanent hearing loss. My sister and brother-in-law are learning as well. Alana is teaching them. And me."

"It's tempting to teach you," Than said. "Considering how much I've suffered at your hands during our sparring, a little retribution might be nice."

Alana wasn't sure what she hoped at that moment. She'd expected to feel relief at the thought of not having to spend that kind of time with Justin, but instead, all she felt was disappointment.

"Actually, I think I'll just stick with Alana. I have a feeling she'll have more patience with me, because, unlike you, languages are not my thing."

"I'm sure you'll do just fine." Than slapped him on the shoulder. "I'm available to practice if you ever need it."

When Than turned to her, he had a twinkle in his warm gaze. He signed, "Don't go too easy on him. He is merciless when he spars with us."

Alana laughed and quickly signed back, "I'll do my best."

Caden captured Than's attention and asked him if he wore guns like Justin. When Than's brow furrowed over the sign for Justin's name, Alana explained the name sign Caden had given him. Than gave him a thumb's up and let Caden know he'd chosen well. And then to answer his question, Than swept one side of his suit coat open so that Caden could see the gun harness there.

Empty? Caden signed.

Than explained that when he was in his office he usually didn't wear his weapon, but when he left the building, he had it on. As Justin interacted with both Than and Caden, Alana had a chance to watch him and realized that while Beth might think he didn't have friends, he most certainly did. The easygoing communication between Than and Justin spoke of something more than just co-workers.

"Well, I'd better go." Than smiled at Alana. "It was a great pleasure to meet you and Caden. Hope to see you again."

After he had left, they continued down the hallway until they came to a large desk. A woman sat there much like Kelsey had at the front, but this one looked a little frazzled.

"You must be new," Justin said to her as he held out his hand. "I'm Justin Morrell."

"Yes. This is my second day. My name is Janice."

"Has he bitten your head off yet?" Justin asked as he motioned to the door.

The woman's eyes widened. "He really does that?"

"I'm sure you'll do just fine. His bark is worse than his bite. Seriously." He gestured to the door again. "Is he in?"

The woman nodded. "Should I let him know you're here?"

"Sure. Just tell him Justin wants to see him for a couple of minutes."

She lifted the receiver of the complicated looking phone on her desk and stared at it for a moment before punching a button. "Mr. Black, Justin is here and would like to see you for a couple of minutes." She listened for a moment and then replaced the receiver. "He said to go on in."

Alana was curious about the man that seemed to be something of an enigma. Justin opened the door, but this time he walked in ahead of them and then waited for them to join him.

"Justin? What's up?"

Alana looked toward the voice and saw a man stand from behind a large desk. Once again she felt Justin's touch on her back as he moved them toward where the man stood. She felt his intense blue gaze sweep her from head to toe and then move to Caden. When he looked back at Justin, his expression revealed nothing.

"Hey, Marcus..." The words of a new male voice trailed off behind them.

Alana turned and saw another man in a suit. This man had blond hair and icy blue eyes. Like Marcus, he looked her over but unlike the other man, he made no attempt to hide his curiosity. However, his expression changed as he looked at Caden. His gaze seemed locked on her son as his mouth tightened, and it wasn't until Caden took a step toward her and she slipped her arm around his shoulders that he looked away.

"Justin," he said with a nod at him.

"Hey, Alex. I was just introducing Alana Jensen and her son, Caden, to Marcus."

Alex walked past them to stand at the edge of Marcus's desk. He held out his hand to Alana. "I'm Alex Thorpe."

The name registered in her brain. Marcus Black and Alex Thorpe. Top guys in the company, Alana realized. She shook his hand and smiled. "Nice to meet you."

Marcus held out his hand as well. "Marcus Black."

She leaned across the desk to shake his hand as Justin said, "Alana is working with Beth, Dan, and Genevieve."

Caden chose that moment to tug her hand. She looked down at him, and he asked her if these were Justin's friends. His brow furrowed then he signed that they were scarier than Than. Alana quickly explained who they were in relation to Justin.

When she looked up again, she noticed both Alex and Marcus were watching them. Marcus looked like he'd put the pieces of the puzzle together once he saw Caden signing to her. Alex, on the other hand, still looked a bit perplexed.

"Anyway, I won't keep you guys from your work," Justin said. "See you next week."

Alana was relieved to leave Marcus's office, and she sensed that Caden was too. Justin led them back to the elevator.

"Sorry about that. I didn't expect Alex to show up too. I was going to introduce you to Marcus since you already knew a little about him, and he is aware of the situation with Genevieve."

"They're the two top guys?" Alana asked just to make sure her assumptions were correct.

Justin nodded as he motioned for her and Caden to step out of the elevator when it stopped. "He and Alex founded the company when they got out of the military just over ten years ago. It was originally a group of four of them, but the other two left when they had a difference of opinion on some things. Not sure exactly what, but that's the story. They changed their name to BlackThorpe, and the rest is history. It was small at first but then grew as they made a name for themselves."

Alana looked around at the floor the elevator had brought them to. This one appeared to be empty.

Justin waved his hand. "The main boardroom is down there. There are also several smaller boardrooms along the wall. Sometimes we use this middle area for larger events." He walked to the closest door and turned the knob to open it. "I thought maybe we could meet in one of these rooms for the sign language lessons. They all have televisions so I could bring a gaming system for Caden if he likes to play video games."

Alana smiled down at Caden and signed to him. When Caden's eyes lit up, and he nodded vigorously, she said, "Well, I guess you can probably figure out his answer without my help."

Justin laughed. "Yeah. Seems he likes the idea."

She wished she had a gaming system for him, but it was just a treat he got when he went to spend time with Peter. Maybe she'd be able to save up enough money to get him a used one for Christmas. A gaming system had been at the top of his list for birthday and Christmas ever since he'd figured out what one was.

Justin crossed his arms over his chest and said, "So? Do you still think this is something you want to do?"

The main reason *to* do it centered around Caden—being able to defend him. Of course, he would also be thrilled to spend more time with Justin and to be able to play video games. The reasons *not* to do it all centered on her, which meant that of course she'd do it. Every decision she'd made had been with him in mind. She hadn't left Craig in spite of the abuse because she believed the lifestyle he provided for Caden was better than anything she could. But once he'd started to hint that he'd use Caden to keep her under his control, she started her plans to leave. And the day he'd come right out and said that Caden could benefit from a little more discipline especially if she didn't fall in line, she'd packed their bags and left.

8

WHILE GRATEFUL Justin was giving her a way out, there was no way Alana could take it. "Yes. Like you said, it is beneficial to both of us. Even Caden, if he gets to play video games."

A smile moved across Justin's face so quickly Alana wasn't completely sure it had even been there. "We can start next week. Would this time work okay for you?"

"Yes, it works perfectly." Then she frowned. "Do I need to get some ID before I come back?"

Justin stared at her for a moment then jerked his head toward the elevator. "Come with me."

As the doors whooshed open, Alana realized they were back on the floor where they'd met Marcus and Alex. This time they walked past his office to one that opened off a large reception area with yet another desk and receptionist. Justin said a quick hello to the woman as they passed by her then lifted his hand and rapped his knuckles on the open door.

"Hey, Justin. What's up?" a male voice said. " You're usually back at the compound by now."

Justin motioned them forward. "I'm giving a tour and had a question for you."

As Alana and Caden stepped toward him, a dark-haired man came around a large desk. The man smiled and when he saw Caden, he said, "Well, aren't you a handsome young man?"

When Caden looked up at her, Alana quickly signed what the man had said. Caden smiled and signed his reply. "He says thank you."

"Alana is helping my family out," Justin said. "Oh, Alana, this is Eric McKinley. Eric, this is Alana Jensen."

Eric held out his hand first to her and then to Caden. "Pleasure to meet you both."

"Not sure I've mentioned to you that my niece has been diagnosed with hearing loss," Justin said.

Eric's expression immediately turned to one of concern. He laid a hand on Justin's shoulder. "Wow. That has to be difficult news to get. I'll sure be praying for you guys. How are her parents doing?"

Justin crossed his arms again and braced his feet, but Eric didn't move his hand. "They're doing fairly well. They've had a few months to get used to the diagnosis. Alana is teaching them—and me—sign language. In exchange, I'm going to teach her some self-defence, so I had her come by to see the facility here."

"That sounds like a great trade," Eric said, lifting his hand from Justin's shoulder. "I know that Staci appreciated those classes you gave last year. Hey, did I ever tell you her first impression of you?"

Justin glanced at Eric and shook his head. "Was that when we came to her house after you got back from the Middle East?"

"Yep. She said you looked like a guy that never passed an exercise machine without trying it out." Eric chuckled. "I told her that was probably a pretty good guess."

A broad smile flashed across Justin's face. "There are a few I can pass up, but, for the most part, that is true."

"I assured her that for all your muscles and chiseled good looks, you were a gentle giant."

Justin sent a look Caden's way and winked. "Good grief, Eric, I have a reputation to uphold."

"Well, it's true. Sarah likes you, and you know what they say about kids being a good judge of character."

Justin turned to her. "Staci is Eric's wife, and they have a daughter named Sarah. How old is she now?"

"She's six," Eric smiled proudly.

"Caden is seven," Alana said as she brushed her hand over Caden's hair.

"It's a great age, isn't it?" Eric said.

Alana nodded. It was true. She loved the curiosity Caden had developed for things beyond his own little world as he'd gotten older. And communication was so much easier now that his ability and desire to learn more signs had also increased.

"Actually, Eric, I had another reason for stopping by to see you. I was wondering if we could do a hand scan of Alana so she can get through security for the next little while."

Eric shoved his hands into his pockets. "She can't just show ID? Once you put her on the approved list, all she has to do is flash some photo ID."

"I don't have photo ID," Alana said.

Eric looked at her in surprise. "No driver's license?"

Alana shook her head. "Nor any other photo ID. I do have a bank card and a library card."

She watched as Eric and Justin exchanged glances and knew Justin would be explaining more in detail later.

"Sure, we can do that." Eric moved around his desk and sat down. "I'll just call down to security and give them a head's up that you're on your way and what for, okay?"

Justin nodded. "Thanks, man."

"Anytime." Eric looked at Alana and Caden. "Be sure to stop in and say hi when you're in the neighborhood again."

It wasn't long before they were on a different floor, and the atmosphere had changed completely. The understated elegance of the previous floors had been replaced with more practical decor and a much noisier environment. Several people called out a greeting to Justin as he led them through the hallways flanked by workstations. He lifted a hand in response to each one but didn't slow to talk.

At least not until a woman stepped out in front of them, and he had no choice but to stop or run her over.

"Justin." The woman's voice was low. "I didn't know you were still here."

Alana and Caden stood off to the side and watched as the woman ran her hand over Justin's shoulder and then gave his upper arm a quick squeeze with her beautifully manicured hand. The woman's appearance seemed like it would fit much better on the floors they had been on earlier. Her jet black hair was worn in a shiny, sleek bob that just brushed her shoulders, and even though her makeup was understated, there was no doubt it had been expertly applied. Her suit looked like the female version of what Alana had seen on the guys Justin had introduced them to. The spiked heels she wore gave her a good four inches on Alana and brought her to Justin's eye level. Feeling Caden's hand tighten briefly in hers, Alana glanced down in time to see him scowl at the woman.

"Hi, Jacey." Justin took a step back, bringing him next to Caden. "I had some personal stuff to take care of before I headed back to the compound."

Jacey's gaze moved to Alana and after looking her up and down, she glanced at Caden before turning her attention back to Justin. Though the woman wasn't outright dismissive of them, Alana was sure she didn't see her as any competition. Not that there was any to begin with.

"Give me a call next time you stay after your meeting. We can do lunch."

Justin made some sort of noise as a response that didn't seem to be quite an agreement or a refusal. "If you'll excuse us, we need to finish up here."

Jacey nodded as she stepped to the side. As they walked past her, the woman's face remained impassive, but Alana knew that expressionless didn't mean emotion didn't lurk beneath the surface. She wished she could assure the woman that she wasn't a threat to anything she might want to have with Justin. However, Alana got the feeling that even if she weren't there, Justin wouldn't have acted any differently. His reaction wasn't that of a man who was interested but constrained by the workplace setting or the presence of her and Caden.

Justin didn't say anything more until they reached the security office and then it was only to talk to the man seated behind the desk. Eric had obviously arranged it all because it didn't take long to get her hand scanned and a picture taken. The man updated everything and then had her test it out. As soon as the scanner had recorded the image of her hand, the picture they'd taken as well as her name popped up on the screen.

"Does Caden want his done too?" Justin asked.

"Can he? I think he'd love that."

She'd already explained to Caden what was going on as they'd done her file so when she asked if he wanted to do it too, he nodded vigorously. The security man was great with him, and Alana found her heart expanding with gratitude for all the people that day who had made the effort to connect with Caden.

"Well, that's about it for the tour," Justin said as they walked back through the hallways leading to the elevator. This time there was no sign of Jacey. "I'm heading back out to the compound. Can I drop you off somewhere?"

———◈———

Justin waved at the guard as he pulled his truck through the gates of the BlackThorpe complex and out onto the street. He glanced over at the passenger seat, a little surprised that Alana had taken him up on his offer of a ride. Of course, she still wasn't having him drop her off at home, but at least it was a step in the right direction, and hopefully it would shorten the time she and Caden had to spend on the bus.

"Thank you for showing us around. I hope you won't get into trouble for taking time away from your work. Today or in the weeks ahead when we come to meet with you there."

"I don't get into trouble," Justin said as he shot her a quick smile. "I put in a lot of hours, and they all know it. No one will get on my case for a taking a little bit of time during the day once a week for personal activities. Plus, I'm still at the office and if something comes up, I always have my cell with me."

"Well, that's good, but if you ever need to cancel, just let me know."

Justin glanced into his rearview mirror and saw Caden looking all around the truck. Between his fascination with guns and Justin's truck, the little guy was definitely all male. Watching Than interact with him had sharpened Justin's desire to be able to communicate with the boy as much as he did with Genevieve. Usually, he steered clear of kids—with the exception of Genevieve—but Caden was slowly but surely worming his way past Justin's defenses. And he found he wasn't as opposed to that as he might have been at one time.

"So, you've seen where I work," Justin began, "how about telling me about your work."

When Alana didn't reply right away, Justin figured she wasn't going to reveal anything, but then she said, "I work from home so I can homeschool Caden and not have to find someone to watch him."

"What exactly do you do from home?" Justin had started out planning to get to know Alana because of her involvement with Beth, but now he found he wanted to know more about her...just because.

"I do a few different things. I write blogs with reviews and links to books and other stuff that I earn money on if people click on the links and buy things. I also do some freelance writing."

"And teaching sign language?"

"No. I don't charge for that."

Justin shot her a look as he slowed to a stop at a red light. "You don't?"

"No. Usually, the people I work with are like Daniel and Beth. It doesn't feel right to me to make money off people who are dealing with something already so stressful. People have helped me through difficult times when I couldn't pay them. I'm just passing it on."

Well, that shot down any thoughts he had that she might be trying to scam Beth. He'd just assumed his sister was paying her for the lessons. She'd turned down his offer to pay too. Thankfully, she had accepted his offer of teaching her self-defence. It didn't sit right with him for her to teach him something without some sort of payment in return.

"So those other things you do earn you enough money?" Justin told himself it shouldn't matter, but knowing what he did about her past, he found it hard to keep his protective side from showing.

"Yes."

When she didn't expand on that, Justin let that subject drop. "Do you home-school Caden because he can't go a regular school? Is that something Beth will need to do with Genevieve?"

"No, there are schools for deaf students. I'm actually considering putting Caden in one for the next school year. He needs more than what I've been able to offer him at home. He loves being around people."

"Does he have many friends?"

"Not many, no. He has a friend named Peter, who is also deaf, so Peter's mom and I try to arrange playdates for them a couple of times a month." Alana paused then said, "I do tend to be a bit more protective than perhaps I should be. I just couldn't handle the thought of anything happening to him if I'm not around to communicate with or for him."

"Being a parent is hard work," Justin said. He'd had to play that role way before he was ready to, but he wouldn't do anything differently if he could go back. Well, if he could go back, he'd tell his family to stay far, far away from the family cabin that weekend, but barring that, he would step into that role of parent anytime Beth needed him to.

"Caden makes it easy. I just worry a lot."

Silence filled the cab of the truck for a few minutes then Justin said, "Hey, I didn't get much of a lunch today, you want to join me for something before I drop you off and head back to work?"

"I don't know..."

"My treat," Justin assured her. "You'd be doing me a favor. I don't want fast food and hate sitting on my own in a restaurant."

Actually, neither was really a true statement, but Justin found himself not wanting the time with Alana and Caden to end. He named a restaurant that was on the way and near to where she'd wanted to be dropped off.

"If you're sure..."

"Wouldn't have offered if I wasn't." Justin was glad Beth wasn't there because he had a feeling she'd be wondering if he'd been taken over by an alien or something. Usually, he steered clear of women, but it was fairly clear Alana didn't have the interest in him that Jacey had shown earlier. That made it easier for him to relax a bit more with her.

Justin had to admit that he admired her. Even though he'd basically forced her to reveal her past to him, he was glad she had. Understanding where she came from helped him see her in a different light.

"Okay. Thank you."

When he spotted the restaurant he wanted, Justin exited the highway and drove into the parking lot. He made sure he parked where he would be able to see his truck since he was leaving the bags that contained his guns and laptop. Normally, he would have put his weapons back on before leaving BlackThorpe but with Caden around Justin had settled for strapping one of his guns into an ankle holster and a knife on his other leg. The boy couldn't see the weapons, but Justin felt more at ease knowing he was armed.

Once inside the family-style restaurant, Justin requested a booth for them and soon they were seated along the wall that was mainly windows and gave him a good view of his truck. Alana slid Caden into the booth first and then followed him while Justin settled onto the padded seat on the other side.

"Feel free to order whatever you're hungry for. Breakfast. Lunch. Dessert."

Even though he held his menu open in his hands, Justin watched the mother and son duo across the table from him. Alana was pointing to things on the menu and signing to Caden. The boy's brow was furrowed as he signed back to her. He wondered how many lessons it would take him to be able to follow along when they communicated with each other.

"Is he not finding anything he wants to eat?" Justin asked when it became quickly apparent that they were in disagreement over something.

Alana sighed. "He doesn't want a kid's meal. For some reason, he thinks being almost eight means he shouldn't have to order off the *baby menu*."

Justin glanced at the boy to find him sitting back against the booth, arms crossed, an uncharacteristic frown on his young face. "Is there a reason you don't want him to order from the regular menu?"

Alana paused then said, "It's more expensive, and I don't know if he'll eat it all."

"Don't worry about the cost," Justin said. "And if he doesn't eat it all, you can get it packaged to go, and he can eat it later."

Alana looked from him to Caden. The boy's green eyes widened, and his expression took on a pleading look as he made a circular sign on his chest. He wondered if the look worked on his mother because it sure was working on him. Justin was ready to give the kid just about anything he wanted at that point.

Apparently it did, because after staring at Caden for a moment, Alana nodded. A huge smile wreathed his small face as he reached out to give her a tight hug. There was something about the scene that had Justin sitting back and considering. It seemed a bit odd for a kid to get so excited about being able to order off the regular menu. The little guy acted like he'd just been given a gift.

He didn't have much time to mull that over before the waitress returned to take their order. It appeared that Alana had already known what Caden wanted because he hadn't signed anything more after giving her a big hug.

As the waitress jotted down what Alana said, Justin frowned. If the breakfast meal was what Caden wanted— even in the middle of the afternoon—that meant that Alana was only ordering a salad. A *side* salad. He was again reminded of how thin her arm had been when she'd shown him her scars. Was there a reason she wasn't eating more? She seemed to eat fairly heartily when at Beth's.

When the waitress asked what he wanted, Justin tacked on a couple of appetizers in addition to the country fried steak he'd planned to order. Once she'd left them alone with the promise of returning shortly with the appetizers, Justin scrambled for something to talk about.

"So, what kind of games does Caden like to play? I'll try and bring some that are appropriate for him."

Alana signed to Caden and also spoke the words. "Justin wants to know what games you like."

Caden glanced at him then lifted his hands to respond to his mother.

"He likes anything Mario. Does that make sense?"

Justin nodded. "Yep. I know the Mario games. I'll bring a few different ones so he can pick which one he likes best. Does he have a gaming system at home?"

Alana's mouth tightened briefly as she shook her head. "He's played the games at his friend's house."

Caden touched Alana's arm as he shot Justin a slightly embarrassed look. Alana bent down to him as he signed. She nodded and then said, "Please excuse us. Bathroom break."

Justin watched as they slid out from the other side of the booth. He leaned back and stretched out his legs, keeping an eye on them as they made their way across the restaurant to where signs indicated the restrooms were. As he sat there, he mulled over how his view of Alana was changing. He wasn't just looking at her as Beth's friend or Caden's mother. It had started, he realized, the moment he'd found out that someone she'd trusted to take care of her had done the exact opposite. That was just wrong on so many levels.

His first instinct had been to try to take care of her, but that wasn't his place. And it certainly wasn't a role he was looking to fill with her—even if she wanted him to, which he really didn't think she did. If she had wanted that, she wouldn't be turning him down every time he tried to help her out.

He was still a bit surprised she'd agreed to come here for a meal with him, but he suspected it had more to do with Caden than with her wanting to spend time with him. Something told him that pretty much every decision she made was weighed against how it would impact Caden. He knew how that was. He'd lived a lot of years doing that with Beth.

He wondered if she ever did anything just because she wanted to or because it would be something she enjoyed. At the thought, he gave a short laugh. He wasn't exactly the poster child for doing things he enjoyed outside of what he did for work.

When the waitress showed up at the end of the table with their appetizers, Justin pulled his legs in and straightened.

"Will your wife and son be back?" the waitress asked. "I'll be bringing out their food shortly."

Wife?

Son?

9

JUSTIN BLINKED and then swallowed hard before saying, "They just went to the bathroom."

Wife?

Son?

He couldn't seem to shake the scenarios that suddenly popped into his mind. He should have told the waitress that Alana wasn't his wife. That Caden wasn't his son. Why hadn't he corrected her?

Because it really didn't matter in the long run. It was a natural assumption for someone to make, but explaining the real relationship would have just been too complicated.

At least that's what he told himself.

Before he could think much more about it, Caden dashed into the booth with Alana right behind him. As promised, the waitress showed up with the rest of their order and suddenly the table was full of food.

Caden looked at Alana and then they began to sign together. Matching each other sign for sign. When they finished and Caden began to eat, Alana met his gaze.

"We were just saying grace before we ate."

Just nodded his understanding. He bowed his head and said a quick prayer as well.

"Here, help me with these appetizers," Justin said as he pushed a plate of nachos toward Alana.

She glanced at the salad in front of her then reached out to snag a couple of the chips. Meanwhile, Caden was tucking into the meal he'd chosen. French toast. Eggs. Sausage. As he watched the boy eat, Justin had a flashback to when he'd been about that age. During the week, they tended to have oatmeal, toast and fruit, but on Saturdays, breakfast was a treat. He remembered having all the things Caden was eating. His mom and dad would work side-by-side in the kitchen preparing a larger than usual breakfast for him and his siblings.

Justin didn't often think about his childhood—so much of the time before the loss of his family was fuzzy—but watching Caden was bringing them into focus. In his mind's eye, he could see he and his mom having discussions like Alana and Caden had. It was hard to think that even though he and Caden had both faced tragedy in their lives, Caden had experienced it at a much younger age.

Justin didn't know how much the young boy might have known about what went on between his parents, but at some point, obviously he'd suddenly been without a father. Likely Alana had hidden her bruises from people outside the home, but no doubt there had been days when she was in a lot of pain. Caden would have seen that when no one else would have. And yet the boy seemed so happy, and no matter what his father had done, Caden had a caring and gentle nature that Justin had seen when he'd spent time with Genevieve.

Caden offered his mom a bite of sausage which she took after a moment's hesitation. Justin was glad to see her picking at the appetizers in addition to her salad.

"What exactly do you do at BlackThorpe?"

Justin swallowed the bite he'd taken and took a gulp of his water. "I am in charge of the training division. That includes hand-to-hand combat training as well as weapons training. We have a large area of land that's been set up to facilitate training, with buildings and different things that represent situations the groups we're training might run into. We train in all types of weather and terrain, and we're out for twenty-four hours straight sometimes. The compound also has an obstacle course along with the gym where people can work out."

Alana plucked another chip from the plate of nachos. "Who do you work with?"

"We have our own teams that we've trained for security—corporate and personal. Our guys have also been hired to help with search and rescue among other things. And there are companies that send us groups of employees to train as well as some military teams."

"Do you lead the training yourself?"

"I'm definitely more hands on than I likely need to be. I have a good team that works with me. I just prefer to be involved. Keeps me on my game."

"Have you taught self-defence before? Is that what Eric was talking about?"

Justin nodded. "I offer courses a couple of times a year for employees and their family and friends. For the most part, it's women who take it. I believe strongly in equipping people with the ability to keep themselves from becoming victims if at all possible."

Alana tilted her head. "And that's what you're going to teach me?"

"Yes."

"I would like to get Caden involved in Karate or something similar one day. Is that something you'd recommend?"

"Definitely. At his age, he can learn the basics of it without any problem."

"I worry that his being deaf might impact his ability to learn."

Justin thought about his team, knowing that a couple of them, at least, had training in Karate. They could probably help Caden. "It might, but you won't know for sure unless you look around for courses to see what sort of set-up they have and how willing the teacher is to work with Caden."

"You don't know Karate?" she asked, her eyes on her salad.

"I took lessons when I was a little older than Caden, but my interest drifted away from that as I got older, so while I remember some of the moves, I've forgotten a whole lot more."

Out of the corner of his eye, Justin saw their waitress approached and looked up when she said, "How's everything?"

"It's great, thanks," Alana said with a smile. She looked at Caden and gave him a thumbs up. He grinned and gave her a thumbs up in return. At least Justin didn't need her to interpret that.

"Yes, everything is good," Justin agreed.

"Can I bring you anything else?"

After a moment's thought, Justin asked her to do up a couple burgers and fries to go. "And then the bill, thanks."

He was pleased to see that the appetizers were basically gone, and both Alana and Caden had finished what they ordered. Justin wasn't sure why he was concerned about what they ate, but the memory of Alana's too-slender arm wasn't something he'd been able to push from his mind.

"Looks like he was hungry enough to eat the whole meal," Justin commented as Caden carefully lifted his cup of chocolate milk and sipped it through a straw.

"Yes. He didn't eat much for lunch. Once he found out where we were going and that he'd get to see you... Well, his appetite kind of got lost in the anticipation."

Warmth spread inside Justin as he thought of Caden's excitement at seeing him. He didn't know what it was about him that drew the boy, but he couldn't deny he enjoyed the feeling.

Once the waitress brought the two orders he'd placed and he'd taken care of the bill, they left the restaurant.

"Thank you for the ride and for lunch," Alana said as they approached his truck. "I guess we'll see you next week."

"I wish you'd let me drive you home," Justin said as he opened the driver's door.

She smiled at him, her full lips turning up at the corners just enough to bring out small dimples in her cheeks that he hadn't noticed before. Long dark lashes framed her green eyes that held none of the wariness of the past as she said, "You've done plenty. We appreciate it very much."

And yet he found himself wanting to do so much more for her. Them. He rubbed a fist across his chest, fighting a sudden tightness there. "Well, like I said earlier, if you do need a ride or anything, just give me a call. You have my number."

"I do," Alana agreed with a nod of her head then reached out and grasped Caden's hand. The boy smiled and waved at him.

Justin waved back and then watched as they turned and walked toward the bus stop. When he swung around to his truck, he realized he still held the bag with the take-out in it. "Oh hey, wait up." When Alana turned, he jogged toward her and held out the bag. "Supper's on me."

She looked at the bag and then met his gaze. He thought she was going to refuse, but then she reached out and took it from him, their fingers brushing lightly as he let go of it.

"Thank you. Again."

"Anytime." He jogged backward a couple of steps before turning and heading back to the truck.

———⟨⟩⟨⟩———

Alana tried to focus on Caden's stream of signs as they rode the bus home. Her thoughts kept drifting to Justin and the time they'd spent together. And now, more than ever, she was certain she should spend as little time in his company as possible. She obviously had a type...she hadn't really thought about it since she'd only dated Craig. But now that she was finding herself attracted to someone who was physically very similar, she knew it was more than just a coincidence.

But it was just physical attraction. And that she knew she could ignore. Unfortunately, his kindness toward Caden was more difficult to brush aside. She was a sucker for anyone who treated her son well. They were immediately a friend in her mind. Too bad her heart wasn't as content to have Justin as just a friend.

Back in the apartment, Caden grabbed the book she'd told him he had to read two chapters of before he could play on his tablet. She was so grateful that he'd picked up reading quickly and easily and read well above his grade level. It meant he could follow along with the closed captioning for some of the shows and movies he liked to watch on her laptop.

He sat on the daybed, scooting back until he reclined against her pillows. Bending his knees, he planted his feet flat on the mattress and propped the book against his thighs. Whenever she looked at him, his blond curls hanging over his eyes, concentration on his beautiful little face, Alana absolutely couldn't regret that she'd gotten involved with Craig. Her sweet boy filled her heart and life with more love and joy than she could have ever imagined. When her parents had told her to get an abortion or else, Alana had chosen the "or else" and every day she was grateful she had. If it hadn't been for Caden, she might never have had the strength to leave Craig.

As she slid the bag with take-out containers into the small fridge, she said a prayer of thanks for Justin's generosity. Alana had no idea what had prompted him to make the gesture, but since she hadn't made it to the store yet that week, she was glad for the food that would help stretch what they had until she could get some grocery shopping done.

A knock on the door drew her attention, and Alana let out a sigh. She had a feeling she knew who would be there and was tempted to ignore it, but he wouldn't go away. She'd tried that approach one day. There was no peephole to see who it was but opening the door confirmed her suspicions.

"Hello, Mr. Dean." Alana tried to keep her tone friendly.

The man swayed slightly as he lifted a cigarette to his lips. The smell of booze and cigarette smoke wafted her way, and Alana had to steel herself from taking a step back. Though the smell was overwhelming, she tried to be grateful that at least today the man was wearing a T-shirt in addition to his boxers. He'd appeared on her door in less, much to her dismay. His brown hair was thinning and looked like it could use a good wash. He blinked a couple of times as if to clear the blurriness from his reddened eyes.

"Ello, Alana." He held up a cup that looked to be about half full with a dark beverage she was going to assume was coffee. "D'ya have any cream?"

"I'm sorry. I don't use cream." She'd long since learned how to drink her coffee black. He knew she never had any, but it was just one of the excuses he used to pound on her door. Not for the first time, she wished she could afford an apartment in a slightly better building.

"Milk?"

The *love thy neighbor* verse was going around in her head as she stood there. He knew she'd have milk. And that she would give him some because she'd done it each time he'd asked. "Just a minute."

She closed the door and locked it before going to the fridge to pull out the milk. There wasn't a lot in the jug, but there should still be enough left for Caden's cereal and drink in the morning even after giving the man some. When she opened the door again, Mr. Dean thrust the mug at her. Mindful of how the cup shook in his hand, she poured some into it.

"Thanks, Missy," he said then put the cigarette back in his mouth and ambled back to the stairs that led to his apartment on the floor beneath theirs. She worried that one of these days he'd stumble on the stairs and break his neck.

When she returned the milk to the fridge, Alana spotted the take-out containers and was reminded of the generosity of Justin and others in their lives. If a little milk made the man's day brighter, it was really the least she could do.

Mr. Dean never seemed to want to make conversation beyond what they'd just had, and she'd never gotten the feeling that he was coming on to her. It just seemed that every few days he needed some sort of human contact, and he'd chosen her for that. She had no idea what drove him to drink—she'd yet to see him sober—but clearly something had.

It was at times like these she was reminded how much she had to be grateful for. Sure her lifestyle now was nowhere near what she'd grown up with or even had when she'd lived with Craig, but her boy was healthy and happy. They were safe. They had a home. She glanced over to where Caden still sat, his nose in the book he held.

Yes, she was blessed.

"Where is your head at, man?" Justin slammed his fists onto his hips and glared at the guy bent over beside him, his hands braced on his knees.

Sweat slid down Justin's forehead and dripped into his eyes. Blinking away the sting, he lifted his arm to use his sleeve to wipe away the perspiration from his brow. "We never lose."

Than straightened and took a deep breath. The usually well-groomed man was a mess. Splatters from the volley of paintballs he'd taken from the opposing team spread across every part of his body. He took a swipe at a hunk of black hair that fell over his dark eyes, leaving a mixture of paint and mud across his forehead. "Sorry, dude."

"Sorry?" Justin jerked his hand toward where the opposing team had gathered. "You just handed out the first victory ever against the BlackThorpe team. Do you have any idea how many years it's gonna take to live that one down?"

They didn't always use paintball weapons since they had laser ones available, but every once in a while they'd pull them out. Usually, no matter what the weapon of choice, they won, but this time, the winning team was a military one who had come to BlackThorpe to do some training before their next mission. They were definitely going to take bragging rights and run with them. Yeah, it was going to take a while to live this one down.

Justin crossed his arms and stared at Than. The man truly did look miserable. "Still no word from the lovely Lindsay?"

Than's brows drew together as he gave a quick shake of his head. "When she asked for a little time, I thought maybe a day or two not ten."

"Maybe you should have given her a more precise time frame."

"Seriously?" Than gave him an exasperated look. "You think I'm going to take advice about women from you? When was the last time you took a woman out on a date?"

The man had a point. He didn't really understand women any better than the next guy. His own sister left him totally mystified sometimes. "Then I guess I should say better you than me?"

That got him another look, but Justin just laughed and slapped Than on the back. "Let's go get cleaned up and brace ourselves for the gloating."

Justin had planned to go to Beth's for supper but when the exercise had turned super competitive, he'd texted her on one of their breaks that he couldn't make it. And he was glad now that he had because all he wanted was a long hot shower, not just to wash away all the paint but to ease the aches from the harder-than-usual workout.

In addition to Than, his group had included Alex, Trent and two of his team at the compound. Though the three guys were mainly desk jockeys, they worked to keep their skills up and usually the six of them were a good team. Justin shook his head. Taken down by a lovesick guy. He felt a bit of sympathy for the other man, but not enough to prevent him from ribbing Than about it every chance he got.

As he stood in front of his open fridge looking for something to eat after his shower, Justin thought of the time he'd be spending with Alana and Caden the next afternoon. He was still trying to figure out his reactions to the pair. If he didn't have room in his life for a woman, he certainly didn't

have room for a woman and a child. There was no sense in
allowing any thoughts but those viewing her as Beth's friend
to enter his mind.

That protective side of his nature had tried to convince
him that Alana and Caden needed him to keep them safe, but
Justin knew better. He would give Alana the tools to protect
herself and Caden, because, given her past, that was the best
thing he could do for her. And in return, she'd give him the
ability to communicate with his niece.

And Caden.

Justin shut the fridge door with a little more force than
necessary. If truth be told, he'd been struggling with his own
distraction throughout the exercise earlier. Fortunately for
him, he'd practiced the moves and positions so often his
body had reacted even when his mind had been a little slow
on the uptake.

And if he was honest with himself, his decision to skip
supper that evening had been partly avoidance. After the
previous week when he'd wanted to prolong their time
together, Justin had a little talk with himself about letting his
thoughts and emotions go in that direction. He couldn't go
back on his promise to help them, but he could limit the
other time he spent with them until he got a handle on what
was going on inside of him.

The next afternoon Justin met Alana and Caden down by
the main desk. Alana wore her usual outfit of a long skirt and
a loose, long-sleeve blouse, but she clutched a bag that Justin
hoped included clothes more appropriate for what they
would be doing.

Hi, Justin!

Justin grinned when he realized he understood the two
signs Caden had just made. "Hi, Caden." He lifted his gaze to
Alana, not too surprised to see wariness in her eyes. "Hi. So
do you want to do the sign language part first?"

Alana nodded. "That would probably be best."

Justin led the way into the elevator and once the doors
closed and the car began to rise, he said, "No problems with
security this time?"

She shook her head. "Caden enjoyed having his hand scanned."

"Good. I figured that would be the easiest way to give you access to the complex."

The elevator came to a stop and the doors silently opened. The floor was empty as he led them to the small board room where he'd set up the gaming system for Caden earlier. He figured that since the boy wouldn't need to have the sound on, he could be in the same room as them. Not that Alana was likely to let him out of her sight regardless.

He took a few minutes to show Caden the games he'd brought. After what appeared to be some internal debate, Caden pointed out the one he wanted. Justin got it set up and then handed him the cordless controller.

"Does he know what to do?" Justin asked as he glanced over his shoulder to where Alana stood watching them.

"Yes. I think he'll be fine."

Justin watched for a minute and saw that Alana was right. Caden was soon starting a race of some sort on the screen. Satisfied that he would be okay, he turned his attention to the woman hovering a few feet away from him. "Ready to teach me some sign language?"

She stared at him for a moment, her green eyes large in her face. "Uh...yep."

Justin motioned to the end of the table furthest from Caden. "Why don't we sit there?"

Alana followed and claimed a seat across the table from him. She opened her bag and took out a binder and laid it on the table in front of her. When she looked at him, her gaze was more focused. "I figured I'd give you a bit of an overview before we get down to the actual signs."

As she explained the grammar of sign language and a few other things, Justin felt a bit of tension creep up his shoulders into his neck. His strengths did not lie in this area. He really didn't want to make a fool of himself as he struggled to learn even the most basic signs.

"I'm going to teach you what I've taught Daniel and Beth so far. Because Genevieve is so young, you can get away with some fairly simple signs at first, but we'll move on from those once you're comfortable with them." She slid a piece of paper across the table to him.

Justin reached out and pulled it close so he could look at it. There were drawings of what he assumed were the first signs he would be learning.

"We're going to concentrate on the top five today which are mom, dad, milk, eat and more. Those are signs Genevieve is already doing so at this point it's probably more about you understanding her when she makes those signs so you know what she's asking for."

Over the next half hour, Alana showed him the signs, repeating them with her hands and watching without a spark of judgment or impatience on her face as he fumbled his way through them. Justin was aware it would take time for him to grasp it, but he sure hoped that at some point his hands would move with more fluidity and less stiffness.

At the end of the thirty minutes, Alana gave him a smile. "That's great! Now when you're with Genevieve and you see her making these signs, you'll know what—or who—she's wanting. Keep practicing them this week. We'll add a few more next time we're here."

Justin knew he was scowling, but he couldn't help it. Did she really think he'd done well? Or was she just trying to keep him upbeat and not discourage him? He sure didn't feel like he'd done all that great, and he was very relieved they were finished this part of their teaching deal. Now they would move into an area where he was much more confident, but first he needed to clarify something with her.

He shifted in his chair and cleared his throat. "I'm not sure how to ask this, but it came to mind that it's something I needed to address."

Alana sank back into her chair, her brows drawn together, but she didn't say anything.

"I was...uh...wondering if Caden had been witness to any of the abuse you endured." Justin hated to bring this up, but he felt it was something he had to know before they went on to the self-defence lessons.

Alana's face paled as she crossed her arms over her stomach. "Why does it matter?"

Justin leaned forward, bracing his elbows on the table. "Because part of the self-defence training involves you being approached in such a way that you can practice the moves. I don't want to trigger anything if it brings back a memory that could be harmful to him. In fact, that's true for you as well."

She caught her lower lip between her teeth as her gaze shot briefly to where Caden sat with his back to them. "We'll both be fine."

"You're sure? I think it's important you learn to defend yourself, but not if it's going to bring back bad memories for you or Caden."

Alana straightened, pulling her shoulders back. "We'll be fine. I talked to Caden about what would be happening. He understands what we'll be doing."

Justin stared at her, wanting to make sure she really was okay with it. In the end though, all he could do was take her at her word. "Okay. Let's see if Caden's willing to wrap it up so we can head down to the gym."

Once they'd pried Caden away from the game, they headed down to the floor where the gym was. He'd put out word earlier that the gym was off limits for part of the afternoon.

"The change room for women is through there," Justin said as he pointed toward the door to their right. "Caden can sit on the bench over there if he'd like. Or he can sit on the mat near us. Whatever you and he will be most comfortable with."

Alana reached into her bag and pulled out a tablet. "I brought this in case he gets bored."

"Does he need it connected to the wireless so he can get on the internet?" Justin asked as he held out his hand for it.

Alana hesitated and then let him take it from her. "He can access his games without the internet."

As he looked at the tablet, Justin realized it was an older model. Without making a comment or touching the screen to bring it to life, Justin handed it to Caden. "Can you ask him where he wants to sit?"

She set the bag on the floor and signed to him. When he signed back, she said, "He said he'll sit on the bench."

"Okay. I'll stay with him until you've changed."

Alana signed something more to Caden and he nodded and looked up at Justin with a grin.

"I'll be back in a minute."

Justin rested his hand on Caden's shoulder as they walked to the bench and sat down. Caden tucked his legs cross-legged under him then bent over the tablet for a minute, tapping on the screen. Justin couldn't see past his tousled curls to what he was doing. When Caden lifted his head, he handed the tablet to Justin.

Justin glanced at him and then looked down at the tablet. Caden had opened a program where he could type, and he had tapped out a question for Justin.

Are you going to teach my mom to fight bad guys?

Justin thought about nodding as his answer but then decided to take advantage of this way of communication with the little guy.

Yes. I will teach her things that will help her protect herself and you too.

He handed the tablet back to Caden, wondering as he did if a seven-year-old was usually that good at reading and writing. Caden bent over the tablet again, resting it in his lap so his hands were free.

When Justin looked the question once Caden handed it to him again, his stomach clenched.

Mom said it would look like you were attacking her, but you wouldn't hurt her. Is she right? You won't hurt her?

His gaze met Caden's and this time there was no smile on the boy's face, just a serious questioning look in his eyes.

I won't hurt her. I promise.

When Caden read his answer, the smile was back and it reached clear to his eyes. Then he quickly typed out another message and handed it back to Justin.

Thank you. I love my mom. I don't want her hurt again.

Justin's stomach rolled at the last word Caden had typed. *Again*. So he had seen the hurt she'd endured because of the abuse. Justin swallowed hard and typed, **You're a good son to want to protect your mom, Caden. I know she's proud of you.**

After he had handed it back to Caden, Justin slipped an arm around his thin shoulders and pulled him into a side hug. When Caden looked up, Justin smiled at him. This kid was growing on him in ways he'd never imagined a child would—with the exception of his niece.

When he heard the delicate clearing of a throat, Justin lifted his head to find Alana standing a few feet away, her expression unreadable.

10

"EVERYTHING OKAY?" She said the words at the same time as she signed.

Justin glanced down at Caden then gave Alana a thumbs up. Caden grinned as he turned to his mom and gave her the same gesture. She gave a small shake of her head, but a smile played at the corners of her mouth.

"Ready to go?" Justin asked as he stood up, taking in her attire for the first time.

While she had changed into something besides a skirt, it all still hung on her like it was a size or two too big. She wore loose pants and a long sleeve T-shirt that covered her waist and hips. Her hair was still tucked up in the braid she always seemed to wear it in.

"As ready as I'll ever be, I guess," Alana said. She signed something to Caden, who nodded in reply and once again turned his attention to his tablet.

Justin touched her elbow and guided her to the middle of the mat. "Okay, before we start anything, let's talk a bit about potential threats and being aware."

Alana tried to keep her gaze on Justin's face as he talked to her, but it was a struggle. She kept fighting the urge to lower her head. Why hadn't she realized sooner that was something she still carried with her? Craig had towered over her and had always taken her meeting his gaze as challenging him for some reason. Justin was the first man where she'd been in a position to experience those feelings again.

Justin stopped talking for a moment as his gaze narrowed then he said, "Breathe."

She stared at him. "What?"

"Breathe. You're holding your breath." Justin took a step back from her. "Relax."

Alana became aware of how tightly her crossed arms pressed against her rib cage. And she gripped her upper arms so forcibly she was probably giving herself bruises. Dipping her head, she took a couple of deep breaths and lowered her arms. "Sorry."

"You don't need to apologize." Justin's voice was gentle. "What am I doing that is making you uneasy?"

Look him in the eye. He's not Craig.

She lifted her gaze to meet his. His blue eyes didn't show any anger or displeasure with her for what she'd done. Just concern.

"Here do this with me," Justin said. "Take a breath in for two counts then hold for two counts and exhale for two counts. Can you do that?"

Alana nodded. Breath in. *One. Two.* Hold. *One. Two.* Exhale. *One. Two.* She held his gaze as she did it again and he did it along with her.

After doing it a few times, Justin smiled at her. "Feeling better?"

"Yes."

"Breathing like that can help to calm you down, but it can also help you to concentrate and focus." Justin put his hands on his hips as he looked down at her. "You know, I wanted to do something in return for your help in learning sign language, but I realize now that maybe I pressured you into something you're not comfortable with."

Alana really just wanted a few minutes to gather herself back together. She was reacting on so many different levels it felt like there was a cacophony of emotion going on inside her. How could she find herself drawn to a man who, at the same time, brought back reactions that were tied to such a bad time in her life?

Standing this close to him, the scent of his cologne or soap teased her senses and made it difficult for her to focus on what he'd said. Part of her knew it would be wise to take the out he offered. Neither she nor Caden needed to be around him this much. It was only going to lead to heartache for one or, most likely, both of them. She glanced over at Caden and found that he was watching them, his expression serious.

What a mess.

She took a deep breath and let it out before looking at Justin. He hadn't moved. It was almost as if he was afraid he'd spook her if he did. "I want to learn this. For me. For Caden. It's all just very new."

Alana paused, but Justin didn't say anything. He just stood there watching her. She knew she needed to put it all out there so he'd understand. Trying again to keep her gaze on his, she said, "Craig—my ex—was very much into body building. He was a...large man."

If she hadn't been looking at him, she wouldn't have seen the moment comprehension dawned on him.

"Like me." It wasn't a question.

"Yes. Like you."

His brows drew together. "Are you afraid of me?"

She hesitated, her thoughts going back to when they'd first met, but since getting to know him, that fear had faded. "No."

Apparently her hesitation hadn't gone unnoticed. "You need to tell me the truth."

"When we first met, yes, I was a bit fearful. Especially because you wore your weapons. But then I saw you with Beth and Genevieve and even with Caden and knew that although you might have similar physical characteristics, you weren't like Craig."

"You're right. I'm not. I know next to nothing about the man, but I can say with total confidence that I'm not like him at all." His gaze moved from her to Caden then back. "I would never hurt you or Caden. You have my word on that."

Physically maybe, but Alana was pretty sure that if she didn't keep her heart protected, she'd be feeling hurt in other ways. "I do understand that. My reactions caught me off-guard, to be honest. It's been awhile since I've dealt with that type of thing."

"I'm sorry if I was the one who triggered it," Justin said. "Do you want to stop for now?"

"I think it's the talking part." Alana motioned between the two of them. His looming over her seemed to be what was causing most of her issues. "If there's more you want to explain to me, it might be better if we did it sitting down."

Justin seemed to contemplate her words before nodding. "We can do that." Without saying anything further, he lowered himself onto the mat, crossing his denim-clad legs. He rested his hands on his thighs as he looked up at her. "Better?"

With a smile of relief, Alana settled onto the mat facing him with her legs crossed as well. "Yes, this is better."

❧

Figuring Alana didn't need another possible emotional hurdle to overcome that day, Justin settled for just talking her through some of what they'd be doing. He was glad she'd told him what had been bothering her.

When he'd first noticed the tension rolling off her in waves, he'd been pretty certain she'd just tell him nothing was wrong if he asked about it. That she'd opened up to him about her ex was more than a little surprising. It was a bit difficult to hear though. An average man could do damage enough to someone like Alana, but someone who was focused on body building and who was built like him could do so much worse.

It had suddenly become very important that Alana know she never had to fear anything like that from him. He'd assured Caden that he wouldn't hurt his mom and now he needed Alana to know the same thing.

"I guess you changed for nothing," Justin said as he leaned back on his hands. "Next time, we'll work on some actual self-defence moves. As long as you feel up to it."

"I think I'll be okay with it. Having talked to you about it—my reaction earlier—has helped."

"Well, if something is making you uncomfortable, you only need to say the word."

"I will."

As he pushed to his feet and held out his hand to her, Justin asked, "Can I give you a ride?"

When she hesitated before slipping her hand into his, Justin wasn't sure if it was a reluctance to touch him or a reaction to his offer to give them a ride once again. The feel of her soft, delicate hand in his started a warmth that spread from his fingertips up his arm. Before Justin could relish the feeling too much, she took a step back from him, and he let her fingers slide from his.

"You could just drop us off at the same place as last time," Alana said as she clutched her hands together.

He wondered how long it would be until she would actually let him drive them home. "Sounds good. Do you want to change again before we leave?"

Alana looked down at herself. "Yes. I won't be long."

Justin nodded then watched as she spun around and headed for the changing room. He went back to where Caden sat. With a glance in the direction Alana had gone, Justin gestured for Cadent to give him the tablet.

After tapping the screen, Caden handed it to him. Justin knew he was going behind Alana's back, but he wanted to know where they lived, and he figured the boy might give up the information a bit more readily than his mother.

Do you know your address?

When Caden nodded, he tapped out **Can you tell me what it is?**

Without hesitating, Caden took the tablet and tapped on the screen. Justin didn't recognize the address the boy had typed out, but he committed it to memory before taking the tablet once again. **Thank you.**

He handed it back to Caden and watched as the boy glanced toward the change rooms and then pressed a finger to the backspace key on the screen keyboard. Pretty soon, their whole conversation was gone. Sneaky little guy.

They shared a grin then sat back to wait for Alana.

Alana was glad for her busy schedule over the next week. It kept her from thinking too much about Justin. At least during the day. Nothing could stop her from curling up on her bed in the darkness and imagining what it might be like to be loved by a man like him. She saw the depth of his ability to love when he was around Genevieve and Beth. Even when he'd been upset with his sister, he hadn't hurt her or withheld his love.

She'd only ever experienced that from Caden. And while she was extremely grateful for his unquestioning love, Alana wondered what it would be like to have someone *choose* to love her like that. To *choose* to give her a special place in their life. To protect her instead of inflict pain. To love her son as if he was their own.

"God, could you please bring us such a man?" Alana whispered the words into the silent darkness. She wasn't foolish enough to ask for Justin. Even though she felt that he was a good man for her...for them, Alana knew that there was no room for them in his life. Seeing him at Beth's earlier that evening had reinforced that in her mind, but her heart still felt far more than it should for this man she was only getting to know.

It wasn't often she let her emotions get the better of her, but it was so hard when she had a particularly long day. And with Caden's birthday looming—he'd mentioned it to her again that morning—all she could think about was how hard it was. She wanted—for just a few minutes—to have a pity party. This wasn't the life she'd envisioned for herself as a young girl. Kicked out by her family. Abused by her husband. Struggling to provide for a son she loved more than anything.

Alone.

Hot tears burned her skin as they slid from her eyes to soak the pillow beneath her cheek. She rubbed a hand over her chest, trying to ease the pain and tightness there. But the tears wouldn't stop, and the tightness wouldn't free her from its grip.

I am strong. I am capable of doing anything. I am worth loving. I will survive.

It was a mantra she'd begun to repeat to herself in the months leading up to her escape from Craig.

"You are weak." He would shout at her when he'd try to get her to work out with him, ignoring the fact that most the time she was in too much pain to do much of anything. Never mind that she really had no interest in bodybuilding.

I am strong.

"You're just lucky you have me. You'd be useless on your own."

I am capable of doing anything.

"I don't know why I keep you around. You don't even know how to please a man. Maybe if you could figure that out, I'd love you."

I am worth loving.

And when he would strike out at her, she'd let her mind drift away as she told herself *I will survive.*

And she had. Survived and thrived.

It took a long time, but finally her emotions were spent and her thoughts stopped whirling. But clearly she hadn't completely let go of what had been drifting through her mind before falling asleep as she woke several times during the night. Often it was nightmares of being back with Craig that roused her, trembling and desperate to know that she and Caden were safe.

She woke in the morning to find Caden shaking her shoulder, concern on his face.

What's wrong, Mama?

Alana pushed up to a sitting position and pulled him into her lap, wrapping her arms tightly around him. It was at times like this she wished they could talk instead of relying on signing. She wasn't able to comfort him and talk to him at the same time.

They sat that way for a few minutes before Caden pulled back from her, concern still on his face.

With a sigh, Alana moved her arms from around him to sign her response.

I'm fine, love. Sometimes I get sad, but seeing you always makes me happy.

The tension on Caden's face eased a bit, and he smiled at her. *Do we get to see Justin again today?*

Even as she nodded, Alana wished there was some way she could cancel. Especially after last night. But she could hardly tell Caden that. It was apparent her son had a serious case of hero worship going on with the man. And with him having so few good male role models in his life, Alana couldn't bring herself to limit Caden's exposure to Justin.

Let's eat breakfast and do a little schoolwork before we go.

Caden's vigorous nod set his curls dancing. Alana gave him one last squeeze before they climbed off her bed and made their way to the kitchen.

Justin sat down on the bench beside Caden. He held out his hand for the tablet. Without hesitation, the boy gave it to him, the screen already showing the app they'd used last time for chatting.

Is everything okay with your mom?

Caden's shoulders slumped as he looked down at the tablet when Justin gave it back to him. He glanced up, his eyes worried. Then he started to tap on the screen.

Justin glanced at the door leading to the changing room, hoping he'd get a response from Caden before Alana showed up. He'd noticed immediately that she was different this morning. There had been tension on her face he hadn't seen the night before at Beth's. And she looked like she hadn't slept at all during the night. But most concerning of all was how she hardly held his gaze. During their sign language lesson, she'd focused on his hands as she'd taught him another set of signs.

And he wasn't the only one concerned. He'd seen the way Caden had kept glancing over at her even while he played his video games. It was the first time he recalled seeing worry like that on the young boy's face.

Caden took so long to type his reply Justin was worried he wouldn't be able to read it before Alana joined them. Finally, Caden handed him the tablet, his lip caught between small teeth.

I had to wake Mama this morning. Usually, she wakes me. I think she had been crying. I asked what was wrong. She said she was sad but that looking at me made her happy. I don't know what made her sad. She never cries. I just want her to be happy.

Justin felt something tighten in his chest as he read the words. He took a deep breath to ease it, but it didn't help. It was the same tightness he'd experienced a few days ago when he'd driven past the address Caden had given him, and he'd seen where the two of them lived. His first instinct had been to park his truck, find their apartment and take them away from there. But that wasn't his place. And he didn't doubt she was doing the best she could to provide for her son.

Before he could type out a response, Caden took the tablet back and erased what he'd written. Instead of typing anything more or giving it back to Justin, Caden drew his knees up and wrapped his arms around them, trapping the tablet between his chest and thighs.

Justin tried to remember what it had been like to be seven or eight years old. Most the memories from that time were fuzzy, but as he thought back now, more came into focus for him. Times when he'd seen his mother crying. No doubt she'd cried sad tears at some point, but he couldn't recall a time when he'd seen her cry anything but happy tears. The tears that had come because his dad had brought her some unexpected gift or one of the kids had done something special. It hadn't been his job to make sure that his mom was happy, his dad had taken care of that. They'd all just been able to exist in a world of love and joy most of the time.

The responsibility of making someone happy fell on his shoulders when he'd had to step into a parental role for Beth. That had been hard, but at least he'd been old enough to understand what was going on and how to read Beth's emotions—most of the time. Caden would have no idea what might cause his mom to be sad or worse yet, how to make her happy again. It was a big responsibility for such a little guy. One that Alana likely didn't want her son to have, but one he'd taken on regardless.

Justin slid an arm around Caden's shoulders. The boy sat stiffly for a moment, hunching over his knees before he turned slightly and relaxed into Justin's side. At that moment, there was no denying this little boy had successfully bypassed all the defenses Justin had placed around his heart and claimed a part of it, much in the same way Genevieve had. He hadn't wanted to think about having a family of his own. His job was his life. He didn't have time for the things that being with Caden and Alana made him think about.

He was jerked from his thoughts when Alana suddenly appeared and dropped to her knees in front of Caden. Her hands ran over his head then cupped his face.

She looked up at Justin, concern clear in her eyes. "What happened?"

Justin debated what he should tell her, but without much time to weigh the pros and cons, he settled on the truth. "He's worried about you. He said you were sad."

Immediately, all emotion disappeared from her face. Just like that, Justin could no longer read anything in her eyes, and it made him uneasy. Had he stepped over a line?

Alana's hands slid from Caden's face, and suddenly she was signing way too rapidly for Justin to have even a hope of understanding. Caden relaxed his grip on his legs and settled them on the bench, the tablet still in his lap. As Caden straightened, Justin let his arm slide away.

Knowing this had to be dealt with before they could move on to anything else, Justin leaned back against the wall and crossed his arms. The only emotion he could see on Alana's face now was love for her son. Caden was signing back to her as quickly as she'd signed to him.

This went on for a couple of minutes before Caden set his tablet on the bench and slid into Alana's arms. She buried her face into his shoulder and held tight. Justin swallowed hard and looked away from the two of them huddled on the floor. This was not what was supposed to happen. This was not part of his plan. He'd let two people into his heart—three, if he counted Daniel—and that should have been more than enough for him.

What was this woman doing to him? She and her son were drawing out emotions he didn't know he had for anyone but his family. Everything had changed when he'd lost his family. To have four people ripped from his heart in one blow had been almost unbearable for him. He didn't want to be that vulnerable again. It was bad enough he took that risk with Beth and Genevieve, but these two? In his heart, he knew they had the potential to mean even more to him than his sister and her family.

After Alana let Caden go, the boy slid back on the bench and picked up his tablet. Alana stood up and looked at Justin. And once again her face held no emotion.

"Ready to go?"

Justin hesitated. "Are you sure you're up for this?"

"Yes, I am."

He wanted to offer to talk if she needed to, but he knew that wouldn't help his need to keep his emotions from getting mixed up in hers. Putting his hands on his knees, Justin pushed to his feet. "Then let's do this."

11

ALANA LET OUT a sigh as she followed Justin onto the mat. Though most the time she was grateful for Caden's soft heart and the way he was sensitive to the feelings of those around him, sometimes she really wished he was a little less sensitive to hers. She thought she'd been able to reassure him that everything was okay. They'd talked about it and then moved on with their day just like they usually did. She was dragging a bit because she hadn't gotten much sleep, but she had hoped Caden had forgotten about the rest. Apparently that had been too much to hope for.

As they reached the center of the mat, Justin turned toward her. She knew he was searching her face for any sign that she wasn't as fine as she'd said.

"Are you sure you don't want to talk about anything?" Justin asked.

Alana recognized the irony in the situation. There was no way she'd discuss what had upset her with the person who was responsible for some of that turmoil. "Only one thing. How exactly did Caden tell you he was worried about me?"

Justin's brows rose slightly. "He has some app on his tablet that lets us type our conversation. He's a very resourceful little guy, plus he seems to read and write quite well for his age. Is he ahead of where most seven-year-olds are?"

"Yes. He learned to read fairly young, and I've worked hard with him to expand his vocabulary so he could communicate like he did with you."

"Well, he certainly reads and writes way better than I can sign," Justin said with a rueful grin.

Her heart skipped a beat at the sight of his smile. "You'll get there. By the time Genevieve is his age, you'll be able to communicate with her just like I do with Caden."

Too bad I won't be around to see it. The words wound their way through her mind and into her heart. The sadness she'd worked so hard to push aside started to seep back in. She couldn't let that happen. Justin was as perceptive as Caden and would notice right away.

"I hope I'm half as good as you are. Watching the way you and Caden sign is crazy."

"Lots of practice," Alana said with what she hoped was an encouraging smile. "So, what are we working on today?"

Justin's eyes narrowed briefly then he said, "Do you have any questions about what we talked about last week?"

Alana shook her head. And even if she did, she wasn't going to be asking him. She needed this session to be done and over with as quickly as possible.

"Okay. We're going to work on one move today. Like I mentioned last week, most confrontations initially take place face-to-face, but today I'm going to show you how to free yourself from an attack from behind."

Alana watched as he explained the moves to her then he motioned for her to turn around. It slowly dawned on her that he was going to walk her through it while actually making contact with her. Why had she not thought this through better?

"If I come up behind you and get my arm around your neck like this," Justin looped his forearm around her neck, "you're going to automatically lift your hands to try to pull my arm away. But I'm stronger than you, and just pulling on my arm won't free you in time."

As her hands came up to grip his arm, Alana had to keep reminding herself this was Justin. He wasn't going to hurt her. She felt the strength in his arm around her neck and in his chest where it touched her shoulders.

He won't hurt me.

"So at the same time as your hands come up, you need to turn your head to the side like you're trying to look at me. This will make sure that only one of the arteries in your neck is being compressed so you can maintain consciousness. Give it a try."

Alana turned her head to the left and glanced up to find Justin was so close she could see the dark flecks in his blue eyes. *Too close.* She lowered her gaze but kept her head turned to the side. Hopefully, he couldn't hear her heart pounding because right then the rush of blood in her head seemed way too loud.

Justin continued to give her directions step-by-step until she was free of his grasp. "Good. Let's do it again. The best way to make sure you'll be able to use these moves is to practice them so much that they become automatic to you. Then if you feel an arm around your neck, your body will already know how to react."

Alana tried to focus on the moves in her head while she continued to remind herself it was Justin, and he wouldn't hurt her. And yet, at the same time, she had to ignore that it was Justin's arm around her neck. His chest pressed against her shoulders. Being this close to him wasn't helping her resolve to not get her emotions any more tangled up where he was concerned.

After a few times through it, she found herself doing what she had done in the past. When she couldn't trust her emotions, she distanced herself from the situation that was forcing her to feel. She had never in a million years imagined she'd be employing the same method she'd used to avoid the physical and emotional pain inflicted on her by Craig to escape the feelings being close to Justin brought her.

Would she ever get to the point where she wouldn't have to hide how she felt? Maybe in a couple of weeks she could make up a reason to avoid any further lessons with Justin and then send him links to videos he could watch to help him with his sign language. But then what would that do to Caden?

"Alana?"

She blinked, surprised to find him in front of her. After the last go around, Alana had been expecting to feel his arm around her neck again. "Sorry. What?"

Justin stared at her for a moment. "Where did you go?"

"Go? When?"

"Just now. You were going through the motions, but it was like your mind was someplace else."

She crossed her arms and made sure to keep her gaze locked onto his. "I thought that's what you said. Practice so my body would do it automatically."

He nodded slowly. "Yes. True. I just didn't think you'd actually check out."

There was no way she was going to tell him how she'd learned to do that and why she'd chosen to do it with him. "Do you think I have the hang of this?"

"Yes, I do. You caught on to the moves very quickly." He glanced past her to where Caden sat. "I think we can call it a day."

"Okay. I'll go get changed," Alana said as she turned to check on Caden before she headed for the changing room.

———⊱✦⊰———

Justin waited until Alana disappeared into the change room before going back to Caden. The boy smiled as Justin settled on the bench beside him. Whatever had been bothering him earlier seemed to have disappeared. Justin waited to see if he would write anything on the tablet, but this time Caden just held it in his hands.

He found himself more than a little mystified by Alana's reaction to their practicing. *His* reaction to being near to her, he'd understood. The scent of her shampoo had teased him when he'd move closer to put his arm in position around her neck. He hadn't touched her anywhere else but around her neck and shoulders, but it had been enough to send his mind in a direction it shouldn't have gone.

He'd found himself wanting to pull her into his arms, to tuck her in against his chest and tell her that she didn't need to learn these moves because he would be right there with her to make sure she never needed them.

But while he'd been struggling to keep his reaction to her nearness under control, she'd basically checked out. At first she'd been paying attention, but the last few times, he knew that he may have held her body, but her mind was gone. He was pretty sure her ability to do that was a remnant of the abuse she'd endured at the hands of her ex.

Justin didn't want her to do that with him. It made him feel like he was doing something with her that she wanted to block out of her mind.

How did all of this get so messed up? And how many times was he going to ask himself that before he realized there was no answer...it was just a mess.

When Alana came toward them, bag in hand, Justin got to his feet and noticed that Caden did as well.

"Can I give you a ride somewhere?" he asked as she approached even though he knew what the answer was going to be. One of these days, he hoped she would surprise him.

"Thank you, but I think we'll just take the bus today."

Justin nodded. "Okay. Guess I'll see you next week." He walked with them to the elevator, and after they had reached the main floor, he turned to Caden and held out his hand for a fist bump. Caden grinned and bumped his much smaller fist against Justin's. "See ya, buddy."

He then watched through the large glass windows as they walked toward the main gate. Justin had seen the flash of disappointment on Caden's face when he'd realized they weren't going in his truck. Unfortunately for the little boy, he was getting caught in the middle of whatever his mom was dealing with and Justin's own confusion over things.

With a sigh of frustration, Justin turned to the men sitting behind the security desk to retrieve the bags he'd left with them earlier. There was nothing he needed to hang around there for, so he would just head back to the compound to deal with stuff that actually made sense.

Over the next week, Alana finished up the homeschool year with Caden. Though she never really stopped teaching him—even in the summer—she tried to make a big deal out of an official end of the school year so he felt he was getting a break like his friends.

On Friday, Peter's family picked him up to go to the amusement park at the Mall of America with them. It had been terribly difficult to allow him to go with them without her, but she knew this was something she wouldn't ever be able to give him. If Peter hadn't been deaf as well, Alana might not have let Caden go, but it helped that she knew he could communicate with Peter and his parents.

With Caden occupied, Alana hoped to accomplish several things. She'd made her list the night before in hopes of maximizing the time she had to run her errands before she had to pick Caden up.

After dropping Caden off at Peter's house, she caught the bus that would take her to the deaf charter school she'd researched online. She'd been going back and forth on whether or not it would be a good idea to send him in the fall, so she hoped the appointment would help her figure that out. He was such a social child, and she wasn't sure she could provide enough social stimulation for him especially since they didn't know that many deaf children his age. Plus, it would free her up to look for a job that would fall within the hours he was at school.

She'd prayed about it and hoped she could get enough information to make the best decision. It was at times like these that she missed having someone to help her make decisions. She was worried that there might be a perspective she overlooked, but all she could do was gather as much information as possible and then pray she made the right choice for Caden.

When Alana left her appointment an hour later, she was definitely leaning toward seeing this as a good thing for Caden. And if she could continue to do her online work in addition to getting a job—even part-time—while Caden was in school, she might be able to afford to move them to a better apartment. Feeling encouraged, she tucked all the information she'd received into her bag, planning to review it again at home later then caught the bus to go get some groceries.

Though grocery shopping was usually depressing, Alana found that having something positive to focus on made it easier. In preparation for Caden's upcoming birthday, she spent some of her grocery budget picking up a cake mix and frosting. Picking up what she'd need one or two things at a time meant it wasn't such a strain on the budget. She would have preferred to make it from scratch, but it was cheaper to just buy the mixes since they were on sale. She was pretty sure that Caden wouldn't care as long as it was chocolate and sweet.

She was just about to the end of her relatively short grocery list when her phone rang. Fumbling for it in the pocket of her skirt, Alana hoped nothing was wrong with Caden. The name on the display, however, had her hesitating over the icon to accept the call. *Justin.*

Before she could talk herself out of it, she tapped the screen and pressed the phone to her ear. "Hello?"

"Alana? This is Justin."

She swallowed hard and said, "Hi, Justin. What's up?"

"I was calling to see if you and Caden would be interested in coming to the BlackThorpe company picnic with me."

"Uh...I'm not part of the company." She felt a little stupid pointing out the obvious.

"It's open to family and friends of the employees and the people who are involved in BlackThorpe's wounded veterans program. I thought maybe Caden would enjoy it. From what I hear, they'll have lots of fun things like those inflated slides and bouncy houses along with some games and lots of food. There's also fireworks at the end of the evening."

"When is it?"

"Tomorrow. I realize it's kind of short notice, but Melanie got on me again today about inviting people. Beth and Dan have said they'd come, so if you need a ride, they can give you one, and Beth said you're welcome to stay the night since the fireworks will likely run late."

Alana moved her cart to the side of the aisle so she was out of the way of the other shoppers. "I don't know..."

There was a beat of silence on the other end of the line before Justin said, "Well, consider yourself invited. If you decide to come, just give Beth a call about getting a ride. The picnic starts at four and the fireworks will be around nine o'clock."

"Okay. I'll think about it. Thank you for the invitation."

"You're welcome. Hope to see you there."

After Justin had ended the call, Alana tucked the phone back into her pocket. He was right, of course. Caden would absolutely love something like that. And it didn't mean Justin would be hanging around with them just because he'd invited them. She wasn't sure she'd be able to handle that without having even more of her emotions get tangled up where he was concerned.

Maybe it would be better—safer—to turn down the invitation. Caden wouldn't know. And given that he'd just been to the Mall of America, it wasn't like he hadn't done anything fun. Yeah, it would be better if she just passed on it.

Alana looked down at her list and pushed her cart forward.

Oh, who was she kidding? There was no way she wouldn't accept Justin's invite. Having accepted that truth, Alana found herself finishing off her shopping with a knot of excitement in her stomach. By the time she got back to the apartment with her groceries, she'd gone back and forth several times, but each time her heart got the better of her. Not just because she really did want to see Justin again, but because it was something that would bring Caden joy.

After she had put away her purchases, Alana sat down at the table and called Beth. As expected, the woman was thrilled that she planned to join them at the picnic. They made arrangements for Alana and Caden to meet them at their house at three the next afternoon. She also accepted Beth's invitation to spend the night and go with them to church the next morning.

Now that she'd locked herself into that, she only had one more thing to figure out. What was she going to wear?

⸺⊷⊰⊱⊶⸺

The flow of people through the gates of the compound made Justin uneasy. Usually, things were locked down pretty tight, so having it this open didn't make sense to him. He stood next to Melanie Thorpe, arms crossed, watching the groups of people approach the sign-in table where their names were matched against the ones provided by employees.

"Justin." Melanie jabbed her elbow into his ribs. "Stop scowling. You're going to scare off the kids."

He glanced down at her, not bothering to change his expression. "This really is ridiculous. What were Alex and Marc thinking?"

Melanie grinned at him. "Well, to be honest, it was more me and Adrianne who broached the idea with them."

"What on earth did you do that for? Doesn't this strike you as a bit of a security nightmare? Did you vet all the people who said they were coming?"

"We thought it might keep the morale high among the employees. And it's not like they have access to top secret information here. All buildings remain secure and there are clear boundaries marked to keep people within the area we've set up for the picnic."

Justin scoffed. "Like that's going to keep someone from ducking past them and doing some exploring."

Melanie patted his arm. "It will be fine, but I give you permission to say you told me so if this goes south."

Before Justin could respond, he felt something attach itself to his lower leg. Looking down, he spotted Genevieve hugging him. A grin chased the scowl from his face as he bent down to scoop her up.

"Who is this cutie?" Melanie asked as she reached out to touch Genevieve's curls.

"This is my niece, Genevieve," he said as Beth and Dan walked up with Alana and Caden. He hoped his happiness at seeing the two of them with his sister didn't show too much on his face. "And this is my sister, Beth and her husband, Dan. This is Melanie Thorpe. The apparent mastermind behind the mayhem today."

"It's a pleasure to meet you." Melanie held out her hand and greeted them with a wide smile. "I'm already discovering a big upside to this picnic, Justin. I'm meeting members of your family I never knew existed."

He looked past Beth and Dan to where Alana stood with her arm around Caden. Her gaze was on Melanie, but Caden's was on him and the boy gave him a wave. When Justin gestured with his hand, the boy darted away from Alana's side to stand next to him, a big grin on his face. His green eyes—so much like his mother's—sparkled with excitement. Alana followed a little more slowly, and Justin could read her unease in the tension around her mouth and eyes and the way she held her hands clenched in front of her.

He noticed the pair of jeans she wore fit her better than anything he'd seen her in so far, but her arms were still covered by the see-through long-sleeved blouse she wore over a pink tank top. And for the first time that he could remember, her hair was down. And it was long—longer than he would have imagined—and curly. He shoved his hands into his pockets when they itched to touch her hair to see if it felt as silky as it looked.

"Melanie, this is Alana and her son, Caden." Justin rested his hand on Caden's shoulder. "They're family friends."

He could see the curiosity on Melanie's face as she studied them. She held out her hand to Caden and waited until he slipped his into it. "Nice to meet you, Caden."

Caden glanced at his mother and Alana moved to stand next to him. She quickly spelled out what Justin assumed was Melanie's name. He had only just begun to learn the alphabet, but the motions she made with her hand looked familiar.

When Melanie shot him a wide-eyed look, Justin said, "Caden is deaf."

It wasn't often something caught Melanie off-guard, but she quickly regained her composure and held out her hand to Alana. "It's nice to meet you, Alana."

A small smile lifted the corners of Alana's mouth. "You too."

"There's a lot of fun stuff for kids Caden's age." Melanie motioned with her hand towards to the picnic area. "I saw Lucas and Brooke arrive a little while ago. You should introduce Caden to Danny."

"That's a good idea," Justin said as Dan took Genevieve from him and got her settled into the stroller he'd been pushing. He gave Melanie another hard look. "But I still think the whole picnic thing is the opposite of a good idea."

This time Melanie reached up and patted his cheek. "Relax. You might actually enjoy yourself." She gave a little wave to the rest of the group. "I'm going to go make sure everyone is doing their job. Have a good time."

As Melanie walked away, Justin gazed across the crowd in search of Lucas Hamilton and his family. When he didn't immediately spot them, he turned back and said, "Why don't we wander around and see what sort of stuff they've got for the kids?"

Justin had barely taken a step when a small hand slipped into his. Looking down, he saw Caden standing at his side, his eyes wide as he took in all the people and activity ahead of them. Tightening his grasp on the boy's hand, Justin moved toward where they had set up some activities for kids.

He glanced over his shoulder and saw that Alana had fallen in step with Beth. She didn't look nearly as happy or excited to be there as her son was. Though he'd known she'd likely accept his invitation for Caden's sake, Justin had hoped she would enjoy herself as well. Hopefully, as the afternoon wore on she'd relax.

This was a mistake.

Though Alana figured Beth would have mentioned if Justin had gotten a girlfriend in the past few days, seeing him with the beautiful blonde was still a harsh reminder that at some point, he just might. She told herself the sadness she felt was for Caden. When he'd slid his hand into Justin's, she'd held her breath, wondering how Justin would react. Though Caden hadn't come right out and said it, Alana knew from a few subtle things he'd mentioned that he really wanted Justin in his life more. If Justin had a girlfriend, Caden wasn't likely to get that wish.

She saw that Justin had shortened his strides so Caden could keep up with him as they crossed the grass together. For too long she'd convinced herself that Caden was just fine without a father. Unfortunately, Caden's actions showed that he was craving a male influence in his life. And not just any male, but Justin. Though he seemed to enjoy being around Daniel, he'd never reacted to him the way he had to Justin.

"Hey, guys."

Justin's greeting drew Alana from her thoughts and onto the group of people he'd stopped beside. She recognized a couple of the men from her first visit to BlackThorpe.

"Hey, man. How's it going? I see you got my buddy with you again."

Than dropped down to Caden's level and signed to him. Caden pulled his hand from Justin's to reply but even though Than was engaging him in conversation, Alana noticed that Caden didn't move from Justin's side.

As Than and Caden talked, Justin introduced them like he had with Melanie. Then he motioned to a pretty woman with straight brown hair and a friendly smile. "By the way, Alana, this is Lindsay, who just recently put Than out of his misery and agreed to be his girlfriend."

"I just had to wait until I was sure the line had disappeared." Snickers sounded around the group as Lindsay grinned.

With a smile, Justin drew her attention to another familiar face. "Beside Eric over there is his wife, Staci and their daughter, Sarah. And this is Eric's sister, Brooke, who is married to Lucas and their son, Danny. Lucas is Lindsay's brother." He laid his hand on the shoulder of the man next to him who held the hand of a woman who appeared to have dwarfism. "This is Trent and his fiancée, Victoria, another of Eric's sisters. They're just keeping it all in the family here at BlackThorpe."

Alana noticed the young boy Justin had introduced as Danny had approached Than and was watching his conversation with Caden intently. The little girl—Sarah—also moved toward him and slid her hand into Danny's. Quickly reviewing the relationships Justin had just explained, Alana realized that the two of them would be cousins. She saw the affection on Danny's face as he glanced at Sarah before turning his attention back to Than and Caden.

There was no missing the curiosity of the group as they shook hands with her. Alana stayed close to Beth. Everyone seemed very friendly, but she found it hard to think of things to say even though Beth was chatting easily with Lindsay.

"Hey, why don't I take the boys to the slide," Than suggested. He looked at Alana. "Would that be okay? I'll be able to translate if Caden needs it."

"Sure. That would be great. Thanks." She quickly signed to Caden what Than had suggested and that she had given her permission.

Than flashed Alana a smile before taking Lindsay's hand and then reaching for Caden's. Danny took his aunt's other hand and the four of them set off together. Sarah seemed a bit upset at being abandoned but then she spotted Genevieve and made a beeline for the stroller. Beth squatted down next to the girl and told her Genevieve's name and answered the questions Sarah had about her. Staci moved to stand with her daughter and began to chat with Beth.

Alana took a deep breath and let it out, trying to ease the tension in her body. There was a longing growing in her for something like this. A group of friends. An easy camaraderie. A sense of belonging. But there wasn't a place for her here. Justin belonged because he worked with these people and, if his current conversation with Trent was any indication, they were also his friends. As his family, Beth and Daniel also fit in easily. Daniel chatted with Eric and Lucas like they were old friends even though Justin's introduction made it clear they had just met.

A gentle touch on her arm drew her attention, and she looked over to see Victoria at her side. The woman gave her a friendly smile. "So have you known Justin long?"

12

"**N**O. ONLY A few weeks. I originally met Beth and Daniel since we go to the same church. I've been helping them with...some stuff, and I met Justin as a result of that."

"He's a great guy," Victoria said, her gaze going to where her fiancée stood talking to him. "Your son seems to sense that as well."

Alana nodded. "Ever since Caden saw him with his guns, he's decided Justin is his hero."

"Couldn't ask for a much better hero, if you ask me," Victoria said. "He helped me learn to shoot a while back. Never once told me I couldn't do it because of my size. He and Trent just figured out the best way to make it work for me and then let me go to town. He's a good man."

As she listened to Victoria talk Justin up, Alana wondered what she was trying to accomplish. It wasn't as if Alana needed to hear all about Justin's good points. She knew a lot of them already, but his life didn't have room for an instant family, so it really didn't matter what she felt about Justin. He wasn't the man for her.

"It seems most the men I've met who work for BlackThorpe are good men," Alana said, trying to move the conversation away from Justin.

Victoria grinned. "Well, I'd have to agree since I'm engaged to one and related to another."

"Have you set a wedding date?" Alana asked.

"Yep. It took us awhile, but we finally decided on one." Victoria tilted her head, her eyes suddenly sparkling. "You should come. You could be Justin's plus one."

Alana was sure her eyes widened significantly at that remark. No subtly at all there. "Um...wouldn't it be up to Justin to invite a date? He might already have someone in mind."

Victoria shrugged. "I doubt that, but if it will make you feel better, I'll ask him about it just to be sure."

Alana held up her hand. "No. No, that's okay. We don't really have that sort of relationship. It's more of a teacher-student kind of thing."

"Really?" Curiosity bloomed across Victoria's face. "So who's the teacher and who's the student?"

Alana glanced toward where Than had taken Caden before answering. When she spotted her son's curly mop, she looked back at Victoria. "We kind of both are. I'm teaching him sign language, and he's teaching me self-defence."

"Sign language? Why is Justin learning sign language?"

Not sure if it was her place to say anything about Genevieve, Alana just said, "Someone close to him is hearing impaired, and he wanted to make sure he was able to communicate with them. I'm also teaching his sister and her family."

"Has your son been deaf since birth?" Victoria asked.

Alana told her a bit about Caden's deafness and then they shared stories of trying to navigate in the world with something that set them apart from most others. She found herself relaxing the more they chatted. Victoria was easy to talk with, and Alana was glad she didn't try to bring Justin up again.

A light touch on her back startled Alana, and she looked up to see Justin beside her, his head bent down. "Should we go see what Caden is up to?"

Alana glanced around and saw that the others in the group had begun to move in the direction Than had taken Caden and Danny. Trent took Victoria's hand and after she shot Alana a mischievous smile, Victoria began to walk away, tugging on Trent's hand.

With a nod of her head, Alana followed them, acutely aware of Justin at her side. It had been her plan to stick close to Beth and not get into situations with Justin that fueled the fire of emotions within her. As they neared the large inflated slide, a couple of kids dashed past, bumping into her in their apparent eagerness to get to their destination. Alana stumbled as she took a step to the side which brought her right up against Justin. This time his touch wasn't light as he laid an arm across her back and his hand came to rest on her hip, keeping her on her feet.

"Sorry." The word slipped out as she quickly stepped away from him. His hand slid from her side without any further attempt to hold her. "Guess they were in a hurry to get to the slide."

"Yep, seems so." Justin's voice was steady. "It looks like Caden and Danny are having fun on it."

They stopped next to Than and Lindsay, who stood at the foot of the slide looking up.

"C'mon, boys!" Than yelled up to them then motioned with his hand.

Alana noticed Caden and Danny were each seated on one of the dual slides and after a glance at each other, they pushed off and slid down to the bottom. As they climbed off, they high-fived each other. Spotting her, Caden ran to where she stood with Justin, his cheeks flushed and his eyes bright with excitement.

It's so much fun! Can I keep going with Danny?

Alana nodded. *As long as it's okay with his parents.*

Caden's gaze darted to Justin then back to her. *Can you tell Justin thank you for inviting us?*

I will. She'd no sooner finished the signs when he darted away again to where Danny waited for him at the steps that led to the top of the slide.

Alana took a deep breath, the scent she'd come to associate with Justin alerting her to how near her he was. She turned to look at him. "Caden wanted me to tell you thank you for inviting him today. He's having a great time."

A quick smile transformed his face as his blue eyes warmed. "I'm glad. I wasn't sure it was a good idea to have something like this, but seeing Caden having fun makes it all worthwhile."

Alana nodded her agreement as she watched the boys climb up the stairs. It had been awhile since she'd last seen Caden having so much fun. And she was very thankful that Danny had taken Caden under his wing. "Danny seems like a neat kid."

"He is." This pronouncement came from Lindsay. "I'm his aunt, so one might think I'm biased but honestly, he just an all-around terrific kid. Made me rethink the whole 'not having kids' thing."

"I'm sure Than was glad to hear that," Justin said, his gaze going to the man at Lindsay's side.

Than laughed. "Well, I would have taken her regardless, but yes, I was glad to hear that." He slid an arm around Lindsay's waist and tucked her into his side. Lindsay laid her hand on his chest as she leaned her head against his shoulder.

Alana stared at them, wondering what it would be like to be in a relationship where affection came so easily. She hadn't seen it in her parents' marriage, and it certainly hadn't been present in her relationship with Craig.

It was the confidence Lindsay and Than had in each other that Alana found most intriguing. Than had reached for Lindsay with a confidence that said he knew she wouldn't reject his advances. Alana had never been confident enough in anyone's feelings for her to approach them like that.

Except for Caden. She knew he'd never rebuff her affection, but would she ever be able to feel that way about anyone else? A man? Like Justin?

Alana pushed aside her thoughts. Being around Justin like this was putting too many things into her mind. She needed to just concentrate on Caden and the fun he was having. Today was about him. Not about her screwed up past. Not the longings in her heart. No, it was about Caden being able to just be a little boy doing fun things.

She crossed her arms over her torso as she watched Caden go up and down the slide a couple more times. Eventually, Lucas stepped toward the slide as Danny and Caden reached the bottom. The tall man waved the boys over. Reluctantly, they abandoned the slide and made their way to Lucas. Before Alana could move, Than slid his arm from around Lindsay and walked over to join Lucas and the boys. She saw him signing to Caden and then reached out to take the boy's hand.

As they walked back toward them, Alana saw that the excitement had dimmed some on Caden's face, but his gaze was darting around, no doubt looking for the next thing they would do. When he reached her, he let go of Than's hand and signed to her asking if they could go do more.

At her nod, Caden took her hand and then slid his other hand into Justin's. The corner of Than's mouth lifted as he looked at Caden and then Justin. They continued to move as a group, taking in the carnival-like setup of the event. When they came upon a booth that offered the opportunity to shoot, Caden jerked his hands free and quickly signed that he wanted to try.

"Let me guess," Justin began before Alana could say anything, "he wants to have a go at the shooting game."

She nodded. "Yeah, he wants to give it a try."

"Well, then let's go." He took Caden's hand then looked over at Than. "You think you can beat me, man?"

Than groaned. "Probably not, but I'll give it a whirl."

As Alana watched, Justin and Caden were joined by Danny, Than, Trent and Victoria. She walked to where

Justin and Caden stood so she could interpret for them if need be.

Justin picked up the gun and gave it to Caden. He glanced at Alana and then gave instructions on how to do it.

Do you understand? Alana asked Caden once she finished interpreting what Justin had said.

Alana waited for Justin to pick up a rifle, but instead, he dropped down to his knee beside Caden and put his arms around him to show him how to position the rifle and then helped him hold the gun. After Caden had fired off a couple of shots, Justin lowered his arms but still stayed on his knee, his hand on Caden's back. Than and the others had taken up their rifles and began to shoot as well.

Justin stayed with Caden for a bit and then when it was apparent he had a handle on it, he stood and picked up another free rifle.

"How's it going there, Than?" Justin called. "Shot out the star yet?"

"Shut up, man, and start putting some shots in your own star."

Alana smiled as the insults flowed between the men. Justin settled in with the rifle pressed against his shoulder and began a steady stream of shots at the small target. She moved closer to Caden and Justin to watch them. Caden's shots were a little wild and he rarely hit the target, but she could see the smile on his face as he pulled the trigger over and over. In contrast, every time Justin pulled the trigger, he hit the target.

She wasn't sure how many of the BBs they had to shoot, but by the time all was said and done, only two had managed to shoot out the red star. Justin, of course, but more surprising was that the other person was Victoria. She and Justin slapped hands in celebration.

"You've been my best student, Tori," Justin said with a grin at the woman.

Even though Caden's target showed that he'd only managed to hit it a handful of times, Alana could see the excitement coursing through him. Already, his gaze was moving toward the other games that were set up. He slipped his hand into hers and pointed to the next booth, looking up at her with a question in his eyes.

Alana noticed that Justin was still standing with his friends, so she walked with Caden to the next game. There were already several people playing it so they had to wait. As they did, she tried to explain to him what to do.

They stood for a couple of minutes before he tugged at her hand again. She looked down at him with a smile that faded when she saw the serious look on his face.

What's wrong?

Caden's brows drew together and it took him a moment then he slid his hand from hers to answer. *Can Justin be my dad?*

A band wrapped around Alana's lungs and squeezed all the air from them. This was what she had been afraid of. Tears blurred her eyes, but she blinked them away as quickly as she could. She struggled to take a deep breath to ease the tightness in her chest. How did she explain this to him?

Justin is just a friend, sweetheart. Don't you like to have him as a friend?

Caden stared at her, his green eyes so full of emotion for one so young. *I love him, Mama.*

The shot of pain that pierced Alana's heart had her reaching for her son as much to comfort him as to keep her balance. She hadn't expected to hear something like that from Caden, but he had never been one to hide how he felt. And the way his face lit up whenever he was around Justin should have warned her of the growing affection he had for the man.

His revelation stunned her, and she had no idea what to say. She always thought her son's first heartbreak would be because of a girl. Alana had never imagined it would be because he loved a man he wanted to call dad.

"Everything okay here?"

At the sound of Justin's voice, Alana's breath caught and she tried to steady her nerves as she nodded. She looked at

Caden and signed that they would talk about it later. He stared at her then gave a slow dip of his head.

Glancing around, Alana tried to avoid Justin's gaze. Unfortunately, the gaze she did meet was even worse. *Than*. He would have been able to follow her conversation with Caden. She didn't want to see pity in his gaze, but there was nothing there but understanding. He gave her a quick smile before looking down at Caden and signing to him.

Want to try this game?

Caden glanced over at the game then back at Than, a smile spreading on his face as he nodded. When a spot opened up, Caden took his place and began to shoot the water pistol. Alana approached Than and when he turned to look at her, she signed *Please don't say anything to Justin.*

Than nodded and signed back *I won't. I'll try to distract Caden from him, but I'll have to explain to Lindsay. Is that okay? She doesn't really know Justin.*

Alana nodded then turned her attention back to Caden, but her thoughts and emotions were scrambling to find firm ground again. She crossed her arms over her waist, wishing they could leave. But she was trapped with no way home until Daniel and Beth decided to leave.

"Well, that's hardly fair," Justin said.

She looked up to see that he had been addressing her. "Fair?"

"You not only get to hold private conversations with Caden but now with Than too?" Thankfully, she saw the quick smile on his face that told her he was just joking.

"Yeah. We're sharing state secrets," Alana said, hoping her tone was light even though it didn't sound that way to her.

"Well, that's a good incentive to learn sign language. All those secrets I'll be privy to."

At that moment, Alana was very grateful he hadn't been able to understand the secret Caden had shared with her. She glanced over at Than and saw him standing with his arm around Lindsay, their heads close together. When she looked back at Caden, she saw that Danny had joined him.

As they moved through the game booths, Alana tried to avoid being close to Justin. Since she was trying to do it without making it seem obvious, her body was tense and her nerves were on edge. If it had been just her, she wouldn't have worked so hard at it, but every time Caden finished something, he'd turn around to find her and then she'd see his gaze search for Justin.

Thankfully, Than, Danny, and Lindsay kept him busy and in spite of that one serious moment, he seemed to be back to having fun. And there was definitely nothing wrong with his sense of smell. As they approached the area where the food was, Caden darted over to her to ask about getting something to eat. The smell of hotdogs and hamburgers was definitely tantalizing, and Alana hoped her stomach would settle down enough to allow her to enjoy the food.

Justin was beginning to think Alana was avoiding him. He felt like he was constantly looking around to locate her. One minute she was standing near him and the next she was gone. It was as if she was making sure there was distance between them, and he couldn't figure out why.

The conversation she'd had with Caden and then with Than was also bugging him. He'd been watching closely enough to see Caden use the sign for his name and then Alana had used it again when she'd signed with Than. Unfortunately, he hadn't been able to decipher anything else. One sign had looked familiar, but he wasn't sure because it hadn't really made sense.

Even though he'd started out not really wanting to be some kid's hero, as he watched Caden interact with Than, Justin felt a twinge of jealousy. He hated that he felt that way because Than was a friend, and he could see how much Caden enjoyed being able to communicate with him.

On top of the jealousy was the frustration that this time together wasn't really working out as he'd hoped. He'd thought that in addition to being fun for Caden, it would give him a chance to get a little closer to Alana in a more casual way. Instead, he felt like he was following her around like a love-sick pup, and that was not him. She had alluded to the fact that he was like her ex-husband physically, so maybe she just wasn't interested in seeing beyond that to how much he wasn't like him.

As they approached the food area, Justin once again went to where Alana and Caden were. Yeah, he wouldn't be following her everywhere after this, but she and Caden were still his guests so he'd make sure they had what they needed for supper.

Beth and Dan were standing with her which made it a bit easier to approach them. There were several barbecues set up behind long tables loaded with food and all the condiments needed for the hamburgers and hotdogs. There was a large white tent with no sides just beyond the food that looked to be filled with tables. Alex and Marcus had definitely spared no expense for this gig.

"Ready to get some food?" Justin asked as he joined them.

Beth nodded. "This is just great, Justin! I only wish Genevieve was a little older so she could enjoy it more."

"I had my doubts about this, but it appears that Mel and Adrianne managed to pull it off." He looked at Alana. "Is Caden enjoying himself?"

She signed to Caden then he looked up at him and vigorously nodded his head. His hands flew as he signed back to Alana. "He says that it's the most fun ever. Which is high praise since he was just at the Mall of America yesterday."

As they moved into the line for the food, the others joined them. It didn't take too long to load up plates with food and then find a table. Justin settled into a chair next to Caden, who sat with Alana on the other side of him. He had a feeling that Caden was going to hurry through his meal in order to get back out to the fun and games. Not that he could blame the kid. At his age, he probably would have done the same.

"Hey, Justin. How are you enjoying everything?"

Justin looked up to see Adrianne standing behind Beth and Dan across the table from him. "Everything is great. You and Mel did a fine job pulling it all together."

"And I see you brought some family," Adrianne said as she looked down at Beth and Dan with a smile.

"Yes. That's my sister, Beth and her husband, Dan. The little cutie is their daughter, Genevieve." Then he laid a hand on Caden's shoulder. "And this is Alana and her son, Caden. They're family friends."

He could see the curiosity in her gaze as she looked at Alana and Caden. It was the same one expression he'd seen from everyone he worked with when he introduced them.

"Nice to meet you all. Be sure to stick around for the fireworks. This company came highly recommended, and we're hoping to end the evening on a high note." With another smile at them, Adrianne moved on to chat with Trent and Than a little further down the table.

As Justin ate, he looked around at the people who were in attendance. He spotted a few people in the crowd that he recognized as employees at BlackThorpe, but the majority were unfamiliar faces. He still had some security concerns, but all areas with access to confidential information were behind doors that needed codes and hand scans to gain entry to. At Melanie and Adrianne's request, none of them were visibly armed, but as usual Justin wore his ankle holster along with his knife. It had been too warm to wear a jacket that would have covered a shoulder holster.

Caden shifted on the chair next to him, and Justin looked down to see the boy's plate was empty. He tapped Caden on the shoulder and when the boy turned to him, Justin hesitated and then made the sign for more. A huge grin wreathed Caden's face even as he shook his head. Justin couldn't stop the warmth that spread through his body at Caden's obvious delight when he saw him make the effort to communicate using signs. It made him more determined to work harder to learn the language that would allow him to communicate with Genevieve *and* Caden.

"Nice one," Dan said with a smile. "I see you've been paying attention to Alana's lessons."

"Not sure one word warrants quite this much enthusiasm, but I'm working my way up."

"Gotta start somewhere," Beth said as she handed Genevieve a piece of hotdog.

Unfortunately, he had a ways to go still because he couldn't understand the conversation Alana and Caden were currently having. It seemed to be another serious discussion from the look of the expression on Alana's face. Then she reached out and put a hand on either side of Caden's face and pressed her forehead to his. The little boy's shoulders slumped. Whatever they had been discussing, it didn't appear to have gone Caden's way.

When Alana lifted her head to press a kiss to Caden's forehead, their gazes met briefly. He caught a glimpse of emotional turmoil before she looked away. It made him wish yet again that he could figure out what was going on. Even before he asked her if everything was okay, Justin knew what her response would be.

"It's fine." She ran a hand over Caden's curls.

Seeing Caden's hunched shoulders and bent head, Justin wondered how Alana could actually refuse the little guy anything. "Is there anything I can help with?"

Something flashed in Alana's eyes before she shook her head. Her gaze slid past him for a moment and he looked over to see that Than and Lindsay were watching them. Once again, Justin got the feeling that Than knew what was going on and it bothered him that he didn't.

Suddenly, Than grinned and said Caden's name. Alana touched his shoulder and pointed at Than. The boy lifted his head and as he turned to look at Than, Justin could see that his green eyes were damp with unshed tears. What on earth was going on?

As he signed, Than said, "Want to go to see what other games they have?"

Caden looked at Alana, who nodded. He slid off his chair and headed to where Than stood with Lindsay and Danny. Justin waited for Caden to look at him, but it seemed that Caden was doing what he could to avoid him...just like his mother had been doing.

Justin moved into the chair Caden had just vacated, bringing him closer to Alana. She shot him a surprised look but didn't say anything. He shifted in his seat so he could face her, his hand gripping the back of her chair. "Did I do something that has upset Caden?"

13

"**N**O." ALANA'S answer came quickly. Almost too quickly.

"Then why didn't he even look at me when he left? That's not how he is normally."

Alana picked at the hotdog bun on her plate. "He was just excited."

Justin looked across at Beth to see if she had some answers, but all she did was shake her head and shrug. A glance at Dan resulted in a similar response. He bit back a growl of frustration. Somehow he was going to figure this out because he couldn't shake the feeling that he was a part of what was going on with Caden. Only two people besides the little boy knew what had happened, and thankfully, one of those was a friend. A friend he would be questioning if Alana didn't shed some light on the situation herself.

It bothered Justin more than it should that Caden was upset. And he could see that Alana was bothered by whatever it was that was happening with her son. These two had definitely become more important to him than he'd ever imagined they might be. He stared at Alana for a moment, taking in her profile. The way her dark lashes fanned out to frame her deep green eyes. The gentle slope of her nose. The smooth texture of her skin. The silky loose curls.

As if sensing his gaze on her, he saw her lips part slightly and a tinge of pink sweep up her cheeks. Though she didn't look at him, Justin sensed she was as aware of him as he was of her. Was it possible that there was something worth exploring between them? Up until then, any thought of a relationship had been shoved aside in favor of his job. But now he was finding himself considering that very thing with not just a woman but also her son.

He heard the soft clearing of a throat then Dan said, "Well, I think we're going to keep moving along."

Alana reached for her purse as she got to her feet. "I should probably see how Caden is doing."

Justin stood up as well and began to follow her. He felt a tug on his arm and glanced down to see Beth there. She slid her hand into the crook of his arm as Dan pushed the stroller with Genevieve in it, catching up to Alana.

"Do I detect some sort of interest on your part for our teacher?" Beth asked, her head tipped up to look at him.

Justin watched Dan bend down to say something to Alana. Denying it would be pretty stupid. If Beth had figured out that much, it meant he hadn't done a very good job hiding how he felt—particularly from someone who knew him very well. "She is an interesting person. I'm glad that she decided to bring Caden today."

"Yes, he does seem to be having a great time." Beth walked in silence for a few minutes then said, "I don't know much about Alana and her past. She never talks about it and not just with me. I asked a couple of the other ladies at church and they said the same thing. She's very generous with her time and talents, refuses to take payment for teaching sign language and will do anything for anyone who asks. But no one has ever been to her home and though it's clear it's inconvenient for her to take the bus, she always—always—refuses a ride. I think she has something in her past that makes it difficult for her to trust people. She does plenty for others but rarely, if ever, allows anyone to do something for her."

"I know a bit about her background and understand why she might be that way." Justin patted Beth's hand. "But that's not my story to tell."

She looked up at him, her expression serious. "I do consider her a friend though, and I think she considers me one too. Having said that, I hope you won't do anything to hurt her."

Justin scowled at her. "It's not my intention to hurt her. Or Caden, for that matter."

"I know you wouldn't mean to, but there's a lot of potential for hurt here." Beth slowed her steps which made Justin pull up as well. "I think you see her as someone needing protection and help. That can be misunderstood—particularly by a woman. I just don't want you having one idea in mind while Alana might be getting another."

She squeezed his arm before slipping away to catch up with Dan and Alana. Justin lingered behind, his thoughts on what Beth had shared. Was it just his desire to protect two people who seemed so vulnerable? He didn't think it was *just* that. He really didn't. He'd been trying to move slowly. Let her get used to him being around. Get used to him interacting with her. Because he wanted her to see—to understand—that he wasn't like her ex. He needed her to know he would never, ever, use his strength against her or Caden.

He couldn't deny it was Alana's vulnerability that initially drew him—once he'd gotten past the point of thinking of her as someone out to scam his sister and Dan. But even though there was an air of vulnerability around her, he knew now there was a core of steel within her. She did what she had to to take care of her son even when it was no doubt more challenging given Caden's deafness. She'd stood up to him

and basically called him out about looking into her past.
Yeah, she had some steel in there.

Justin noticed they'd caught up to Caden and the others.
Instead of approaching Alana like he'd been doing earlier, he
hung back and just watched. He rubbed his chest to ease the
sudden ache there. For a brief time, he'd moved willingly
into contact with someone, but now he was back to the
fringe. Drifting along the edge, watching to make sure
everyone was safe. Only this time, the fit didn't feel right. It
wasn't where he wanted to be.

Alana found herself in conversation once again with
Victoria as the group continued to make its way to the games
and other fun stuff that they hadn't had a chance to see yet.
They stopped at a face painting booth, and Caden was
thrilled to have them paint a Spiderman mask on his face.
Danny got a pirate look while Genevieve and Sarah each got
butterflies.

Glad to see that Caden was distracted from their earlier
conversation which had once again centered on Justin, Alana
glanced around for the man. Before they'd stopped to eat, it
seemed that every time she'd turned around he'd been within
arm's reach of her. But since their brief conversation at the
table, he was nowhere near either of them. She tried to tell
herself that it was for the best, just like she'd tried to
convince herself that avoiding him was a good thing. But
regardless of what her mind was telling her, her heart was
saying something else.

"Is this a good spot?" Beth asked as they came to a stop in
a big grassy area behind the tent where they'd eaten earlier.

Justin nodded. "Mel said the fireworks would be best
viewed from anywhere in this area."

"I brought a couple of blankets." Beth pulled them out
from under the stroller and handed one to Justin. "I used to
like to lie down to watch the fireworks when I was a kid.
Remember that, Justin?"

Alana looked over in time to see Justin give a quick nod
as he flicked the blanket out and let it settle on the grass.
Clearly, he wasn't in the mood for a trip down memory lane.

She held Caden's hand, uncertain of where to sit. The blankets were plenty large enough for all of them, but Alana was waiting to see what Justin would do before settling onto one of them.

There was still enough light that they could see, but twilight was quickly falling on them. The area they were in was rapidly filling with people. Most just settled on the grass, but some had folding chairs and a few had blankets like Beth had brought.

"I'll be back," Justin said once the blanket Beth had given him was spread out.

Alana watched him walk away. Even as he moved through the crowd, he was easy to track because of his height. Caden squeezed her hand and she looked at him. Releasing his grip, she signed that Justin would be back even before he asked where he was going.

"C'mon and sit down," Beth said as she settled on the blanket with Genevieve. The little girl looked a little tired and burrowed into her mother's arms.

Alana could only imagine how Caden was going to crash after this. All the excitement plus the exercise was sure to have worn him out. She kind of wished they were going home to their own apartment afterward, but she wasn't going to change their plans now.

After she had slipped off her shoes, she settled onto the blanket, glad that she had worn pants instead of a skirt. She pulled Caden onto her lap and then took a couple of minutes before the sun was completely gone to explain to him what was happening. Though they'd watched fireworks when they'd lived in Florida, she wasn't sure he remembered much about them.

By the time the fireworks started, Justin still wasn't back. Trying not to dwell on it, Alana leaned back on her hands and let Caden rest against her so he was in a good position to see the sky. She felt his excitement as his body tensed and he'd clap when a particularly beautiful display lit up the night sky. Alana was glad that he could still enjoy the beauty of the fireworks even though he couldn't hear the sound that went along with them.

A beam of light fell on the blanket, and Alana looked over to see Justin lowering himself to the blanket on the opposite side. He stretched his legs out and reclined back the way she was. His movement must have caught Caden's attention because his head whipped to the side. When she felt him start to sit up, Alana wrapped an arm around his waist to keep him in place.

He leaned his head back to look at her. Alana pushed to a sitting position and grabbed Caden's hand and placed it against her cheek and shook her head. She felt his shoulders slump as she loosened her grip on his waist. After she was sure he was going to stay put, Alana resumed her earlier position to watch the rest of the fireworks.

It was the perfect end to a relatively great day. The only downside was the emotional angst she'd waded into, all because she and Caden found themselves drawn to a man who had no place for them in his life. The man spent every day at his job basically. How did a family fit into that? Even Beth—before Alana had met Justin—had mentioned how much she'd like him to have a family, but that she doubted that would ever happen since his life barely had room for her. If his own sister saw him that way, Alana didn't figure that would be changing anytime soon.

Once the fireworks had ended, lights came on and there was a surge of people toward the parking lot. Alana kept a tight hold on Caden and walked right behind Beth and Dan. She wasn't sure where Justin was, but when they reached the van, he materialized beside Dan.

Beth reached out to hug him. "Thanks for a wonderful time. I'm so glad you invited us all. It was nice to see that you do have some friends after all."

"Friends? You mean the guys I work with?"

Beth laughed and reached up to pat his face. "Yeah, you may consider them co-workers, but what I saw today...they're friends. And I'm glad I got to meet them."

Alana almost smiled when Justin gave a grunt and crossed his arms. The man did seem to like to make it appear as if he was keeping his distance from everyone, but clearly he'd managed to make connections with the guys he worked with. Even Victoria considered him a friend.

After he'd buckled Genevieve into her seat, Dan opened the back of the van to put the stroller in. Grateful for the light in the parking lot, Alana signed for Caden to thank Justin.

Caden walked to where Justin stood and reached out to touch his hand. Justin lowered himself to Caden's level when he saw who it was and watched as the boy signed *thank you*. It was one of the signs Alana had taught Justin so she hoped he understood it without translation. She realized that he had when he signed *you're welcome* back to Caden. Before she could stop him, however, Caden threw his arms around Justin's neck and buried his head into his shoulder.

Wrapping his arms around Caden, Justin stood with ease. Alana's first instinct was to grab her son from the man, but her feet were rooted to the ground, her arms pinned to her side. She swallowed hard against the emotion that crowded its way up her chest into her throat. Tears pricked at her eyes as she was faced with proof—once again—of how much Caden longed for this man to be his father.

Justin's head was bent as he held Caden for a minute before stooping to put him back on his feet. He held out his fist and waited for Caden to bump his much smaller fist against it. "See you soon."

As Caden came back to her side, Alana said, "Thank you, Justin. We both had a wonderful time."

Justin gave a quick nod of his head. "Glad to hear it."

As Daniel moved to his side, Alana helped Caden into the van and made sure he was buckled before taking her own seat. It wasn't long before Beth and Daniel were in the front seats, and they were joining the line of cars exiting the compound.

They were almost to the house when the text alert went on her phone. Alana pulled the phone from her pocket and stared down at the message on the screen.

This is Victoria. I hope it's okay I asked Justin for your number. Would like to get together for coffee sometime.

Alana smiled as she tapped out a response. *Would love to get together. Let me know when it might be convenient for you.*

Terrific! It was great to meet you and your son. Look forward to visiting more with you. Have a good night!

Alana ended the conversation as Daniel pulled the van into the garage. She had thought Caden might fall asleep, but he was still awake and quickly crawled from the back seat. Beth had shown her to a guest room in the basement before they'd left earlier so after saying goodnight and thanking them once again, she headed down the stairs with Caden.

The room was decorated in sage green and chocolate brown and had a large queen size bed that looked so much more comfortable than her daybed. It had an ensuite bathroom with a deep tub that was a temptation she wasn't even going to bother trying to resist.

It took a few minutes to get Caden through his nighttime routine and then settled onto one side of the queen size bed. While she waited for him to fall asleep, Alana laid out their clothes for church the next day and set the alarm on her phone. Once Caden had drifted off, she went into the bathroom and began to run the water. There were some bath salts there that she added and then with a sigh of appreciation, she slid into the warm water. It had been so long since she'd enjoyed a good soak and after the day she'd just had, it was a welcome relief.

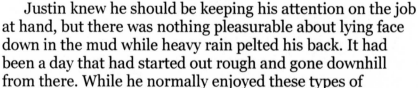

Justin knew he should be keeping his attention on the job at hand, but there was nothing pleasurable about lying face down in the mud while heavy rain pelted his back. It had been a day that had started out rough and gone downhill from there. While he normally enjoyed these types of exercises, his mood going into this one had already been awful and now the rain-soaked night just added to his misery.

He listened as his team reported in from various locations across the BlackThorpe land. The only thing that made this thing marginally better was knowing that Marcus was out there enduring the same misery as he was. Alex was part of the team as well. Every couple of months, the two of them would join the teams for an exercise like this. Justin assumed it was to make sure they didn't lose the edge from their military days.

Lifting his night vision goggles, he searched for any sign of the other team approaching his location. This was a hostage extrication exercise with the opposing team being the ones trying to make the rescue. They were a top special ops team with a couple new members they wanted to put through their paces, so Justin knew they were going to be difficult to take down. Which was all the more reason to keep his thoughts on the task at hand instead of playing the past twenty-four hours over and over in his head.

Though he'd hoped to see Alana and Caden at church, it hadn't been too surprising when he hadn't given the size of the church and the fact that it had more than one service. But it had all really started to go downhill when he'd shown up at Beth and Dan's for supper on Monday night and discovered that Alana and Caden weren't there. Beth hadn't given any reason, and he hadn't asked.

Then, after another boring staff meeting, he'd been looking forward to spending some time with Alana and Caden, but she'd shown up alone. Something about Caden being at a playdate. That was also the reason she gave for why she couldn't stay for the self-defence part of their agreement. After they were finished with the sign language lesson for the day, she'd told him she needed to go pick Caden up. He'd offered to drive her but, once again, she'd refused him.

Even during their lesson, any attempt at conversation not related to what she was teaching him had been met with vague responses and an immediate return to the lesson. She hadn't avoided his gaze, but there was a distance there that hadn't been present since their first couple of meetings. Basically, she'd confused the heck out of him. And disappointed him as well. He'd been looking forward to talking to Caden. Those few minutes each week while Alana got changed and they chatted using his tablet had been fun for Justin. And he would try out a few signs on him as well.

Given how enamored Caden was with him, Justin had a hard time believing the boy hadn't wanted to be there. Especially since he hadn't been around for supper the night before.

The sound of shots and a sudden burst of chatter in Justin's earpiece jerked his attention back to the muddy situation he was currently in. He heard a sudden burst of swearing as another shot rang out. Recognizing the voice as one of his regular team members, Justin swung his head in the direction of where the guy was supposed to have been hiding.

Those shots had sounded...real.

Another burst of swearing had Justin scowling. "Stow the language, Delane, and report."

"Live ammo! I'm hit." Pain laced Delane's words, and Justin felt a lightning bolt of shock race through his body.

Live ammo? They were on a training mission. Only laser-equipped weapons were being used.

The chatter in his ear increased dramatically as men reported in locations at Justin's demand. Once all of the team had reported in, he ordered them to pull back to the building where the hostage was being held. Justin barked out an order to Trent, who was monitoring the exercise from inside the compound, to call for an ambulance. They had a nurse standing by in case of injuries during the exercise, but a gunshot wound was beyond her abilities. Plus, who knew if Delane was the only one who was going to need attention before they took out whoever was firing with the live ammo.

"I've got Delane." Marcus's voice sounded strong and sure in his ear.

More shots rang out, freezing Justin in place.

"Marcus!" Delane's shout came through his earpiece. More swearing and then, "They got Marcus. We need some help here."

"Trent, I need positions on everyone. Who's closest to help Marc and Delane?"

Justin listened as Trent gave him the information he needed, his friend's voice steady amid the ever-increasing mayhem. When Justin realized he was closest to their location, he said, "I'm going to them."

"I'm coming from the opposite direction," Alex said. "Meet you there."

"Justin, I've been in contact with the leader of the other team, and they have no idea what's going on."

"Tell them to get out of the field," Justin ordered Trent.

It was hard to believe a rogue shooter had managed to make their way so deep into the compound and on a night when a training exercise was scheduled. This was not a random thing, and it seemed the shooter had just a bit too much information about what was going on.

Justin's mind raced as he grabbed for the gun on his ankle. He jerked the strap of the laser enabled weapon so it was on his back and moved toward where Trent had said Marcus and Delane were. He tried to contain his thoughts regarding Marcus being injured or possibly worse. Their family didn't need any more death. Marcus's sister wouldn't survive if something happened to him, Justin was almost sure of that.

Please, God, keep him alive.

As he neared the location Trent was guiding him and Alex to, more shots rang out. He was close enough to hear the sound of someone stumbling and then heavy breathing in his ear.

"Alex? Report."

"Hit."

What on earth was going on? Someone was picking them off like sitting ducks.

"The Ops team has gone back into the field, Justin," Trent said. "They're circling around and will try to locate the shooter. Medical support is on its way."

"I can't move three of them, Trent. I'm just going to have to assess the situation and stay with them. We can't risk anyone else until we get a bead on the guy."

"Are you armed, Justin?"

"Yes."

Another shot rang out, and he jerked. The searing burn of a bullet hitting his left bicep knocked him to his knees. He dropped flat to his stomach and breathed through the initial agony then he began to crawl forward. Trying to keep the pain from fogging his thoughts, Justin managed to say, "How close?"

"You're almost there. Keep straight."

Justin knew Trent could see them all on his screen. Right now he would see his dot approaching where Marcus and Delane were. Keeping his voice low, he asked, "How far away is Alex?"

"Close. He's moving toward Marcus as well."

A tendril of relief wove its way through his pain. At least Alex wasn't dead and from what he was hearing, Delane was still alive. Marcus was the only silent one.

"I'm here." Alex's voice sounded strained. "Marcus is unconscious. It looks like he was hit in the thigh and must have knocked his head when he went down. Delane took a bullet to his shoulder."

Thigh? Shoulder? Arm? "Where were you hit, Alex?"

"He got me in the leg."

The shooter wasn't going for kill shots.

"The Ops team just spotted someone, but they're on the move at a pretty fast clip. Heading north."

North? Justin pictured a map in his head. He knew more about the layout of the BlackThorpe land than anyone else. There was a road on the northern border of the land. It was possible someone had breached their perimeter from that direction. Unfortunately, they didn't have cameras to monitor every inch of the land beyond the BlackThorpe compound. There was a fence around the outer perimeter, but it wouldn't keep out anyone who was determined to get past it.

"I'm sending the team in to help you guys out," Trent said. "And notified the emergency response to send additional ambulances."

Justin settled onto the ground beside Delane as Alex bent over Marcus. He touched a hand to his upper arm and felt the stickiness of blood. Well, there was no arguing that this day would go down as one of his worst in recent memory. As he sat there listening to his team make their way towards them, he wondered at yet another attack on BlackThorpe and its team. First what went down with Eric and then the hacking attempt and now this? It seemed too much to be simply coincidence.

He didn't have any more time to ponder the issue as they were suddenly surrounded by the other members of the BlackThorpe team. Marcus was the first one carried out. Delane followed and then Alex leaned on one of the other guys. Justin was able to walk under his own steam even though the shot in his arm hurt like the dickens.

"The Ops team lost the shooter. I'm thinking from the direction he was moving that he has wheels waiting for him on that northern road."

"Yeah. You're probably right. Call the Ops team back. It's not likely they'll catch him now."

The flashing lights of the ambulances were visible as soon as they walked through the entrance to the compound. Medical personnel immediately surrounded them, evaluating their condition. Marcus was whisked away on a stretcher first, still not having regained consciousness. Alex was the next to go followed by Delane. Justin waved off the ambulance workers and found the nurse. Missy Grant shoved him into a chair as soon as she spotted him.

"You should go to the hospital, Justin," she said as she bent over his shoulder. "Just to get this checked over."

"It barely grazed me, Missy. I think I'm fine with a cleaning and some bandages."

Missy shook her head as she tsked him. "You boys think you're so invulnerable."

"Don't think that at all, but the others were wounded more seriously than I was. I need to talk to Trent and the Ops team to figure out what went down out there."

Missy fell silent as she cleaned the wound from where the bullet had sliced across his upper arm. She put some medication on it and then covered it all with a bandage. Once done, she straightened and began to gather up her supplies. "This certainly wasn't what I thought I'd be dealing with tonight."

"You and me both." Justin stood and looked around. He spotted members of his team and the Ops team standing in groups. His gaze landed on the Ops team leader and he approached him. "Up for a debriefing on what went down?"

The man nodded. "Sorry we didn't get hands on the shooter." He had a few choice words for the person who had infiltrated their training exercise. "It was like he just vanished. Although I think he had knowledge of the area which gave him the ability to give us the slip. We're usually better than this."

"So are we," Justin said with a scowl. "Let's head to command and see what Trent saw on his screens."

14

SINCE HE'D LEFT his phone with Trent in the
command center, Justin had to wait until he got there to use
it. He called Eric first to ask him to meet Alex and Marcus at
the hospital. After that he called Adrianne, knowing she'd
take news of Alex's wound better than Melanie probably
would.

The only person he wasn't sure what to do about was
Meredith. It was likely she wasn't expecting Marcus home
that night, but something told him Marcus would have called
her at some point. Justin stared at the floor as conversation
swirled around him. He didn't even have a number for her.
Maybe Adrianne would have it and could give him some
ideas on how to approach his cousin with the news of her
brother's shooting.

He placed another call to Adrianne. After hearing what he
had to say, she assured him she'd take care of contacting

Meredith. Relieved he could focus on what was happening at the compound, Justin grasped his phone tightly and turned to Trent.

"Than's on his way to the hospital too," Trent said as Justin stepped to his side. "Figured he needed to know what was going on and he said he'd go there first and then come here if necessary."

Justin nodded, his gaze fixed on the cluster of dots on the monitor that represented all the men involved in the training...except Alex, Marcus, and Delane.

"Should you have gone to the hospital, man?" Trent asked, his gaze going to Justin's arm.

"No. I'm fine." It hurt like crazy, but this had happened on his watch, on his land. He needed to figure out who had managed to infiltrate their exercise. Justin was glad that whoever had decided to take aim at BlackThorpe had done it now and not in the middle of the friends and family event they'd had just a few days earlier. Could someone have come in that way to scope out the place?

"I sent Rodriguez and Tyler out in a Hummer once we realized the direction the guy was headed in," Trent said. "And as soon as it's daylight we'll get a team out to comb for anything this guy might have left behind."

Justin rubbed his forehead. "We're going to have local authorities all over this too. Three gunshot wounds isn't something they're just going to brush over."

"Hopefully Eric and Than can deal with them."

They passed the next few hours waiting for reports on Marcus and the guys at the hospital. The guys in the Hummer were still out...possibly chasing down nothing. Justin hated the feeling they weren't going to able to get the guy. They were supposed to be better than this. No one got the drop on BlackThorpe guys. But this person certainly had.

The gnawing in his gut told him that whoever had been responsible for it had taken lots of time to plan it out. And likely they had help on the inside. It would be the only way they would have known about the nighttime exercise with the Ops team.

After word had come that Marcus had regained consciousness, Justin felt some of the tension ease from his shoulders. But the return of the guys with the Hummer and their report of not finding anything in the direction they'd gone did nothing to rid him of the frustration that ate at him.

It was coming up on four o'clock when he and Trent left the now-empty command center. Trent had decided to stay at the compound for the night in order to be there in the morning when the teams went back out to look for more clues. Both men were quiet as they made their way to the apartments. Justin had no doubt that Trent was also thinking about a possible connection, but neither of them actually put that thought into words.

Though he normally would have taken a shower, Justin only took the time to get out of his muddy clothes, swallow a couple of pain killers and fall into bed. He hoped he could catch a few hours of sleep before he had to be back up again.

A sudden high pitch steady shrieking jerked Alana from sleep. When she opened her eyes, they burned as did her lungs when she tried to draw in a deep breath. Panic filling her, she scrambled to her feet and raced for Caden's bed. Without even trying to wake him up and explain what was going on, Alana snatched him from the mattress on the floor, holding him tight when he woke and started to squirm against her.

Oh, how she wished she could talk to him, but she didn't have the time to explain what was happening. She skidded to a halt just feet from the door to the hallway as she realized that was where the smoke was coming into her apartment. There was no way they'd be able to go out into the stairwell.

When flames flickered on the carpet under the door, Alana began to back away. Outside, she could hear shouts and the sound of sirens growing louder. Panic tightened around her lungs, and she struggled to draw in air even as it stung to breathe. Her only choice was to try a window and hope that someone would be there to help them get from their second story apartment to the ground.

Turning, she ran back to Caden's room and set him on the floor by the window and worked to lift it up.

"Mama?" Hearing the fear in the raspy voice of her son increased her efforts to raise the old window that seemed to be stuck in place. Caden rarely spoke though he knew a few words. Mama being one of them.

She paused in her efforts to quickly sign *everything will be okay* then turned her attention back to the window. Her nails ripped at the wood, but she didn't stop. She had to get Caden out safely. He was pressed against her legs now, and she could feel his body shaking badly.

Suddenly, there was a loud rush of noise in the main part of the apartment. Figuring it was nothing good making that kind of noise, Alana started to beat against the glass, hoping that maybe she could break the window and get them out that way.

"Please, God, help me." Tears blurred her vision, as much from the smoke as from her own emotions getting the better of her. "Help us."

The smoke started to gather in the room now, creeping toward them with ominous intent. *Please, God. Please, God. Please, God.* She just couldn't stop repeating it over and over in her head.

Suddenly, Caden's grip on her legs tightened. She looked down, barely able to see him in the thickening smoke. She managed to blink away tears and saw him pointing toward the door. Afraid of what she would see, Alana glanced over her shoulder as she pounded harder on the glass. But instead of a wall of flames, she saw a huge hulking figure in firefighter gear coming towards them.

Relief flooded her as she plucked Caden from the ground and shoved him into the firefighter's arms. "Please, save my son!"

"I'll get you both out, ma'am. Follow me." His voice was muffled as he turned to go back toward the main part of the apartment.

Alana froze. That was where the flames were.

She could hear the man talking as he disappeared into the smoky haze that filled the living room. Alana began to shake, fear rooting her to the floor. Unable to save herself, her only thought was that at least Caden would be safe.

Justin dragged himself out of bed after managing to get six hours of sleep. He took a shower, trying his best not to get the bandage on his arm wet and then made some phone calls. He heard a knock on his door and opened it to find Trent there.

"You got food in here? The fridge in that apartment is empty," he said as he walked into Justin's kitchen.

Justin nodded. "And there's coffee, too. Help yourself to whatever you want."

Though he usually ate supper in the cafeteria, he had food for breakfast and lunches in his apartment. He leaned against the counter as he placed the call he was dreading.

"Hey, Beth."

"Justin? What's wrong?"

"What do you mean?"

"You don't usually call at this time of day. What's up?"

Justin took a deep breath and let it out before he said, "We had a little incident during the training exercise last night."

There was a pause and then Beth said, "What kind of incident? Are you okay?"

"I'm fine. I got winged by a bullet, but it's just a scratch, basically."

Trent lifted an eyebrow at that description and clearly Beth didn't believe it either.

"You were shot? Are you at the hospital?"

"No. I'm at the compound. I told you it wasn't bad. The nurse bandaged me up. In a few days, I'll be good as new." He knew she probably wasn't going to be convinced until she could see him in person. "But there were others more seriously injured, Marcus being one of them."

"Oh no! Is he going to be okay?"

"I just spoke to him, and he's also going to be fine, although it might take a bit longer for him to recover. He took a bullet to the leg. Alex and one other team member were also shot, but we're all going to be okay."

"What on earth happened? Aren't you supposed to use fake bullets or something for the training?"

Justin gave her a quick run-down of what had transpired and then once again tried to reassure her he was fine. He promised to stop by later that day to let her see that for herself. "I've got to go. Still have some phone calls to make, but I'll see you later."

"You better. If not, I'm going to come there."

"I promise I'll be there. How about I come for supper?" He would try his hardest to make it by then.

When Justin hung up, Trent picked up the remote for the flat screen in the living room and turned it on. In the small apartment, the television was visible from the kitchen as well as the living room.

"Checking to see if our little shooting made the news?" Justin asked as he went to the fridge to pull out stuff to make sandwiches since it was nearly noon.

"Yeah, but I'm hoping that it didn't. You just never know what got out once the guys arrived at the hospital. Three gunshot wound victims might stir some interest."

Justin hoped Trent was wrong, but in this day and age, it was better they prepared for the worst. With the volume up, they worked to make their sandwiches as they waited for the local noon news to start.

Justin had just gone to grab them a couple of drinks when the news started.

"An early morning fire has claimed the life of one person. Around four o'clock this morning, a fire broke out in an apartment complex in the 300 block of—"

Justin spun around, his gaze pinned to the television. "What?"

As footage showed the building the fire had ravaged, Justin felt his empty stomach heave. That was Alana's building. The one she and Caden lived in. One person was dead.

No, God, please.

"Justin? What's wrong?" Trent moved to his side and put a hand on his shoulder.

Justin grabbed his phone and called Alana's number. It went immediately to voicemail. Dread built inside him as he called his sister again.

"Have you spoken to Alana this morning?" he asked without preamble.

"Justin? No. Why?"

"I just saw on the news that there was a fire in the building where she and Caden live."

"What? Wait...how do you know where she lives?"

"Caden told me. And I drove by there one day just to see. They said one person is dead."

There was silence on the other end. "They didn't say who?"

"No. They didn't. I tried her phone, but it goes right to voicemail."

"I'm going to call Daniel and see if he can find out any more information. I'll call you as soon as I hear something," Beth said and then hung up.

Justin stood there, his phone clutched in his hand. The debacle from the night before was pushed aside as all his thoughts focused on what had happened to Alana and Caden. He just couldn't even wrap his mind around what he'd do if one of them was the "one person" who hadn't survived the fire. He had to get to them. If the worst had happened, he needed to be there for whichever one was left.

He dragged in a ragged breath at the thought that something might have happened to either of them. Reaching out with a hand to grasp the counter, Justin pressed his other hand to his chest. In what seemed from a very distant place, he heard Trent speaking and tried to focus on what he was saying. The thump of blood as it pulsed through his body blocked out everything but the pain that rode along his veins, spreading to every inch of him.

"Let's go, man," Trent said as he grasped Justin's uninjured arm and tugged him toward the door. "Than's going to meet us at the apartment. Eric is going to come out here to deal with this end of things until I get back. Alex has been discharged, but he's staying at the hospital with Marcus."

Justin numbly followed Trent down the hallway to the stairs that led them out to the parking lot. He wanted to take his truck but figured he was in no shape to drive without endangering other drivers on the road in his haste to get to Alana and Caden. It took everything in him to not urge Trent to go faster. He knew they weren't likely to still be at the apartment building, but it was the best place to start until Beth let him know if Daniel was able to get more information.

"I know it's easy to assume the worst," Trent said, "but let's trust that God's kept His hand of protection on them."

Justin longed to take comfort in Trent's words—he really did—but he knew better than most people that sometimes God removed that hand of protection and allowed the worst to happen. He'd lived this once already. He didn't want it to be God's will that He take either of them this time around. Justin wanted both of them to be alive so they could be in his life for years to come.

He had known the Jensen duo had managed to work their way past his defenses, but Justin hadn't realized just how far they'd gotten into his heart until faced with the very real possibility that he might have lost one of them.

Leaning his head back against the headrest, Justin closed his eyes and tried to focus on his breathing. Before he came face to face with whatever lay ahead, he had to pull himself back together. They—both of them—would need him to be strong.

If Alana would allow him to help them.

Something told him that Caden would be fine with him showing up. Alana...he had no idea. But that was really too bad if she didn't want him there. He didn't just want to help them, he needed to. The same protectiveness he had for Beth and Genevieve now extended to Alana and Caden in a way he'd never thought it would.

Hearing Trent's phone ring, Justin opened his eyes and straightened in his seat. Thankfully, the man put the call through his vehicle's hands-free so Justin could hear both sides of the conversation.

"Are you there yet?" Trent said by way of greeting.

"Just pulled up." Than's voice filled the interior of the vehicle.

"What does it look like?" Justin asked, not entirely sure he wanted to hear the answer even though he'd see it for himself shortly.

"Looks pretty bad, man. Sorry to say." Than cleared his throat. "There are still some official vehicles here. Do you want me to ask them about Alana and Caden, Justin?"

Justin blew out a breath. Was it better to hear it before or after he got there? "Wait for me."

"Will do," Than responded quickly.

Trent shot him a look as they came to a stop at a red light. "You sure you want him to wait?"

"Yes." Justin wasn't sure why, but he suspected it had to do with living with the unknown for just a little while longer in case the news was the worst. Hope was a crazy thing. He was braced for the worst, but there was still a spark of hope that until someone told him differently both of them would be safe and sound somewhere.

"We're almost there, Than," Trent said.

"I'll be waiting." The call ended abruptly.

Justin let out a long breath and closed his eyes again. He prayed for God to give him strength. If there was only one of them left, he was going to need strength to comfort them.

But please, God, let them both be safe. I can't imagine my life without them.

He opened his eyes as the vehicle slowed, and they came to a stop behind Than's truck. They'd barely stopped when Than got out and walked toward them. Justin released his seatbelt and pushed the door open. By the time he got around to where Trent and Than stood, they were already talking.

Than's gaze met his and the usually light-hearted expression on the man's face was missing. He laid his hand on Justin's shoulder. "Praying we get some good news here, man."

Justin nodded and then made his way across the street toward the burnt-out apartment building. Than and Trent flanked him as they approached a group of people on the sidewalk. Justin figured they probably made quite the trio. Him in his T-shirt and jeans, Trent in his rumpled clothes from the previous day and Than decked out in his business suit.

"Excuse me," Justin addressed the group. "Can I speak to whoever is in charge?"

A man wearing a suit separated himself from the group and approached them. "I'm Dave Saunders. I'm in charge of the investigation into the fire. How can I help you?"

"My friend and her son lived in the building. We heard that one person passed away. Can you tell me if they're okay?"

The man stared at him. "We're not releasing the name of the deceased at this time."

Justin's hands curled into fists. Surely the man wouldn't be that cruel. He felt a hand on his shoulder and then Than stepped forward.

"We understand that completely. All we'd like to know is that our friend and her son are okay. Can you at least tell us that much? We are desperate for information on them. We assume she lost her cell phone in the fire because we can't get in contact with her."

Than's gift was dealing with people, and he was working it. Justin's gift, on the other hand, was using his strength and it was taking everything in him—and Than's tight grip on his shoulder—to not try to pound the information out of the man.

15

THE MAN'S GAZE went from Than to Justin to Trent and then back to Than. "The deceased was an adult male."

Justin's legs buckled as relief crashed over him. Trent and Than each grabbed an arm and held him upright.

"Thank you so much," Than said to the man. "And I hate to impose on you more but is there any chance you could tell us where the people who were displaced by the fire were taken?"

"Some were taken to the hospital, others went to a motel, but I'm not sure who went where." When the man rattled off the name of an organization, Trent released Justin and reached for his phone. "You could start with them. They should be able to let you know for sure who's at the motel."

"Thank you for your help. We appreciate it very much," Than said as the man turned to walk away. He looked at Justin. "You okay, man?"

"I am now. I need to find them, though." He shoved his hand through his hair. "They've lost everything."

"I'm with you. Trent's going to head back to the compound, but I'm going to go with you."

Justin looked at the man. "Thank you."

Than gave a quick nod. "That's what friends do."

Friends. Yeah, he was coming to see that the guys he'd put in the co-worker category really were friends. He just hadn't acknowledged it.

Trent kept talking on his phone as they walked back to where they were parked. "Yes, we're trying to locate Alana Jensen and her son, Caden. They were residents of the apartment building that burned earlier today."

They stood between the two vehicles waiting for Trent to finish his call and hopefully give him the information he needed to find Alana and Caden. Justin shoved his hands into his pockets, wincing slightly at the burn as the muscles of his upper arm pulled. And he was suddenly feeling strangely naked as he realized he hadn't strapped on any of his weapons before leaving the apartment. Probably just as well. Given how on edge he'd been, he might just have pulled a weapon to get information if someone had tried to prevent him from finding out what had happened to Alana and Caden.

His phone beeped, and he pulled it from the holder on his belt. He saw it was a text from Trent that contained a name and address.

Trent lowered his phone. "That's the motel where they took the apartment's residents. The person I talked to didn't have names, but she said we should be able to find them there."

Than took Justin's phone and looked at the address before walking toward the driver's door of his truck.

Trent pulled open the door to his vehicle. "I'm going to swing by my place and then head back to the compound to work with Eric."

"Sorry to have bailed on you. I hope Marcus understands."

"He will. I'll call you if I need more information. Just concentrate on doing what Alana and Caden need."

"Thank you."

Trent reached out to clap him on the arm but then froze, clearly remembering that was the arm with the wound. "You're welcome."

As Trent climbed into his car, Justin went to the passenger side of Than's truck and pulled himself up onto the seat. Than was focused on the navigation system and glanced over as Justin joined him.

"It's not too far from here. Should be there in less than ten minutes."

Justin stared out the window, noting that the area was not improving much as they drove. He hoped he could convince her to leave with him. She had other options than a motel in a run-down neighborhood.

His sister's ringtone pulled his attention back inside the vehicle. Realizing he should have called her as soon as they had news about Alana and Caden, Justin tapped the screen to accept the call.

"Justin, I haven't been able to get through to Daniel. He's in a meeting."

"It's okay, Beth. We think we've found them. We're on our way now to where they said the residents of the apartment block were taken."

"So she and Caden are okay?"

"As far as we know. The one person who was killed in the fire was an adult male, so at least we know it wasn't either of them."

"Will you call me again once you've talked to her?" Beth asked.

Justin agreed to let her know what was going on once they connected with Alana.

"And if they need a place to stay, you know we have plenty of room."

"I'll let her know that." Justin had a feeling it was going to be a fight to get Alana to accept any sort of help, but he would play dirty if he had to in order to get her to agree to leave with him and Than.

Than pulled into the parking lot of a two-story motel that looked as if it had seen better days. The only good thing, Justin supposed, was that the likelihood of the manager giving up Alana's room number in exchange for a bill or two was fairly high. Any reputable place wouldn't have given out that information, but this place looked to be a step or two below that. They got out of the truck and headed for the front office.

"You shoulda left the suit coat in the truck, man. You're a little overdressed for the neighborhood." Justin said as they approached the grungy glass door with "OFFICE" stenciled on it.

Than reached out and grabbed the door handle and jerked it open. "No can do, man. Unlike you, I'm carrying."

Justin almost chuckled at that. Definitely a reversal of positions, that was for sure. "I kind of left the apartment in a rush."

"And apparently you didn't get the memo. Alex sent the word out that we're all to be armed now."

"I hadn't heard that," Justin said as his gaze moved over to the man sitting behind the counter. What had this organization been thinking putting Alana and the other apartment residents in a place like this? "I'm looking for Alana Jensen. She was one of the people brought here after their apartment building burned down. Can you tell me what room she's in?"

The man regarded him for a moment. "We're not permitted to give out that information."

Before Justin could say anything more, Than jabbed him in the ribs. He turned to see Than facing the door they'd just come in. "Isn't that them?"

Justin's breath caught as he got a glimpse of two familiar figures making their way along the walkway of the upper floor. Without another word to the man behind the desk, Justin pushed the office door open and headed for the stairs leading to the second floor, his gaze still tight on the duo.

He had almost reached the staircase when Caden's gaze landed on him. For an instant, the boy froze and then took off running. Justin heard Alana's shout for Caden even though the boy couldn't hear it. He'd just stepped on the bottom step when the little guy came flying down the stairs and launched himself at Justin.

Without hesitation, Justin opened his arms and pulled the boy close. Like he had the night of the family event at the compound, Caden buried his head into his shoulder but this time his grip on Justin's shoulders was tighter. Almost as if he was determined to never let him go.

Justin slid one arm under the boy's thighs and used the other to rub his back. The scent of smoke still clung to him, and Justin had to swallow hard at the thought of how close he'd come to losing them.

"Justin?" Alana's voice drew his attention from Caden. She stood a couple of steps up which brought them to eye level. He ran his gaze over her to make sure she was okay.

She wore a large T-shirt that came to mid-thigh with sleeves that reached just to her elbows. When she tugged at one of the sleeves, Justin knew she was trying to hide the scars she'd showed him that day in the restaurant. Her legs were encased in black leggings, and her feet were bare. That she was out of their room in an outfit that he was pretty sure she'd never wear in public just brought home to him the fact that they had lost absolutely everything.

Pulling back a bit from Caden, he glanced over at Than. The man nodded and approached them. He tapped Caden on the shoulder and when the little boy looked up, Than signed something to him. Caden hesitated for a moment before he loosened his grip around Justin's neck and let himself be lowered to the ground.

Than reached out and gave the boy a quick hug before signing to him again. Satisfied that Than would take care of Caden, Justin turned his attention to the woman still standing on the stairs, watching them with wary eyes.

Justin stepped on the first step, bringing them closer and once again putting him above her. She looked up at him for a moment then dropped her gaze to Caden and Than.

"How did you find us?"

Justin wanted to pull her into his arms to assure himself she really was okay, but he had a feeling she'd resist that. "We went by the apartment and they told us which organization had provided a place for you to stay. Trent phoned them and found out that they'd brought you here."

Her brows drew together. "But how did you know about the fire? That it was our building?"

"Uh...I knew your address and recognized it when we heard it on the news."

Alana crossed her arms, a key card clutched in one hand. "I guess you got that from the background check."

"Actually, no. I asked Caden and he gave it to me."

One of her eyebrows lifted at that revelation, and she glanced over at her son again then murmured, "I think he'd tell you pretty much anything you wanted to know."

Justin couldn't find it in himself to feel bad about pumping Caden for information. If he hadn't, they might never have known what had happened to them. "Are you guys okay? Were you hurt at all?"

She shook her head. "They checked us out at the scene because they were worried about smoke inhalation. They gave us both some oxygen but then let us go once they determined we were okay."

Relief flowed through him. He'd been so focused on them being alive, Justin hadn't really thought about what other injuries they may have sustained as a result of the fire. He was glad that it appeared that at least physically, they were okay. "Can we go to your room to talk for a few minutes?"

Alana hesitated, biting her lower lip for a moment before she nodded. She turned and moved away from him quickly. He glanced over at Than as he started up the stairs behind her. Than took Caden's hand and followed them.

Acutely aware of what she was wearing, Alana tried to get to the top of the stairs before Justin got too close. They'd been on their way to try to find some coins to use the vending machines to get something to eat and drink. She wasn't thrilled for them to be walking around barefoot, but she'd had no choice.

The room seemed to shrink as Justin and Than stepped inside. She noticed they both looked around, but neither of them made a comment. Meanwhile, she was just trying to keep her emotions in check. When she'd first spotted Caden in Justin's arms, the tumult of emotions that went through her had robbed her of breath.

"I'm just going to step outside for a minute," Than said as Caden settled onto the bed in front of the television. "I need to make a couple of phone calls."

Justin nodded at the man before turning his attention back to her. His arms were crossed over his broad chest, and Alana realized he was unarmed. She also spotted what looked like white gauze peeking out from under the edge of one sleeve of his T-shirt.

"What happened?" Justin asked. "Do you know how the fire started?"

Alana rubbed her forehead. "One of the tenants had a habit of smoking while inebriated. From what I heard, it sounded like it started in his apartment. I woke up when the smoke alarm in our apartment went off." She bit her lip. "I had bought that alarm myself. I hate to think what might have happened if I hadn't."

Justin's arms dropped to his sides, his hands curling into fists, but he didn't say anything.

"I grabbed Caden and went to the door, but there was too much smoke. It was too hot." Her heart thudded at the memory, and she found the fear of that moment rushing back. She pressed both her hands over her mouth for a moment then tucked them under her chin. "I went back to the window in Caden's room and tried to open it. Break the glass. I couldn't do it."

"Alana..." Justin's voice was low and soothing.

He reached out and took her arm. Slowly—as if giving her an opportunity to stop him—he drew her toward him then wrapped his arms around her and pulled her close. Her arms were trapped between them as she dipped her head to rest it on his chest. Alana drew on the strength of his embrace, willing herself not to cry. She couldn't remember the last time—if ever—that someone had held her like that.

She took a deep breath, inhaling the fresh, clean scent that she would forever associate with him. It helped for just a moment to clear the smoky odor that clung to both her and Caden. For a few minutes, she let herself not be strong. She allowed Justin to hold her and be the strong one. But finally, she took another deep breath and pulled back from him. He held onto her for a moment then let his arms slide from around her.

She stepped back and crossed her arms over her waist, feeling more able to continue. "I didn't know what to do. But then a firefighter came and took Caden from me. At least I knew he was going to be safe."

"But what about you? How did you get out?"

She remembered the rush of relief when she'd seen that second firefighter and realized that she would be saved too. "Another firefighter found me."

Justin didn't say anything right away as if he was waiting for her to go on. When she didn't, he said, "Why didn't you call Beth or me? We were...worried."

"My phone was in the apartment, and I didn't know either of your numbers by memory."

Justin seemed to consider her explanation before nodding. "You don't need to stay here."

Alana glanced around the room. It wasn't bad—definitely better than some places she'd stayed—but the neighborhood left little to be desired. And having to walk to get food for them would be a challenge. Still, it was one she was willing to take on.

"Seriously, Alana. Beth has room or if you'd rather be on your own, you can have my apartment."

Alana stared at him. "I don't want to impose."

Justin scowled at her words but then seemed to make an effort to soften his reaction. "It is no imposition. Absolutely none." He pulled his phone from the holder on his belt and swiped on the screen. "Here. Why don't you call Beth? You can hear for yourself that she has no problem with you guys moving in with them for as long as necessary."

Alana hesitated then took the phone he held out to her. She looked down and saw that he brought up Beth's contact information. She just had to tap the screen.

"I'm going to step outside with Than while you talk to her," Justin said as he nodded his head in the direction of the open door.

Alana watched as he walked away then she looked down and tapped the screen to call Beth.

⸺⸺⊰✕⊱⸺⸺

Justin took a deep breath and let it out as he joined Than by the railing outside the room. He hadn't even had a chance to say anything to Than when he felt a small hand slip into his. Glancing down, he saw Caden at his side, his fingers gripping his tightly as if afraid he was going to leave them. Justin wanted to reassure him that he wouldn't, but until Alana said the word, he had no idea if they'd be in the back seat of Than's truck when they left.

Than smiled at Caden before looking at Justin. "I started the ball rolling to circle the wagons."

Justin arched a brow. "In what way?"

"I contacted Linds to let her know what's happened, and she said the charitable arm of their company will step up and help in any way they can. Victoria called to say that she, Brooke and Staci would be willing to go buy clothing and anything else Alana and Caden might need. I told Lindsay to get in contact with them and organize that."

Warmth spread through Justin. These people barely knew Alana and Caden, and yet were offering their help. He was proud to be able to call them friends. "She's on the phone now with my sister, and I'm hoping Beth can convince her to go stay with them for a while."

Than glanced around at the neighborhood. "Yeah, it would be better if they weren't here."

Justin looked down again at Caden and wished that he could talk to him. It was then that it dawned on him that the little guy had lost his tablet. And Alana had lost her laptop.

He knew those two things were important to them. He would have to take care of replacing those as soon as possible.

"Here's your phone."

He turned to see Alana standing behind him. Her gaze dropped to where Caden held his hand, and he could have sworn he saw a flash of pain on her face, but Justin was at a loss to understand what would have caused it.

"So, are you going to stay with Beth and Dan?" Justin asked as he took the phone from her. "Or would you rather go to my apartment. I hardly use it so it won't be an inconvenience at all."

"I think it would be good for us to stay with Beth."

Justin was actually glad she'd taken Beth up on her offer rather than going to his apartment. Being at Beth's meant he could stop by more frequently without it being awkward like it would have been had they stayed at his apartment.

"Then let's get this show on the road. Than will drop us off at Beth's." Justin was eager to leave the rundown motel and get them somewhere safe.

"I'll go pull the truck around," Than said as he strode away from them.

Justin followed more slowly. With Caden holding one hand, he laid the other lightly on Alana's back as they moved toward the stairs. He knew Than was bringing the truck closer so they didn't have to walk across the parking lot in bare feet. He would have carried Alana if he thought she'd accept that, but Justin was fairly certain that at this particular point, she'd rather walk over hot coals than let him pick her up.

By the time they got to the bottom of the stairs, Than had the truck pulled around and stood with the back door open. While they got themselves situated, Than went into the office, presumably to tell the desk clerk that Alana and Caden were checking out. Alana helped Caden climb up and then got in behind him. Once he was sure they were buckled, Justin closed the door and slid into the front passenger seat as Than got behind the wheel.

He gave Than Beth's address so he could plug it into his navigation system then Justin pulled out his phone and sent a text message to Victoria.

Than said you're going to shop for Alana and Caden?

Yep. I'm meeting the others in twenty minutes.

Justin hesitated then typed, *When shopping for Alana, she prefers long-sleeve shirts. They can be lightweight, but she prefers her arms to be covered.*

Okay...I'll see what we can find. Might be a bit difficult this time of year.

And not to be difficult, but she also prefers longer skirts to pants. But if you do buy her pants, I don't think she'd want skinny jeans.

:D Wow, Justin, you really know this girl.

Justin grinned at her comment. *Well, I also know Caden likes Spiderman.*

I guess we'll just wing it on sizes. How old is Caden?

He's seven.

Okay. Hopefully, Brooke will be able to help with his stuff since she had Danny.

Justin glanced over his shoulder and saw Alana staring out the window, almost as if she was in shock. They needed to get her and Caden settled as soon as possible.

Thank you for helping.

Any time! Just wish it weren't necessary because of something like a fire.

He was typing a final message to Victoria when suddenly Than put his blinker on and swerved the truck into a parking lot. Justin looked up in surprise and glanced at Than.

"I'm hungry. Didn't get lunch yet. How about you?" Than arched a brow at him.

"Yeah, me too," Justin agreed as he looked up at the fast food sign then glanced back at Alana. "How about you guys?"

He saw Alana signing something to Caden and waited for her to decline the offer. It didn't take a rocket scientist to figure out that she didn't like people doing things for her. She was going to have to come terms with that in her current situation, though. She was about to get a lot more than fast food.

As Than pulled up into the drive-thru lane, Alana said, "Caden would like a plain cheeseburger with fries and a chocolate milk."

"What about you?" Justin asked.

She stared at the board with the menu and then asked for a salad with chicken and ranch dressing.

"What about something to drink?" Than asked after he relayed his order and Caden's.

"A vanilla milkshake." She said the words in a rush as if she knew if she thought about it too long she'd change her mind.

Justin gave her a grin then told Than what he wanted. Within a few minutes, the aroma of fried food filled the interior of the truck. He didn't make any mention of helping with the cost of the meal but planned to talk to Than about it later.

"We'll just wait to eat until we're at Beth's," Alana said when they handed her the bags with her and Caden's food and their drinks.

"We should be there in a few minutes," Than said.

As Than got back on the road, Justin called Trent to find out what was going on at the compound. The good news was that Marcus had been released from the hospital even though he was on crutches given the damage the bullet had done to his leg. The bad news was that they had absolutely no further leads on the shooter or who might have given him the information on the exercise.

"Can you run me out to the compound to grab my truck?" Justin asked Than as they neared Beth's house.

"Sure thing. I had planned to head out that way anyway," Than said. "Am I the only one wondering if this is all connected to the hacking and kidnapping attempt on Eric?"

Justin sighed and lifted a hand to press against the bandage under his T-shirt. "No, you're not. It can't be a coincidence, can it? We've never had any significant issues and then suddenly within the space of a year we've had three fairly serious attacks."

"I think it's something we're going to have to address. It's like someone is toying with BlackThorpe. They never came after Eric again even though we were fairly certain the threat originated in the US. And the hacking attempt. It was just the once and then nothing more. And this...well, he was either a bad sniper or he intentionally shot you guys with non-lethal shots."

"Yeah, Trent said they found the spot where the sniper had been and from that distance he should have been able to make a kill shot."

"How is your arm, by the way?" Than asked.

Justin lifted the edge of the sleeve, wincing as he saw the blood that stained the white gauze. "Hurts some. Looks like I need a bandage change."

"You were shot?"

Alana's voice had him turning in his seat so he could see her. For some reason, he'd assumed she wasn't paying attention to them.

"Yeah, but not seriously. Just grazed my arm." He lowered the sleeve so the bandage was covered again. "We had an incident during the exercise last night. Everyone is okay, though."

Alana frowned. "But you were shot."

"That's kind of a risk of the job. I don't carry weapons just for the fun of it." Before Justin could say anything more, Than pulled into Beth's driveway and came to a stop.

Gathering up the food, they got out of the truck and headed for the front door. Beth had it opened before they even reached the door. Justin saw his sister's gaze take in the way Caden and Alana were dressed along with the lack of footwear. He saw compassion in her eyes and knew that it hurt her to see them this way as much as it had hurt him. But now, between them and their friends, things would be better for the Jensens.

Alana held onto her own emotions by just a thread when she saw Beth's emotional response when they walked in her door.

"C'mon inside," Beth said with a wave of her hand. "Go ahead and take your food to the table."

Once she'd set their drinks and food on the table, Alana found herself engulfed in a tight hug. As Beth held her, Alana lost it. The fear she'd experienced from the first moment she'd awoken fighting to breathe finally loosened its hold on her, and her emotions unraveled in the process. The gratitude she felt for what these people were doing for them overwhelmed her.

"You're safe now, sweetie," Beth said, her voice soft and low. "Caden is safe too. You are such a good mom. Everything is going to be okay. I promise."

As she took several shuddering breaths, Alana felt a hand rest between her shoulder blades.

"*We* promise," Justin said, his voice gruff. "You've done a great job taking care of Caden. Now you need to let us take care of you both."

The warmth of his words washed over her. She didn't know what she'd done to deserve these people in her life but right then she was so very grateful for them. And for the first time since she'd realized that they'd lost everything, Alana felt a spark of hope.

Finally, feeling a little more in control of herself, Alana lifted her head and saw that Beth's cheeks were damp with tears too. She gave her a weary smile. "Thank you."

"You're welcome," Beth said as she lifted a hand to smooth Alana's hair. "Now you need to eat. I'm sure you must be starving."

Alana nodded and turned toward the table, happy to see that in the midst of her emotional meltdown Than had stepped in. He sat with Caden eating their burgers and signing.

Justin urged her toward a chair and then sat down next to her. As she ate her salad, Alana was glad the conversation stayed away from the fire. Instead, she listened as Beth

berated her brother for not telling her about the shooting as
soon as it had happened.

"I did eventually tell you. Isn't that good enough?" Justin
asked as he held out a fry, an apparent peace offering.

Beth snatched it from his hand and after she had eaten it,
she said, "I suppose, but I'm still worried about Meredith."

"I'll give Marcus a call later to make sure they're doing
okay."

Alana let the conversation swirl around her, surprised at
how...normal it felt. Not at all like they'd just gone through a
horrifying experience and lost everything but the clothes on
their backs. She was eager, however, to get rid of the smoky
stench that seemed to have permeated her hair and clothes.
They'd taken showers at the motel but with no good
shampoo and having to put on the same clothes, the acrid
scent still clung to them. She knew she could probably
borrow some clothes from Beth, but Caden wouldn't have
anything clean to change into since there were no boys his
size around. As long as he had nothing to replace his smoky
clothes, she would continue to wear hers.

Once Justin finished his meal, he said, "I'm going to have
to go for a bit. Need to get back to the compound to check in
with the guys and pick up my truck. I'll be back in a few
hours."

Than signed to Caden that he was going and her son's
gaze shot to Justin. When he looked at her, she signed
quickly that Justin would be back a little later. Her plan to
keep Caden away from Justin had gone up in flames—quite
literally. And with him having lost so much already, she
wasn't going to deny him the opportunity to be around the
man he admired so much.

Justin's hand rested briefly on her shoulder before he
bent to give Caden a hug. Once the men had left, Alana
turned to find Beth watching her with a bemused expression
on her face. "What?"

16

BETH TILTED HER HEAD and smiled but was prevented from answering her question by the sound of soft cries coming over the baby monitor that sat on the kitchen counter. "Sounds like the princess is up. Be right back."

Alana finished the last of her salad, watching Caden as he sat in his seat still working his way through his fries. Usually, she just got him the kids' meal, but she'd figured he was probably pretty hungry having missed breakfast on top of everything.

He glanced up and when his gaze met hers, he signed *I wish I had my tablet.*

Pain sliced through her. Since rent wasn't currently an issue, she planned to use the money in her account to get them some clothes from the thrift store. Unfortunately, a tablet—and a laptop—were a bit more than she'd be able to afford for a while. If she'd had her wits about her, she would have thought to at least grab that for him. But she'd been so focused on just saving Caden's life that nothing else had crossed her mind.

I know, baby. I'm sorry.

Alarm crossed his features as his eyes went wide in distress. *How can I talk to Justin without the tablet?*

Alana felt her shoulders droop as if a weight had just been dropped on them. How had she not realized how important that piece of electronics had become to Caden in relation to Justin? Until Justin had a larger vocabulary of signs, that tablet would have been Caden's only method of direct communication with him. Something told Alana that Caden had enjoyed not having to rely on a translator.

She could have tried to find a used one, but without her laptop, she was limited in finding even that. It was possible that Beth would let her use her computer, so she took a deep breath and hoped she wasn't lying to her son. *I will get you another one as soon as I can.*

Some of the distress faded from his eyes, but enough remained that Alana felt the prick of tears. She held her arms out to him, and he slid out of his chair and right into her embrace. Resting her cheek against his curls, she made the shorthand sign for I love you and waited for him to do the same, pressing his smaller hand against hers so their fingertips touched.

When Beth came back with Genevieve in her arms, Caden immediately straightened and left Alana's embrace. The little girl clapped, a huge smile on her face when she saw Caden. Beth set her down on the floor and Caden took her hand and led her to the toys that were piled in a corner of their living room.

"Do you want to take a shower?" Beth asked. "I have some clothes I can loan you."

Alana took a moment to try and formulate a plan. She hadn't wanted to change until Caden could as well, but she needed to be able to go out in public so she could get what he needed. "Yes, I would appreciate a shower and a change of clothes."

Though they were about the same height, Beth had curves that Alana didn't so likely anything she gave her to wear would be a bit baggy...which was just fine with her. Beth didn't take long to find her some clothes and then sent her down to the bathroom she'd used during their previous stay with them. Though a bath in that lovely tub was tempting, Alana resisted and showered instead, using the shampoo and conditioner Beth had told her were there for her.

Once finished the shower, she dried off and pulled on a pair of capris and a T-shirt and then used the towel to remove as much of the moisture from her hair as she could. Lowering the towel to the counter, Alana looked into the mirror and took a deep breath. The shower had helped to lift the remaining fear and worry which allowed her to focus on her plan of attack. Knowing that Caden was now in a safe place with people she trusted gave her the most comfort. Everything else she could fix. It wouldn't be the first time they'd started over.

She didn't plan to stay with Beth and Daniel indefinitely, so she needed to get a plan in place that would allow her and Caden to find another home of their own. First things first...she would ask Beth if she could watch Caden and then use the money they'd been given for food for bus fare. Once she had a couple of outfits for both her and Caden, they would be that much closer to feeling normal.

Alana closed her eyes briefly and prayed. "God, please let there be some good deals at the thrift store today. Thank you for providing us with a place to stay and good friends. And, if possible, please provide a tablet for Caden. Please."

As she opened her eyes, verses that she'd clung to in the past whispered through her mind.

Be anxious for nothing, but in everything by prayer and supplication, with thanksgiving, let your requests be made known to God.

So many times she'd murmured that verse—particularly the first part—when she'd been worried about how she and Caden would survive. *Be anxious for nothing.* And God had provided for them time and again.

I can do all things through Christ who strengthens me. How often had she wondered if she'd be able to cope with the weight of responsibility of Caden's care once they'd left Craig? Time and again she'd managed to pull through even the most trying and difficult situations, and she knew it was only with God's strength.

But the verse she'd clung to the most during the two years they'd been on their own had been *And my God shall supply all your need according to His riches in glory by Christ Jesus.* And He had supplied all their needs. Sure what they'd had hadn't been fancy or expensive, but they'd had clothes to wear and food to eat and a roof over their heads. Things might have changed, but God had already begun to provide for them again through Beth and Daniel's generous offer of a place to stay. And she was confident that He would continue to provide as she sought to replace what had been lost.

Her thoughts went to the fire and this time to the man who most likely had been responsible for it and how he'd paid for that with his own life. Was he at peace finally? She realized that she could have done more for the man. Though he'd made her uncomfortable, she could have extended friendship to him. She hoped that this experience would make her more sensitive to those around her who might be hurting.

With one final press of the towel to the damp ends of her hair, Alana hung it on the rod and left the room with her smelly clothes in her hands. Once Caden could change, she'd ask Beth if she could do a load of laundry. As she looked around the room where she and Caden had stayed not that long ago, she could hardly believe how much had changed in their lives.

Suddenly eager to get her plan underway, Alana left the bedroom and headed for the stairs. She had just set her foot on the bottom step when she realized there were voices coming from the main floor. Lots of them.

A little self-conscious about the short sleeves on the shirt, Alana didn't really want to see anyone, but Caden was up there and wouldn't be able to communicate with anyone. Resolutely, she walked up the stairs and into the living room.

Her eyes widened as she recognized the group of women sitting in the living room with Beth.

Victoria slid off the couch when she spotted her and came over, arms outstretched. Alana bent over to hug the woman, still not really used to affectionate embraces from anyone but Caden.

"I'm so sorry to hear about what happened," Victoria said as she stepped back. "We all are."

"Thanks. We're both still alive, and that's really all that matters," Alana said, meaning every word of it.

"Well, we're thankful you're okay." This time it was Lindsay who spoke. "And we want to help you get back on your feet."

Alana's eyes widened as Lindsay motioned to a pile of bags by the coffee table. She looked at Beth, who was grinning.

"If you don't like what we bought, you can take it back, but first you can blame Justin," Victoria said with a laugh.

"Justin?" Alana asked, watching as Brooke and Lindsay began to pull items from the bag.

"Yeah. He was the one who told us what to buy you." Victoria grinned. "He said you preferred longer skirts and to skip the skinny jeans."

Heat rushed into Alana's cheeks. "Really?"

"Sure thing." Victoria wiggled her phone in the air. "I have the text messages to prove it. And he said that Caden liked Spiderman."

Oh, that man tugged at her heartstrings like no one else ever had. Even before all of this, she'd been teetering on the edge of falling for him. It may have been a small thing that he'd noticed what she preferred to wear and what Caden liked, but it was just enough to shove her off that cliff.

Tears pricked at her eyes as Lindsay and Brooke held up some of the items they'd bought for her. It didn't escape her notice that several of the blouses had long sleeves, something else he'd noticed and cared enough to mention. Was it more than just caring for her and for Caden?

"We have a whole bunch of stuff for Caden too," Brooke said. "I hope we got the sizes right. He looked to be about the same size Danny was at that age."

At the mention of Danny, Alana's gaze went to the corner where Caden had been playing before she'd gone for her shower and she noticed that two more kids had joined them. Sarah and Danny were now bent over a pile of blocks with Caden while Genevieve was doing her best to knock them over.

"I don't know what to say." Alana brushed at the dampness on her cheeks. "Thank you seems so...inadequate."

"Thank you is more than sufficient," Lindsay said with a smile. "I'm just glad that we were in a position to be able to help. I want you to take these things and don't look back."

"Thank you," Alana said again as Victoria took her hand and guided her to the growing pile of clothes on the coffee table.

When Justin pulled his truck into the driveway of Beth's house, he recognized Trent, Eric and Than's vehicles on the street. Beth had called him a little earlier to let him know that they had shown up and the decision had been made to order pizza for everyone that was there.

He got out of the truck and opened the door to the back and lifted out the three boxes that sat on the seat. After closing the door with his elbow, he made his way to the front door and let himself in. He stowed the boxes on the top shelf of the closet where he usually put his weapons and laptop. This time around, he'd left them at his apartment at the compound even though he still wore a weapon in his ankle holster as per Alex's request that they be armed.

The smell of pizza tantalized him as he walked into the living room and saw the group of people gathered there. It looked like all the women who'd gone shopping for Alana were still there as well as their husbands. The only one still missing appeared to be Lucas Hamilton. He'd had no idea when he'd taken Beth, Daniel and Alana to the company family day that the collision of his co-workers and his family would be something that would come to mean so much more. Looking at them all gathered there warmed his heart in a way he wouldn't have thought possible not that long ago. He'd spent a lot of years keeping his work life separate from his family.

A sudden impact against his hip had him reaching for the wall to keep his balance. Even as he looked down, Justin knew whose face he'd see smiling up at him. Returning the smile Caden had for him, Justin slid his hands under his arms and lifted him up. As the boy buried his head into Justin's shoulder once again, he realized that he no longer had that acrid smoky smell clinging to him.

Justin hoped the memories of the fire would also no longer cling to Caden, although he had a feeling it might take a little longer to get to that point. But he was going to make sure that if—or when—Caden wanted to talk to him about it, he'd have that ability with the new tablet he'd bought him.

"Thank you." The softly spoken words drew his head up, and Justin found Alana standing in front of him.

Her big green eyes regarded him warily. He wondered what it would take to get rid of the wariness she seemed to have whenever she was around him. Did she not realize yet that he would never ever do anything to hurt her or Caden? He knew he'd been an idiot at the start, but he'd tried to show her that he was different once he realized how far off the mark he'd been. Yet she still seemed to expect him to lash out at any moment.

He gave a quick nod of his head, his hand splayed across Caden's back. "You're welcome."

"It was very unexpected and thoughtful." Her fingers twisted together in front of her. "I'm not sure what I would have done if you hadn't found us."

Justin reached out and covered her hands with his. "You're a strong and competent woman, Alana. I have no doubt that you would have done what was best for Caden and moved forward."

Her eyes widened a bit more, but her fingers remained still beneath his. "Some days I don't feel very strong. This morning when I couldn't manage to get Caden out of the apartment, I didn't feel very strong."

"Being strong doesn't mean you can do everything perfectly without feeling fear or weakness. It just means you can face what comes your way and deal with it, even if that means just setting one foot in front of another until you get things figured out. Knowing something of what's brought you this far, I can say without a word of a lie that you're strong. Just like Beth is. I don't think I've met two stronger women in my life."

Some of the wariness eased from her expression, but she still held herself rigidly and perfectly still. Slowly, he let his fingers slide from hers. Suddenly, the little boy in his arms held his hand out to his mom, his fingers in what looked like the sign people made to *rock on*.

A smile curved Alana's lips, and she lifted her hand and made the same sign before pressing it against Caden's. All wariness was gone from her expression as she made that connection with her son.

"What does that mean?" Justin asked, figuring there was significance to it just as there was to anything Caden did with his hands.

Alana's gaze swung to his as she moved her hand from Caden's. "It means *I love you*."

Justin studied the position of her fingers until she lowered her hand and when he looked at her face, he saw a sweep of pink in her cheeks. Maybe she wasn't as unaffected by him as he'd thought she was.

"Why don't you come get something to eat?" Beth came to stand next to Alana, a wide smile on her face. "I tried to save you a few pieces before your buddies ate them all."

He bent to place Caden on his feet then followed Alana and Beth to the table where large boxes covered its surface. Genevieve sat in a high chair near the table, and her face lit up when she saw him. His heart clenched when she signed *Hi* to him. He dropped down to his haunches in front of her and signed it back to her then leaned forward to place a kiss on her curls.

"You, my man, are a softie," Than said with a chuckle.

Justin straightened and took the plate Beth held out to him before she went back to the living room with Alana. He shot Than a look and grunted in response as he put a couple of pieces of pizza on the plate.

Than just laughed. "I always suspected you might have a soft side, but this is way more than I imagined."

"Loving my family doesn't make me soft," Justin said then took a bite of his pizza.

Than tilted his head and regarded him with a serious gaze. "Caden isn't your family. Neither is Alana."

Justin glanced around to make sure no one else heard Than's softly spoken words. "No, they're not."

His thoughts went to the company family day and the conversations that had gone on between Alana and Caden. He set the piece of pizza back down on his plate and said, "What were Alana and Caden talking about at the compound the other day?"

Than's expression changed, closed off and he shook his head. "That's not mine to share, man."

Justin stared at him, wondering if there was anything he could say or do to change Than's mind. But as frustrating as not knowing was, he appreciated that Than honored the privacy of the conversation between Caden and Alana, and he would do the same. He gave Than a nod and turned to look at the group gathered in the living room. Some sat on the furniture while others, like Trent, were seated on the floor. They had all made themselves comfortable in his sister's home and it felt right.

Once they had finished eating, they began to clean up their dishes and the guys took the pizza boxes out to the trash. Eric and Staci were the first to leave with Sarah, but it wasn't long before the rest followed. Soon it was just him left. He thought of the boxes in the closet by the front door and hoped that Alana would receive them in the way she'd accepted the clothing and other essentials that had been given to her and Caden.

This was more than just giving them some electronic toys. From previous conversations, he knew that she used her laptop to earn money and he had personal experience of what Caden used his tablet for. These weren't frivolous items. They were necessities.

Since Daniel had taken Genevieve upstairs to give her a bath, Alana was in the kitchen with Beth. Caden sat at the table, his legs swinging as he colored in a book someone had bought him. From what he could see, it appeared to be filled with pictures of his favorite superhero.

While they were all distracted, Justin went to the closet and pulled the boxes down. He stood there for a moment and sent up a prayer that Alana would accept these gifts. He needed to do this for her. For them.

Back in the dining room, Caden's eyes grew wide when he saw Justin put the boxes on the table. He set the smallest box aside without opening it, focusing instead on the medium-sized one.

"What you got there, Justin?" Beth dropped the dishtowel she'd had in her hands onto the counter and came around to where he stood.

Alana followed her, and Justin knew the moment it registered with her what he had in front of him. He heard her swift intake of breath as her gaze darted to his. She gave a slight shake of her head, but Justin held up a hand.

"You need these things, Alana. They are vital to both you and Caden, so please, just accept them."

"It's too much," Alana said even as she reached out and ran her fingers along the box that held Caden's tablet. The label clearly marking it as the most up-to-date one on the market. She looked up at him, her green eyes shining with moisture. "It's too much."

Justin stood there, needing her to accept the gifts. Wanting her to see that he really did understand that she and Caden needed these things. Her gaze went back to the boxes, and Justin could almost hear the internal conversation she was having with herself.

He saw her lips move as if reciting something to herself and then her gaze lifted and she nodded. "Thank you."

Justin wanted to fist pump his victory in the air, but instead he gave her a quick smile and then lifted the lid on the box. He freed the tablet from its packaging and took a second to bring the screen to life. "You're going to need to put your information in the login so you can download his apps from the app store."

Since this was the same type of tablet he had, Justin was able to quickly hook up to Dan's wireless and then handed it to Alana to put her information in. She quickly tapped the information in then handed it back. He sat down on a chair to download Caden's apps and immediately the boy was at his elbow watching the screen.

The boy signed something to his mother, looking from the tablet to Justin to Alana. When Alana nodded, his gaze jerked back to Justin and a big smile spread across his face. Then he signed another sign that Justin recognized. *Thank you.*

Justin signed *you're welcome* in return. It was the one sign he felt fairly confident using.

Once again, the sparkling in Caden's eyes told Justin just how much the little guy appreciated his efforts to communicate with him. As he did a few more things on the tablet, he felt Caden rest his head against his shoulder.

After he was done, he handed it to Caden and watched as he stared down at the screen and then pressed the tablet against his chest. When Justin thought of how much he'd had when he'd been Caden's age, it touched him that Caden hadn't taken for granted what he'd been given.

When Caden lifted his hand, Justin expected him to hold out his small fist for a fist bump like they'd done before. Instead, the little boy gave him the same sign he'd given Alana earlier.

I love you.

The air whooshed out of his lungs as he heard Alana's gasp beside him. He almost glanced at her, but his gaze was held by the look in Caden's eyes. A serious expression had taken over the sparkling of just a few minutes ago. Time stood still as Justin realized the ramifications of that moment. But he wasn't going to dash the boy's hopes, especially when he realized that he could respond honestly.

Lifting his own hand, he copied the gesture and then pressed his fingers to Caden's the way he'd seen Alana do it earlier. A smile spread across Caden's face and as their gazes met, the little boy nodded and then pulled his hand back. He returned to his seat, his head bent over the tablet.

Justin almost laughed. It had been that simple for Caden.

I love you.

I love you too.

And that was enough for him.

Not wanting to make a bigger deal out of the exchange than Caden had, Justin picked up the smallest box and opened it. He lifted out the phone and handed it to Alana.

17

ALANA TOOK THE phone from Justin as he said, "I know you also lost your phone in the fire. You will need to go and get this one activated for your number and the plan you have. Beth can give you all our numbers again."

Beth reached out and took the phone from Alana's slack fingers. "Why don't I just add them myself? Then you can show her that last box there."

Justin glanced at Alana, noticing the slightly shell-shocked look she wore. He wasn't sure if it was still because of the items he'd purchased for them or if the exchange between him and Caden had caused it.

He opened the box containing the laptop and removed it from the packaging. When he set it on the table in front of the empty chair next to him, he rested his hand on top of it, his gaze on Alana. She wasn't looking at him, and he could see her gnawing on the inside of her lip. He waited for her to make up her mind.

Leaning back in his seat, he fought the urge to cross his arms since he figured that would give him a dominant appearance that wouldn't be helpful at the moment. There were plenty of times when he wanted that dominant position, but right then wasn't one of them. An electric silence settled between them as Alana's hands gripped the back of the chair.

Finally, Justin reached out and covered both of her hands with one of his. He waited until she looked up at him. "How about we do it this way? Consider it a loan until you can get something for yourself. At least it will give you the opportunity to get back to work."

He thought about asking her if she had enough money set aside to purchase a new laptop, but he doubted she did and he didn't want to embarrass her like that. Though Alana usually kept her emotions from showing on her face, this time he could pretty much read everything going through her mind. He figured it had something to do with the emotional overload she'd gone through in the past twenty-four hours.

Justin had to admire her stubbornness even as he wished she'd just accept the gift. She was used to taking care of herself and Caden, and while she'd do anything for her son—including accepting the tablet—she obviously didn't feel comfortable doing the same for herself. He may not have known her long, but he had a pretty good idea of what made her tick.

Finally, she moved her hands from beneath his and slid into the chair. She looked at him, her green eyes determined. "A loan."

Justin fought to keep his expression serious as he nodded. "A loan."

With that settled, she reached out and lifted the lid of the laptop. The guy at the computer shop where he'd bought it had assured him it was ready to go. He sure hoped that was the case or he'd be getting Dan to help her out. While he knew enough about computers to operate his own, doing updates and such was more Dan's or Trent's territory.

"The guy at the computer shop said it had the latest

operating system on it. And it's touchscreen."

It quickly became apparent that he didn't need to worry about updating the laptop. Alana clearly knew her way around the machine.

"You're pretty knowledgeable about this stuff," Justin commented. "Did you take classes for this?"

She glanced at him, surprise on her face. "No. I had to kind of learn as I went. If something wasn't working, I would Google it or watch videos. I couldn't afford to take it to someone."

"Well, I know next door to nothing about how computers work, so if you have any issues, Dan or Trent will be your best bet. I'm sure either would be happy to help you."

Alana lifted a brow. "Trent? Really? He doesn't really know me."

"Trent loves computers. I think that after he's done working on them at BlackThorpe, he goes home to work on them some more. Of course, Victoria might have changed that a bit now."

Daniel walked into the kitchen then and slipped his arm around Beth's shoulders. "Geni wants you before she'll sleep."

"I'll be right back," Beth said as she went up on her tiptoes and pressed a kiss to Dan's lips before walking out of the kitchen.

Dan took in the boxes and equipment on his dining room table and then looked at Justin. "Did you get them setup on the wireless?"

"I got Caden's tablet on it, but I think maybe you should do the laptop."

Dan nodded and sat down on the seat next to Alana. Within a few minutes, he had her logged into their wireless network.

"How much did you lose on the other laptop?" Justin asked as he watched Alana type information into a web page.

Alana sat back and let out a quick breath. "Actually, not a whole lot. Everything I did was online. If I ever had files I wanted to save, I emailed them to myself since I didn't have an external drive to save to and couldn't afford online backups."

Justin was glad to hear she hadn't lost everything. Well, she had, but at least some of it was salvageable. He was quite sure that having a way to continue making money was pretty important to her.

Realizing there wasn't much left for him there, Justin pushed away from the table and stood. "I'd better head back to the compound."

He laid a hand on Caden's shoulder. When the boy looked up at him, Justin glanced at Alana. Once her son looked at her, she quickly signed something to him.

Caden laid his tablet down and stood up to hug Justin around the hips, and when he stepped back, he signed *thank you* once again. After signing back to him once again, Justin looked at Daniel and Beth. "Thanks for everything today."

"I'm just glad we were here to help out." Beth gave him a quick hug. "And you take care of yourself. No more getting shot. You know the house across the street is up for sale. Maybe you should take a look at it."

"Maybe I will," Justin murmured as he walked past her.

Justin was nearly at the front door when he heard Alana say his name. He turned to face her, prepared for her to try to thank him again, but as soon as he got a look at her face, he knew this was something else.

"First of all, I want to thank you for everything you've done for Caden and me. Victoria said you made sure they knew what to get for me clothes-wise and for Caden too."

Justin shoved his hands into his pockets and shrugged. "I wanted to make sure you had things you were comfortable in. And that Caden had clothes he liked."

"They did a great job and what they chose was exactly right. Thank you."

"You're welcome." He stood there, waiting for her to continue because he was pretty sure he knew what else was on her mind.

Her gaze slid away from his and her fingers twisted together at her waist. "About what Caden said earlier..."

Justin thought of just brushing it aside. No doubt it would be easier for her to not have to acknowledge that her son had told him he loved him. And though Caden himself hadn't made a big deal out of it, the moment had been significant and as surely as he knew it, so did Alana. He was fairly certain Caden didn't make a habit of telling people—particularly men—that he loved them. In the time since he'd met them, he'd only ever seen Caden make that sign with Alana.

As the silence stretched out once again, Alana shifted her weight and lifted her gaze to his, wariness back in her green gaze. She cleared her throat and swallowed. "What Caden said...he has become very attached to you. His dad didn't pay him very much attention, and there hasn't been much male presence in his life until we met Beth and Daniel. He likes Daniel a lot, but you...you...he loves." Her head dipped so he couldn't see her eyes. "I appreciate you responding the way you did with him even if it isn't how you feel. He's had a lot of heartache in his short life. The fire was just the latest."

"It *is* how I feel." Justin crossed his arms, a little defensive given she didn't appear to think he was capable of actually feeling something for her son.

Alana's head shot up and her eyes widened. "What?"

Justin shrugged. "What can I say? The little guy has grown on me. And I know I love him because I feel about him like I do about Genevieve. And I definitely love her."

Alana seemed to be contemplating his words as she didn't reply right away. But as usual, the woman had pulled her emotions back inside her. For a few minutes there she'd showed her nerves and wariness, but now she was back to keeping everything hidden.

She lifted her chin, her shoulders pulling back slightly. "Okay. Well, I just want you to know I won't get in the middle of your relationship with Caden. I think...I think you'll be good for him. And maybe he'll be good for you too. But you don't have to worry about me reading anything more into this thing between you and Caden."

Justin stared at her for a moment then nodded his head as he turned and gripped the doorknob to leave. He twisted it and opened the door, but then swung back around and looked at her. "But what if I want you to read more into it?"

Her jaw sagged even as her eyes widened at his question. There was no hiding the shock on her face. Justin wasn't actually looking for an answer right then, but he did want to give her something to think about because in the panic that had followed the news of the fire, he'd come to the realization that this woman—and her son—had found their way into his heart. Now he just had to be patient and see if she felt the same way.

He quietly closed the door behind him and walked to his truck, his eyes going to the house Beth had mentioned earlier. As he drove around the cul-de-sac, he paused to write down the information on the realtor. Maybe he'd give them a call in the morning and get a few more details on it.

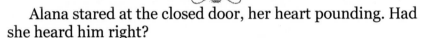

Alana stared at the closed door, her heart pounding. Had she heard him right?

But what if I want you to read more into it?

Maybe he'd misunderstood what she meant by her comment. And now she was left wondering if she was reading more into his departing statement.

Frowning, she gave her head a shake and turned around to go back to the dining room to get Caden since it was already past his bedtime. She froze when her gaze fell on Beth. Her friend leaned against the door jamb of the opening to the kitchen. From her expression, it looked as if she'd heard most—if not all—of her conversation with Justin. Honestly, if she'd realized where their conversation was going to go, she wouldn't have started it when there were other people around.

Beth lifted an eyebrow. "So are you going to give Justin a chance?"

Alana rubbed her palms down the rough denim of her brand new jeans. "A chance?"

Her friend pushed away from the door jamb. "Justin basically just told you that he's interested in something more with you. And that's a pretty big thing for him."

So he must not have misunderstood her if Beth had come to the same conclusion she had. She would know her brother better than Alana. And while that cleared up one thing...it left her filled with uncertainty.

"I don't know." Alana felt she had to be honest with her friend. "I don't know that I would be the best woman for him. He needs someone...stronger."

Beth's eyebrows rose at that. "You don't think you're strong?"

"I spent years with a man who beat me. If I'd been stronger, I would have left the first time he did it. Instead, I stayed...for almost six years."

"But you did leave, Alana. That took real strength. I think you're stronger than you realize."

"Any strength I have comes from Caden. I did what I had to do for him."

Beth tilted her head, a look of curiosity tinged with sadness on her face. "Did you not think you were worth being strong for?"

She wanted to be able to deny what her friend had said, but the words stuck in her throat. There was no denying she felt that anything bad that had happened to her was what she'd deserved. But nothing bad that had happened was Caden's fault, so she'd done her best to protect him.

"Do you ever do anything for yourself? Accept anything for yourself?" Beth approached her and ran a hand down her arm. "Even tonight. You accepted the tablet outright for Caden but would only accept the laptop as a loan. And I'm pretty sure that you only agreed to stay here and accept all the clothes because of Caden."

Alana looked away from Beth, not wanting her to see the anguish that was slowly building within her. She'd never had anyone grasp her inner struggles like Beth just had. Trembling had started in the pit of her stomach, and she fought to keep it from showing outwardly.

The burden of responsibility for the bad things that had happened in her life rested squarely on her shoulders. And even as she strived to give Caden the best she could, there were times when she did wish she could grab onto something good for herself.

"Alana," Beth said her name softly. "Though I would love to see you and Justin together, all I ask is that if you do give him a chance, make sure that it's for you and not for Caden. Justin hasn't had an easy life either, and he deserves a woman who accepts him for who he is, not for how he treats her son."

Alana glanced up to meet her friend's gaze. She nodded that she understood. Justin did deserve what Beth wanted for him.

And she didn't.

It took a little while, but finally Caden was settled for the night in the big bed they'd shared the last time they'd stayed the night. Once she was sure he was asleep, Alana took the laptop Justin had given her and went to sit on the soft couch in the rec room. Beth had told her to think of the lower level as their home for as long as they needed it.

She sank onto the couch, pulling her feet in to sit cross-legged and propped the laptop on her knees. It was stunning to consider the past twenty-four hours. It had been a roller-coaster ride of emotion the likes of which she'd never known. From terror to worry to thankfulness to...maybe love?

As she sat there staring blankly at the laptop screen, Alana wondered if she dared hope. Hope for something good for her—not just Caden—because although it was a definite bonus that Justin and Caden had a connection, there were emotions she had for the man that had nothing to do with her son.

She'd fallen hard and fast for Craig when they'd met when she was in high school. The youngest—the "surprise baby"— she'd never achieved the successes of her older brother and sister. Her parents had invested their time and resources in her much- older siblings, and Alana had been left to find her own way through school and any extracurricular activities she'd wanted to be involved in. So it was no wonder, really, that when Craig began to pay attention to her she'd fallen for him so quickly. Gave in to him physically far too easily.

And boy, had she gotten her parents' attention when she'd wound up pregnant.

Her gaze drifted to the slightly open door to the room where Caden slept. They'd told her that keeping the *fetus* would be the worst decision she'd ever make. When she'd gone ahead and made that decision, they made theirs and cut her out of their lives. All of them.

People told her that she was lucky Craig had agreed to marry her and then had gone on to provide her and Caden with such a wonderful life. All they saw was the outside trappings of the life they lived...never the terror that occurred behind closed doors.

Realizing that her hands had clenched into fists, Alana took a deep breath and relaxed her fingers. That was over now. No longer a part of her life. After that last horrific beating where Craig had threatened Caden, she'd called the police. They'd taken one look at her and arrested Craig. Though his family's lawyers had worked their magic for him, she'd gotten what she wanted from him. In exchange for no spousal or child support as part of the divorce, he would terminate his parental rights. He'd been more than happy to oblige. With the help of an abused women's support group, she'd been able to get the sealed file for her name change as an extra layer of protection in case Craig changed his mind. She was sure he never would, but all of that added to the maelstrom of emotions she was dealing with now.

She'd thought that Justin's physique being so similar to Craig's would be a deterrent, but it seemed that the opposite was actually true. This man didn't use his strength to inflict pain on those around him. But there was no doubt in her mind that if Craig ever bothered to track her down, Justin wouldn't hesitate to go to her defense. He protected those he cared for and that was a big draw for her.

Once they'd gotten past that rough start, Alana had found herself looking forward to being around him. He'd become a part of the life she only allowed herself to dream of as she'd lay in bed late at night. She hadn't lied to Beth when she'd said that she thought she wasn't the right woman for him. That's why Alana had only allowed herself to dream about it, not to ever really consider it might come true. But when Caden had revealed how important Justin was to him, Alana had become scared that unlike her ability to relegate Justin to the "wishful thinking" part of her heart, her son would not be able to realize that his feelings might not be returned.

Alana couldn't stop the smile that edged up the corners of her mouth. Caden was braver than she was. He'd taken the bull by the horns and ended up with the result he wanted—well, part of it anyway. She would have let fear hold her back. Fear of being rejected again. Fear of not being enough for Justin.

And yet...

But what if I want you to read more into it?

Suddenly, she wanted to talk to Justin, but she had no way to do that. Her phone wasn't hooked up yet so she couldn't call or text. And she'd lost his card that had his email address on it.

Alana slid the computer off her lap and got to her feet. She walked quietly up the stairs to see if Beth was still awake. She found her friend curled up in an easy chair, a ball of yarn in her lap as her hands worked a crochet hook. The TV played on low. A crime drama from the look of it.

Beth looked up and smiled at her, lowering her hands. "Hey. Caden go down okay?"

"He went down just fine. I think he was pretty wiped from everything of the past day."

"I would have thought you'd be wiped out too," Beth commented.

"I am, but my mind is kind of whirling around right now." She paused, swallowing the lump that had suddenly grown in her throat. "Actually, that's why I'm here. Do you have Justin's email address?"

Beth's eyes widened briefly as she jabbed the tip of the crochet hook into the ball of yarn and set it on the small table at her elbow. "Sure. I can also give you his instant messenger username."

Alana wasn't sure she was ready for that type of chatting just yet...especially if he wanted to video chat. For now, she just wanted to be able to write him an email to kind of break the ice in the new direction they seemed headed.

She followed Beth into the kitchen where the woman pulled a pad of paper and a pen from a drawer. She scribbled something on the top sheet then pulled it off and handed the paper to Alana.

Alana stared at it for a moment and then folded the paper, her fingers trembling slightly. Trying to quiet the fluttering in her stomach, she looked back up at Beth, her fingers working the crease of the folded paper. "Do you really think...?"

Beth leaned a hip against the counter and crossed her arms, the movement making her look more like Justin than she normally did. "Do I really think you and Justin would be good together?"

Alana nodded, suddenly realizing that if she did get involved with Justin and things didn't turn out well, she'd likely lose a friend too. Beth was the first really good friend she'd had since...well, forever. She'd connected with her and Daniel in a way she hadn't with the other couples she'd worked with.

"Actually, I think you would. I'm sure you call to Justin's protective nature even though he knows how strong you are. And I do think his protective nature draws you to him as well. But you need to understand and accept that wanting that protectiveness in a man doesn't make you weak. You've already proven how strong you are. I also think you have plenty of love to give. And I saw Justin's face tonight with Caden...I don't doubt for a moment that he loves Caden.

"Justin has been responsible for so long, putting aside his own desire for a military career to take care of me. I think he loves his job now, but he needs more than that even if he won't come right out and say it. Though if tonight was any indication, I think he's coming to that realization himself." Beth walked to her and wrapped her arms around her. "I know this isn't easy for you, but it will be worth it in the long run. I'll be praying for you both."

"Thank you," Alana said as she returned her friend's hug then stepped back. "Well, I'll let you get back to your evening." She lifted the paper. "And thanks for this."

"Feel free to come to me if you need someone to talk to about all this. Yes, I want to see Justin happy, but I want that for you too. I'll do what I can to help you both."

As she made her way back downstairs, Alana thanked God for bringing Beth and Daniel into her life. It seemed wrong to be thankful for Genevieve's hearing loss, but that was what had brought them together. Hopefully, she and Caden had brought joy to their lives as much as they'd brought to hers.

Back on the couch, she resumed her position from earlier. She opened up her email and clicked to compose a message then sat and stared at the blank white space trying to gather her thoughts.

------⊷⊶------

Steam filled the bathroom from the water he'd turned on and cranked to hot in the shower. Justin reached back and grasped his T-shirt between his shoulder blades to pull the wet fabric over his head then dropped it to the floor. His muscles were screaming at him for the punishing workout he'd just put them through. He hoped the hot water would ease some of the pain.

As soon as he'd gotten to the compound, he'd gone right to the weight room to start pumping. Thankfully, the room had been empty at that time of night. Although maybe it would have been better if he hadn't been alone with his thoughts.

It seemed all he did was replay the evening over and over in his mind and wonder if he'd messed up by saying what he had to Alana as he was leaving. She'd seemed so shocked at his words, making him contemplate the possibility that she hadn't considered him in that light.

And even now, he couldn't get the whole evening out of his head. In the past, he hadn't had to pursue women. They were usually the ones coming after him. He knew it was a combination of his physique and the gruff, bad-boy image he seemed to portray to the world even though nothing could be further from the truth.

Okay, gruff, maybe, but a bad boy? Not really. Not in the way the women had thought he'd be apparently since none of them had stuck around very long when they'd discovered his idea of a good time was sparring with his co-workers or watching sports on television. Preferably football or NASCAR. So trying to figure out how to convince Alana to give him a chance was a challenge.

This was probably the reason he was better off single than trying to navigate the waters of a relationship.

Justin growled in frustration as he grabbed a towel to dry off. After pulling on a pair of sweats and another T-shirt, he ventured into his small kitchen and pulled a bottle of water out of the refrigerator. He swiped a banana from the bowl by his coffee maker and settled down on a chair at the small table in front of his laptop. After pressing the button to bring it to life, he peeled the banana and took a bite.

Trying to push aside his thoughts of the past hour, Justin opened his email program to see if there were any work-related emails he needed to deal with. He had no doubt his attention for the rest of the week would be divided between the training already scheduled and working with the rest of the team to figure out who was targeting them.

Several emails popped into his inbox, but the most recent one caught Justin's attention. The sender was A. Jensen and the subject line read *This is all new to me.*

He frowned, wiggling his finger on the touchpad and sending the pointer all over the screen. Did he want to open it and see what she had to say? Well, that was a dumb question because of course he did. But was he ready for it?

After circling the subject line a few times with the pointer, he told himself to buck up and be a man. It wasn't as if it said something like *Please leave me alone* or *You must be insane.* To be honest, her subject line was one he could have used himself in reference to this whole situation.

Saying a quick prayer that he hadn't made things even more awkward between them, Justin clicked on the email and watched it fill his screen. It wasn't a short and sweet *let's do this,* but it also wasn't a to-the-point *not interested* either.

18

HI JUSTIN ~ First of all, let me thank you once again for all you did today for Caden and me. I know others were involved, but I also know that you were the driving force behind it. I appreciate your efforts on our behalf more than you'll ever know.

What happened tonight with Caden was no real surprise to me. At the family day with you, he told me then that he loved you. I was scared to let him get even more attached to you, so I tried to keep him from you. I didn't want him to get hurt. But apparently he was determined. All he knows is how he feels and he wanted to share it with you. Thank you for taking it all in stride.

If I had to choose a better role model than you for Caden, I don't think I could. I'm sure he has some memories of his father, though I haven't talked to him much about it, but the fact that he attached himself to you in spite of the physical similarities to his dad makes me think he sees beyond that to the man you are inside. And he apparently thinks that man is worth admiring...loving.

Beth tells me you are a good man, but I already knew that. Caden and I have been blessed to have you in our lives. Maybe we can see you again sometime this week?

Take care ~ Alana

Justin read the email over a couple of times. She still didn't seem to be separating herself from Caden when it came to him, but maybe he would have to be the one to initiate that. And he was okay with that. She'd opened the door a crack, and he was going to nudge it a bit further.

He clicked the screen to send a reply, pausing for a bit to formulate what he wanted to say.

Hi Alana ~ Thanks for the email. I would like to see you and Caden again this week. I have a team in this week and it's going to be pretty busy with them, so it might not be until Friday. I'll come by Beth's as soon as I'm done work. ~ Justin

He would have loved to be more specific about a date, but Justin had a feeling that vague would do better at this point. And he wasn't one for writing long emails anyway, so short and sweet would have to be good enough.

Though he wished it wasn't going to be a few days before he saw Alana again, Justin knew it was probably better to let her get through the emotions of the past day and get back on her feet. Hopefully by Friday, she'd be feeling like her life was closer to normal. His biggest concern at this point was that she would likely not want to stay with Beth and Dan too long. That would mean she'd be looking for another rundown apartment in another rundown part of the city. He knew she couldn't afford anything more, but he really didn't like the idea of her returning to a place like the one that had just burned down.

Knowing there was nothing else he could do right then about that particular problem, Justin turned his attention to the other emails in his inbox.

Alana had been working on her blog for the next day when the alert went letting her know she had a new email. She clicked to bring the program up and smiled even as a group of butterflies started fluttering in her stomach when she saw Justin's name.

She hadn't known what to expect from him in response to her email. Thankfully, it looked like he was willing to take it slow and spend some time with them. She knew that would make Caden happy, and she had to be honest with herself—it would make her very happy too.

Humming to herself, she finished her blog and set it to post late the next afternoon then worked on the email she'd send out with the same information. It was these small tasks that helped settle her and made her feel like they were well and truly over the worst of what the fire had wreaked on their lives.

She did one last round of her social media and email before closing the laptop. As she leaned her head back, Alana knew she couldn't stay that way long or she'd end up spending the night on that oh-so-comfy couch. With a sigh, she pushed to her feet and went into the bedroom. Beth had given her a small nightlight and it cast just enough glow for her to see that Caden still slept soundly. She'd wondered if he might have bad dreams after what had happened the night before, but so far, so good. Of course, the night wasn't even half over.

After a quick trip to the bathroom to brush her teeth, Alana slipped between the sheets and as she sank into the mattress, she let out a long sigh. It felt good to finally be able to just let everything go.

Thank you, God, for bringing us through this awful day. Thank you that neither of us were hurt. And thank you for the provision of what we needed and even more and for friends. Thank you so much for friends. Alana's thoughts went to the conversation with Justin. His blue eyes had been so serious as he'd delivered his line right before walking out of the house. *And if this...relationship with Justin is Your will for us, I pray You'll make that clear to each of us.*

And as she finally said Amen, Alana curled onto her side and let her gaze linger on her son's sleeping form on the other side of the large bed and then slid into slumber.

The next day, Beth took her to get her new phone activated then the two of them spent some time wandering around a mall with Caden and Genevieve. It all felt so...normal. Like the fire and losing all their stuff had happened in a dream, not in this reality. But here she and Caden were, dressed in clothes provided by people who considered her a friend, and though they'd lost everything they'd owned, it wasn't only the replacement of those things that made her grateful, but the friendships that had developed because of their circumstances. Although, if she really thought about it, some of those friendships had started back that day when they'd gone to the BlackThorpe family event.

Beth didn't ask anything more about Justin nor did she ask if Alana had emailed him. Their time together at the mall was relaxing and a good distraction from all that had gone on lately. They stopped at the grocery store on their way home and picked up some food for supper. As they carried the groceries into the house a short time later, Alana was reminded again of how much generosity was involved in Beth and Daniel opening their home to her and Caden.

Not wanting them to feel as if their privacy had totally been invaded, once dinner was over and clean up was completed, Alana took Caden downstairs where she spent some time working with him on a few of the educational apps he had on his tablet. Though she'd technically finished homeschooling him for the year, she still liked to keep up with some subjects, particularly reading. It wasn't just a way to make sure he could communicate with people who didn't know sign language, but to also increase his own vocabulary of signs.

He was reading a story about a boy and his dad, and partway through, he paused and looked at her. *Will we see Justin soon?*

Yes. He said Friday hopefully.

Caden's face lit up then he turned his attention back to the book in his lap. Alana reached out and ran her fingers through his curls. He shot her a sideways grin before continuing to read. She bent her knees and tucked her feet under the hem of her skirt. She realized as she sat there that part of the peace within her came from feeling secure in a way she never really had in the apartment.

Even though she'd had more than the one lock on the apartment door, Alana had never fully trusted they would keep out someone determined to get inside. Being in this house in a nice neighborhood and knowing that Daniel could protect them if anything happened gave her a sense of security. Unfortunately, it wasn't going to last too long. She had to start looking for a new place soon. There was enough money in her account to pay for one month's rent since she'd saved it to pay for the next month but after the apartment had burned, it was still sitting there. She'd had no calls or messages from the landlord of the building and figured she wouldn't be getting anything out of him.

Her phone chirped a text alert. Alana picked it up and smiled when she saw a message from Justin.

How was your day?

Relaxing back against the soft cushions, Alana tapped out a reply. *It was really good. Got my phone activated—obviously—and spent time with Beth and Genevieve walking around the mall. How was yours?*

It took a couple of minutes before another message popped up on her screen.

Tiring. I'm training along with this group and they're strong. Really push themselves and me. There's been a change in plans tho. They're staying two more weeks, but they'll be off official training Friday night through Sunday, so we're still on.

Alana's heart skipped a beat, wondering what—if anything—he might have planned for them. To be honest, just being together even if they stayed in the house was fine with her. *That sounds good. Caden was just asking if he'd see you again soon. He was happy when I said you'd be here on Friday.*

Justin's reply was there almost immediately after she'd sent hers. *And you?*

And me what? Even as Alana hit send on the message, she knew what he was asking. Playing dumb wasn't something she should do with him. Quickly, she tapped out another message. *Yes, I'm happy to know you'll be here Friday too.*

Time stretched on as she waited for his reply, certain that it must be a long one if it was taking this long to send it back. But when the message came, it was short.

That makes three of us.

Alana wondered at the delay in his response but then pushed it from her mind. She couldn't allow herself to start focusing on things that weren't obviously important. He said he was happy to be seeing them on Friday too, so she'd take him at his word.

She bit her lip as she stared at the small screen, trying to figure out what to type in reply. But before she could formulate a reply, another message popped up.

Must head for bed. Have to be up at 4 tomorrow morning. Sleep well & have a good day tomorrow.

Alana experienced equal parts relief and disappointment, but at least now she knew what to type. *Have a good night & stay safe!*

Despite having not even heard his voice, Alana found herself to be ridiculously giddy over their conversation. That he'd thought about her and texted to chat touched her more than she thought it would. And the feelings she had for the man swelled within her heart.

Please, God, let this be what's right for us both.

Once she'd put Caden to bed, Alana spent some time on her work and then browsed through the available apartments online. She kept one browser window open with the listings and another with a map so she could see where they were located. Even if they did have to rent a somewhat run-down place for the first few months, she hoped that come the fall when she was able to get a job, they'd be able to move into a better apartment in a nicer neighborhood.

Regardless of what may or may not happen with Justin, Alana needed to focus on taking care of Caden and herself. She'd accepted a lot of help already—more than she was really comfortable with—but at some point, she needed to stand on her own two feet once again.

But for the first time in a long time, she actually allowed herself to look beyond just a few months into the future. Looking into the future now meant considering that maybe she and Caden would have a man in their lives who would love and protect them. She wasn't interested in casual dating. If she was going to get involved with Justin, it meant she would be willing to marry him.

The thought sent a frisson of excitement up her spine, but it was quickly followed by a flash of fear. Marriage hadn't been the best thing in her experience. Would it be different with Justin? If that was even what he wanted...

They hadn't known each other all that long. Maybe it was too soon to even let thoughts like that enter her mind. But it was hard not to when she'd seen things in Justin that called to parts of her that she'd kept buried for so long. And images captured in her mind that she didn't think she'd ever forget. Like seeing Justin gather Caden into his arms when he found them at the motel. And pressing his fingers to Caden's to tell him he loved him.

As a young girl, all she dreamed of was finding someone who would love and care for her in a way no one had in her family. She'd thought—for a brief moment in time—that she'd found that with Craig. When she realized it was going to be nothing like she'd hoped, Alana had shoved those dreams deep down because dwelling on them hurt too much. Then she'd met Beth and Daniel and in them she'd seen what a real, loving relationship looked like. More than any other couple she'd worked with, they had let her into their lives, opening her eyes to possibilities that slowly drew her dreams to the surface again. It was very hard not to want to give Justin a starring role in those dreams.

Sifting through those images and feelings, Alana recalled Beth's concern that she might be attracted to Justin just because of how he treated her son. She really couldn't deny that was a big part of it. But there was also the thought that maybe Caden played a big part in Justin's feelings for her as well. Alana rubbed at the twinge of pain that went through her heart. She wanted him to want to be with her because of who she was, not just because she was Caden's mother. It was clear he loved her son, but would he come to love her as much?

Knowing she'd likely drive herself crazy trying to figure it out at this early point in things, Alana tried to focus on her work again. She had a couple of days yet before she'd see Justin, so there was no sense in making any assumptions until they actually spent some time together.

⸺◈⸺

By the time Friday rolled around, Justin hoped he'd make it through the evening without falling asleep. He was beat. Between training on things like the obstacle course, sparring and mock drills, his body had taken a beating. The members of the team were in excellent shape and pushed him farther than most teams that came to the BlackThorpe training compound. Usually, he would have enjoyed the challenge, but right then, he was just hoping to have enough energy to last the evening.

He took a quick shower—even though it had been tempting to linger under the hot water—then pulled on a pair of faded jeans and a black short-sleeve Henley, tucking it in before feeding his black leather belt through the loops on the jeans. Knowing he wouldn't be wearing his shoulder harness, Justin sank down on his bed to put on his socks before securing the ankle holster to his leg. He slid his gun into it then lowered the hem of his jeans. Grabbing his heavy-duty black watch from the nightstand, he fastened it as he got to his feet.

In the living room, Justin shoved his feet into a pair of black topsiders and grabbed his cell phone and keys from the counter along with the bag he'd packed the night before in anticipation of spending time with Caden. He was still attaching the cell phone case to his belt as he left his apartment. Beth had said supper would be at six, but at the rate he was going, he was going to be a few minutes late.

Hopefully, the traffic wouldn't be too bad since more people were heading out of the Twin Cities than into them on a Friday afternoon.

Before he pulled his truck out of its parking spot, Justin sent Beth a quick text to let her know he was running a bit behind. The twenty-minute drive gave him time to think about the evening ahead. He planned to spend time with Caden and Alana after supper. He'd brought his game console along with a couple of games he thought Caden might enjoy. Figuring Alana would want to put her son to bed herself, he hoped that once he was asleep, she'd be willing to go see a late movie with him. Though, when he'd originally come up with the plan, he hadn't known he'd be half dead with exhaustion.

Beth had agreed without hesitation to listen for Caden while he and Alana were out. He just hoped he didn't drift off during the movie...especially if she chose the romantic comedy that was showing at the theater he planned to take her to. And while a movie wasn't the best place to talk, Justin thought it would be a good start for the dates he hoped they'd have in the future. He didn't want to rush her, but he was surprised by the strength of the feelings he had for her already.

Justin could only hope she felt something for him as well. This could get awkward really fast if she didn't.

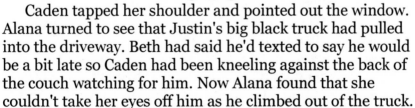

Caden tapped her shoulder and pointed out the window. Alana turned to see that Justin's big black truck had pulled into the driveway. Beth had said he'd texted to say he would be a bit late so Caden had been kneeling against the back of the couch watching for him. Now Alana found that she couldn't take her eyes off him as he climbed out of the truck.

He slammed the truck door then stood there with a bag in his hand as he stared across the cul-de-sac. With an abrupt turn, he opened the door to his truck and put the bag back inside. After shutting the door again, he made his way across the cul-de-sac. Alana's gaze followed him as he approached a woman with long curly blond hair who was wearing a business suit.

She watched as Justin held out his hand to the woman and then stood talking to her for a minute, his arms crossed over his chest. When she motioned to the house and began to walk toward it, Justin followed her. Alana frowned.

Caden tapped her on the shoulder. *Why is he going there, Mama?*

Alana just shrugged and shook her head. She didn't need any other sign to let him know she had no idea what Justin was doing.

"Is Justin here?" Beth asked from behind them.

Alana turned around. "Yes, he's here, but he went to a house across the street to talk to someone."

"What?" Beth leaned over the couch, bracing a hand on the back of it. "Which house?"

"The one with the stone front," Alana said as she pointed to where Justin and the woman had disappeared.

"Really? The one that's for sale?" Beth asked, a thread of excitement in her voice.

Alana looked more closely, realizing as she did that there was, in fact, a FOR SALE sign on the front lawn. From the angle they were looking at it, the sign hadn't been facing them so she hadn't realized it was there. "He's looking at a house that's for sale?"

"I guess so. I mentioned it to him last week and said he should look into it. He didn't say anything about having made arrangements to meet the realtor, though."

"What are you guys looking at?" Daniel's voice had the three of them turning from the window.

"Justin is here, but he went across to that house that's for sale," Beth explained to her husband as she reached to take Genevieve from him. "I think he's getting a tour of it."

Alana couldn't help the tendril of jealousy that wound its way through her. Even from a distance she had seen that the agent had been attractive. And she knew exactly how attractive Justin was. With one last glance out the window, Alana pressed a hand to her stomach and told herself to get it together.

First, she had no claim to Justin. They were still in those tentative steps of a relationship. It could go either way at this point. Second, she really didn't think Justin was the type of man to show interest in more than one woman at a time. For whatever reason—whether it was because of Caden or because of her or a bit of both—his attention was on her for the time being. And Alana was pretty sure that Justin would end things with her before moving on to another woman. The thought caused her stomach to clench, but she kept a firm grip on her emotions. Finally, the other woman could be married or involved with someone already. Alana was doing them both a disservice by assuming the worst.

Guess we can start putting the supper out since we know he's here. I'm guessing he won't take too long."

Beth pushed away from the couch, leaving Genevieve beside Caden peering out the window.

"What can I do to help?" Alana asked as she followed her friend into the kitchen.

By the time Justin strode in the door ten minutes later, everything was on the table ready to go. Alana was pouring water into the glasses when she heard him greet Caden and Genevieve. Her heart picked up speed as she waited for him to appear in the kitchen.

She wondered what he'd think of the outfit she'd chosen. The maxi dress had been among the clothes the women had bought for her. It was made of the lightest material that swirled around her as she walked, the hem of the dress brushing the tops of her feet. Pastel swirls of color painted the fabric of the dress. She wore a sheer soft pink long sleeve blouse over top of the dress. It gave her enough coverage to feel comfortable without being too hot.

Beth had insisted on treating her to a mani-pedi, so her nails were all beautifully shaped and covered with a light pink that complimented the colors of the dress. She'd even made use of the makeup someone had bought for her. The only things missing were some jewelry. Even though she hadn't had anything expensive, she'd picked up a few pieces over the years. Splurging on herself had seemed wrong but at Christmas last year she'd allowed Caden to pick out a necklace, bracelet and earring set for her. It hadn't been real gold, but to her it had been priceless.

She lifted a hand to her bare neck, mourning the loss of Caden's gift to her in the fire. And it left her without anything sparkly to wear. Still, even without the presence of any type of jewelry, the outfit made her feel feminine and almost pretty for the first time in way too long.

"Hey, Justin." Beth's greeting drew Alana's gaze to the doorway between the kitchen and the other room.

Justin bent to give his sister a hug, and Alana drank in the sight of him. In her mind, she remembered what he looked like, but every time she saw him again, he seemed to be even more attractive to her. When he turned in her direction and his blue eyes landed on her, a smile eased the harsh planes of his face.

19

"**H**I," JUSTIN SAID as he moved to the table, standing on the opposite side of her. "You look very pretty."

Alana felt the heat rise in her cheeks as she set the water pitcher on the table. Her other hand still rested on the base of her neck and her newly-free hand gathered the fabric of her dress into its grasp. "Thank you."

It had been so long since a man had complimented her, she wasn't entirely sure what else to say. Thankfully, Daniel joined them then with Caden and Genevieve.

"We ready to eat?" the man asked as he lifted his daughter into her high chair.

Feeling the vice-like tightness in her chest ease, Alana moved the water pitcher to the center of the table. She waited for Caden to slide into his chair before she sat down. They all settled into the chairs they'd sat in that very first night they'd met and had kept each time they'd eaten together since.

As she ate yet another delicious meal, Alana knew she was going to be gaining weight if they stayed there much longer. The conversation was mostly about things that Alana knew nothing about, but she listened with interest as Justin described the week he'd had with the team he was training with. Then Daniel shared a few things that had happened during his week as an FBI agent.

Whenever Justin spoke, Caden would watch him. She knew he was torn between watching Justin and wanting to know what he was saying which would mean he'd have to turn his attention to her. Maybe, one day, Justin would be fluent enough in sign language to be able to sign as he talked so Caden could be part of the conversation.

Maybe.

If this really did turn into something more serious between them.

"So you went to check out that house, Justin?" Beth asked as she added some more cut-up chicken to Genevieve's plate.

Justin's eyebrows rose slightly. "Maybe moving across the street from you isn't such a good idea after all. Would you be monitoring me?"

Beth laughed. "Nope. The only reason I knew was because Caden was watching for you."

"Yeah, I took a chance that the woman was the agent when I noticed her there when I pulled up. She'd just finished showing the place to someone else so was happy to let me have a look."

I'll bet she was happy to. Alana winced at the thought and immediately worked to shove it from her mind. It had been years since she'd felt jealousy over a man. In the beginning, she'd felt that way whenever Craig had showed another woman any type of attention. But later—once she'd realized that other women distracted him from hurting her—she'd welcomed his wandering attention.

"So did you like it?" Beth's question pulled her back from the detour into her past.

Justin shrugged. "It's big. Has a decent layout. Lots of space for me to set up a gym if I wanted to."

Beth groaned. "I didn't mention it was for sale so that you would buy it and turn it into a man-cave."

"Well, now I kinda like that idea," Daniel said with a grin at his wife.

"You guys," Beth said with a disgusted look. "I just thought it would be nice for you to be closer. You hardly ever go to your apartment. This place would be closer for you so maybe you'd actually go home at night instead of staying out at the compound all the time."

"The apartment at the compound is home, Beth," Justin said as he leaned back in his chair. "It's got everything that house has."

"Everything except room for..." Beth's gaze darted around the table. "Everything except room."

The conversation slipped to other things and soon they were clearing off the table.

Alana was setting a stack of dirty plates on the counter when Justin appeared at her side. "Is it okay if Caden plays some video games for a bit?"

"Sure, that would be fine. I think he'd like that."

With quick movements of her hands, she told Caden what Justin wanted. Seeing the way her son's face lit up helped ease the disappointment Alana had felt when she'd realized what Justin's plans for the evening were. She'd hoped that at the least it would involve all three of them or at the most, just the two of them. Instead, he'd planned an evening of video games...with her son.

Alana tried to keep an amicable look on her face as she helped Beth load the dishwasher even though her heart ached. She had hoped that maybe, finally, a man would want her just for her, but it seemed that once again, she wasn't enough. Maybe she never would be. She swallowed the lump of pain that lodged itself in her throat. She could do this. She would do this. Because being with Justin made Caden happy, and she'd do anything for him.

She transferred some cookies and brownies from a container Beth had given her onto a plate. Beth poured coffee into four mugs and put them on a tray along with cream and sugar.

"Let's go see what the boys are doing."

Alana followed Beth downstairs with the plate of dessert in her hands. She could hear Daniel and Justin ribbing each other over the noise of the game they were playing. As she stepped off the last step, her gaze went to the floor where the guys and Caden sat. Genevieve was actually in her dad's lap, Daniel's arms around her as he manipulated the controller in his hands. Caden sat between the guys, his gaze intent on the screen, unable to hear or participate in the good-natured smack talk.

She allowed herself to look briefly at Justin, her breath snagging in her lungs at the expression on his face. He looked more relaxed and at ease than she'd ever seen him. Seeing this side of him, this lighthearted, teasing side made her heart tumbled a little further into emotions and feelings she was scared to acknowledge.

Was God not listening to her prayers at all? Why had He allowed her to stumble into yet another situation that was sure to leave her heartbroken?

Beth settled onto the couch behind her husband, her hands lightly caressing his shoulders. Alana ignored the rest of the space beside her friend and sank into a chair to the side but still behind where the guys sat. Drawing her knees up, she tucked her skirt under her toes with one hand as she held the mug of hot coffee in her other. She took a sip as she stared at the bright colors on the television, her mind drifting away.

Her thoughts weren't coherent or focused on any one single thing. They just passed through her mind like tumbleweeds in the desert. It had been something she'd learned to do when she found her emotions spiraling out of control. She wasn't sure it was healthy, but until she was in a position to fully experience and work through her feelings, this was the next best thing. She forced her mind to jump from thought to thought.

Have I made the right decision to register Caden for school in the fall?

I hope that one of the apartments I plan to look at will be our new home.

Alana took another sip of her coffee, enjoying the warmth that eased its way down her throat.

I wonder what type of work I would enjoy.

Will anyone hire me when I have no degrees or real work experience?

Is it my turn to sign at church this Sunday?

Another sip of coffee. Another slide of warmth down to her belly.

What am I going to do for Caden's birthday?

"Alana?"

She blinked and turned her head toward Beth. "Hmmm?"

"Are you okay?" Her friend's brows were drawn together.

Alana realized it wasn't just Beth watching her. Daniel, Caden and Justin were all looking in her direction as well. Caden put his controller on the floor and got up. She lowered her legs as he approached and placed the mug on the table next to the chair. He crawled onto her lap, his green eyes wide with worry.

What's wrong, Mama?

Absolutely nothing that her son would understand, Alana realized. She slid her fingers into his curls and pressed a kiss to his forehead. Then she signed to him. *I'm just thinking about lots of things, sweetie. It's what moms do.*

Caden tilted his head. *Are you sure?*

Very sure. Are you having fun?

Her son's bright smile warmed her heart. *Yes. But I think they're letting me win.*

Alana buried her face in Caden's curls to muffle her laughter. No matter what else was going on inside her, this little boy was her heart and could make her smile like no one else.

Feeling a bit like her emotions were giving her whiplash, Alana let out a sigh when Caden slid from her lap and

returned to where he'd been sitting. He glanced over at her
with a grin as he picked up his controller.

Alana slipped her hands under her thighs and leaned
forward, trying to keep her attention on what was going on in
the room. She noticed that Justin had looked at his watch a
couple of times and wondered if he needed to leave. Easing
her phone from the pocket of her skirt, Alana checked the
time herself. It was past Caden's bedtime, so maybe it was
time for the evening to wind down.

Caden's disappointment was clear when she finally got
his attention and let him know it was time for bed. He stood
up and gave Daniel and then Justin a hug. Alana slipped an
arm around his shoulders and led him into the bedroom
while the guys cleaned up the game. Beth had disappeared
upstairs to put Genevieve down as well. Maybe a later
bedtime for the kids would mean they'd sleep in a bit in the
morning. One could always hope.

Caden wasn't in any rush to get to bed. He seemed to take
forever to brush his teeth and change into his pajamas.
Though it was a bit awkward, with their home-school year
done, Alana had been trying to read to him each night. They
were currently reading through the Chronicles of Narnia.
She'd bought the ebooks on his old tablet and had been able
to re-download them onto the new one. Caden would hold
his tablet so she could see the words and sign them for him.
She tried to be even more animated than normal as she read
about Aslan, Lucy, Peter, Susan, and Edmond.

Finally, he snuggled down under his covers, his eyelids
drooping. Alana bent over and brushed a kiss on his cheek.

"Love you, baby."

When she left the bedroom, she discovered the rec room
was empty and everything had been cleaned up. She listened
for any sort of movement from upstairs, but when she heard
nothing, Alana tried to keep her disappointment from
spreading. With a sigh, she returned to the room and quietly
picked up her laptop from where she'd left it earlier. She
might as well try to get some work done.

She also grabbed the earbuds that had come with her
phone so she could listen to some music. Caden knew to

come find her if he woke up. Telling herself to be grateful that her son had had such a great evening, Alana sat down on the couch with her legs crossed to support her laptop. She plugged the earbuds in and then slipped them into her ears. Once she'd loaded her YouTube playlist, she opened up her blog and began to work on the one for the next day.

She'd been working for about five minutes when someone moved into her line of sight beyond the laptop screen. Alana jerked in surprise, her leg almost kicking Justin where he'd lowered himself into a crouch in front of her. He moved quickly, however, and grabbed her before she made any contact, his fingers wrapping completely around her ankle. When he didn't release her foot right away, Alana pulled the earbuds from her ears.

"What are you doing?" Justin asked, his thumb stroking the skin on the inside of her ankle.

"Working. Uh...I thought you'd left."

His eyebrows rose before drawing down. "You thought I'd leave without saying goodbye?"

Her gaze dropped from his for a moment. That was exactly what she'd thought. "I realize it took me a little while to put Caden to bed."

He seemed to consider that before saying, "I had planned to take you out to see a late movie. Beth said she and Dan would stay down here to listen for Caden. Did you still want to go?"

Alana's heart skipped a beat. Not only had he not left, he had actually planned something for just the two of them. "Yes. I'd like that."

She slid the laptop from her lap onto the couch beside her and shut the lid. He gave her ankle a gentle squeeze before releasing it.

"If we leave now, we can still make the show," Justin said as he straightened.

"Let me just grab my purse and my shoes."

"I'll meet you upstairs."

She watched him walk away then snatched up her laptop and hurried to the bedroom. She put it on the dresser and found her sandals and purse. Unable to help herself, Alana took a quick detour into the bathroom to make sure her hair was okay and to swipe on a bit of the lip gloss the ladies had bought her. By the time she came out again, Beth and Daniel were settling on the couch with a big bowl of popcorn. Daniel had the remote in his hand.

"Have fun." Beth grinned at her. "And don't worry about anything here. If he wakes up and needs you, we'll send a text."

"Thank you," Alana said as she tried to keep her nerves under control. She went up the stairs and found Justin waiting by the front door.

"Ready to go?" Justin asked as she joined him.

She nodded, grasping the strap of her purse tightly. Justin opened the door and motioned for her to precede him out of the house. They walked in silence to his truck where he also opened the door for her and waited as she settled herself into the seat before closing it.

Since it was already after nine, the sun had pretty much disappeared, leaving only the gray of twilight behind. Alana couldn't remember the last time she'd been out so late, and it was going to be even later when she got home.

"Thank you for playing those video games with Caden earlier," she said as Justin backed his truck out of the driveway.

"To be honest, it was even more fun than I thought it would be. It's been awhile since I've done something like that."

"He thought you might be letting him win."

Justin glanced over at her. "Did he now?"

"Yep. Were you?"

"Well, here's the thing. I did tell Dan that we should take it easy on him at first, but that was before we realized that the kid needed absolutely no help in beating us."

"Really? I'm surprised he did so well since he doesn't have a machine to play on regularly. Or were you guys just that bad?"

Justin's chuckle took her by surprise. "Well, I am better with shooting games than I am driving Mario karts. Actually, though, while Dan and I probably aren't the most adept at that game, Caden more than held his own."

"He had a lot of fun and really, that's all that matters. I think he would have had just as much fun if he'd lost every race."

"I'm glad to hear it." Justin lapsed into silence for a bit then said, "What are some other things he might enjoy doing? Does he like to ride bikes or swim?"

Alana sighed. "He did enjoy those things but hasn't had much chance to do either in a couple of years. Once a month or so he goes to his friend's house and they have a pool so he swims there. But there wasn't really anywhere for him to ride a bike where we lived. I've taken him mini-golfing a couple of times, and he's enjoyed that."

"I haven't been mini-golfing in years," Justin commented. "That might be something fun for us to do."

"I'm not the greatest golfer," Alana admitted. "We usually just play the holes without keeping score."

Alana felt warmth spread through her. She just wanted to pinch herself to make sure she was really awake and not dreaming all of this. Loneliness over the past two years had filled her with a longing to one day have someone who understood that she and Caden were a package deal and would care for—maybe even love—them both. She found herself hoping with all her heart that Justin might be that someone.

"Definitely something worth looking into," Justin said. "I was going to give you a choice of movies tonight, but it looks like we'll miss getting there in time for the romantic comedy. I hope action adventure is okay with you."

Action adventure was more than okay with her. Romantic anything wouldn't have been her choice to watch, especially on a first date. "That's fine. I enjoy action adventure and, depending on the film, even sci-fi."

"Well, that's good. Beth had thought you'd want to see the romantic comedy. That sister of mine is into all the chick flicks and romantic stuff. I don't know how Dan watches movies with her."

"I'm guessing through his eyelids," Alana said with a laugh. "When I went upstairs the other night, Beth was watching some movie that was making her cry, but Daniel was asleep next to her on the couch."

They discussed movies they'd enjoyed for the rest of the trip. It sounded like Justin didn't go to the movies any more frequently than she did. When he pulled the truck to a stop in the parking lot outside the theater, he told her to wait then he got out of the truck and came around to open her door.

He held her hand as she slid out of the truck but released it once she was on her feet. She missed the warmth and strength of his grasp as they started toward the doors of the theater, but then she felt his hand land lightly on her back and decided that that was nice too.

Inside the theater, Justin bought them tickets and then moved her in the direction of the concession stand. "Do you want some popcorn?"

Her pause as she inhaled the scent of buttery goodness was obviously enough to convince him that she did indeed want the treat. She stood beside him as he ordered popcorn with extra butter and two drinks. Once he'd paid, he handed her the drinks and picked up the popcorn. Again his hand rested on her back just at her waist as he guided her to the theater where their movie was showing.

As they walked into the theater, Alana stared at the seats. They looked like recliners. Exactly how long had it been since she'd last been in a theater? Last time she'd gone they'd had nothing like this.

Since the movie had been out for a few weeks, there wasn't much of a crowd and they ended up being alone in their row. Once the movie started, they reclined their chairs. Alana drew up her legs and turned slightly in her seat to make room for the bucket of popcorn. Justin reached across periodically to grab a handful.

When several minutes had passed without him reaching for more, Alana glanced over at him, surprised to see his eyes were closed and his chest rose and fell in even breaths. As she thought back over their dinner conversation, she realized in all likelihood that he'd been up since early that morning. No wonder he was tired.

She set the popcorn on the empty seat next to her and then shifted so her head rested near his shoulder. His right arm lay on the divide between their seats while his left hand was on his abdomen. Before Alana could question the wisdom of such a move, she reached out and let her hand rest lightly on top of his. When his hand turned over, allowing their fingers to intertwine, she shot a look at him, but his eyes were still closed.

Deciding not to read anything into whether or not it was a conscious movement on Justin's part, Alana snuggled closer to the arm rest where their hands lay. She turned her attention to the action on the screen and found herself actually enjoying the movie for the next little while.

It didn't bother her at all that Justin had fallen asleep. She was actually touched that he'd been willing to let his day go so long just to spend some time with her. This week had been the first time she'd ever experienced people doing things for her because they wanted to. She'd always felt like anything her parents, siblings or even Craig had done for her had been from a sense of obligation or expectation.

Craig had always expected her to show off any gift he gave her. Maybe others thought the jewelry and nice clothes had meant Craig was a good husband who loved her, but Alana had known better. Those gifts had not been motivated by love for her. They had all been to make Craig look good. She would gladly have given it all up if he'd just showed her an ounce of affection or love. At least in the first couple of years of their marriage. By the time their third anniversary had rolled around, she didn't want anything from him but to be left alone.

Suddenly, she became aware of Justin's thumb stroking the back of her hand. Alana realized her grip had tightened as her thoughts had wandered to her past. She relaxed her fingers, darting a look at Justin. His eyes were open now, watching her instead of the action on the screen.

20

"SORRY," ALANA WHISPERED, not certain he could hear her over the movie, but when he gave her fingers a quick squeeze, she thought he might have. Now that he was awake, she started to straighten but when his grip on her hand tightened, she relaxed back, her shoulder brushing against his arm.

When the credits began to roll, Alana was pretty sure the good guys had won, but honestly, her nerves had kicked in again and distracted her from the last part of the movie. As they stood to leave, she waited for Justin to pull his hand from hers, but instead, he didn't release it until they reached his truck.

Alana struggled with the nerves fluttering in her stomach and the rush of emotion that holding hands with Justin brought to the surface. Had she ever held hands with someone the way she had with Justin? Oh, she'd held hands plenty with Caden, but it had always been about her keeping him close. This time around, it had felt like Justin was keeping her close to him.

"Sorry about drifting off in there," Justin said as he pulled the truck out into the late-night traffic.

"There's nothing to apologize for. I'm sure you've had a long day."

"I have. I just don't want you thinking it was because of the company."

"I didn't think that at all. I figured it had more to do with those super comfy seats."

Justin chuckled. "They were pretty amazing, weren't they? I haven't gone to a movie in...years, I think, so they were a surprise to me."

"Me, too."

"So in spite of my falling asleep, you had a good time?"

"A great time, Justin, thank you."

"Great enough that you might want to do it again sometime?"

Alana looked over at him just as he glanced her way. "Yes. I would like that."

"Good. I'd like that too."

By the time they pulled into the driveway at Beth and Daniel's, the nerves and emotions she'd been experiencing earlier had almost faded away. At Justin's request once again, she waited for him to open her door. He took her hand to help her out but didn't release it this time until they were inside the house.

Alana walked down the carpeted steps to the basement, Justin behind her. She came to an abrupt halt at the bottom of the stairs, glancing up at Justin before looking to where Daniel sat on the couch with Beth curled up in his lap, kissing her.

She was too embarrassed to interrupt them, but Justin clearly had no problem doing it. He grinned at her then cleared his throat.

"I think you've scandalized Alana," he said as Daniel helped Beth off his lap.

Daniel laughed. "No need for that. We were just kissing. We're allowed."

Alana had witnessed the affection of these two before and had actually appreciated seeing proof of how a real loving marriage should be. But somehow witnessing it with Justin at her side made it a bit more awkward.

"Caden was okay?" she asked as Beth leaned into her husband's side when Daniel slipped his arm around her.

"Never heard a peep out of him," her friend assured her.

"Well, we'll leave you two to say goodnight," Daniel said as he and Beth walked toward the stairs. "Justin, come up and see me before you go."

Justin stepped aside to let them pass him. "Will do."

Alana gripped her purse, the nerves from earlier were back in full force. She looked at Justin and found him watching her. "Thank you again for this evening. Both Caden and I really enjoyed it."

"I did too. I'll give you a call to set up something else."

Alana nodded. She watched as his gaze dropped to her lips momentarily and for a moment she thought he might kiss her. But instead he took a step back. She was equal parts disappointed and relieved—a feeling she was getting very familiar with. He seemed to understand that she needed this to move slowly. After all, they hadn't known each other all that long. Holding hands was about all she could handle right then.

He reached out and cupped her cheek, his thumb sweeping across her cheek. His features softened as he looked at her. "Sleep well."

She laid her hand on top of his and pressed her cheek against his palm. "You too. Drive safe."

He gave her a gentle smile before turning to climb the stairs to the main floor where Daniel waited to talk with him. Alana scooted into the bathroom and closed the door. She leaned back against it, pressing the palms of her hands against the smooth wood. Closing her eyes, she let out a long sigh. She couldn't remember the last time she'd felt this way. Even though she'd been nervous, being with Justin had also felt right. There had been no fear or anxiety that he'd suddenly turn on her. She'd felt...safe.

Relishing the warmth that spread through her at the thought, Alana went to the vanity and looked in the mirror. Her cheeks were flushed and her eyes were bright. She couldn't help but smile at herself. And the smile stuck even as she removed her makeup and brushed her teeth.

She pulled on a pair of leggings and a baggy T-shirt and quickly braided her hair before slipping between the sheets and curling on her side. Slowly the excitement of the evening mellowed and left her with a drowsy happiness.

Though Alana knew she should have worked on her blog, she pushed it out of her mind. She didn't publish it until later in the day anyway, so she'd tackle it in the morning. Right then she just wanted to savor the memory of her evening with Justin. For the first time in a long time, she had a feeling of hope and anticipation for the future.

Justin laid out the strips of bacon on the cookie sheet, keeping one eye on Caden as he made circles with the pancake batter on the griddle. When the oven signaled it was at the right temperature, he opened the door and slid the two cookies trays in. It certainly wasn't the way his mother used to make bacon, but he'd seen the women in the cafeteria at the compound do it this way and had asked them about it. He wasn't the world's greatest cook, but he had a pretty good handle on the breakfast menu.

Caden glanced over at him once he'd finished pouring the last pancake. Justin smiled and gave him a thumb's up. The boy was a quick learner and now on this second batch, he already had the circles looking nearly perfect. He picked up the spatula and with careful movements lifted the edge of a pancake to check it just like Justin had showed him.

He hadn't planned to still be at Dan and Beth's this morning, but when Dan had offered him a place to crash the night before, he had been too tired to turn him down. Unfortunately, his internal alarm clock had still had him up at six o'clock, so after spending some time on his phone reading email, he'd decided to make breakfast for the household.

He'd been in the middle of pulling out the ingredients to make the pancakes when he'd spotted Caden watching him from the doorway, his tablet clutched to his chest. He had waved him over and after a short conversation on the tablet, he'd scored himself a helper. They made quite a pair—Caden dressed in Spiderman pajamas and him wearing a pair of long, athletic shorts from Dan and one of his tank tops that read *Keep Calm and Love Your FBI Agent* across the front. He hadn't even realized what it said until after Dan had disappeared into the master bedroom. He didn't doubt that Dan had had a good chuckle at his expense.

The shirt revealed his tattoos, and Caden's eyes had gone wide when he'd first seen them. Justin had stooped down to his level so the boy could see them more closely. He'd traced his finger along the black ink, curiosity clear on his face. When he'd asked what they meant, Justin had taken the time to type out what each tattoo represented to him. Now he had to hope Caden didn't go asking Alana for a tattoo. He could only imagine her reaction to that.

He moved to stand next to Caden as the boy carefully flipped each pancake. They were a perfect golden brown. The kid was a natural. This time he gave him two thumbs up. Justin was glad that some signs were universal. He still had a long ways to go before he'd be able to communicate with Caden without having to use the tablet, but he had a stronger motivation than ever now. In the coming years, he wanted to be able to talk with not just Genevieve but Caden as well.

He'd just closed the fridge with an egg carton in his hand when Alana appeared in the doorway of the kitchen. Justin froze in place at the worried look on her face. It eased slightly when she spotted her son, but then her gaze jerked to him, her green eyes going wide.

"Good morning," Justin said as he carried the eggs to the counter. "Hungry?"

He watched as she moved a little further into the kitchen. She looked like she'd rolled right out of bed and come in search of Caden. Some of her hair had come loose from her braid and framed her faces in curls. Her cheeks were flushed and one sported a couple of creases. The outfit she wore was similar to what she'd been wearing the day they'd found her and Caden after the fire.

His stomach knotted at the memory of that day, but then it eased as he reminded himself that they were safe. The reality was that the fire had brought about a shift in things between them, and though Justin felt bad about the damage and loss of life it had caused, he didn't regret that it had facilitated the closeness now growing between him and Alana.

Alana walked to the other side of the counter and watched as Caden began to pour more pancake batter after having moved the cooked pancakes onto the platter next to the griddle. "I didn't realize you were staying the night."

"It wasn't the plan—hence the shirt—but when Dan offered, I was just tired enough to take him up on it."

Her gaze went to the front of his tank top and a smile curved the corners of her mouth. But instead of commenting on it, she just said, "I see Caden has been helping you out."

Justin nodded. "And doing a terrific job."

Alana signed to her son, and he set the spatula down before signing back to her. The proud look on Caden's face was mirrored on his mother's. As he watched them together, Justin was struck again by how much these two were a team. Caden's devotion to his mother was clear, and he already knew that Alana always put Caden's well-being before her own. Was there a place for him in their relationship?

In some ways, his relationship with Caden was stronger than the one he had with Alana, but if he wanted any chance of a future with the three of them together, he needed to change that. If their date the previous night was any indication, they were well on their way. Feeling her hand settle over his had been a surprise. He'd been dozing, his body finding the comfort of those reclining seats just a bit too enticing, but at her touch he hadn't been able to resist turning his hand to intertwine his fingers with hers. He couldn't remember the last time he'd enjoyed holding hands with someone as much as he had with Alana. He hoped the opportunity arose again soon.

Normally, he was focused on his job at BlackThorpe. If he wasn't in the midst of training with a team, he was planning for the next team that would be arriving. In the midst of it all, he worked with the wounded veterans and BlackThorpe employees like Trent and Than, who liked to spar with him. But right then, standing in Beth's kitchen with a little boy on a stool flipping pancakes while he prepped eggs to scramble, his job at BlackThorpe was the furthest thing from his mind.

"Well, I'm going to invite you to stay overnight more often if this is what I wake up to."

Justin glanced over to see Dan walk in with Genevieve in his arms. Like Alana, the little girl's curls were a tousled mess and her cheeks were still flushed from sleep. She smiled when she saw him and his love for her washed over him. She had been the first person aside from Beth who had breached the walls he'd kept around his heart. Once she'd gotten through, it was that much easier for Caden and Alana to follow.

"Where's Beth?" Justin asked as he worked the eggs in the pan.

"I'm letting her sleep in a bit." Dan sniffed the air appreciatively. "The smell of bacon got to me just before Genevieve woke up."

"It should all be ready shortly."

Over the next few minutes, Alana and Dan set the table while Justin and Caden finished up the food.

"If I were on a diet, heads would be rolling."

Justin glanced over at the sound of his sister's voice. Still dressed in her pajamas, she sauntered to his side and peered into the pan.

"I thought Dan was letting you sleep in."

She put her hands on her hips and glared at him for all of two seconds. "Do you honestly think I could sleep with that smell tantalizing me?"

"Well, let's eat up," Dan said as he buckled Genevieve into her seat.

Easy conversation flowed around the table as they consumed the breakfast he and Caden had made. The boy glowed with pleasure each time someone told him—through Alana—how wonderful the pancakes were. As he thought of all Alana and Caden had gone through, Justin came to understand what a truly amazing job Alana had done of raising her son. He could still see the remnants of the abusive relationship she'd been in through her tentative approach with him and her initial reluctance to depend on anyone but herself.

Slowly, though, he was seeing that change, and he hoped she would continue to become more confident in herself. And he really hoped he was around to see it.

Once Alana had gotten over her shock of not only finding Justin still there the morning after their date, but also that he was letting Caden help him with breakfast, she enjoyed the breakfast they'd prepared. It felt...normal for the six of them to be there.

Beth had already made it clear she thought Alana and Justin would be good together and for the first time, Alana was feeling confident about that as well.

After the breakfast was done, Beth and Daniel had insisted they would clean up since Justin and Caden had made the meal. Alana had tried to help as well, but Beth had shooed her out of the kitchen and told her to go downstairs with Justin and Caden.

She found the two of them setting up another video game. Leaving them to play, Alana went to change. When she got a look at herself in the mirror, she frowned. Her hair was an out-of-control curly mess around her face and she was still in her pajamas. How she looked had been the last thing on her mind when she'd woken to find Caden gone from the bed and not in the basement.

Working quickly, she rebraided her hair and smoothed back the flyaway ends before putting on just a bit of eyeshadow and mascara since she'd always been told her eyes were her best feature. Back in the bedroom she chose a pair of jeans and a long-sleeve lightweight shirt.

She picked up her laptop and went out to where Justin and Caden were playing their video game. Settling on the couch, she opened the laptop so she could finish her blog post for the day.

Alana had just hit the save button when she saw Justin glance at his watch then over at her as he set his controller down. "I'm going to have to leave soon. I agreed to meet a couple people to work out this afternoon."

Caden looked at her, and when Alana quickly signed that Justin had to go, he didn't bother to hide his disappointment.

"We'll do it again," Justin said as he got to his feet. He held out his hand, knuckles up and though his little shoulders were slumped, Caden bumped fists with him.

Alana's heart ached just a little to see her son disappointed, but he would have to get used to Justin leaving and most likely being away for several days at a time. Alana knew he was devoted to his job so she figured it might be the next weekend before they saw him again. She was as disappointed as Caden, but she was old enough to understand their situation in a way that her seven-year-old son couldn't.

"I'm just going to go get changed," Justin said as he headed for the stairs.

Alana slid her laptop off her lap when Caden sat down on the couch next to her, cuddling close. She pulled him onto her lap so that he straddled her knees. Face to face, she was able to sign to him, trying to explain why Justin was leaving.

Why can't he stay here like we do?

Oh, to believe that all life's problems could be solved so easily. In the mind of a seven-year-old, apparently they could.

Justin doesn't live here. He has his own apartment and pretty soon we will too.

Can't we just live with him at his apartment?

Alana shook her head. *No. We need to have our own apartment.*

We're not going to stay here?

Alana was sure they'd discussed the fact that they needed to find their own place. He looked at her, his green eyes worried and a bit sad. She didn't want that for him, but he was asking for things she just couldn't give him. There was no way she could guarantee that one day he'd have Justin in his life the way he wanted. And as nice as it was to live in Beth and Daniel's basement, she couldn't do it indefinitely.

We're going to look at apartments next week.

He scowled, and Alana let out a sigh. It wasn't very often he copped an attitude so she supposed he was due, but it was still difficult to know that the decisions she was making for them upset him. And it was even harder when she knew that his heart was now firmly engaged with not only Justin but Beth, Daniel and Genevieve as well. She never spoke of the family they had but who had rejected them—his grandparents and aunt and uncle—but Caden still knew what he wanted and that was a family, if not by blood, by choice.

She lifted her hand with the *I love you* sign and waited for him to respond. His lower lip poked out a bit and his shoulders slumped, but he lifted his hand and pressed his fingers to hers. Then he sank against her, resting his head on her shoulder and pressing his face against her neck.

Alana wrapped her arms around him, closed her eyes and began to hum knowing he could feel the vibration against his face. They didn't sit this way as often as they used to. When he was a baby, she would hold him with his cheek pressed into the side of her neck so she could hum and sing and he would feel it. Now he only sought her out for that when he was feeling upset or sad.

"Everything okay?" Justin's voice jerked her back, and her eyes popped open. He stood a few feet away, now dressed in the same clothes he'd worn the night before. His hands were on his hips as he stared down at them, his brows drawn together. "Is he okay?"

Alana gave him what she hoped was a reassuring smile. There was no way she was going to repeat the conversation she'd just had with Caden. "He's a little sad his video game time is over."

Justin cocked his head. "He can still play video games even without Dan or I here. I'm leaving my system for him to use."

"I'll be sure and tell him that. I might even take a turn or two with him."

Justin's gaze was still on Caden. "Are you sure he's okay?"

Alana nudged her son and pulled her head back to look down at him. His eyes opened, and he straightened. She quickly signed to let him know Justin was leaving. Alana half expected him to jump off her lap and go hug the man, but instead, Caden just waved to him and settled back down against her. She could tell by the look on Justin's face, he was confused by Caden's reaction.

"I'm afraid he's not too happy you're leaving," Alana told him, deciding to clarify things for Justin. She gave him a rueful smile. "He misses you when you're gone."

Justin dropped to his haunches by her legs and laid a hand on Caden's back. When Caden turned to look at him, Justin held out his arms. Without hesitation, her son wrapped his arms around Justin's neck and allowed the man to stand with him. After a minute, Justin lowered him back to Alana's lap and then ran his hand across Caden's hair.

He cleared his throat and looked back at her. "My week is pretty busy with the team that's at the compound for training, but I'll try to call you to set something up."

Alana nodded, though she hoped maybe he'd also call just...because. She knew his job was important to him, just like Daniel's was to him, and yet Daniel always made time for his girls, as he called them. If Justin felt she and Caden were important enough, he'd make the time for them too. But she understood it might take time for him to come to that realization. And then he'd have to decide what to do about it.

After saying goodbye, Justin headed up the stairs. Alana watched his long legs take him from view. Things had seemed to be going so well, but she was feeling the weight of her son's expectations of his own relationship with Justin. She could understand and accept things that Caden couldn't. Unfortunately, he was going to have to learn how to accept that this relationship was going to move at a slower pace than he wanted.

Over the next several days, Alana worked hard at several freelance writing jobs she'd picked up. Thankfully, there was a small park near Beth's house and she would take her laptop and work while Caden played. The sunshine was good for him, and he never seemed to tire of swinging and sliding. Sometimes there were other children there, but often it was just the two of them. Sometimes she brought Genevieve with them or Beth would come along, but usually it was just her and Caden.

By Wednesday, she was anxious to turn in the biggest of the freelance jobs she'd done. If they paid promptly, she'd have more than enough money for another apartment. She'd made a list of places to look at, and she had phoned and made appointments to go on Saturday to see three that looked promising.

There had been no call from Justin though Alana knew he'd spoken with Beth when she'd mentioned he wouldn't be coming for dinner Monday night. She'd done her best to keep Caden occupied with countless races on his favorite video game. They'd finished the Narnia book they'd been on and started the next one. And they'd spent hours at the park each day.

Caden had asked about Justin the first couple of days, but then he seemed to realize that the answer was going to be the same each time. Justin had told her that the week would be busy, but Alana had thought he'd at least text. After all, he'd been able to do that the previous week when he'd been busy. And he *had* found the time to phone Beth. Maybe it was just going to be too much for him. Juggling a busy career with a relationship that included two people not just one. Sometimes even when something seemed doable or even desired, in the end it just didn't work.

Or maybe she was just expecting too much too soon? What did she know about how relationships were supposed to work? She hadn't had anything like this before. But if Justin was, in fact, realizing this relationship wouldn't fit into his life, it was better that he realize it now before things got serious.

Although, who was she kidding? In her and Caden's minds, things were already serious.

Thursday when she checked her freelance account, Alana was excited to see that the payment had been made through a payment site. She quickly logged in and had the money sent to her bank account. Finally, she felt like she was going to be able to get her life back. She was so thankful for what Beth and Daniel had done for her, but they needed their life back too. The one without a needy pair living in their basement and eating their food. She didn't know if she'd ever be able to repay them, but she hoped someday she could.

In the meantime, finding a place of their own would be the first step in getting things back to the way they'd been before.

When Saturday morning rolled around, she made sure she and Caden were up early and ready to go. Beth looked at them in surprise when they came upstairs.

"Heading out?"

"Yes. I've got some errands to run so we'll be gone most the day."

Beth stared at her. "You weren't planning to go to Trent and Victoria's wedding?"

"That's today?" Alana hesitated. "Uh, I wasn't invited."

Beth frowned. "You weren't?"

Alana wasn't about to tell her that Victoria had told her to come as Justin's plus one. She would have only done that at Justin's request...and she hadn't received that. And she wasn't confident enough in either her relationship with Justin or her friendship with Victoria to just show up. "I really don't know them that well."

"I still think they'd be happy to see you there. Victoria said it was a casual wedding."

"I've already kind of made some plans for today." Alana smiled, hoping Beth would see she was okay with it. "You can tell me all about it later. Take some pictures! And give my congratulations to the happy couple."

Beth still looked a bit unsettled as she said goodbye. Alana breathed a sigh of relief once they left the house. It took a little while, but her excitement for the day returned when they got off the bus not far from the first apartment, and it seemed to be catching as Caden skipped along beside her as they walked hand in hand along the sidewalk.

Justin couldn't believe he'd forgotten about Trent and Victoria's wedding. It had been one of those weeks where he questioned why he didn't delegate more. But right then he needed to get himself changed into something more than jeans and a T-shirt. Since the invitation said casual, he hoped the black pants and button down light blue shirt would be good enough. There was no way he was pulling out his one and only suit. He'd worn it to Eric's wedding and then shoved it back into the closet where, as far as he was concerned, it could stay.

He was anxious to see Alana and Caden. Trent said Victoria had invited her, so they'd be there along with Beth and Daniel.

Doubts pricked at him as he threaded his belt through the loops on his pants. Would Alana be upset that he hadn't contacted her through the week? He'd dropped the ball on that. No doubt about it. And what excuse could he give that didn't sound like a cop-out? Truth be told, he'd been a little...scared after he'd said goodbye to Caden and Alana last Saturday. Seeing Caden upset because he was leaving really brought home the seriousness of the situation. This wasn't a game. Wasn't a casual fling. No matter what his and Alana's thoughts might be about the direction of their relationship, Caden had a long-term plan for Justin in his life.

Justin adjusted the collar of his shirt as he stood in front of the mirror. He scowled at his reflection, suddenly wishing he had a do-over for the week. He hated the thought of letting anyone down—least of all a kid who had dealt with so much in his life already. And while he wasn't one to admit to fearing much, the thought of letting Caden down did scare him a bit. What if he couldn't live up to the boy's expectations?

And Alana... She'd already been let down in such a big way when it came to men. And now he'd let her down too. Oh, no doubt she accepted it because she likely didn't think she deserved better, but she did.

He ran a hand through his hair. One week into the relationship and he'd already screwed up. Big time. He hadn't contacted her the first couple of days because he truly had been crazy busy. At the end of the long days of training, he'd come back to the apartment and crashed. Literally, taking a shower and falling into bed. Excuses aside, he had to make this up to Alana. To both of them.

Justin left the bedroom and grabbed his keys and cellphone from the counter where he'd left them earlier. He sure hoped that the reception included a big meal. He was starving and with the wedding starting at six, he didn't really have time to eat anything beforehand. The thought of going through the drive-thru on the way to the ceremony was enticing, but he was already running later than he should be.

He left the BlackThorpe compound feeling a bit like he was a day late and a dollar short on a few fronts in his life right then. Not used to that out-of-control feeling, he had a burning need to get everything back on solid ground. Hopefully, step one would be seeing Alana and Caden at the wedding.

Justin let out a quick breath when he finally pulled his truck into the driveway of the Hamilton mansion shortly before six. Apparently Lucas and Brooke had let Trent and Victoria hold their small wedding in the large backyard. There was a smattering of cars, but nothing like the number that had been present for Victoria's brother, Eric's wedding. He spotted Beth and Daniel's SUV as he strode toward the walk that led to the back of the house.

As Justin rounded the corner of the house, he ran into Than. The man was all smiles every time Justin saw him these days. Ever since Lindsay had put him out of his misery and agreed to give him a second chance. Than had also been a good listening ear when Justin had shared a bit about what was going on with Alana and Caden. The man definitely had more experience in dealing with women than he did.

"Alana's not with you?" Than asked as they shook hands.

Justin frowned. "She's not with Beth and Dan?"

"Not that I saw."

He looked past Than to the people in the backyard, his gaze searching for Alana or Beth. "I'm going to have to figure out what's going on. Talk to you later."

Justin strode across the perfectly mowed lawn in search of his sister. When he spotted her and Dan talking with Eric and Staci, Justin changed direction to join them.

"Hey, Justin," Beth said as she slid an arm around his waist and gave him a hug. "I was beginning to wonder if you were going to make it."

"Where's Alana?" he asked, his gaze still scanning the crowd.

"Um...she and Caden left the house this morning to run some errands."

"She didn't plan to come to the wedding?"

"She said she wasn't invited," Beth said, her voice so low Justin had to bend down to hear her.

"But Trent said that she was."

Beth shrugged. "I don't know what's going on. All I know is that she came upstairs with Caden and said they had some errands to run and would probably be gone most the day."

A pit opened in the bottom of Justin's stomach. How much more messed up could this get? When Trent had reminded him at the beginning of the week about the wedding and mentioned that Alana had been invited as well, Justin had felt a sense of relief in knowing that even if his schedule kept him away from her during the week, he'd see her again on the weekend. Of course, the training during the week had pushed everything about the wedding from his mind yet again, so it was only because of Trent's call earlier that day that he was there.

"Where's Genevieve?" Justin asked as they settled into folding chairs that had been set up. There weren't a lot of them, but there were more than Justin had anticipated when Trent had said it was going to be a small wedding.

"She's staying with Emily tonight. She wanted to have her for a sleepover."

"Does she know sign language?" Justin asked as the gentle sounds of a string quartet began to play.

"She's learning too. Someone at the senior's center she goes to mentioned that they knew it so she decided to learn from them instead of with us."

Justin pulled his phone from the holder at his waist and before he could think too much about it, he tapped out a message to Alana...something he should clearly have done earlier.

Everything okay with you and Caden?

There were still people milling around, so Justin hoped he had enough time for a quick conversation with Alana before the ceremony got underway. The minutes ticked by without a response, and Justin had just about given up on getting one when a message flashed on his screen.

Everything is great. We had a good day together out running errands. Another message came on the heels of that one. *How have you been?*

Though he wanted to question her about the wedding, he couldn't very well ignore her question. *Super busy. This team is one of the best. We've been running through lots of training exercises and scenarios. And they've decided to stay one more week.*

Sounds exhausting.

The change to the music had Justin lifting his head. He spotted Sarah, Eric's daughter, and Danny, Brooke's son, beginning to make their way down the aisle. Knowing he couldn't continue to text now that the wedding was starting, he sent one last text.

It is very exhausting. I need to go now. I'll talk to you later.

Okay.

Justin stared at the one-word reply and felt uneasy. The situation was just getting worse and worse. Something told him making contact with her like this only to have to abruptly shut it down had done more harm than good.

Maybe he'd been wrong to think he could juggle a relationship with Alana and still be able to do his job. That had been the downfall of his last relationship. Maybe it was just him. After all, he had plenty of examples of people who juggled busy careers with family.

21

JUSTIN LET OUT a puff of air and tried to focus on the wedding. Brooke passed the end of their row, followed by another young woman. Both of them joined Trent at the front where he stood beside Eric and the minister. When he spotted Victoria coming down the aisle on her dad's arm, Justin couldn't keep his lips from turning up. She was radiant with her gaze fixed on Trent, a beaming smile on her face.

He remembered the first time Trent had brought Victoria to the compound to learn to shoot. Though she was a little person, her determination to be able to learn hadn't been daunted at all by her lack of height. Trent had given her the opportunity to learn, and she had tackled it and excelled at it.

As he watched, Mr. McKinley stooped to kiss his daughter on the cheek before giving her hand to Trent. The minister then welcomed them and spoke a bit about Trent and

Victoria and offered them thoughts about marriage. Justin had never really paid a whole lot of attention to this part of the weddings he'd attended in the past. Mostly he was just biding his time until the reception where he could relax and enjoy some good food.

This time Justin couldn't—and didn't even bother to try to—block out the minister's words as he spoke to Trent and Victoria.

"The Bible talks about the two becoming one. Of a man loving his wife as he loves himself. And of a woman submitting to her husband. People like to look at each of those things individually when, in fact, they all tie together. Some people don't like the submitting part and want to reject that, but in a truly God-honoring marriage, all of the pieces must be put in place. The best way to make sure that happens is to give God first place in your life and then make each other a priority. A relationship cannot grow and flourish when you don't make it a priority and that's true of your relationship with God *and* your relationship with your spouse.

"In the busyness of life, it's easy to put your relationship last on the long list of things to do, assuming it will still be there when you have the time. That may work for a short time, but if it drags on too long, it will almost guarantee that you'll begin leading separate lives when you are supposed to be one. So take the time—make the time—to connect with each other on a daily basis. Pray together. Talk to one another. Be affectionate with each other. In this day and age, there's really no reason you can't be in contact during your day."

Justin winced and dropped his gaze to his phone where it still rested in his hands. He wasn't married to Alana, so maybe the daily contact wasn't necessary, but he really should have tried harder to reach out at least once every couple of days. But also he'd done what he always did when it came to his job. He immersed himself in it. That was the way he'd always worked.

And nothing had ever tempted him to change that...until now.

"Alana didn't make it?" Victoria asked a short time later when she came to the table where Justin sat with Beth and Dan and some other BlackThorpe employees.

Justin glanced at Beth and then looked at the bride. "She told Beth she wasn't invited."

Victoria frowned. "Well, I guess that's technically true. When I mentioned it to her, I told her she should come as your plus-one."

Justin's eyebrows rose. "My plus-one?"

"Yeah, you know. Come as your date." Victoria sighed. "Guess I should have told you that too, eh?"

"Possibly. Although, to be honest, I should have thought of it myself."

Victoria tilted her head, a smile teasing the corners of her lips. "So is there actually something between the two of you? Alana kind of brushed me off when I suggested that the day we met at the compound."

Justin drew circles on the tablecloth. "We're getting to know each other a little better."

Trent laid a hand on his shoulder. "We'll be praying that you'll both find God's will in your lives."

As Trent and Victoria moved on to talk to some of their other guests, Justin contemplated Trent's parting comment. It was an odd way to put it, almost as if Trent wasn't sure that it would be God's will for them to be together. On the guy's wedding day, Justin had expected a more romantic comment. Like how great it was to find the person who completed him. Or how blessed he was to have found the woman God had planned for him. Did Trent doubt Justin's ability to find the balance he'd clearly been able to reach between his job and Victoria?

Well, now that did nothing to appease his own worries on the subject. Maybe he really wasn't cut out to be more than just a friend and the best employee BlackThorpe had ever had. So what did he do about what he'd started with Alana?

Was it too late to take it back to the friendship they'd had before he opened the door to what he'd thought he could handle but apparently couldn't? Or was that just a cop out?

Maybe their relationship wouldn't be easy, but that didn't mean it wasn't what God wanted for them. And it didn't mean it couldn't be good. Hard work had never scared him when it came to his job. He just needed to keep that in mind for a relationship too.

Justin shifted on his seat as he grappled with the mess of thoughts and feelings that spun through his mind. He listened as toasts were made. Watched as the bride and groom kissed...several times. And through it all he questioned if he had the ability to be the man Alana needed him to be. Oh, he knew he'd never hurt her the way her ex had, but there were others ways of hurting that could be worse than physical.

The thought of hurting her or Caden made him feel sick. He rubbed his finger across his forehead. In considering a relationship with Alana, he wasn't just committing to the possible role of husband but also that of father. Two people to let down. Two people to disappoint if he couldn't manage to find that necessary balance between his job and a family.

"Are you okay?" Beth's soft words brushed across him. She laid her hand on his arm and gave it a squeeze. More than anyone, she would understand the struggle he was having.

Once she and Dan had married and Justin's role as guardian/parent had ended, he'd thrown himself even more into his job. She'd seen what was happening and had been after him to pull back and hand over some of his responsibilities so that he could have a life outside of BlackThorpe. He tried to do as she suggested, had even gone so far as dating someone, but even scaling back some of his work hadn't been enough for her. The woman had told him she felt like a mistress that he fit in when his "wife" didn't need him. That idea left him with a bad taste in his mouth, but not enough to try to change more for her. It had been easier to just let her go.

He supposed that was the question he had to ask himself. Was it easier to just let Alana and Caden go than to do what he had to to change his devotion to his job? The unfortunate thing was that he couldn't make any changes until this next week was done, regardless. He had committed to working with this team personally, and they still had one more week to go. Maybe he'd just have to talk to Alana and let her know that he needed another week and then he'd be making some changes.

He just hoped he'd be able to follow through. For sure he wouldn't be able to do it on his own. That was difficult to come to terms with as well. Control had always been important to him. Perhaps what had happened with Genevieve and now Alana and Caden was God's way of showing him who really was in control. Something told him that trying to keep that control would only lead to more stress than he was currently feeling.

Justin followed Beth and Dan home once the reception had ended. By the time they pulled into their driveway, it was almost ten o'clock. He hoped Alana would still be up, but the sight of the darkened basement dashed those hopes.

"Do you want me to go see if she's still awake?" Beth offered. "She might just be in the room with Caden?"

Justin shook his head. "No. I don't want to bother her if she's ready for bed. I'll talk to her tomorrow."

Beth's gaze went to the darkened basement then came back to him. "You need to make some time to talk to her. Really talk. Not go to a movie or even out for dinner where you can't have a decent conversation."

Justin ran a hand through his hair. Beth was right, of course. She'd figured out the relationship stuff much better than he ever had. Ten years younger than him and she already had a healthy marriage to a man who loved her and their beautiful daughter.

What did he have? He stared down at his bare, empty hands. Nothing. That's what he had. Yes, he had a job that paid well and gave him a certain amount of fulfillment. But the money from the job just piled up in his bank account because he had nothing aside from a few toys—like his truck and weapons.

"I'd better go." Justin turned and reached for the door handle. Before Beth could say anything more, he twisted the knob and walked out into the dark night. Alone.

Ever since that horrible night when his commanding officer had told him what had happened to his family and everything had spun out of control, Justin had prided himself on having brought everything back under his control. Beth's life—until she'd married Daniel. His own life. And certainly his emotions.

But as he climbed behind the wheel of his truck and headed back to the compound, Justin had to finally admit that since the day he'd walked into Beth's house and seen Alana and Caden and had heard the news about Genevieve, his life had once again spiraled out of his control. His emotions were much too near the surface, and he hated that more than anything. How could he be confident in his ability to make quick decisions and deal with the tough stuff if he allowed those emotions to surface?

He wasn't a soft man. Nor was he a gentle one. But he couldn't have proved that in his dealings with Alana and Caden. They called to a part of him that he'd thought was long gone. Except that wasn't entirely true, he reminded himself. He'd dealt with Beth and Genevieve with that gentleness, but they were family. He loved them.

His heart sputtered to a stop and then started up again at a galloping pace. The "L" word tended to do that to him. Surely just because he also felt the need to treat Alana and Caden with that same gentleness didn't mean he loved them. Only...

His hands tightened on the steering wheel as he remembered Caden holding up his hand with his two middle fingers bent down. And he'd known what it said when he'd pressed his fingers against the little boy's. And he'd meant it. But Caden's demands on him were easily managed. What he didn't know was if he could meet the ones Alana would have for him. Those perfectly normal demands within a relationship between two people.

By the time he pulled into the compound, Justin hadn't figured out any answers. He wanted Alana and Caden in his life, but rising to the surface was his fear that when all was said and done, he wouldn't be able to give them what they needed. Alana hadn't escaped from one man who treated her poorly to end up with one who wasn't able to give her the time and attention she deserved.

If he'd been smart, he would have waited until this team was finished up before making his move. But no, he'd stepped right into the middle of it during one of the longest and most stressful training sessions he'd had in a long time, and he still had one more week to get through.

The next morning, Alana and Caden were up early and went upstairs to make some breakfast before church. She'd brought home some groceries the night before because she felt bad that they had eaten so much of Beth and Daniel's food. What she bought wasn't as much as she would have liked, but between needing to make sure she still had enough money for an apartment and not being able to carry much on the bus, it had ended up being only a couple of bags.

They'd finished cooking the bacon and scrambled eggs just a few minutes before Daniel put in an appearance.

"Smells delicious, guys," he said with a smile. He wore a pair of gray pleated slacks and a dark blue button down short sleeve shirt. "How did your day go yesterday? Beth mentioned you had some errands to run?"

Alana smiled at him as she slid some eggs onto a plate with several strips of bacon. She pushed the plate across the counter toward him and then laid a fork alongside it. "It was good. I think we've found an apartment. It's in a better neighborhood than the other one and will be closer to the school I hope to send Caden to in the fall."

Daniel settled on the stool, a frown on his face. "You've been looking for an apartment?"

"Well, yes. I didn't expect to continue to live here with you guys indefinitely. I can't even begin to thank you for being so generous in offering us a place to stay, but I'm sure you'd like to have your life back."

He took a bite of the scrambled eggs and seemed to take the time while he chewed to consider his response. "We never lost our life with you and Caden moving in here. You have been the perfect house guests, and I know Genevieve has loved having Caden around to play with. We're in no rush to have you leave. Are you sure you're in a good place financially to do this? I think I speak for Beth too when I say that we don't want you to feel you need to rush to leave us." Daniel paused then said, "Have you talked to Justin about this?"

Alana dropped her gaze to the pan and pushed the scrambled eggs around. "I'm not sure why I would have. Yesterday was the first time I'd heard from him since last Saturday. I'm sure he has a lot going on. He doesn't need me talking to him about stuff like this."

She felt an arm around her waist and knew without glancing over that it was Beth.

"What Daniel said is exactly right." After giving Alana a quick squeeze, Beth went to stand beside her husband. "Having you here hasn't inconvenienced us at all. If anything, it's been a good thing. We're probably learning sign language faster than we would have since Caden being here helps us too."

Alana dished up a plate for Beth, keeping her gaze on the food. "I just feel like you've done so much for us already. I'm not used to relying on people."

When neither of them replied, Alana looked up to find them both watching her. Beth smiled. "We know you like your independence. We're not asking you to give that up, just give it a little more time before you go back out on your own."

She clutched the spatula. "Will you at least let me pay something as rent while we stay here?"

The couple exchanged glances before Daniel said, "Let us talk about that and get back to you. Deal?"

Alana hesitated then nodded. "And please, if our being here creates any kind of problem, just let me know. I value our friendship way too much to want to overstay our welcome."

"We'll let you know," Daniel assured her.

"There's just one other thing..." Beth's voice trailed off as Daniel cleared his throat. She glanced at her husband who gave her a small shake of his head.

Alana watched as the couple seemed to have a whole conversation without saying a word. Finally, Daniel shrugged and went back to his breakfast.

Beth looked at her and said, "The other thing is Justin."

Alana had figured as much, but she didn't say anything as she waited for Beth to continue.

"I don't want to get in the middle of things between you and Justin." Daniel choked on a cough and Beth turned to glare at him. "I really don't, so all I'll say is to be patient with Justin. I love my brother to death, but I'm not unaware of his failings. Just...yeah, have a little patience with him."

Alana nodded but didn't say anything. At this point, she had no idea what was going on with the man. After the previous date at the movies and then finding him still there the next morning, she'd had high hopes for things between them. That was before the week of silence had gone down. Now she wasn't so sure, even after receiving his texts the night before.

As she rinsed off her and Caden's plates and slid them into the dishwasher, Alana said, "Caden and I won't be home for most the afternoon. He has a playdate at Peter's after church."

"That sounds like fun," Beth said with a smile at Caden. "We'll be going to Daniel's mom's to pick up Genevieve, so I guess we'll see you later this afternoon."

After the kitchen had been cleaned up, Alana went to finish getting herself and Caden ready and then left with

Beth and Daniel for the service. It wasn't her Sunday to sign for the service, but they still sat near the front so that Caden could follow the person who was signing. When it was over, they went to meet Peter's family at the pre-arranged place.

"Thanks so much for allowing Caden to come play with Peter this afternoon," Suzanne said. "Are you sure you don't want to come as well?"

"Thank you for the invitation, but I have a few things I need to take care of. I'll be by to pick him up around four. Is that still okay?"

"That's perfect."

After giving Caden a few last-minute instructions, she watched him walk away, her hands clutching the handles of her bag. It was hard to let him out of her sight, but she knew Peter's parents would take good care of him. He always had so much fun with Peter, and he deserved that.

Standing out of the way of the people walking out the doors of the church, Alana kept her gaze on Caden until she saw him get into the car. She took a deep breath and let it out, picking up a familiar scent when she did. Not wanting to look like an idiot by sniffing the air to find the man who smelled like Justin, she joined a group of people leaving the building.

Outside in the warm air, she paused and tried to decide what to do. Moving slowly toward where the bus stop was, Alana decided she'd get something to eat first and then go to a park and spend the afternoon alone working through some things. Though she loved Caden dearly, there were times when she needed to be able to deal with her thoughts and feelings without him getting upset.

"Can I give you a ride somewhere?"

So she hadn't imagined the scent that had grabbed her attention in the foyer. Turning slowly, she found Justin standing behind her, hands in his pockets. Seeing him again reminded her why she'd agreed to spend time with him the previous week.

"I'm just going to get something to eat and then I plan to spend some time at a park." Alana wasn't sure why she'd told him all that, although she was kind of curious to see what he'd do with the information.

"May I join you?" His expression remained granite hard, but there was a flicker of something in his eyes. Uncertainty? Vulnerability? Hope?

"Sure." No matter how mixed up she felt inside about the past week, Alana just couldn't deny herself the pleasure of being with him.

His expression seemed to momentarily show relief. "My truck is parked over there."

She felt his hand at her back as he guided her toward it. Not surprisingly, they walked in silence. As they approached the truck, the doors unlocked and he reached out to open the passenger one for her. She put her bag on the floor of the truck and then slid up onto the seat.

While she waited for him to come around to slide behind the wheel, Alana inhaled the scent of his cologne. It did funny things to her stomach, and she knew that for the rest of her days, this particular scent would forever bring Justin to mind whether he was still in her life or not.

"Were you going anywhere in particular to eat?" Justin asked as he started the truck.

"I was just going to find a place that had salads and sandwiches. Something I could eat at the park without too much hassle."

Justin gave a quick nod of his head and maneuvered the truck from its parking space and out onto the road. The silence hung heavy between them, but Alana had no idea what to say to break it. He was a hard man to read, although if she had to guess, she would say he might be thinking she was upset with him. Maybe another woman would have been. The underlying message that had been running through her mind all week had been that his work was important. More important than her. She'd never had anyone give her precedence over something like a job...or basically anything. There was no reason to think Justin would be different.

It wasn't long before they pulled into the parking lot of a restaurant. As he got out of the truck, Alana bent over to pull her wallet from her bag. She straightened as the door opened and Justin held out his hand to help her down. The touch of his hand brought back memories of the night at the movie theater and how much she'd enjoyed holding hands with him.

Unfortunately, he let go of her hand as soon as she was on her feet. Gripping her wallet in both hands, Alana walked with him to the door. When he opened it for her, she walked past him without looking at him, afraid of what he might see on her face.

As they waited to place their order, Alana took the time to school her features and hopefully hide the truth of what she felt. She thought she'd be strong enough to deal with whatever he had to say to her, but now she wasn't so sure. Her time this afternoon was supposed to have been for her to deal with all the emotions of everything from the past few weeks—including Justin—without worrying about Caden getting upset. Now she had all these thoughts and emotions sitting right below the surface and a feeling that they were going to spin out of control on her.

When it was time to place their order, Justin motioned her to go first. Alana swallowed and told the woman what she wanted. When she bent to pull money from her wallet, Justin's hand closed over hers and he leaned forward to tell the woman what he wanted. The comforting feel of his warmth at her back and his hand firm on hers pulled her emotions near to the surface once again.

He released her hand to pull his wallet from his pocket and paid for both their meals. As they waited for their food, he bent down to her and said, "I don't understand why you keep doing that?"

She refused to look at him. He was too close, close enough to read things in her eyes she didn't want him to see. "Do what?"

"Paying for yourself. When you're with me, I pay." His voice was low but firm. The warmth of his breath across her ear as he spoke sent shivers up and down her spine. "And don't order the cheapest thing on the menu either. I have plenty of money so buying you a meal isn't going to break me."

There was no way she would argue with him in a public place like this, but if he was wanting to talk to her about how it wasn't going to work between them, this was the last meal he'd ever buy for her.

Once their food came, they returned to the truck. Justin waited until she had buckled herself in before handing her the bags of food.

"I'll be right back," he said then turned toward the convenience store that shared the parking lot with the restaurant.

Alana closed the door then leaned her head back against the headrest, her eyelids sliding down. *God, please give me the strength to deal with whatever is coming. If this is it for us, give me peace about it, knowing that Your plan is always better than mine. But God, if at all possible, let me not get hurt again. My heart's had about all it can handle.*

She felt the warmth of a tear slide down her cheek and then another. Panicked that Justin would return to find her crying, Alana looked around for a tissue. Not finding anything, she scrubbed at her cheeks with one hand.

The stupid tears wouldn't stop coming. What was going on? She didn't even know what he planned to talk to her about. She was assuming the worst, and those emotions that had been pulled to the surface now began to overflow at the worst possible time. Trying to take deep breaths in order to regain control, Alana continued to wipe at her cheeks.

These emotions made her feel weak when she'd worked so hard to be strong. Frustration and anger warred with the sadness. Tears weren't something she indulged in much. Certainly she'd stopped shedding tears over anything Craig had done to her years ago. So why now? What was it about this man that pulled at her emotions so strongly?

The driver's side door opened, and Alana quickly turned to look out the window as Justin slid behind the wheel. She continued to wipe at her cheeks with small movements as she waited for the truck to start. What she heard instead was the driver's side door opening. She glanced over to see that Justin had gotten out again.

22

BEFORE SHE COULD figure out what was going on, her door opened and a gasp escaped her as Justin took the food from her lap and set it on the floor of the truck. He reached over her and pushed the button to release the seat belt then he put his hand on the outside of her thigh and turned her to face him. When he stepped close, his abdomen bumped against her knees.

Alana gathered the material of her skirt into one hand while the other continued to wipe at her cheeks.

"Why are you crying?" Justin asked the question softly as he reached out and brushed his thumb across her cheek.

"I don't know." She gave a half hiccup-half laugh. "I just...I knew I was close to this...due for it even with everything that's been going on." She lifted her shoulders and let them fall. "Or maybe it's just hormones."

Justin's brows rose slightly as humor sparked in his eyes. "Really? Hormones? You're going to go with that?"

Alana let out a sigh and leaned her shoulder against the back of the seat. Was she really having this meltdown in front of Justin? She just couldn't catch a break. "Sometimes it's easier to go with that than anything else."

"Well, let's not have this conversation in a parking lot." Justin reversed his actions from earlier. He turned her in her seat, buckled her in and then returned the bags of food to her lap.

Though she felt a little more in control, Alana struggled to regain the stability she needed in order to have any sort of talk with Justin. Thankfully, he didn't pursue conversation as they drove. She had no idea where he was taking them, but as long as it was someplace outside where she could enjoy the sunshine and the nice breeze the day had to offer, it would be fine.

Her heart hurt though because she knew what she had to do. Alana was almost 100% sure that Justin was struggling with how to fit her and Caden into his life. Which, to her, meant he wasn't ready for a relationship. Or maybe he was ready to be buddies with Caden but didn't have time for anyone else. If he'd truly wanted to be with her, he would have found a way to make it work. And she would have been understanding of the demands his job put on him. Between the two of them, they could have made it work.

But she couldn't do it on her own and for the first time she was going to put her own needs above Caden's. She just couldn't be in a relationship with a man who seemed to be only interested in her because of Caden. Yes, they were a package deal, but she had to feel that a man would want her even without Caden. She really hadn't gotten that feeling from Justin.

So, she would let him off the hook and try to keep from falling even further in love with him while encouraging his friendship with Caden. And then she'd just keep praying God would either give her peace about their current situation or bring along the man who was willing to fulfill the role of husband and father without hesitation, who would be able to do what was necessary for them to make things work.

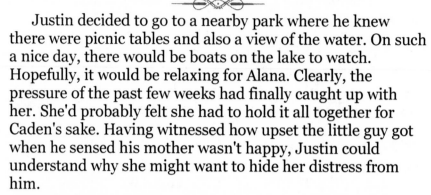

Justin decided to go to a nearby park where he knew there were picnic tables and also a view of the water. On such a nice day, there would be boats on the lake to watch. Hopefully, it would be relaxing for Alana. Clearly, the pressure of the past few weeks had finally caught up with her. She'd probably felt she had to hold it all together for Caden's sake. Having witnessed how upset the little guy got when he sensed his mother wasn't happy, Justin could understand why she might want to hide her distress from him.

He had undoubtedly added to her stress and, for that, Justin felt bad. She needed someone who would help her shoulder the burdens, not add to them. He hoped he could be better about that in the future...if she'd give him that chance.

"Is this okay?" he asked as he pulled the truck into a parking spot.

She glanced around and nodded. "I'm just looking for fresh air and a little sunshine."

"Well, then this should fit the bill." He turned the truck off and jumped out.

Alana had her door open by the time he got there, but she was still sitting there with the food on her lap. He reached to take it from her. "Want to grab those drinks?"

She turned to pull the bottles of water from the drink holder in the console. Tucking them into her elbow, she used her free hand to hold onto the door as she slid to her feet. She closed the door and he used the fob to lock the truck before they headed down a pathway that led to some picnic tables. The first tables they came to were in use, so they kept going.

Finally, Justin spotted an empty one that was shaded by the large trees around it and yet still had a good view of the water. Alana must have seen it too because she began to make her way in that direction before he even said anything. They put the food and drinks on the table then Justin waited for Alana to choose her seat before he settled down across from her.

Once they had their food out, he noticed she bowed her head obviously saying grace for her food. He dipped his head as well, but in addition to thanking God for the provision of food, he prayed that he'd have the right words to say to make things right.

Alana was staring out at the water when he lifted his head. He could see the tension on her delicate features as the breeze lifted the loose strands of hair along her cheeks.

"Did you have a good week?" He wasn't sure how else to start the conversation, but that seemed to be as good a place as any.

"Yes. I spent some time looking for an apartment. I found one yesterday that I thought would be good."

Justin straightened and stared at her. "You're moving out of Beth's?"

Alana gave a one-shouldered shrug but didn't meet his gaze as she jabbed her fork into the salad in front of her. "We can't live there indefinitely, but when I told them this morning that I thought I'd found a place, they both insisted it was no bother for us to continue to stay there."

Tension eased from Justin's shoulders at that news. *Thank God for Beth and Daniel.* He couldn't imagine that any place she found would be better than what had burned down. "They enjoy having you there. Have you felt something different from them?"

Alana briefly met his gaze. "Not at all, but Caden and I aren't their responsibility. I'm perfectly able to take care of my son. We might not be able to live in the best neighborhoods, but he's always had clothes to wear and he's never gone hungry."

"But you have." Justin spoke the words as a shot in the dark. He had no definitive proof of that, but when her gaze jerked up to his and pink stained her cheeks, he knew the shot had hit its mark.

Fire flashed in her green eyes. "But he hasn't. And that's all that matters."

"No, actually, it's not. You need to take care of yourself too." Justin took a bite of the sandwich he held before he said anything more. The purpose of this lunch was to talk through things, not rile her up more.

"Caden and I are just fine." She set her fork down and lowered her hands to her lap, hidden from his view by the picnic table. "And I agreed to stay with Beth and Daniel only if they'd let me contribute by paying rent. But sooner or later, we will move into a place of our own. I have managed to take care of both of us before and there's no reason I won't be able to do that again once I've save up a bit more money. I'm planning to get a job when he goes to school in the fall. We will be fine."

Justin lowered the sandwich, his appetite slipping away. Was she aware of what she was saying? That she was making it very clear—whether she meant to or not—that she saw herself as caring for herself and Caden alone in the future she was laying out to him? She wasn't going to even give him a chance, he realized.

"Listen, about this past week..." Justin tried to find the words in an attempt to get things back on track. "I'm sorry."

"No need to apologize." She said the words as if she'd been practicing them. "I know you have a very busy and stressful job."

"Yes, it is, but—"

She cut his words off with a wave of her hand. "You don't have to explain anything to me. I think right now it's just best if you don't have to worry about us. I know Caden will appreciate any time you can spend with him, but I don't want you to feel stressed out trying to juggle your job and stuff with us. It seems that it works best to just commit to Monday nights."

Justin swallowed hard as he tried to take in what she was saying. He supposed he should be glad she wasn't shutting him completely out of their lives, but the pain he felt was just too much. "I really am sorry about what happened this past week. It wasn't my intention to make you feel like I didn't have time for you."

"But you didn't. Have time that is." She tilted her head as she looked at him. "And I understand that. I think it's pretty clear that you have a lot of responsibility at BlackThorpe. I just don't feel like it will work. Either you'll cut back and I'll feel guilty because I know you'd rather be there for things like the training you've been doing, or you'll continue on as it is, which wouldn't be any good for a relationship. We've already seen that."

"Won't you at least give me a chance to make some changes? We kinda started things off in the middle of something I'd already committed to. And I know I made a mistake not contacting you last week." Justin rubbed his forehead. This talking stuff out was hard. "I think I could make changes that would make this work."

She arched her brow. "You think? And then what happens when you find out you can't? When I let myself get my hopes up only to have you decide that you just can't step away from it enough? It will only get worse the longer we put this off. The bottom line is...you love your job."

That was true, he did. He loved it, and he was good at it. But as he faced the prospect of losing Alana, Justin realized that while he did love his job, he loved her more. Yes, there it was. The L word...but there was no avoiding it. He had to acknowledge the depth of his feelings for her because it was what would propel him forward to make the changes to show her that he could—and would—make room for them both in his life.

He wanted to tell her that he was going to change. That he *wanted* to change so that he could be with her and Caden. But something told him at that moment that his words carried zero weight with her.

No, he was going to have to show her.

"If you're sure that's what you want," he said when he realized she was sitting there waiting for a response from him. He saw the resignation in her eyes but strangely enough, it gave him hope. She wasn't ending things because she didn't want to be with him. He was counting on that as he began to formulate a plan of action. Unfortunately, it wouldn't be as simple as just suddenly switching his job to 9-

5 hours starting the next day. He had to hand off some responsibility and rearrange a few things. Nothing that couldn't be done, but it would take a little bit of time.

"It is." She stabbed a piece of lettuce with her fork and lifted it to her mouth.

They ate in silence for a couple of minutes before Justin said, "So you've decided to send Caden to school in the fall?"

She shot him a wide-eyed look, obviously surprised at the change of subject. She take a quick breath and let it out. "Yes. I went and took a tour of the school, and I think it will be good for him."

"It's a school for deaf students?"

With his questions, Justin grabbed control of the conversation and steered it away from the tense discussion they'd just been having. Though Alana had appeared surprised initially, she seemed to relax as they stayed on neutral ground with the talk centering on Caden, Beth, Daniel, and Genevieve. She ate slowly as they talked, but at least she was eating for which Justin was grateful.

When she finished, he cleaned up their containers and dumped them into a nearby garbage can.

"What time do you need to pick Caden up?" Justin asked as he returned to the table.

"Four."

"You've still got an hour and a half. Want to go for a walk?"

He thought she was going to refuse, but then she nodded and got up from the picnic table. As they walked along the path, Justin found himself wanting to reach for her hand, but that wasn't his place right then. Soon, he hoped it would be, but just not quite yet.

It was during the walk that he tried to delve a little deeper into her life. He found out she did indeed have parents and two siblings, but it quickly became apparent she didn't want to talk about them. It was kind of sad really, given that he couldn't imagine any circumstances—barring death—that his parents would have allowed him to break off contact with them. Unless, of course, it had been her family who'd broken contact. He'd already done the math and figured she had been either seventeen or eighteen when she got pregnant with Caden. She wouldn't be the first person whose family had kicked her out over a teen pregnancy. It was definitely their loss if that had been the case.

It did explain a lot, however and gave him that much more insight into how she'd view things with him. As he walked beside her, Justin realized he'd never thought he'd care enough about a woman to work this hard at a relationship. He'd dropped his last girlfriend when she'd kept after him about working less, and yet now he was already figuring out how to do that in order to be with Alana and her son.

He didn't just take advantage of the walk to ask about her life, but to share more about his. Oh, he didn't come right out and talk about his past, but wound it up with Beth's and delivered it to her that way. Previously, he hadn't wanted people to know much about him, but with Alana, Justin found that he wanted her to know everything.

By the time they'd circled back around to the truck, Justin felt more confident in his plan. And best of all, she was relaxed with him in a way she hadn't been earlier.

"What's the address?" he asked as he started up the truck.

She frowned and opened her mouth to no doubt object, but Justin looked at her and lifted an eyebrow. Alana sighed and gave him the address. He punched it into the navigation system and waited for it to plot the route before pulling out.

"I know you'd probably rather take the bus on your own to pick him up, but I'd like to see him for a little bit." He paused. "If that's okay with you."

He glanced over in time to see her look at him, her brows drawn together over her beautiful green eyes. "Yes, it's fine. I know he'd like to see you, too."

Alana didn't pursue further conversation during the drive to pick up Caden, but this time the quiet wasn't tense like it had been before. He couldn't remember the last time he'd spent as much time with a woman—other than Beth—just talking. Once she'd relaxed, Alana had been surprisingly talkative. He'd enjoyed it and planned to do what he needed to in order to make sure it happened again. And again.

He had no problem imagining them spending time talking each day. Him sharing about his day. Her sharing about hers. It's what he should have done in the week following their movie date.

When they pulled up to the house, Alana turned to him. "Do you mind just waiting here?"

He knew why she wanted that. She considered their relationship over so didn't want to have to explain his presence to whoever was inside. He was fine with that...for now...so he nodded.

He watched her walk in front of the truck and head for the front door. She moved gracefully, the long skirt she wore flowing around her legs. He frowned as he thought of how she always wore long skirts or pants. Did her legs have the same scars as her arms? His stomach clenched at the thought.

It wasn't long before the front door opened and Alana stepped out with Caden. Justin grinned as he saw the moment when Caden realized he was there. The boy froze then darted toward the truck.

Justin opened his door and slid out just as Caden reached him. The little guy flung himself into his arms and he scooped him up. The feeling of Caden's small arms tight around his neck just reinforced how much he wanted these two in his life permanently. He wished he could hold Alana like he held Caden. He wanted to gather them both close.

By the time Alana had joined them, he'd circled around to put Caden in the back seat. The boy's eyes widened, and he gave Justin a questioning look when he spotted what waited for him.

"Can you tell Caden the booster seat is there so he can ride safely in my truck?" When Alana didn't move, Justin looked over at her. Her gaze was glued to the booster seat, her expression conflicted. "Alana?"

She seemed to mentally shake herself and quickly signed to Caden. When she finished, Caden gave him a big smile and a thumbs up before climbing into the truck. Justin moved in to buckle the seatbelt for Caden, essentially trapping Alana between him and the door.

When he straightened and stepped back, her cheeks were flushed, and she moved quickly to the front seat. He waited until she was in and buckled before he closed her door.

Grinning, he rounded the back of the truck. She may think things were over between them, but little did she know.

———⬥———

Alana stared at the addition of SOLD on the FOR SALE sign across the street from Beth's house as she made her way back from the park where she'd spent the afternoon with Caden. She'd wondered if Justin was seriously considering it after he'd gone to look at it, but he hadn't said a word about it in the almost two weeks since. Not that he'd had many opportunities to say anything. After spending the afternoon and part of the evening with her and then Caden, he'd once again dropped off the radar. This time, however, he had given her a head's up that he had another intense week ahead so would probably not be by until the next weekend.

Not that he owed her any explanation now. She'd ended things and he'd taken it pretty well. He hadn't tried too hard to dissuade her from it. He hadn't argued with her logic. But then how could he? Everything she'd said about his job had been true.

As Caden went downstairs to get his tablet, Alana went to the kitchen and found Beth at the counter dumping batter into a cake pan. She looked up and smiled as Alana joined her.

"How was the park?" she asked as she scraped the bowl and then put it in the sink.

"Warm. I think we skipped right over spring and headed for summer." Alana looked at the assortment of bowls on the counter. "What can I do to help?"

"Can you peel the eggs for the potato salad? Daniel's going to try to come home a little early today to help with the barbecue. I'm doing up some steaks and some chicken breasts."

Alana took the bowl of eggs Beth handed her and sat down on the either side of the counter to peel them. "Are you expecting company?"

Beth nodded. "Daniel's family is coming. And so is Justin."

Alana's heart skipped a beat when Beth said his name. "Sounds like a party."

"Yeah. We're celebrating using the barbecue for the first time this year," Beth said with a grin.

Not long after Caden reappeared, noises came over the baby monitor and Beth went to get Genevieve up from her nap. The two little kids settled on the floor to play while Alana continued to help Beth with dinner prep. When everything seemed ready except for the meat that Daniel would barbecue, Alana excused herself to go downstairs to freshen up.

Alana took a quick shower to wash off the sweat from the time at the park then she stood in front of the closet trying to decide what to wear. It shouldn't matter. She wasn't trying to impress anyone, but at the same time, there was a part of her that wanted to look nice when Justin saw her.

But why? She let out a long sigh and briefly pressed her fingertips against her eyelids.

She eyed the handful of short sleeve blouses that had been part of the wardrobe the ladies had purchased for her. Slowly, Alana stretched her arms out, turning them so her hands were palm up. She didn't spend much time looking at her scars. They weren't as visible as they'd once been, but she'd never be completely free of them.

At one time, they had symbolized fear and pain. Now looking at them, they still brought back the memories of how she'd gotten them. But the fact they were healed and fading proved her body was strong and that she was a survivor.

She ran her fingers over the scars on her left arm. The bumps and ridges were still there, but they no longer hurt to touch. There was no need to keep hiding them. Her arms lowered to her side as Alana realized that even after she felt safe from Craig, she'd never stopped hiding. She'd hidden where she lived from people like Beth and Daniel. Hidden what her family had done to her. Hidden her true identity though she knew Craig would never come after them. Hidden her scars. Hidden what they had survived. It wasn't about fear, she realized as her stomach clenched. It was about shame. And, as Beth had pointed out, not feeling worthy.

Alana stared at her feet, curling her toes into the soft depth of the carpet. She was ashamed of the decisions she'd made that had resulted in where they'd ended up. Ashamed of believing a guy who told her he'd make sure she didn't get pregnant. Ashamed of not being good enough for her family to love and support her. Ashamed of having stayed so long with a man who spent every day tearing her down. And despite her statement to Justin the week before, she *was* ashamed that she hadn't been able to provide a better home for Caden.

So much shame.

She took several steps back and when the mattress butted up against her legs, Alana sank down on her bed. The weight of her revelation pressed heavily on her. What did she do now? She hadn't been strong, she'd been desperate to escape not just the abuse heaped on her by Craig, but the shame of her life.

Keeping people at a distance had worked until Beth had butted up against her walls relentlessly, forcing them to cave and allow her, Genevieve and Daniel into her heart and her life. And Justin had followed, bringing with him his friends. They'd swept her along into friendships before she'd even realized what was happening. And now she was struggling to hide her shame when she had no walls left.

God, help me.

She remembered all the sermons she'd heard over the past couple of years that had focused on the type of life God wanted Christians to live. Not a life of shame for sins already forgiven. Nor a life of shame for the ugliness that she'd lived through.

About six months ago she remembered being filled with a longing in her soul following a message at church. It had been taken from Isaiah 61 and had impacted her enough that she'd gone home to memorize the first three verses of that chapter. Shortly after she'd become a Christian, the woman who had shared the Gospel with Alana encouraged her to memorize verses from the Bible. If they were especially meaningful, she told her to commit them to memory.

The woman had gone on to explain how sometimes a person was in need of the comfort of Scriptures but didn't have the ability to read it at that moment. Alana had known what she meant. She'd experienced plenty of times when she would have longed for the comforting words but had no access to a Bible. So she'd memorized anything that touched or moved her.

The verses in Isaiah 61 had filled her with a longing she couldn't really explain. Maybe it had been the desire to trade all the ugliness in her life for beauty. *Beauty for ashes. The oil of joy for mourning. The garment of praise for the spirit of heaviness.*

But she hadn't truly understood what that meant until right then. As if God had known she needed to truly grasp what that beauty would be in her life. Not a life without scars, but a life free from the bondage they'd kept her in.

She wanted to be strong enough to show her scars. To tell people where they came from and then not care if they turned away from her. She'd shown them to Justin and he hadn't turned away...at least she didn't think they were the reason he'd backed off. Maybe he'd discovered, like her family and Craig had, that she just wasn't worth...

Instead of your shame you shall have double honor.

Another part of a verse from Isaiah 61 flashed into her mind and helped to steer her thoughts from a path that was sure to leave her in tears. Alana curled her fingers into the palms of her hands and stood up. Resolving to embrace a life of beauty, joy and praise, she returned to the closet and dragged a blouse off its hanger and slid it over her head.

It was made of a pale green, lightweight material with a peasant neckline and loose sleeves that ended at her elbows. It was gathered just under her bust and fell to her hips in waves. After some debate, she grabbed a pair of jean capris from the dresser and pulled them on. They were just clothes with no spiritual significance, but given her state of mind, they represented the freedom she sought from the shame that had held her soul captive for so long.

She was a bit surprised to see how well they fit. Usually, her clothes hung on her a bit, but it was clear she'd gained some weight while eating Beth's great cooking.

Once she was dressed, she went back to the bathroom. Rather than braiding her hair, she worked it into a high ponytail then added a bit of makeup. Once again, just going for a bit of eye shadow and mascara to accent her eyes. She stood in front of the full-length mirror and took in her appearance. It was the most skin she had showed to strangers in forever, but it was time.

When she rejoined Beth upstairs, her friend gave her appearance the once over and then smiled. "You look nice."

"Thanks." Alana accepted the compliment as a balm to her tattered soul. "What can I do now?"

"Daniel's out back cooking the meat so we can start taking out the other stuff." She slid a stack of paper plates and plastic forks and spoons across the counter. "Just put that stuff on the table with the tablecloth."

"Are Caden and Genevieve out there?" Alana asked, suddenly aware of the quiet.

"Yep. Daniel took them out."

She picked up the things Beth had set out and walked out to the deck. Before her was a beautifully landscaped and expansive yard. The kids were at a play structure a little ways away from the deck. Caden was on his knees in front of Genevieve. As Alana watched, he did two signs for Genevieve and then waited.

"What's he teaching her?" Daniel's voice drew her attention from the kids. He stood at the open barbecue, tongs in hand, his gaze on his daughter and Caden.

"He's signing *swing please.*"

"Okay. I thought I recognized *please.*"

Caden took Genevieve's hands in his and formed her fingers into the sign for swing then he pointed to the swing on the structure.

"Thank you for deciding to stay on with us," Daniel said as he lowered the lid of the barbecue. "I know you think we're doing you a favor, but honestly, when I see things like that with Caden, I think you're doing *us* a favor by staying here."

And yet more balm for her hurting heart. "I think he feels a certain kinship with her since he knows she's deaf too."

"Do you ever think of having more children?" Daniel's question momentarily robbed her of thought.

"Ummm...not really. I mean, I knew I didn't want to have any more children with Caden's father. And now..." Alana shrugged. "There's no reason I would be thinking about more children. But are you asking because of the possibility of having another child with hearing loss?"

Daniel nodded, his gaze on Genevieve. "We always thought we'd have two or three children. But now, I'm not sure what to do."

"Are you worried about having another child face what Genevieve's facing?"

"Actually, I'm more worried about how Genevieve would feel if she was the only one with hearing loss."

"It's all in how you approach their hearing loss. I look at Caden and see him with Genevieve and know that he'd make a wonderful big brother. I think Genevieve will be the same way. And just think how much broader your other children's experiences will be. I tell Caden there's nothing wrong with him, that he's just a little different than people who can hear. But then I point out that being different is never bad because God has made us exactly how He wants us to be."

Before Daniel could reply, a group of people spilled through the gate at the side of the house. A smile spread across his face as he spotted them. Alana put the paper plates on the table next to the barbecue and turned to go back inside when Daniel stopped her. Three of the four people in front of her had blonde hair similar to Daniel's while the fourth had jet black hair that she wore in a pixie cut. All of them were smiling at her.

"Alana, these are my sisters, Rebecca and Abigail, though we call them Becca and Abby. And that tall guy there is my brother, Luke and his girlfriend, Sam. Guys, this is Alana. She's the one who's been helping Beth and me with our sign language. Her son, Caden, is over there playing with Genevieve."

Only the kids weren't still over there. Having spotted familiar faces, the little girl was moving as fast as her chubby little legs would go towards them. Abigail caught the little girl and swung her up in the air. Caden moved more slowly and slipped past Daniel to stand at Alana's side. She looked down at him and smiled as she signed the introductions. Once she finished, he pressed against her hip as he waved to them. Each of them responded with a friendly smile. Luke held out his hand for a high-five. Caden immediately reached out to smack the man's hand, a grin on his face.

"He sure looks like you," Becca commented as her gaze moved between Alana and Caden. "He's a gorgeous little boy. Could I take pictures of him some time? Actually, I'd love to photograph you both."

"Pictures?" Alana looked over at Daniel.

He waved the tongs at his sister and said, "She's a photographer. She tends to view everything and everyone through a camera lens in her mind."

"Well, sure. If you really want to." Alana was still a little taken aback by Becca's request.

"Well, sure, I want to. The pair of you are breathtaking."

Alana was sure her eyebrows nearly reached her hairline. Was this woman serious?

"I knew I should have brought my better camera tonight," Becca groused as she crossed her arms.

"Really, Becca. Why didn't you? You knew I was going to be here," Daniel said with a grin at his sister. He dropped the tongs next to the barbecue and struck a pose with his muscles.

"And that's exactly why she didn't bring it," Abby said. "You would have broken it."

Becca looked unimpressed with Daniel's display as Caden and Luke both started to laugh and any nervousness Alana had about meeting Daniel's family slipped away.

"Now that's what I like to hear. The laughter of my children."

All the adults swung around toward the owner of the voice. After Daniel hugged her and greeted the tall gentleman with her, he once again turned to Alana. "Alana, this is my mom, Emily, and her boyfriend, Elliot."

Alana watched as the woman approached her with arms held wide. Before Alana could react, she was gathered into an embrace that was all softness and Chanel. So this was what a mother's hug felt like. Alana slipped her arms around the woman and fought back tears. How could this woman who had never met her before hug her in a way her own mother never had?

Emily pulled back a bit and looked Alana right in the eyes. "Thank you for helping my loves and their baby. And just so you know, I'm adopting you and your little guy, so if you want, you can call me mom like the rest of them do."

Alana was speechless, and she was sure it showed on her face. Emotion had tightened her throat so all she could do was whisper, "Thank you."

She felt a tap on her hip and looked down, knowing it would be Caden wanting to know what was going on. Moving back from Daniel's mom, Alana signed that the woman was Genevieve's grandma. She watched as his gaze went to Emily then Elliot then back to her.

"Will he let me hug him?" Emily asked. "I don't want to overwhelm him when I can't really communicate with him yet."

Alana smiled and signed to Caden *she wants a hug*. His face lit up, and he instantly moved to wrap his arms around the woman's ample figure. While her son experienced what she just had, Alana's gaze went to the man standing behind the two of them. He was tall and very distinguished looking and wearing an expression of complete adoration as he watched Emily with Caden.

So much love. She wondered if Daniel and his siblings realized how fortunate they were.

"Hey! Anyone want to give me a hand?" Beth's voice grabbed the attention of Daniel's siblings, and they immediately headed for the back door.

Alana moved to follow them, but Emily put a hand on her arm. "Let them work a little."

"Don't even bother trying to argue with Mom," Daniel advised. "She always manages to get her way."

"Daniel Edward Olson!"

Elliot slipped an arm around Emily's waist. "Now, baby, you know that he's right. You do manage to love us all into doing exactly what you want."

Emily grinned then, apparently not at all offended by Elliot's observation. Soon Beth led the others back out with the rest of the food and drinks. In the midst of getting it all on the table, Justin appeared.

23

"**J**USTIN! SWEETHEART! How wonderful to see you again." Just like with Alana, Emily didn't hesitate before grabbing him into a hug.

Though Alana wasn't too sure how she felt about seeing him, she couldn't help but smile to see the tall, muscular man stoop down to return Emily's hug. For just a brief moment, she allowed herself to remember what it felt like to be held in his arms. She turned to help Beth with the food on the table, trying not to let her thoughts go any further down that path.

Out of the corner of her eye, she saw Beth give Justin a quick hug. "Glad you could make it."

"Wouldn't miss it," Justin said. "Looks like you've got enough food to feed an army."

"Well, I think you, Luke and Daniel pretty much qualify."

"Hey there, Caden!"

Alana turned in time to see Justin lift Caden into his arms. Keeping one arm across the back of Caden's legs, Justin lifted his other hand to high five and then fist bump with her son. She let out a sigh. Seeing her son this happy...well, even if it hurt to still have to see Justin so much, it was worth it.

"Hey, Alana. How're you doing?" Justin asked as he set Caden back down.

She saw his gaze travel down her body, his eyes widening slightly as he took in her bare arms. When their gazes met again, she could read the question in them, but she wasn't going to answer it.

"I'm doing good. You?" She tried to hold his gaze, but it was hard. She was grateful when she had to move to get out of Daniel's way as he moved the meat, even though it forced her to move next to Justin. At least she didn't have to look into his eyes.

"I'm doing really well, actually," Justin replied.

"Well, if it isn't my favorite muscle man." Becca greeted Justin with a wink and ran her hand up and down his arm. "When are you going to let me take some pictures of you? I'll even agree to pictures with you not smiling."

"Not gonna happen, Bec. The only way you might get a shot of me is at my wedding or funeral."

Alana took a step away from Justin. The knot in her stomach told her more than anything that she was not okay with Daniel's sister touching Justin like that.

"Well, I can hardly take pictures at my own wedding now, can I?"

Pressing a hand to her stomach, Alana turned away, her gaze searching for Caden. Spotting him on the play structure again, she walked away from Justin and Becca, swallowing several times to keep her emotions under control.

You ready to eat? she signed to him when he spotted her.

Push me first, please? Caden asked with a beguiling look on his face.

Not for too long.

She walked behind him as he settled himself on the swing. Once she was sure he was secure, Alana pulled back on the chains and then let him go. When he swung back her way, she gave him another shove.

He loved to swing. Had even from the time he'd been a baby. He knew how to pump his legs to swing but seemed to prefer to have her do it for him. And she didn't mind. As he came back toward her, she pressed her hands to his lower back and then ran forward, ducking under the swing as he went up. She swung around to see him grinning as he laughed with delight. He didn't make a lot of sounds though he could say a few words so hearing him laugh always lifted her mood. This was what she wanted to see on his face every day of his life. And that was all that mattered. Caden's happiness and joy.

Justin watched Alana as she pushed Caden on the swing. Even from this distance he could tell that Caden was having a blast. It seemed that the boy found joy in everything he did. Justin knew that it was in no small part because of how Alana approached life with Caden. She didn't ever make it seem that Caden was living less of a life because he was deaf.

"Let's eat!" Dan called out.

Alana reached out and grabbed the chains of the swing and brought Caden to a stop. She signed something to him and helped him off the swing. Once his feet hit the ground, he signed something to her before taking off toward the deck. She immediately began to follow him, her long curls blowing in the breeze as she raced after him.

Alana's smile as she chased her son brought a smile to Justin's face. His gaze went back to Caden in time to realize the boy was heading straight for him. Justin braced himself and held out his arms as Caden catapulted himself into them. He couldn't help but laugh as Caden shot a fist into the air in triumph.

"Well, blow me over," Becca said. "Not only do you smile, but you also laugh. Guess you just needed the right motivation."

Justin shifted Caden to his other arm and looked down at Becca, still a little ticked at her for her joking comments earlier. They'd met when they'd been partnered at Beth and Daniel's wedding. She'd flirted outrageously with him, but he'd let her know he wasn't interested in anything but friendship. She still liked to jerk his chain and most the time it didn't matter. But tonight he thought it might have hurt Alana and that wasn't okay. "Guess so."

Alana had slowed to a walk as soon as Caden had reached him, and her smile faded as she joined the rest of them on the deck. She stood off to the side, her arms crossed over her waist. Justin waited for her to look his way, but she never did.

"Thanks for coming, guys," Dan said once everyone had quieted. "In addition to celebrating such a beautiful day to share with family, a little birdy told me that Justin has a reason to celebrate as well."

"Justin?" Beth's gaze bounced between him and Alana, a curious look on her face.

"As of last night, I am the proud owner of a house."

Beth gave a squeal. "You bought it?"

Justin nodded. "Put an offer on it last Sunday and got everything finalized yesterday."

"When's it yours?"

"The sellers were very motivated which helped things to move quickly and it's already empty so I'm getting the keys on Monday."

Beth clapped her hands. "I can't believe this. How cool will it be to have you so close?"

"Very cool," Dan said as he slipped an arm around Beth's waist. "But let's pray so we can eat while you get more details."

Beth grinned as she nodded.

Caden wiggled in his arms so Justin set him down and he made a beeline for his mom. She went down on her knees so they were basically at the same height. As Dan started to pray, Justin kept his eyes open and saw that Alana was interpreting the prayer for Caden. He knew he should close his eyes, but he found himself entranced by Alana's movements as Dan prayed. At the very end, Alana put her hands together and Caden covered hers with his.

As she got to her feet, she was smiling again, and it dawned on Justin that the one thing guaranteed to stir joy in Alana was Caden. He remembered that from his mom and saw it each time Dan's mom was around her kids. Their children moved them. But for both his mom and Emily, the men they loved also brought those smiles to their faces. He wanted to be that man for Alana. After all, she and Caden were able to get him to smile more than anyone else ever had. He wanted to do that for her, too.

Alana bent over to slide the meatloaf into the oven then put the foil wrapped potatoes on the rack next to it. Beth and Daniel had taken Genevieve for a doctor's appointment, so she had offered to make dinner. Meatloaf was the one meal that she felt confident in making. She just hoped they liked it.

She was cleaning up when she heard the front door open and a voice call out, "Anyone home?"

Her hand grasped the cloth she'd been using to wipe the counter. She'd assumed that Justin would be there for supper, but it was only three-thirty. She stood frozen, hoping maybe he'd just leave if no one responded to him. Caden was sitting at the table with his tablet, but of course, he was oblivious to Justin's arrival.

Justin appeared in the doorway of the kitchen. "Hey, there you are."

So much for that hope.

"Hi." Alana gave him a quick smile before turning to rinse the cloth in the sink.

"Hey, Caden."

She glanced over to see that Caden had abandoned his tablet to come greet Justin. They went through their normal high five-fist pump greeting and then Justin straightened and looked at her.

"Look what I got." He held up his hand and dangling from a ring on his finger was a set of keys. Jerking his head to the side, Justin invited, "Come have a look at the house with me?"

Alana searched for a plausible reason why she shouldn't go, but coming up empty she said, "Okay. Just let me get my shoes."

She went to the basement and found a pair of sandals for herself as well as Caden and brought them back up to the front door. Caden had his on first and went out the front door with Justin. When she came out, she found Caden showing Justin the sign for *truck*. The man stood there with his hands on his hips, watching as Caden did the sign, touched the truck and then did it again.

Her heart skipped a beat when Justin repeated the sign Caden had just showed him. Her son nodded proudly when Justin got the sign right. Granted, it was a fairly simple one, but it showed her that he was willing to learn and follow Caden's lead. As she walked up to them, Caden did the sign for *Justin* and then *truck*.

Justin glanced at her then said, "Is that his way of saying it's my truck?"

She nodded, confirming what the two signs represented. "*Justin truck*."

The smile that spread across Justin's face completely transformed the hard planes of his face into something softer and, as always, it took her breath away.

"What's the sign for *my*?" Justin asked.

Alana showed him then watched as he turned to Caden and signed *my truck*. Caden smiled and gave him two thumbs up. She sighed as she watched them together.

"Should we go look at your house?" Alana asked, not so much eager to see the house as she was to escape the emotions that crept to the surface whenever she saw Justin. Especially when she saw him with Caden.

"Sure thing," Justin said as he took Caden's hand. He started toward the house, pausing for a bit when she trailed behind. Once she'd caught up to them, he began to walk again.

When they reached the front door, Justin used his keys to open it. They came right into an entrance way where there was a closet and another door that apparently opened into the two car garage they'd passed on the way to the front door. A set of stairs ran down to the basement and another short flight led to the main floor.

"Let's go up first," Justin suggested.

Even though it was completely empty, Alana had no problem filling the rooms in her mind. She wondered if Justin had enough furniture or if he'd have to buy new stuff. They made their way through an open living/dining room area to the kitchen at the back of the house. There was also a sunken family room with a fireplace. The windows at the back of the house looked out over a backyard, not unlike Beth and Daniel's. The main difference, however, was the presence of a pool.

Alana knew what Caden's reaction would be as soon as he saw it, and he didn't disappoint her. His hands were flying as he tried to express his excitement.

"What's he saying?" Justin asked.

"He's excited about the pool and wants to know if he can swim in it sometime."

Justin grinned and said, "Anytime he wants."

"Uh...I think I'll just tell him yes." There was no way Alana was going to repeat that offer to Caden or he'd never leave Justin alone.

It took a bit, but she was finally able to drag him from the sight of the pool to continue the tour. Back at the stairs where they'd come in, Justin guided them down a hallway where there was a bathroom and two bedrooms.

"You can go on up there," Justin said at the foot of another staircase. "It's the master bedroom."

Alana had lifted her foot to take the first step but faltered. Did she really want to see the master bedroom? But she couldn't very well decline without giving a reason. Taking a quick breath, she climbed the stairs and entered a huge bedroom with windows along the far wall. She realized that the room was directly over the double garage at the front of the house.

"And through there is the master bath and that door leads to a walk-in closet."

Alana couldn't resist taking a peek at the bathroom. She'd come this far already... The bathroom was beautifully done with a huge Jacuzzi tub and a separate shower. At one time, this house wouldn't have wowed her. The house Craig had bought for them in Florida had been bigger and more opulent than this place, but after two years of small, cramped apartments, Justin's home did wow her. Or maybe it was because she could picture living there—if she allowed herself to. Which she couldn't.

After leaving the master bedroom, Justin showed them the basement which had a large rec room along with another bedroom, bathroom, and an office. When they were done, Justin locked the house back up again and they headed back across the cul-de-sac.

"So? What do you think?" Justin asked.

Alana kept her gaze on Beth and Daniel's house. "It's lovely. And I know Beth is thrilled to have you so close. I'm sure you'll be very happy there."

"I'm counting on it," Justin said.

When they got back to the house, Justin disappeared with Caden into the basement and soon Alana heard the sounds of a video game. She went into the kitchen and sat down on a stool at the counter and laid her head down on her arms. Her heart ached with what might have been. If only she'd been enough for him to want to make room in his life for both of them. Instead, he only wanted Caden and somehow she had to accept that.

Resolutely, Alana pushed herself up and took a deep breath. Pushing aside her thoughts, she began to work on the rest of the meal. By the time Daniel and Beth got home, everything was ready for dinner. She was pleased with how the meal had turned out and even more grateful for the opportunity to do something for the couple.

"So how was your day, Justin?" Beth asked as she cut up a piece of meatloaf for Genevieve.

"It was great actually. Spent most of it in meetings, in addition to getting the keys to the house."

Dan looked at him with an arched brow. "You spent most of it in meetings and it was great?"

"Yeah, I know, right? But the meetings were necessary. I met with my team this morning to let them know about some changes coming in how things are done at the compound."

"What sort of changes?" Beth asked, her brow furrowed. "Are you quitting?"

"No chance of that," Justin assured her with a grin. "But I'm going to start relying more on the competent people on my staff to take on more responsibilities. You know...delegate. I mean, if I'm going to come home every night I can't be doing the long training sessions like I have been. These past three weeks have shown me that."

Beth smiled. "It's about time! That's the best news I've heard in ages. Well, next to hearing you got that house."

"I also met with Marcus and Alex this afternoon to let them know how things were going to be changing."

Beth's expression dimmed a bit. "How did they take that?"

"Surprisingly well, actually. They've been after me for a while to use the people on my team more. It doesn't mean that I won't ever participate in the training exercises, but I will pick and choose which ones I do. They were very supportive of the changes as well."

"Well, it's about time, man," Dan said as he leaned back in his chair. "So what's prompted the changes? We've been after you to do this for ages."

"Guess I was just a little slow on the uptake." Justin managed to keep from looking at Alana. "I've realized that I need to make some changes in my life to make room for things that are more important than my job."

"I never thought I'd see the day," Dan said with a laugh. "But you're making the right decision."

Alana had remained quiet during the entire exchange and seemed intent on pushing around the food on her plate rather than eating it. As he watched her, Justin knew he wasn't going to be able to drag out the courtship the way he'd originally planned. Between Becca's stupid remark on Friday night and the fact that Alana had broken it off in the first place, Justin was afraid she wouldn't understand that he was doing this all for her. For them. The three of them.

Suddenly, the idea of waiting to let her know was intolerable.

He chanced a glance at Alana and found her watching him. Their gazes locked, but he couldn't read anything in her expression. Did she understand?

No, maybe she didn't. Maybe her past kept her from realizing that yes, she was *that* important to him. But he'd laid the groundwork with the changes he'd been making and with the house. Now—well, not right then—but soon, it would be time for words. She was ready for it.

Justin couldn't describe the feeling he'd had when he'd seen her arms that night at the barbecue. Bare. Her scars out there for everyone to see. And even now, she wore a short-sleeve T-shirt that fit her better than what she usually wore. Just as he was coming to terms with some things in his life, it appeared she was too. He just hoped it meant that she was open to hearing what he had to tell her.

Alana pushed a chunk of meatloaf around on her plate. What she'd already eaten sat heavy in her stomach. Justin's revelations had taken her completely off-guard, and she was a bit confused. That day in the park, he'd accepted her decision to end things between them. Hadn't he? Was he really making these changes in order to make room in his life for her and Caden? Or was he making these changes so that when the *right one* came along, his life was ready for her?

She really, really hoped it was the former. Every night she'd prayed that God would take away the feelings she had for him, but every single day they were still there, firmly ensconced in her heart. Maybe God hadn't answered her prayers because he had other plans for her...for them.

Those thoughts just kept going around and around in her head as they finished eating and began to clean up. All of them pitched in—even Caden—so it didn't take long.

"Alana?"

At the sound of her name, she looked over at Beth. "What?"

"Daniel and I are going to take Genevieve to get some ice cream. I just asked if it would be okay if we took Caden as well."

"Uh, sure." She motioned Caden over and explained to him about going to get ice cream.

Is Justin coming too?

Was he? Alana had no clue. She had a feeling she'd been so caught up in her thoughts she'd missed part of the conversation. She looked over to where Justin stood, a hip braced against the counter, arms crossed. "He wants to know if you're going too."

"No. But I'll be here when he gets back."

Okay...

She signed Justin's answer and wasn't surprised at the disappointment that crossed Caden's face. *He'll still be here when you get back.*

Alana pressed a fist against her stomach to try and contain her nerves. She wasn't nervous about Beth and Daniel taking Caden out. He'd gone with them on a few different occasions. Daniel had downloaded an app on his phone that Caden could use to communicate if signs weren't working. No, she was nervous about why it seemed that she wasn't going and neither was Justin.

"Let's go, kiddo," Daniel said with a wave of his hand.

With one last look, Caden took Beth's hand when she held it out to him and followed Daniel and Genevieve to the front door. Even after it had opened then closed, Alana stood frozen in place but she managed to say, "Didn't feel in the mood for ice cream?"

She glanced at him, not surprised to find him watching her.

Justin lowered his arms as he straightened away from the counter. "Not really. What I feel in the mood for is a bit of conversation with you." He jerked his head toward the back door. "Join me on the deck?"

She nodded then followed him as he led the way out of the house. The warmth of the early evening air brushed across her skin once clear of the air conditioning inside. And yet a shiver raced up and down her spine.

Justin gestured to a couple of chairs that sat on the end of the deck opposite to the barbecue. He waited while she sat down and then he pulled the other chair so that it faced her. Her heart thudded in her chest as she watched him sit down, his long legs spread so that her knees were between his. She clasped her hands in her lap and took a deep breath.

He leaned forward, bracing his arms on his thighs, his blue gaze on hers. She studied the familiar angles of his face. Any woman would consider him attractive, but Alana knew that his true beauty came from inside. The protectiveness he had toward those he loved. The compassion and love he'd showed Caden.

"I know that you wanted to end things between us because you didn't I could make the necessary changes. As much as I didn't want that, I realized that I needed to show you—not just tell you—that you were important enough to me to make those changes. The house. The changes with my job. I've done it all because...." He stopped and looked down at his hands where they were interlaced nearly touching her knees.

Her breath seemed to catch in her lungs when she saw his jaw tighten right before he looked back at her. Though his expression was tense, his eyes showed the emotion he was feeling. When he reached out to cover her hands where they lay in her lap, Alana stared down at them then slowly loosened her clasped hands. His fingers slipped around to hold hers, his thumbs resting on the backs of her hands. When his fingers tightened momentarily on hers, Alana looked up.

Justin cleared his throat as their gazes met. "I've done it all because I love you."

The air rushed from Alana's lungs. Was she dreaming? She realized she'd tightened her grasp on his hands when she felt his thumbs move across her skin. "Are you sure? I mean, we haven't known each other very long."

Justin's head dropped forward for a moment and Alana wondered if she'd ruined the moment, but when he looked back up, there was a smile on his face. "Yes, I'm sure, but I understand if you need more time. I just need to know that you'll give me a chance to show you how much I love you and that I'm more than willing to do what it takes to keep you in my life. I believe that God brought you into my life to show me that He had a much better plan for me than just focusing so much on my job. People are important. *You* are important. I don't need more time to know that."

"What about Caden?"

"What about him?" Justin tipped his head. "He knows I love him. This right here isn't about him. It's about you and me. All I need to hear from you tonight is that you'll give me—us—another chance. Will you do that, sweetheart?"

Alana stared at him. Did she dare hope? Did she dare take the risk? Did she trust this man to take care of her heart? The answer, of course, was yes. She'd already trusted him with Caden and that boy *was* her heart.

Freeing her hands from his, Alana reached out and cupped his cheek, feeling the roughness of the stubble there against her palm. His hand covered hers, trapping her hand in place. She smiled as she lifted her other hand and made a sign.

Justin's gaze dropped to her hand momentarily before shooting back up to meet hers. When the muscles of his cheek moved, she felt as much as she saw the smile curve his lips. He lifted his hand and made the sign with his fingers and pressed them against hers.

I love you.

Then he leaned forward and pressed his lips to hers in a soft, lingering kiss. When their foreheads touched after the kiss, Alana gave voice to her sign of love. "I love you, Justin."

EPILOGUE

ALANA SMILED as she watched Than's image on the large screen at the end of the room. She and Justin had been invited to celebrate Lindsay's birthday along with other friends and family. Just a year ago she would never have imagined being part of a group like this. A circle of friends— not just acquaintances, but real genuine friends who knew all about her and loved her anyway and whom she loved in return.

Of course, the one she loved the best—aside from Caden— was the man sitting beside her. When the video had started playing on the far wall, Justin had scooted his chair beside hers so he could see. His thigh pressed to hers and he had an arm across the back of her seat. She could feel his fingers playing with a strand of her hair while he held her hand with his other hand.

What a difference a few months made. Since that night in late June when they'd shared their love on the back porch of

Beth and Daniel's house, things between them had only strengthened. She and Caden still lived in Beth and Daniel's basement, but a lot of their time was spent with Justin at his house across the cul-de-sac. The result of them spending so much time together was that Justin's ability to communicate with Caden through signs had improved significantly. Some days Alana was amazed at how easily Justin incorporated signs into his conversations with her and Caden.

A gasp from those around her drew Alana's attention back to the present in time to see that Than had surprised by showing up in person. With a ring. When those around them surged to their feet to congratulate the couple, she and Justin did as well. He kept his hand on her lower back as they moved to where Than and Lindsay stood.

"Congratulations, man," Justin said as he reached out to give his friend a quick hug. "You really managed to pull that off."

"You knew about it?" Alana asked in surprise.

"Well, sure." Justin smiled. "Than recruited several of us guys to help him with the idea."

"And you didn't tell me?"

"Ah...we were sworn to secrecy. Bro code."

They laughed as Alana gave Lindsay a hug. "Congratulations, Lindsay. I'm so happy for the two of you."

Before Lindsay let her go, she whispered, "Maybe you're up next."

Alana felt heat flood her cheeks as she pulled back and smiled at her friend. "You never know."

Not wanting to monopolize the couple, she and Justin returned to the table they shared with Beth and Daniel as well as a Trent and Victoria and Eric and Staci. The conversation that flowed around her filled her with a peace and contentment she'd never imagined might be hers. She knew she was blessed and thanked God each day of her life for that.

Justin pulled his truck into the garage of his house. Some days he had to give himself a shake to make sure it was really real. The shift in priorities over the past several months hadn't left him resentful like he'd worried it might. Instead, having the love of his life and her son at the top of that priority list had filled him with a joy he'd never thought was possible. Though there had been moments of frustration, they had pertained mainly to his job and the inability to track down the shooter responsible for the attack on the training exercise. But the joy in the other part of his life far overshadowed that.

"Want to come sit out back for a bit?" Justin asked as he turned off the truck.

Alana glanced at him as she undid her seatbelt. "What about Caden?"

"He's asleep, right? And Dan and Beth will be there if he wakes up." Justin opened his door which flooded the cab of the truck with light. He knew he wouldn't have to work too hard to convince her.

He rounded the hood of the truck to open her door. Taking her hand, he helped her down from the truck and then they made their way into the house. "Why don't you go on out? I'll grab us something to drink and be right there."

She flashed him a quick smile and squeezed his hand before walking out the back door to the steps that led down to the large deck. When he came out a few minutes later, he found she'd plugged in the little white lights that ringed the deck.

He joined her on the padded bench and set their drinks on the table at his elbow. "Did you enjoy tonight?"

She reached for his hand as she smiled. "I did. That was quite an elaborate thing Than pulled off to propose to Lindsay."

"Yep. I didn't expect anything less for those two." Justin slid his arm around Alana's shoulders, his fingers drifting across the soft skin of her shoulder.

When she turned and leaned into him, lifting her face, Justin didn't waste any time lowering his head to press his lips to hers. One of the most beautiful things of the past few months had been seeing her confidence grow in their relationship. In the beginning, he'd been the one to initiate physical contact with her—even something so simple as grabbing her hand as they walked across the Walmart parking lot. Slowly but surely, however, she'd begun to reach out to him.

The first time she'd hugged him without him hugging her first, Justin had felt like his heart was going to explode. He knew then that the parts of her heart that she'd tried to protect were really and truly his. She trusted him. With her son. With her heart. With her love.

When he slanted his head to deepen the kiss, he felt her hand slide up along his shoulder until it cupped the back of his neck, holding him in place. He loved this woman so much. More than he'd ever thought possible.

Without breaking the kiss, Justin lifted her onto his lap, his hands resting loosely on her waist, enjoying the feel of the curves of her hips that had filled out once she'd begun eating properly. When she sat back from him a short time later, her quick breaths matched his.

"I love you, babe," he said, his forehead pressed to hers.

"Love you, too."

Shifting slightly, Justin reached into the pocket of the dress pants he'd worn for the party for the ring he'd placed there just before coming out on the deck. "I know this might seem less romantic than what we just saw with Than and Lindsay, but this isn't a moment I want to share with anyone but you."

Alana gasped as he held up a sparkling diamond ring. Her hands went to her mouth, her eyes wide.

"Will you marry me, babe?" He knew he should have come up with some flowery speech about all the reasons he wanted to marry her, but she knew them all already. Every day he told her why he was happy she and Caden were in his life. All he wanted right then was an answer to his simple question.

"Yes." Her answer came without hesitation as she reached out to slide her arms around his shoulders and press her face to his neck. "Oh, yes."

He wrapped his arms around her and pulled her close, understanding that this moment would be emotional for her. After the horrors of her previous marriage, Justin knew it took a lot of strength to agree to enter into another one. But every day he showed her how he was different from her ex. And the fact that she'd answered so quickly showed that she knew he was different. That what they had together would be different.

"Let me put this on your finger," Justin said and waited for her to sit back, her hands going to the dampness of her cheeks. "I feel like I've waited my whole life for this moment."

Her smile as she held her left out hand to him filled him with contentment. "Me, too."

"And I want you to know that this ring isn't just a pledge of my commitment to you. It's there for Caden too. I want to adopt him."

If possible, her smile got bigger and tears spilled over. "He's wanted that forever. For you to be his dad."

"I know. It's what I want too. I want both of you."

After he'd slid the ring in place, Alana lifted her hand and made the *I love you* sign. Justin pressed his fingers to hers then leaned in to kiss her. It was the sign they used the most—the three of them—because it was the one they all understood and shared. A sign of love.

The End

OTHER TITLES BY

Kimberly Rae Jordan

Marrying Kate

Faith, Hope & Love

Waiting for Rachel (*Those Karlsson Boys: 1*)
Worth the Wait (*Those Karlsson Boys: 2*)
The Waiting Heart (*Those Karlsson Boys: 3*)

Home Is Where the Heart Is (*Home to Collingsworth: 1*)
Home Away From Home (*Home to Collingsworth: 2*)
Love Makes a House a Home (*Home to Collingsworth: 3*)
The Long Road Home (*Home to Collingsworth: 4*)
Her Heart, His Home (*Home to Collingsworth: 5*)
Coming Home (*Home to Collingsworth: 6*)

This Time With Love (*The McKinleys: 1*)
Forever My Love (*The McKinleys: 2*)
When There is Love (*The McKinleys: 3*)

For news on new releases and sales
sign up for Kimberly's newsletter

http://eepurl.com/WFhYr

Please visit Kimberly Rae Jordan on the web!
Website: www.kimberlyraejordan.com
Facebook: www.facebook.com/AuthorKimberlyRaeJordan
Twitter: twitter.com/KimberlyRJordan

CPSIA information can be obtained
at www.ICGtesting.com
Printed in the USA
LVOW12s1454240816
501678LV00003B/487/P